C000226207

Voices In Darkness

Also by Susan Hepburn

Missing

Voices In Darkness

Susan Hepburn

All the characters in this book are fictitious and any resemblance to real persons, living or dead, is entirely coincidental.

First published in Great Britain in 2002 by
Judy Piatkus (Publishers) Ltd of
5 Windmill Street, London W1T 2JA
email: info@piatkus.co.uk

The moral right of the author has been asserted

A catalogue record for this book is available from the British Library

ISBN 0 7499 0613 8

Set in Times by
Phoenix Photosetting, Chatham, Kent
Printed and bound in Great Britain by
Mackays of Chatham

For Diana, Conrad and D.C.
with love

Prologue

Swifford Maisey, England

It was getting worse.

The Voice.

She heard it almost every day now, clear and persistent.

To begin with, it had just been her name – 'Karen.'

Now, it was talking to her.

Telling her things. *Awful* things.

Trying to get her to do things.

Things she didn't want to do.

Things that were bad.

Really bad.

'You do understand, Karen? They have to be punished. Have to pay for the sins of their ancestors. Your *ancestors.* You *can help settle the score. Bring justice. Only then, can we be free.'*

Karen Peterson shivered, wrapping the duvet around her, rocking backwards and forwards as silent tears squeezed their way from beneath her eyelids. It was no good putting her hands over her ears. She would still hear it. The Voice. It was haunting her.

What could she do? She couldn't tell anyone. They'd think she was mad. Maybe she was mad. Maybe …

'Karen …'

Oh God. It was back.

The Voice was back.

There was no escape …

Chapter One

Broomwood House
Swifford Lea
September 29th

Dear Professor Jackson,

My name is Sally Arnold and I am writing in reply to your letter to the Misses Alice and Molly Webb at the above address. I run the village shop and do their shopping and make their lunch and keep an eye on their mail and bills.

I'm sure I remember them talking about the letter you wrote last year and I'm sorry you didn't get a reply, but things have changed since they got burgled, which was around that time, and I forgot all about it till you wrote again.

Yes, they are still living, but the burglary sent them a bit doolalley, really, which is a crying shame and if I could get my hands on the thieving vandals that caused it – well, what I would do to them isn't respectable to put in writing, but there we are.

Anyway, you wrote again regarding your Oral History and Folklore Study, which is what I'm writing to you about. The thing is, you see, that although the Misses Webb, as I said, have gone a bit doolalley since the break-in, their memory for the past is as good as ever, if not more so, and I'm sure it would do them no end of good to talk about the old days. The only problem I foresee is that they're not very good with men, being spinsters in their nineties, especially not after the burglary because of it being almost certainly men that were responsible.

Could you perhaps send a lady Professor to talk to them? That would go down a treat.

Do please write if I can be of further help. If you can find a lady Professor, I'd introduce her to them, and thinking on what you said about needing time for the research, well my Aunt Ida died recently and we've got her cottage going on the market, but not quite yet, and it's all furnished still, so we (that being me and my husband, Frank) would be happy to let her (the lady Professor) use it for a few weeks at a nominal rent.

Yours sincerely,

Sally Arnold (Mrs)

P.S. I'm not sure about how you actually spell doolalley, but I'm sure you know what I mean.

'Well, lady Professor – what do you say?' Professor Philip Jackson made no effort to hide the amusement in his voice.

'I'm hardly a Professor.' Dr Rhianna Summers smiled wryly as she handed back the letter.

'You're splitting hairs. Come on, Anna – what do you say?'

Philip knew the deliberate shortening of her first name would prickle and hoped he'd not misjudged its effect. They were sitting in the living room of her house, and she looked at him steadily, chewing her lower lip before allowing her eyes to slide off to a point behind him. Photographs, he knew. The room was full of them. Like a shrine.

She sighed and slumped back in her armchair. 'What is this, Philip? An attempt at vocational therapy? I don't need it, you know – I'm writing a book.' She waved vaguely at the desk in the corner where her computer vied for space, half-buried amongst a jumble of files and loose papers.

'Don't insult my intelligence – or your own.' His voice was sharper than he'd intended. 'It is what it says it is – a need to get what these sisters know before they die. As they won't talk to a man, you're the best woman for the job.'

'I've no intentions of coming back to academia.'

'I'm aware of that. I did receive your letter of resignation. But

I'm not asking you to come back. I'm asking you to do a piece of research. God knows, it should be right up your street.'

Philip leaned forward, producing an Ordnance Survey map from his briefcase. 'It's a fascinating part of the country. A remote peninsular, largely untouched by tourism, and Swifford Lea is one of four "related" villages which, I suspect, have more than part of their names in common.'

She hesitated before dropping her eyes to follow the trail of his fingers. He had her intrigued and he knew it.

'See –' He pressed home his advantage. 'Swifford Lea, Swifford Fen, Swifford Holt and Swifford Maisey.'

'What aren't you telling me?'

He grinned and sat back. 'Lots. I want to see if you can get it out of the locals.'

She stood up and walked to the mantelpiece, her back towards him. He had been shocked, when she had answered the door, at how thin she was. She had never been tall – about five foot five, he would have guessed – but she seemed stooped now, shrivelled, and although only in her mid-thirties, her chestnut hair was beginning to show grey.

Was this what grief did to people? He had so hoped that she would come back to work – after a suitable period, of course – believing that it would help her get over the tragedy. She should have been rebuilding her life, not wasting away like a hermit, two years later. Was she really writing a book? He didn't know. Right now, he didn't care. The letter about the Webb sisters had come as a godsend, as he saw it, for both of them. He wanted the information and Anna was the best person to get it. *And yes*, he added to himself – *I* did *think it might work as vocational therapy.*

'You didn't phone before you came, Philip. Why not?' Her voice cut through his thoughts as she turned to look at him. Her eyes, once a vivid shade of blue, had become dull, lost their sparkle.

'Because I knew bloody well you wouldn't agree to see me if I did! And I need you, Anna.'

She frowned. 'It's Rhianna. And don't tell me you haven't any number of willing research assistants.'

Philip shook his head. 'You're out of touch. The cuts have been biting hard. I have two assistants, both men. I need you, Anna. Just for a few weeks. But I do need you.'

She sighed heavily, running a hand distractedly along the mantelshelf, only to look vaguely surprised at the amount of dust it picked up.

'You said yourself I'm out of touch. I'd be no good, Philip. I don't cope well with people these days.'

He tried and failed to fight down the anger and frustration starting to burn in his chest. 'For God's sake, Anna – you're out of touch with the state of play in higher education – not out of your mind! I assumed that there is still a brain inside that head of yours – once one of the sharpest – arguably *the* sharpest in your field.'

He stood up, shoving the map back into his briefcase. 'If you think I'm going to pussy-foot around, forget it! What the hell do you think Guy would make of you being in a state like this? Do you think it will bloody bring them back or something?'

'How dare you!' The shock of his words hit her like a slap, bringing twin spots of scarlet to her cheeks, emphasising the unhealthy pallor of her skin.

'Quite easily. Someone has to say it. *It was not your fault*. How many times does that have to be said? What is this, Anna? Some kind of martyr complex? Do you *want* to carry it for the rest of your life?'

'Get out!' She was shaking now, from head to foot. 'Get out of my house!'

'I'm going. And you leave me no choice. If you won't do the research – these sisters are in their nineties, for Christ's sake – I'll just have to let it go to our beloved rival institution and you know who'll get it – Stella Timpson.'

'What?'

'You heard me.' He slammed the door behind him as he left, cursing himself for having mishandled her so badly.

By the time he arrived back in his office, there was a voice-mail waiting.

'This is Dr Rhianna Summers. I will not allow that woman to be let loose on the Swiffords research project. Make the necessary arrangements and I'll go.'

'You're taking a bit of a risk, aren't you?'

'Pardon?' Philip Jackson looked up from his desk at the unannounced figure standing in his doorway. He frowned at Ted Bridges' casual air. Everything about the man irritated him.

'Rhianna Summers. I heard you're sending her off on a rather important project.'

'That's right. She's the best person for the job.'

Bridges shook his head. '*Was*, maybe. But you're taking a hell of a risk, Philip, and it wouldn't do to bring the department into disrepute. She's hardly been what you'd call stable for the last couple of years.'

While Philip Jackson steepled his fingers and kept his voice level, he was unable to hide the loathing that crept into his eyes.

'She had a breakdown, Ted. Perfectly understandable, given the circumstances. She did not, however, go insane or lose her reasoning faculties. She's one of the finest minds in her field and she's perfect for this work. I have every confidence in her.'

Ted Bridges raised his eyebrows. 'Your loyalty is admirable, Philip – but are you quite sure you're willing to stake your professional reputation on that?'

He smiled before turning and walking away, the intended effect somewhat marred by the fact that he bumped into Steve Graham, one of Philip's research assistants, as he made his exit. Steve watched him go and turned to Philip.

'What did he want?'

'Apart from a punch in the mouth? A cheap rise out of me at Dr Rhianna Summers' expense. Needless to say, he didn't get it.'

Steve took a seat. 'I heard you'd got her for the Swiffords project. How did you manage that?' He had been away at a conference and had just arrived back to find the department buzzing with the news.

Philip smiled. 'I played my weapon of last resort. Told her if she didn't do it, I'd have to hand the whole thing over to Stella Timpson.'

Steve whistled. Although he'd never met either woman, he'd heard the stories. 'You really know how to throw down the gauntlet! Wasn't that a bit below the belt?'

'Oh, I don't think so. It got the desired result, at any rate.'

'Stella Timpson!' Steve gave Philip a searching look. 'You wouldn't really have given it to her? Would you?'

Philip snorted his derision. 'Are you kidding? I'd have

dressed in drag and talked to the old girls myself if I had to. Better yet, sent *you* in drag. No. the only thing I'd give Stella Timpson is a quick hand into hell. One day, Steve, one day – that woman's sins will catch up with her, big style. You mark my words.'

Chapter Two

Swifford Maisey

'Karen . . .'

'No! Go away! I won't listen to you! I won't!' Her father was out for the evening and she shouted the words aloud.

'Karen . . . It is almost time. The Dark Moon is approaching. You know what you have to do. It is God's will. Have you not read His Word in the Bible? There can be no propitiation for sin without blood sacrifice . . .'

'No!'

'YES! It is there in black and white! Would you dispute with God Himself? And do you know what else is there? Do you? That the sins of the fathers shall be visited upon their children. Do you want that, Karen? Their sins to be visited upon YOU? Upon any children YOU may have? It can stop now. You *can stop it. You are called to be the Arm of God.* You *can put an end to all this.'*

The girl rocked back and forth, too terrified to reply.

The Voice was silky now, soft with sympathy and understanding.

'It is the only way, Karen. The only way. You do want me to leave, don't you? Of course you do. But the only way I can leave is for you to carry out God's will. The Arm of God, Karen. That is a great privilege. Once you have exercised your duty as the Arm of God, I can leave you in peace. Not long now, until it shall all be over. Not long now until the Dark of the Moon . . .'

Chapter Three

Saturday November 5th

Rhianna Summers was sitting in a lay-by, drinking coffee from a thermos flask. Not far now. Twenty minutes, perhaps. The map lay open on the passenger seat beside her. Her eyes flickered over the surrounding countryside. She wanted to get there before dark. It must be beautiful here in the spring and summer, she thought, though right now, it had beauty of a different kind. The beginning of November had brought a final, defiant burst of colour to the last remaining leaves, shades of yellow, gold and russet red blazing in the low, late afternoon sunlight.

She sighed, gazing sightlessly for a long moment, then put away the flask and checked the map before restarting the car. She allowed the engine to idle as she told herself, for the umpteenth time, that she must be mad to be doing this, that she no longer had the confidence, concentration or social skills needed for such an undertaking. She gave a little grimace. Philip Jackson had known what he was doing, all right, when he'd played the Stella Timpson card. Had it not been for that, there was no way she would have come. He'd played dirty and she'd let him win. He must really have been banking on getting her agreement. He'd already contacted the Misses Webb's solicitor for consent to speak to them before he'd approached her. Everything was wrapped up and ready. If she'd stuck to her guns and turned him down, he would have had a disaster on his hands.

The research proper had been commissioned by a group of Americans whose forebears had left the Swiffords for the New World back in the 1700s. It was a lucrative contract enabling the 'research within research' with the Webb sisters. Not only would Philip have been devastated to lose it, but it would also have stuck in his – and Rhianna's – craw to know that Stella Timpson could have got it instead. How that woman had managed to survive professionally was beyond understanding. She wasn't called 'Teflon Timpson' for nothing.

Stella *hadn't* got it, however, Rhianna reminded herself, allowing a little *frisson* of anticipation to run through her body as she acknowledged that her own interest really had been fired up. There was even a clause in the agreement with the solicitor allowing her to photograph the house and its contents, on condition that no pictures were published until after the sisters' deaths. What did they have that was so worth capturing on film?

'Come on, girl!' She spoke to herself aloud. 'It's just a couple of weeks. You can do it – just get it over with, and you can go home.'

Home. She realised, as she put the car into gear and pulled away, that there was no longer any comfort in that thought. She had locked herself away for the past two years in nothing more than an empty shell. Bricks and mortar, that was all. She felt a momentary panic. How could she even *think* that? The memories. They were what had kept her going, had given meaning to her continuing existence, but now ... She breathed sharply. It was as if this act of breaking away, however temporarily, had thrown everything into question.

'Shit!' She swore aloud as she rounded a bend to find herself confronted by half a dozen sheep straggling across the road. She edged past them, irritated by their total indifference to her presence. Were the stupid things *trying* to get themselves killed?

Suddenly laughing at her own dour mood, she brought her mind back to the task in hand. Today was Saturday. Get to Swifford Lea, pick up the keys to April Cottage and get herself settled in. Tomorrow, she could orient herself and would be ready to start work with the Misses Webb on Monday morning. Nice and straightforward. Nothing too difficult there. *I'll be all right, once I get into the work. The old professionalism will kick back in. It has to.*

She crested a hill, noting the road sign warning of the gradient. All downhill from here. Down into the wooded plain that held Swifford Lea and its sister villages.

It came up almost out of the blue. One moment, fields and trees; the next, a black and white sign announcing 'Swifford Lea' followed by another asking 'Please drive carefully through our village'.

What village?, she wondered, no sign of habitation having yet come into view. Then suddenly, there it was. A scattering of grey stone cottages, a couple of pubs, a triangular village Green ... She slowed even further, bringing to mind Sally Arnold's written instructions. *Swing round the back of the Green, turn right and head back towards The White Hart. April Cottage is two doors down from that, but this is the best way to approach because of the angle to get into the parking space.* She was right about that. Try to do it from the other way and you'd probably take out half the wall in the attempt.

Parking carefully on the gravelled driveway, Rhianna got out of the car and looked around in the rapidly fading light. On this side of the Green, detached cottages seemed to be the norm whereas the other two sides were flanked by terraces. Probably workmen's homes, originally. She'd find out soon enough. Right now, the priority was to collect the keys to April Cottage and get herself settled in. She used the interior light of the car to check Sally Arnold's instructions again, then set off at a brisk pace, seeking out the village shop.

The pavement soon petered out, the edge of the road becoming muddy beneath her feet. She was wearing sensible shoes, so told herself it didn't matter, but was glad she'd packed Wellingtons, too. As she passed the last cottage on the right, she was treated to an unimpeded view across hedges and fields, trees silhouetted against the darkening sky in which the first few stars were already winking. There were no street lamps here and only the houses to her left reminded her that she was still in the village. Rhianna took comfort in spotting the apparent incongruity of a car showroom, closed but brilliantly lit, knowing from her instructions that the village shop was just a little further down the lane. The air was cool, though not chilled, and carried traces of the pungent smell of manure. The whole place seemed extraordinarily quiet and for one moment, she allowed herself the indulgence of imagining that she'd arrived in a ghost town, apparently normal by outward appearances, yet secretly deserted, no one behind the doors, meals left uneaten on tables, fires still burning in hearths. No sooner had the thought arisen than it was dispelled by a loud bang and a series of sharp cracks. Rhianna nearly jumped out of her skin, right hand flying to her breast as a cascade of lights lit up the sky. Good God! Bonfire Night! She'd completely forgotten it.

Moments later, in the welcoming interior of the shop, it became apparent that Swifford Lea certainly hadn't. A glass-fronted cabinet full of fireworks was being closely examined by several parents with young children, the talk being of taking them – fireworks and children, from the sound of it – down to the display being held in Cooper's Meadow. Ignoring the involuntary pinching in her chest, Rhianna passed them and made her way to the counter.

'Excuse me – I'm looking for Sally Arnold?'

'That's me! You must be the lady Professor? Dr Summers?'

'That's right. Rhianna Summers.'

They shook hands whilst Sally called over her shoulder, 'Frank! Can you come and serve? Dr Summers has arrived!'

Rhianna was acutely aware of several pairs of eyes turning her way, but ignored them as Sally came out from behind the counter. She was a short, attractive woman, younger than Rhianna had anticipated, probably just nudging fifty, sturdily built and dressed, beneath her overall, in black slacks and a fashionable, multi-coloured sweater in striking primary tones. Removing her overall, Sally smiled as her husband took her place at the till, accepting a waxed jacket in exchange.

'I expect it's getting nippy – doesn't take long for the temperature to drop once the sun's gone. Frank – Dr Summers. Dr Summers – my husband – and postmaster – Frank.'

Hands were shaken again, Rhianna hardly able to believe her eyes, acute awareness of her own fragility striking, as her own hand disappeared into one the size of a ham. Frank Arnold was a great, shaggy, bearded giant of a man, grizzled grey, though not much older than his wife, and with the habitual stoop of one for whom doorways and ceilings had always been a problem.

'I'll say it for you, shall I?' Sally laughed. 'He's probably the tallest man you've ever seen. He's technically a giant, you know. Six foot eight.'

'You're quite right. My goodness!'

The ham hand, surprisingly gentle, released her own and the brown eyes crinkled. 'Don't mind me – I'm harmless – honest!'

'That's ... very reassuring to know. I'd hate to have you for an enemy!'

'Be back in a tick!' Sally called as she and Rhianna headed for the door and the firework group made their way to the counter with their order.

'Well – nice night for you to arrive!' Sally pulled a large, rubber-cased flashlight from her pocket as they left the shop, switching it on as they entered the gloom once away from its glass-fronted illumination. 'We always have a good bonfire – the parish council organises it and people take their own contributions as well. Goes down a treat. It's about half a mile down that way, if you want to go.' Sally waved the torch towards a right-hand turning past the car showroom.

'Thanks.' Rhianna's reply was purposely non-committal. Fireworks were lighting up the sky with increasing frequency now, bright streaks and bursts of colour accompanied by a variety of sounds, not all of them coming from the direction of the official display. As they neared The White Hart pub, Rhianna noticed a small knot of people huddled in animated conversation. Sally muttered something under her breath.

'I'm sorry?' Rhianna hadn't caught it.

'Looks like trouble ...' Sally repeated.

Sure enough, one of the group, a man in a knitted hat, grabbed Sally's arm and shook his head.

'Pat's ready to kill someone. Have you seen this? More to the point, can you *hear* this?' Right on cue, a firework lit the sky, exploding in a cascade of green and yellow lights accompanied by a battery of sharp cracks.

Sally sighed. 'Don't tell me – Joe and Hetty.'

'Right. I mean, it's not as if Carol and Bill don't know, is it? And the proper display is only down the road, but no, they have to do it here in their garden, right next to the pub!' He turned to Rhianna. 'They've got the grandchildren over.'

'Aye, and there's still no need for it.' A young man with a fleece over chequered kitchen garb put in. 'The parents live the other side of the village – they could have done it in *their* garden.'

'Oh dear. We'll keep well out of the way, then,' Sally said.

'Don't blame you. There'll be more than one kind of fireworks tonight, the way this is shaping up.' The man with the knitted hat looked from Sally to Rhianna and smiled. 'You must be the lady Professor, come to see the Misses Webb.'

'That's right. Dr Summers. I ...'

Sally pulled on her arm, not giving her chance to reply fully. 'I need to get her settled into the cottage and get back to the shop. I'm sure you'll have chance to speak to her later, Chris.' As they moved out of earshot and started up the garden path, Sally shook her head and said, 'Watch that one. Leader of the Morris Men. He talks the hind legs off a donkey and he'll have your eyes glazed and your brain in neutral before you've had chance to open your mouth.'

Taking a set of keys from her pocket, she opened the front door and reached inside to switch on the light before scraping her shoes and entering. Rhianna copied her as Sally handed her the keys.

'Front door, windows, and back door – which is actually on the side, because it's in the kitchen. Nice and straightforward, eh? I'll just give you a quick show-around and leave you to settle in. I'm sorry about the fires and all, but the electric's still connected and I put the central heating on for you.'

Seeing Rhianna's puzzled look, she led her into the sitting room and pointed to a huge open fireplace. 'One in here, one the other side, in the dining room. Beautiful, they are, and never a year gone by when we haven't had open fires. There was a problem this time, though. When they were inspected. But don't you worry – I've got Adam coming to take a look at them on Monday. He'll soon figure out what's what. Not that I can guarantee they'll be fit before you leave, but we can at least try. Nothing like a good open fire, in my opinion. Nice and cosy.'

Rhianna was busy trying to take everything in, whilst still pondering the interrupted conversation outside the pub.

'What's the problem with those people and the fireworks?' she asked.

'Hetty and Joe. Goats, they are. At the pub. Well, in the field behind it.' Sally laughed. 'My Frank reckons they're not goats at all – says they're llamas. Same thing, really, isn't it? Only bigger. And these are big buggers, believe you me. I expect the fireworks are frightening them, like they do dogs and cats. Now then ...' Leading Rhianna through the sitting room, she opened doors, giving basic information. 'Downstairs toilet with bath – had it put in a couple of years ago. This is the dining room ...' they sailed through it, Rhianna noting dark wood and sepia photographs on the walls '... and this is the kitchen – beautiful, eh?'

'It certainly is.' Rhianna gasped as Mediterranean-blue walls and modern appliances of every kind greeted her eye.

'Weren't expecting this, I bet.' Sally grinned.

'I confess not. It's gorgeous.'

'Oh, she liked her creature comforts, did Aunt Ida. Specially in the kitchen. It's the only modern bit of the cottage. Modern as in both internal appearance and the fact that it's an extension. She said progress should be enjoyed and taken advantage of wherever possible. And so she did. The utility's through here.' Another door was opened, to reveal a washing machine, tumble dryer and freezer.

'This is fantastic.'

'Oh, I think you'll be comfortable.' Moving to a small cardboard box on top of a kitchen surface, Sally said, 'I got the bits and pieces of groceries you wanted – the perishables are in the fridge.' She reached into the box and handed over the till receipt.

'Thanks very much. I really do appreciate it.'

'No bother.'

Rhianna hunted in her handbag. 'Will a cheque be OK, or would you prefer cash?'

'A cheque's fine, with a banker's card. We do most things, I reckon – Visa, Switch and all that. We're open eight till eight every day except Sunday, when it's eight till twelve. The vicar doesn't like it, but there we are. I draw the line at this twenty-four-hour business, mind. Nearest place you'll get that, if you need it, is forty miles away.'

'No thanks!' Rhianna handed her the cheque and card, which were accepted with a nod and a smile.

Leading her back through the other downstairs room, Sally set foot on the steep and tiny staircase. 'Watch your step, here. It twists and turns like nobody's business. I made up the big room for you.'

Rhianna followed her, fascinated by what she saw. The walls, as downstairs, apart from the kitchen, were whitewashed, and ancient blackened beams twisted, propped and butted in abundance. The thin corridor was multi-layered, odd steps up and down appearing every few paces for no apparent reason.

'This is just amazing!'

'Aye – it's served well over the years. It was a butcher's in the 1500s.'

'It's that old?'

'Oh yes. Originally, as I said, a butcher's. Even at the end of the 1800s it was more than just a home. The village shop, in fact.'

'Good Lord!'

'Fascinating history. Aunt Ida had it all traced back – I'll show you her papers, if you're interested.'

'Absolutely.'

'You're sure? I mean, I know the Misses Webb are your first concern . . .'

'Yes, but it's still relevant. Really – I'd love to.'

'Right you are, then. I'll have them ready for you on Monday.'

The upstairs tour was brief and to the point. The big bedroom, made up as Sally had promised, plus two smaller ones and a shower room.

'Just remember these odd steps, if you need to spend a penny in the night!' Sally laughed.

'I'll do my best!'

'Right then!' Back downstairs, Sally took a last look around. 'I'd best be off and leave you to get settled. If I don't see you before, I'll be at the Misses Webb at midday on Monday to introduce you. And don't forget – if you need anything or have any problems – central heating or whatever – just give us a ring.'

'Thank you very much.'

'My pleasure.'

Letting Sally out, Rhianna walked to the car and unloaded the boot. Laptop, suitcase, camera bag, briefcase and wellingtons were quickly installed in the cottage, and she decided to make a cup of tea before unpacking her things. Pushing her hand through her hair, she suddenly felt very tired. *Oh hell! I suppose I ought to make something to eat* . . . Her shoulders slumped at the thought. She had just switched on the kettle when a rapid tapping on the kitchen door startled her. Perhaps Sally had forgotten something? Pulling aside the lace curtain over its pane of glass, she was met by the smiling face of a stranger. She opened the door.

'Yes?'

'Hello there – you must be Dr Summers. I'm Maggie Taylor, your nearest neighbour . . .' the woman gestured towards the next house '. . . and I thought you might like to pop down the pub and meet a few people.' She had a South London accent, Rhianna noted.

'That's very kind, but I was just about to make something to eat and ...'

'Oh, you don't want to be doing that! Sitting in on your own, on your first night! If you want something to eat, my girl, The White Hart's the place for it – we've got our very own celebrity chef!'

'But ...'

Maggie Taylor was not a woman to be thwarted. Grabbing Rhianna by the arm, she pulled her along the side path of the house towards the road.

'You'll enjoy it! Anyway, better to meet curiosity head on, don't you think?' Without giving Rhianna time to reply, she flashed her a smile and asked, 'By the way – what are you like with goats?'

Chapter Four

'Goats?'

'Goats. As in four-footed animals with cloven hooves. Hetty and Joe, their names are. Pete and Pat, that own The White Hart – well, Pat kind of rescued them.' As they approached the pub, Maggie veered down an earthen path to the right. 'What are you wearing on your feet, by the way?' She stopped, snapped on a torch, swung the beam on to Rhianna's shoes and carried on, satisfied. 'You'll be all right in them – it's not too muddy.'

'Where are we going?'

'To see the goats! All these fireworks from next door are upsetting them something rotten. Frightened the pants off the poor things. One of the lads in the kitchen said Joe nearly kicked the shed down, he was so terrified. I want to see for myself, before I go and have a word.'

'Uhmm – is that wise, do you think? If they're upset?' The path was completely dark now, the bobbing yellow beam of the torch their only guide to what lay ahead. Trees and bushes lined their route, casting gnarled and twisted shadows almost as real as themselves.

Maggie laughed. 'It may not be wise, but it needs doing.' She stopped suddenly, causing Rhianna to walk almost into the back of her. She blinked as the torch beam sought out her face. 'You're not frightened of them, are you?'

'Goats? I haven't really come across them, to be honest. Sally Arnold mentioned them, though. Said something about them being more like llamas. Big, I take it she meant.'

'They wouldn't hurt a fly!' Once more, the beam led the way and they moved on. 'They are big, though. Quite surprised me, when I first saw them. And Joe – well, Pete seems to have taken it upon himself to train him in being a proper billy goat – you know, head-butting and all that?'

A flurry of rockets whizzed into the sky, exploding with a boom and releasing three circles of lights which descended with rippling cracks, like gunshots. *Oh great*, thought Rhianna – *I'm in the middle of a field with two wild goats, half-crazed by fireworks, one of which plays alpha-male competitive sports with the pub landlord . . . Terrific!* Glancing back over her shoulder didn't help. The lights of the pub seemed an awfully long way away.

'Here we are.' Maggie came to a halt and swung the torch. Rhianna made out a rudimentary fence in front of them, her eyes following the beam of light across the open space behind it until she was able to make out a three-sided shelter within which two large shapes huddled.

'Hetty! Joe!' Maggie called to them softly. Another crackle of fireworks went off and one of the shapes reared and kicked out at a wall. 'Oh my God! I'll bloody kill Carol and Bill – look at the state of them! They'd normally come straight over when I call them. They eat out of my hand and everything. Bill and Carol are being downright bloody spiteful. Wait here – I'll be right back!' Before Rhianna had time to blink, Maggie, her torch beam bouncing wildly, was jogging back the way they'd come, leaving her in complete darkness.

Oh lovely! Do leave me holding the baby . . . Rhianna took several deep breaths to calm herself, shifting uncomfortably as her eyes adjusted to the inky blackness which seemed to surround her like a blanket. Another salvo of tortuously timpanic fireworks broke the silence and once again, the goats gave vent to their fear. Rhianna squinted across the field, sensing their shapes rather than seeing them as darkness descended once again. *What do I do if they get loose? What – what the hell . . . !*

She blinked hard, thinking her eyes had been deceiving her. For a moment, there seemed to be no sound but her own rapid breathing. As another explosion lit the sky all too briefly, her eyes widened in disbelief. Someone was in the field with the goats. A fizzing hiss and bang, this time unaccompanied by illumination, cut the silence. Rhianna glanced behind her and to her left. *Come on, Maggie – what's keeping you?* Two long sounds like the wail of a banshee followed, and unconsciously, Rhianna used the noise to mask her own movement to the right, where she took refuge behind a stunted tree. The darkness seemed all enveloping. Her eyes swept the cloudless sky punctuated only by the pinprick pattern of stars. Why couldn't there be a moon? She could at least see more if there was a moon ...

Where sight failed, hearing had become acute. She was aware of a low, muttering sound and peered around the tree. As she did so, another starburst rocket flared overhead and she caught her breath. A man – she was sure it was a man, despite his long hair – stood in the middle of the field with his arms aloft. He was no longer muttering, his voice clear but the words indistinct, intoning something in a foreign language. The hair on Rhianna's scalp prickled and goose bumps seemed to rise all over her body. It was surreal. One moment in darkness, the next in a lurid burst of illumination as rockets rent the sky, she watched as he proceeded to pace out the field, drawing a huge circle on the ground. Frustrated by the alternating light and dark, both of which hampered vision, she was unable to make out what he was using to do so.

She closed her eyes, the smell of cordite pungent in her nostrils. *Good God – I've lost it!* Forcing herself to look again, she watched as he turned in four directions. Arms aloft once more, the man seemed to be chanting again, the sense of his words tantalising even as their meaning eluded her. Then, apparently having completed whatever it was he was doing, he melted away into the darkness on the other side of the field.

Bewildered, Rhianna exhaled, realising that she must have been holding her breath, physically jumping as she heard a crackle behind her.

'Anna? Where are you? Are you all right?'

She turned, relief flooding through her as she saw the approach of Maggie's bobbing torch.

'Gawd – it never occurred to me till I was half-way back that I'd left you in the dark – what must you think of me?' Rhianna was blinded as the beam of light hit her face. 'That's me, I'm afraid – once I'm on me high-horse, there's no getting me off it till I've had my say! I do apologise. Anyway, let's get you to the pub and I'll buy you a drink.'

'Thanks. I ... there was a man in the field – with the goats – and ...'

'Oh? Somebody else came to check on them, eh? That's nice.

Bloody Bill and Carol! Only been here five years and why the hell they've stayed that long, I don't know. Nothing's right. Too many cows. Too much mud. Too much noise – can you believe it? If they're not moaning about birds roosting or cocks crowing, it's the cows mooing. The goats were just the last straw.'

'For them or you?'

'Watch your feet.' Maggie linked her own arm through Rhianna's as the pub lights came into view. 'Both, I think. I really like Hetty and Joe. They're characters and this is the country and they've got as much right – more right, if you ask me – to be here than anybody else. But oh no. Carol and Bill don't like it. They set themselves against Pete and Pat from the start. They only took over the pub a year ago, see, and they've transformed it. You wouldn't believe – talk about spit and sawdust – it was the pits and now – well, they got stars in the *Good Food Guide* when they'd only had the place five months. Jealousy, that's what it boils down to, and when Pat rescued the goats, as I said, it was the last straw. Bill and Carol tried to get them shut down and everything.'

Rhianna's head was reeling from the overload of information. 'But these people are putting on the fireworks for their grandchild or grandchildren?'

'Oh yes. When they moved here, they decided it would be a nice place for their daughter and son-in-law as well. I tell you, I dread it every time one of the old ones dies – we just get these people with more money than sense, coming in, putting bugger all into the local economy, commuting to work and trying to change everything.' She laughed. 'Now I know how people must have felt when I moved here.'

At last they came to the road and Maggie switched off her torch.

'Which was when?' Rhianna asked.

'Nearly twenty years ago. Which certain people on the parish council remind me of when they pull rank because they've been here for thirty! There's hardly any Swiffords born-and-breds left.' They approached the door of the pub. 'Right then!' Maggie grinned. 'In at the deep end, my girl! Welcome to Swifford Lea, and welcome to The White Hart!'

It was like a scene from an old Western. Not the sight, but the silence which descended the minute they walked in. It was as if there was a collective holding of breath as every eye swivelled to mark their entrance. As swiftly as it occurred, it was over. The murmur of conversation started up afresh, but a couple of men at the bar shook their heads and wagged fingers at Maggie.

'Watch out – here comes Scrappy!'

Maggie, pulling off her hat to release a tumble of blonde curls, blushed to the roots of her hair and groaned. 'Don't tell me ... what have you heard?'

'Well, if you don't want to be told ...'

'Don't get clever with me, Paul Mitchell. Spill the beans!'

The man's face, ruddy above a thick navy sweater, assumed an air of hurt innocence. 'Just that you had a bit of a contretemps with Carol about the goats.'

Maggie shook her head and rolled her eyes at Rhianna. 'Jungle drums have got nothing on a village like this – don't you let anybody tell you otherwise.'

'Proper upset, she is, from all accounts,' the second man put in.

'Right. And I'm the bleeding Pope. All I did was go and ask – politely, mind – how much longer the noisy sort of fireworks would be going on because the goats were getting a bit upset. And it was Bill I talked to, and he was quite reasonable, before Carol appeared and crossed her arms across her chest as if she'd got a 40DD – which she hasn't – and demanded to know, was I making a complaint?' Conversation had died away again, all ears now tuned to Maggie's account. 'I said no, I wasn't making a complaint, just asking a question. So she slammed the door in my face and let off a load more rockets and a couple of things that sounded like a cat being skinned alive. All right?'

'Well done, Maggie, and thank you for trying.' A tall red-headed woman who looked to be in her mid-thirties appeared behind the bar. Maggie beamed at her.

'No problem. I only wish I could have done more. This is Anna, by the way – the Professor come to see the Misses Webb. She stood guard over Hetty and Joe while I was off contretemping. Anna, this is Pat, who rescued the goats.'

Rhianna opened her mouth to correct her name but was cut short.

'Thank you, Anna. That has to deserve a drink! What will you have?'

'Uhmm ... a glass of red wine if you have one, but ...'

'Oh we have plenty. A wine drinker, eh? Civilised woman – Pete will like you.'

Moments later, seated in a beautifully upholstered blue wing chair in front of a roaring log fire with a menu in her lap, Rhianna realised how close she'd come to making a total gaffe. This was no longer a spit and sawdust pub. More to the point, it served real ale, had an extensive and very fine wine list and, by the look of the dishes listed in front of her, a very fine chef to match. *First rules of the job – don't make assumptions and don't think in stereotypes. And I would have known better anyway, if I'd been paying proper attention to what Maggie was telling me.* She glanced at her companion, taking in her appearance for the first time since being dragged out of April Cottage. Maggie was tiny in stature, barely making five feet, but rounded rather than angular. Not that she carried extra weight, but she was womanly with no shadow of a doubt. What would Guy have said? *Small, but perfectly formed.* She snapped her mind shut on that train of thought. Blonde, curly hair – natural, by the look of it – was complemented by blue eyes and pale skin. Her age? Difficult to judge. Older than herself, but anywhere from five to fifteen years older. She had a porcelain complexion which was giving nothing away.

''Scuse me for a minute – I should have done this before we came in.' Maggie pulled a mobile from her jacket pocket and headed for the back door, to the right of the bar. As she opened it, Rhianna heard her bark, 'Where *are* you?' Rejoining her just a couple of minutes later, Rhianna gave her a puzzled look. Maggie raised her eyebrows. 'Pete doesn't allow mobiles in the pub – not switched on, at any rate. Reckons they're the scourge of modern society.'

'What?!'

'I know, I know ... Anyway, I had to check up on number one son. He's my only son, actually. Only child. Jack, his name is. Only he's not a kid any more – hit seventeen a few months ago and passed his driving test just the other week and I worry myself stupid. Not that I'd let him know that, of course. He just thinks he's got a total dragon for a mother. Gawd, the trials and tribulations, eh?'

Rhianna, swiftly setting her own mobile to 'Silent', was saved from comment by the arrival of a tall willowy girl with the widest smile she had ever seen.

''Ello there, Maggie. Dr Summers. Are you ready to order yet?'

Someone had at least given her the correct title. That had to be a step in the right direction.

'Yes please, Ellie. I could eat a horse!'

'I'm not sure that's on the menu, Maggie, but Pete would more than likely give it a go if you asked!'

'So long as he doesn't cook Hetty and Joe, I don't really care what he does. He'd still turn it out a treat.'

Rhianna hadn't realised how hungry she was until she'd read the menu. Somehow it had seduced her salivary glands back into action after what seemed an eternity of disinterest in food.

'Everything looks so good – we're spoiled for choice!'

Maggie leaned towards her conspiratorially. 'Just one word of advice, Anna – don't ask for meat "well done"'.

'Why not?'

Ellie and Maggie looked at each other and laughed. 'Because Pete would kill you by inches after calling you a total Philistine. Or hit you round the head with a saucepan. What was it he said last time, Ellie?'

The girl's mouth quivered as she quoted. 'If you want it ruined, do it yourself. Don't waste my time and talents and your money on incineration. Meat is to be savoured, not blackened, charred to a cinder or otherwise bastardised.'

'Ah. I'll perhaps change my choice, then,' Rhianna laughed.

Maggie glanced at Ellie and grinned. 'She's a "well done", eh? You could always ask for it "without blood", Anna. I think it's just the phrase "well done" that sets him off.'

'I won't risk it, thanks. I see braised pork is on the menu though – I'll try that . . .'

Two hours later, Rhianna was in a sated stupor, replete and more relaxed than she could remember. After three courses in the upstairs restaurant, she and Maggie returned to the bar for their coffee and hand-made chocolates. She stretched out her legs in front of the fire and sighed.

'I just do not believe that meal . . . !'

'I know. You sounded like, *When Harry Met Sally*, with food.'

Rhianna chuckled. 'I've never felt so embarrassed. I just couldn't help it – it was all so good. I don't usually make orgasmic noises when I eat!'

'You do now! I have to say, Anna, you look a whole lot better than when we arrived. And I'm glad to see you had such an appetite. There's not exactly a lot spare on that frame of yours, you know. I was worried you might be anorexic.'

'What? Good Lord, no!'

'You're not going to throw it all up, are you?' Maggie looked at her anxiously.

'I'm not bulimic, either!' Rhianna laughed. 'Honestly! I've just . . . been working too hard lately.'

She would have been offended by such questions back at home. Here, however, and with a virtual stranger, the concern seemed genuine and was strangely touching. She yawned. First-rate food and a couple of glasses of wine had loosened her up far more than she would have expected. Last orders had been called a while ago and people were now being encouraged to leave. Ellie, the waitress, dumped a rucksack on to a nearby chair and stretched with a feline grace that belied her tiredness. Rhianna had noticed her throughout the evening, commenting to Maggie on the girl's demeanour and ready wit, not to mention her strong local accent, which, like Sally's, reminded her of the buttery tones of Wiltshire, many miles to the south.

'Oh she's an absolute love, Ellie is. One of the few whose family goes back here for generations. She went to school with my Jack. Don't be fooled by the way she talks – she's got a bloody good head on those shoulders. Wants to own her own restaurant one day.'

'And what does Jack want?'

Maggie rolled her eyes. 'To be a musician. God knows where he gets it from. He's doing a course at college in Market Eaton.'

'That's a long way to go every day.'

'That's why he drives and I worry!'

Rhianna watched now as Ellie got ready to leave. She pulled a pair of jeans and a sweater from her rucksack, smiling at the women.

'Gone bitter, it has, with all that rain, and my car heater's broken.'

'Rain? I never noticed.' Maggie peered towards the door in surprise.

'Started just after you two turned up. Sure you weren't singing to Hetty and Joe out there, or doing a rain dance ritual or summat?'

A vision of the man in the field flashed before Rhianna's eyes.

'Maggie – about that . . .' She was interrupted by the muted peal of Morse code. Ellie flashed a glance over her shoulder and pulled a mobile from her bag.

'Sorry – that's me. It's a text message.'

'Splitting hairs about the use of mobile phones, eh?'

Ellie grinned at Maggie before reading it, frowning slightly as she did so. She shook her head, muttering to herself, 'What is she on about? Daft bat!' Stuffing the phone back into the bag, she slipped off her shoes and pulled on the jeans under the modesty of her skirt. Three male stragglers, the last customers left besides Maggie and Rhianna, ogled her with undisguised interest.

'What you lookin' at?' Ellie challenged.

'Anything you're doing, gorgeous!' one of the men replied.

'Dirty buggers – you're older than my dad!'

'That's right – so bugger off – we're closed!' The men turned in the direction of the voice. Rhianna watched as a man emerged from behind the bar. Tall, lean and with prematurely receding dark hair, he didn't have to speak twice. The men scuttled out without a word.

'This is Pete, what owns the pub with Pat,' Ellie explained to Rhianna. She had wriggled into her extra sweater and was now pulling a fleece over her head. 'Cheers, then – see you all tomorrow!' She flashed them a smile, picked up her bag and headed out of the back door towards the car park.

'Ah – we'd better go!' Rhianna looked at Maggie and stood up to leave.

'Ah – you'd better not. Not if you're Dr Summers, that is,' Pete told her.

'Anna,' Maggie chipped in helpfully.

'It's . . .' Rhianna never got time to finish the correction.

Pete Barker pulled a bottle of wine and two glasses from behind his back as Pat appeared with a brandy and coke for Maggie and a glass of mineral water for herself.

'I've been hearing about you all night, Anna Summers. Left in the dark with our goats. Getting orgasmic over my food. You *will* join me in a glass of wine.' Despite the twinkle in his eye, it wasn't really a question.

'Oh, I've had too much already, thanks! Besides, you're closed!'

'To the public.' He grinned and pulled up a bar stool. 'You're no longer the public. You're a friend of Maggie's and protector of our goats.' He set the glasses down and began to pour. 'Welcome to the lock-in . . .'

Chapter Five

The house in Swifford Maisey stood well back from the deserted road and over a mile from its nearest neighbour, surrounded by trees, fields and low hedges. Lights were lit in the upstairs hall and above the stairs, but its inhabitants no longer had need of them. It was eerily silent, not even the dripping of a tap to be heard, the air inside its walls heavy with the smoke of incense.

Had they tried to flee, it would have been futile, against such a force as had overtaken them, but they had not. Death, whilst savage and silent, had at least been mercifully swift in one case, at least.

It had been an orderly house; a place for everything, and everything in its place, until the ultimate disordering of their lives had overwhelmed them. Now, they who had lived here for so many years were themselves the only disorderly components.

Seth Peterson – most of what remained of him – lay hacked and sprawling across the double bed, his lower left leg, still clad in its pyjama bottom, almost three feet away in the middle of the carpet.

Karen Peterson's bedroom, however, was strikingly clean and tidy in contrast. Karen's body, minus her mangled left arm, was not here, but was lying sprawled on the path outside the back door. The missing limb, along with the axe that had severed it, lay on the kitchen table; all the more grotesque, were that possible, because of the small, black, leather-bound Bible still clutched in her lifeless hand.

Blood was everywhere. Gobbetted, splattered, sprayed, whilst under the now lifeless bodies, it lay in blackening, viscous pools beneath those through whose hearts it had once pumped life.

Gone now.

All gone.

A different kind of blood adorned the kitchen walls. This was the blood of warning, streaked in occult symbols and letters which spelled out a terrible message.

Vengeance is mine, saith the Lord, and mine Arm is long and mighty, reaching from generation to generation.

Think not that thou canst escape my wrath or flee my judgement, for the sins of the fathers SHALL be visited upon the children.

As it was written, they that live by the sword shall perish by the sword, yea, verily, it is so. They that here lived by the sword HAVE perished by the sword.

The soals of the corrupt shall rise as the smoak of incense being a sacrifice pleasing before the Lord.

As spoke the curse for the sins of 1732, so shall they ALL be punished. Let the sinners tremble, for there is no escape. What is here begun shall be completed ...

Chapter Six

Anna stirred and stretched before finally opening her eyes. She blinked, confused. *Where am I?* Memory returned and with it, the realisation that she had a headache. Correction – hangover. *Oh my God – the lock-in* ... She sat up in bed and groaned, trying to piece things together. Goats. Maggie. The meal. The lock-in. Straightforward enough. Sort of. But what about the man with the goats? And what about the piano ... ?

She got out of bed and padded across the room to her suitcase, retrieving her washing kit and a bath towel before heading down the corridor. *Watch the steps*, she reminded herself. Seconds later, she stood beneath the jet of a power shower, luxuriating in the pummelling of the water on her muscles, the scent of her shower gel heady in the steamy confines of the cubicle. *So*, she thought. *Swifford Lea may look sleepy, but it isn't. And one of my new neighbours pounds out classical music on the piano at a quarter-to-two in the morning*. She'd heard it as she'd fallen into bed, peering at the clock, confused, but too tired – and too drunk, truth be told – to let it keep her awake. She lifted her face to the spray, grinning wryly as one memory hit her with full clarity. She had made the decision, last night, to give up trying to correct people's use of her name. She would be *Anna* Summers in Swifford Lea. It had irked her beyond belief in academia and yet here, for some unfathomable reason, it didn't.

As she walked back to the bedroom, she noticed a window in the corridor and pulled back the curtains. *Perhaps there's a house behind – that could explain the piano* ... There was not. She had a sweeping view as far as the eye could see, of fields leading to a distant, wooded hillside. The sky was blue and clear, the previous evening's rain banished by an overnight change of wind direction.

No house behind. How odd ... She stood with her eyes closed, picturing the front of April Cottage. It was the first – or last – house in the village, depending on which way you approached it. Maggie was next door, then the pub, then the couple who'd caused the commotion with the fireworks. *Maybe Maggie's son plays. She said he wants to be a musician ...*

She looked at the clock as she dressed. 10 a.m. Good God! She couldn't remember the last time she'd slept so late. Come to that, neither could she remember the last time she'd slept so well. *Better not make late nights and red wine a habit ...* She grinned to herself, unpacking her suitcase before going down to the kitchen. She filled the kettle and popped bread into the toaster before taking the laptop through to the dining room. Yes. She'd remembered accurately. A large and beautiful oval dining table. *This will do nicely.* She hunted for a power point, found one close to the huge open fireplace, and plugged it in. Satisfied that it was working properly, she went to the kitchen, eating at the breakfast bar.

Washing up her things and leaving them to drain, she looked out of the window and over the Green. A middle-aged man was walking two large, rough-coated dogs. A young couple made their way along the road, two small children in tow, the bright, woolly-hatted head of a baby peeping from a carrier on its father's back. Suddenly, the world seemed inviting. There was a village to explore.

Moments later, Anna was outside, her camera slung around her neck and with a notebook and pen in the pocket of her waxed jacket. As she walked around the Green, getting her bearings in daylight, a couple of cars drove past and she was greeted by several people laden with Sunday morning newspapers and cartons of milk. She smiled in return and started taking photographs, making notes as she did so. The front of April Cottage. The fronts of Maggie's house and The White Hart. The Green, from all angles, showing the layout of the roads it intersected. The old war memorial in its centre, topped by a far more ancient-looking cross. Again, she photographed it from all angles, moving in close and using the sophisticated metering and autofocus facilities which would allow her to read clearly the names of those whose memory was engraved upon its stone. Satisfied, she turned and photographed the car showroom, intrigued, as she focused, by a tiny, winding alley to one side of it. She walked across and made her way along it, marvelling at the higgledy-piggledy buildings on both sides whose tops leaned out precariously over the footpath between. No room here for vehicles. She wondered where the householders parked. She worked her way methodically along several lanes before arriving back where she had begun. She glanced at her watch. What time had Sally said they shut the shop today? She still had time, surely? Best be on the safe side …

'Good morning,' Sally greeted her. 'Settling in all right?'

'Yes thanks. I slept like a log.'

Sally laughed. 'I heard you get Barkered.'

'I'm sorry?'

'Barkered,' Frank chipped in. 'It's Pete at the pub's surname, with the ending added to indicate you got held after hours and probably woke up with a bit of a headache …'

'Ah. Got it in one.'

'It'll be paracetamol you're after then?'

'No, actually. A couple of newspapers and, if you sell them, I need a torch and some batteries.'

'No problem.' Frank moved out from behind the counter as Sally served someone else. 'Over here …'

For such a huge man, he was light on his feet. This was a bear with a natural grace, rather than the lumbering gait one would have expected. *Another first line rule of the job. Appearances can be deceptive, so don't be fooled.* Purchases made, Anna returned to April Cottage, where she made a cup of coffee and settled down to read the papers.

The ringing of the phone startled her, not least because she hadn't yet noticed where it was. Finally locating it in the opened-up space beneath the stairs, she was able to answer it.

'Anna? Blimey, you took so long to pick up, I thought you'd forgotten and gone out!'

'Ah – remind me of what I may have forgotten, Maggie …'

'That good, eh? Have you got a hangover?'

'I think it's fair to say I had a bit of a headache when I woke up, but I'm all right now. And you still haven't told me what I may have forgotten …'

'That we're booked in for lunch at the pub today. Which you obviously did forget!'

Anna laughed, remembering her grandmother's catch-phrase, which she repeated to Maggie. 'It's not that I forgot – I simply didn't remember it!'

'Right – well you know now! Just keep it in your head for the next half-hour, OK, and I'll be round to collect you – just in case you haven't remembered it – again!'

No point in settling down with a newspaper, then. Anna went through to the dining room and quickly entered details of her short, photographic jaunt into the newly created Swiffords project folder in the laptop, along with the date and time she was due to meet the Misses Webb the following day. She had barely finished when Maggie arrived.

'Well – you don't look too bad for someone who had a hang-over and forgot about lunch!' Maggie told her.

'I'm fine, really. I was out for the count.' Anna wondered if she should say anything about the piano playing, but decided to let it lie for the time being.

'Good girl. Nothing like letting your hair down once in a while. Come on – I'll introduce you properly.' Maggie veered off down the path they had taken the previous evening.

'To the goats?'

'Who else? It was really good of you to come, and I still feel bad about leaving you on your own. What must you have thought of me?'

'Just "hurry up and come back"!' Anna laughed.

It all seemed so different now. Ordinary. Pastoral. What a difference daylight made. She couldn't believe how spooked she had felt in the dark.

'Anyway, Carol and Bill got their come-uppance with that change in the weather, eh? Apparently the proper display wasn't affected.' Maggie shook her head. 'Just half a mile down there . . .' she waved an arm '. . . and it didn't rain at all. But Carol and Bill got all washed out. Serve 'em right, too. I don't approve of cruelty to Hetty and Joe. God was on our side, I reckon!' She grinned impishly as they approached the goats' field. 'Here we are. Hetty! Joe!'

This time, her call was answered immediately, the animals trotting over to nuzzle her outstretched hand. 'See – I told you – they wouldn't hurt a fly! Well, they might eat it, if it got in their way – they'll eat anything, goats will. Say hello to Anna!'

Anna dutifully stroked them, marvelling again at their size. Joe was tawny with white flashes, whilst Hetty was the reverse. Their strange eyes seemed to be sizing her up, and she suddenly shivered, glancing across the field to where she had first seen the strange man with them. He must either have approached from the open fields, or come across the back of the nearby houses.

'Right then! Let's go and get some lunch.'

As they walked into the pub, Anna looked at Maggie in surprise. 'I didn't think it would be this busy so early – it can't have been open long, surely?'

'Right. But they shut at half-past three on Sunday. Gives them the afternoon and evening off. You're too used to town or city pubs – they believe in having some time off, here.'

Maggie headed for the place they'd been seated the previous evening, already occupied by two men. Anna watched in amazement as they gave up the seats without a word.

'How the hell did you do that?' she asked Maggie. 'Telepathy?'

'Nothing so subtle,' Maggie snorted. 'Those two are part of the local Morris Men and let's just say we don't always see eye to eye.'

'Oh?'

Maggie grinned. 'You wouldn't believe it. There I was, this last May Day morning, minding my own business, fast asleep in bed at 6 o'clock, and what happens? I hear bells and all that other clap-trap. Obviously, I wasn't best pleased at having my beauty sleep disturbed, so I looks out the window to see what's going on and there they are, dancing about on the Green, waving their hankies and bladders on sticks – you know the stuff? Well, down I goes ...' She giggled. 'Can't have been a pretty sight in my dressing gown and no make-up, and I asks them what the bleedin' hell they think they're doing? And do you know what the prat said?'

She indicated the taller of the two men and Anna remembered that he'd been wearing a bobble hat the night before, and that she'd met him with Sally.

'That's Chris, their leader,' Maggie told her. 'He said they were reviving the tradition of greeting the sun on May Day! To ensure fertility! First I've heard of it, I told him, and also told him, in no uncertain terms, to bugger off and greet the sun elsewhere – he wasn't doing it outside my house or he'd likely have nothing left to be fertile with! Here – what you having, by the way? We'd better get to the bar before it's three deep.'

'No, no – my shout.'

'Thanks. I'll have a brandy and Coke, and you'll need to ask what they're doing for lunch.'

Anna returned with the lunch menu and Maggie looked at her mineral water askance. 'You didn't have *that* much last night!'

'I had more than I'd normally drink in a month! I'll stick to this at the moment and maybe – maybe – have a glass of wine with my meal.'

They settled back to make their selection and Maggie looked up in surprise when Pat came to take their order. 'What – no Ellie?' She looked around, trying to spot the girl.

'No. And I don't even know why. Their phone seems to be constantly engaged.'

'That's not like her.' Maggie frowned.

'She's never even been late, never mind not turning up. We could do without it, though. We're run off our feet today.' Pat scribbled down their order. 'I'll give you a shout when we're ready for you.'

'Oh dear – I hope it's nothing serious.' Maggie watched Pat make her way to the bar, then turned to Anna. 'So – you'll be starting work with the Misses Webb tomorrow – you all set?'

'Yes, I think so. I've checked the laptop – oh God – and I *haven't* checked the tape machine, so I must do that later – and I have plenty of batteries for everything as well as mains chargers, so, yes – I think we're up and running. What do you do, Maggie? Or did I ask you last night, but can't remember?'

'No – you're all right. We didn't get round to that. We were too busy pumping you for information! I work largely from home, as a translator. I'm often accused of murdering the Queen's English verbally, but believe it or not, I'm impeccable in French, German and Italian, written and verbal, and in written English. Which is why . . .' she grinned, '. . . I'm a translator rather than an interpreter.'

Anna shook her head. 'I wish I could say the same. Languages were not my strong point.'

'Different strokes for different folks, eh? It's stood me in good stead, though, bringing up Jack by myself. I was fortunate, back then, to find a firm that would let me work from home, and now, with e-mail and the Web and all, it's even easier.'

'Are you divorced?'

'Yes. He ran off with a younger model. He's run off with a couple more, since, as well. How about you?'

Anna's chest constricted. 'Widowed.'

'Blimey – you're young for that. I'm really sorry.' Maggie touched her arm. 'Looks like we're about to be seated for lunch.' As they stood up, the two Morris Men approached, obviously eager to reclaim their former seats. 'You're worse than a bloody vulture, Chris!' Maggie scowled. 'Bet you wouldn't be so quick to jump in my grave!'

'Wouldn't dream of it, Maggie – I'd be jumping up and down *on* it, in full bells and regalia.' He smiled before intoning, 'Ultimately, there is no escape . . .'

'Right – I love you, too!' Maggie laughed as they made their way upstairs. 'God! Who'd live in a village, eh?'

'Don't try and fool me – you love it!'

'Yeah – it has its downside, believe me, but it's a bloody sight better than being abandoned in a tower block or something. Ah – here we go . . .'

Once again, the meal was perfect. As they returned to the bar, Anna plucked at her waistband and said, 'I'm going to look like the Michelin Man by the time I leave here!'

Maggie laughed. 'I know what you mean. I used to be skinny until Pete and Pat took over and I gave up cooking Sunday lunches!'

Only a few hardy stragglers were left at the bar now, time having been called, and as they approached, both women were startled by a huge clattering sound from the kitchen.

'Blimey – that sounded expensive!' Maggie was about to continue when Pat rushed out from behind the bar.

'You! Out, now!'

The men addressed did as they were told, Anna and Maggie transfixed by the stricken expression on her face. Wordlessly, she turned to the bar and pressed a glass against the brandy optic. Anna and Maggie were nearly out of the door when she spoke.

'Not you! Maggie – where's Jack?'

'Jack? He's at work – at the egg factory. What . . . ?'

'Sit down.'

Maggie clutched at Anna's arm as she did as she was told.

'He's not had an accident? What . . .'

Pete joined them, his arm around Aaron, the young pot-wash, whose face was blotchy and tear-stained. 'You get off home, lad. We'll clean up here.' The boy stumbled out of the back door without a word.

'He's not driving?' Pat asked.

Pete shook his head. 'Walking.' He set a large brandy down in front of Maggie, whose own face was now ashen. 'Jack's all right, Maggie, as far as we know. That is to say, the bad news isn't about Jack – but you'd best be the one who breaks it to him.' Once again, a bottle of red wine was produced. He raised his eyebrows at Anna, who nodded, eyes darting from one face to another. He poured a glass for Anna and one for himself, before turning to his wife.

'You'd best tell it, babe.'

Pat's eyes were brimming. She took a deep swallow of her drink before she composed herself enough to be able to speak.

'You know Ellie didn't turn up today?'

'Oh my God . . .' Maggie began.

Pat shook her head fiercely. 'It's not her. It's Karen Peterson – Seth, too. They're dead.'

'What . . . ?' Maggie looked at her in disbelief. Turning to Anna, she said, 'Karen's at college with my Jack. She's Ellie's best friend. Lives in Swifford Maisey, like Ellie.' She looked back at Pat, confused. 'What do you mean, they're dead? Not that poisoning from faulty gas heaters or something? Dear God . . .'

Pat shook her head and took another deep draught of brandy. 'It's worse, Maggie. They've been murdered.'

'What?' Maggie's voice shot up an octave. 'Don't be so daft! Who'd . . .'

Pat broke down and blew her nose noisily. Pete, out of his depth, looked helplessly at her before taking up the story.

'It's true, Maggie.' He shook his head. 'We don't know much, obviously, but Ellie's mum phoned. Seth – Karen's dad – was supposed to go out with a friend today. Early. The friend called round for him.' He struggled to control his voice. 'There was no reply at the front, but the back door was open. Karen was on the path . . . he went inside . . . apparently . . . apparently it was a blood-bath.'

'*Both* of them? You're sure?' Maggie's voice was barely above a whisper.

'That's what Ellie's mum said.'

'Oh my God ...' Maggie drained her glass and shut her eyes. 'Karen was – what? Seventeen, like my Jack. They've gone through school together. Little Ellie's just a year older. They ...' Suddenly rising from her seat, she dashed into the toilets. Pat rose swiftly and followed her. Pete and Anna sat silently, looking at each other.

'Christ! I can't believe this.' Pete exhaled noisily. 'I know rural crime is supposed to be rocketing, but we get next to nothing around here. Barely a break-in. And now ... some bloody homicidal maniac by the sound of it! I just don't believe it.' He leaned forward, blinking rapidly. 'Right. You and Maggie have no man in the house – I'm not counting Jack – you know what I mean. The point is, you're right next to us. Any problem – even a whiff of trouble – you phone me. *Me*, you understand.' He pulled a pen from his pocket and scribbled a phone number on a beer mat. 'I'll be round in a shot and Pat will call the police as I'm leaving. That's the trouble with living in a place like this – these bastards can be in, take their time – make themselves a cup of tea, for all I know – and leave at their leisure, knowing the police have to come from miles away.' He thrust the beer mat at Anna. 'I want you to promise me.'

Anna took it from him. Their eyes locked. Swallowing hard, she nodded.

'I promise.'

Chapter Seven

Monday November 7th

Philip Jackson was absorbed in a report when the telephone rang and he reached for it absently, his mind elsewhere. The moment he heard the voice on the other end, however, his attention focused entirely on the diatribe being aimed into his left ear.

'Well, Philip – I always believed that nervous afflictions were non-contagious, but it seems I have to revise that opinion in light of what I've heard. Are you out of your mind?'

'Stella. I would say it's nice to hear from you, but it isn't. If you have a point to make, make it and get off the line.' *Shit! This can only be about one thing . . .*

'Insanity. Madness. Sending Rhianna Summers on a high-calibre research project. You know she's mad. One can only assume, therefore, that you yourself have become afflicted, to even think of sending her.'

'I really don't know what you're talking about. I was also unaware that you hold a doctorate in diagnostic medicine.'

The bark that passed for Stella Timpson's laugh made him wince. 'You can't fool me, Philip – I know. The Swiffords project. Whoever financed it has been severely misled. They should have come to me. She'll screw it up. You know it, and I know it. And who'll be left to pick up the pieces? You've gone too far, this time. Out on a limb. I can't wait . . .'

'And may I ask how you came to hear about this, Stella?' Philip's voice was as dry as the Sahara. He knew perfectly well what her reply would be. She didn't disappoint him.

'You may ask, Philip. But I don't have to answer.'

She hung up abruptly, well satisfied. *That should have rattled his cage nicely* ... She sat back for a moment, eyes narrowed, before picking up the letter which lay on the desk in front of her. It wasn't often she received anonymous letters. When she did, it was usually hate mail. This, however, was from 'a well-wisher'. Quite an occurrence, then. She didn't think she had any.

> *You should know that Philip Jackson's unit has been contracted to carry out research into four villages – the Swiffords (see map). He has hired Dr Rhianna Summers to do the groundwork. A well-wisher.*

She looked at the map, then at the photocopied document that accompanied it. How enticing. Handwritten. Probably nineteenth century, from the look of the script, and probably torn from a book of some sort. She put on her glasses and held it under the desk lamp. Yes, she had understood it correctly. *A most shameful and wicked episode in the Year of Our Lord 1732* ... her pulse began to race as she read on ...

'Hi, Philip – I was hoping I'd catch you, rather than your voice-mail!'

'Rhianna – is there a problem?' Hard on the heels of Stella's phone call, Philip's anxiety was palpable as the object of her derision came on the line.

'No – should there be?'

'Ah – of course not. I just wasn't expecting to hear from you yet.'

'I'm just calling to let you know that I'm settled in OK and shall be meeting the Misses Webb in a couple of hours' time.'

Philip's blood pressure subsided. She was sounding fine. Her old self. Before the accident, even. He breathed a sigh of relief. Better not tell her about Stella's poisonous call, then. He didn't want to upset her.

'Great!' he enthused. 'One always worries, with situations like this, that they died in the night or something, and that what they know is lost forever.'

'Not as far as I know! But talking of deaths, though – it shouldn't affect the project, of course, but the national papers will probably get hold of it – a father and daughter in Swifford Maisey were murdered either Saturday night or the early hours of yesterday morning.'

'Good God!' *Christ! Nothing ever happens in the Swiffords and the minute I send her there* ... Philip didn't even want to *think* about Stella's reaction.

'Mmm. It's shaken people rigid, as you can imagine. But – as I say – I don't see that it should affect the project.'

'What was it – a bungled burglary?'

'I don't have any details, Philip – only heard about it yesterday afternoon. All I was told is that they're dead, and that it was – and I quote – "a bloodbath". He was a widower, apparently. Brought the girl up on his own since she was tiny.'

'Shit! Have they caught whoever did it?'

'Not as far as I know, but ...'

'Are you all right security-wise? Plenty of locks and stuff?'

'I'm fine, Philip. Really. I also have very good neighbours. Anyway, I'll let you go. I'm sure you're up to your ears in work. I didn't mean to alarm you.'

'Yes, well – I'm glad you're OK. Do you want to give me a ring later and tell me how you've got on with the old girls? Just an overview, you know?'

'Sure. Will do. 'Bye for now, then.'

Philip let out a long breath as Rhianna hung up, uncomfortably conscious of a fine sheen of cold sweat across his upper lip and brow. *She'll be all right. She* has *to be. There's too much riding on this.* Ted Bridges' words came back to haunt him. *Yes,* he acknowledged to himself. *Like my reputation* ...

Anna sat for a moment, pondering Philip's reaction before replacing the phone on its base unit, under the stairs. *Perhaps I shouldn't have told him about the murders. I don't want him worrying about me. Not any more than he normally does, anyway* ... She glanced at her watch. As usual – or as used to be usual – she was way ahead of herself. Everything she needed for her introductory interview with the sisters was ready hours before she needed it. What to do? She frowned, thinking of Maggie. *I wonder how she got on with her son yesterday? It can't have been easy, breaking news like that.* She had offered to go home with her, but Maggie had refused, obviously deeply distressed herself. *Maybe I should ring her, check she's OK.* She picked up the phone again, then frowned and replaced it, call unmade. *No – she works in the mornings. What did she say – something about getting work out of the way first thing, then she knows she can do what she likes with the rest of the day? Perhaps this afternoon, then. After I've talked to the Misses Webb . . .*

She decided to look over the project information Philip had furnished her with and was still happily absorbed in it some time later when there was a rap at the kitchen door. She looked up in surprise. Maybe Maggie wasn't working after all, or had finished early. *Damn! I have to go and see the sisters in half an hour – I can't spare time for her at the moment.* When she answered it, however, she was faced with a tall man of about her own age, dressed in a fleece jacket, jeans and a beanie hat. His skin was tanned and his eyes were a piercing shade of blue. He smiled at her.

'Dr Summers? I'm Adam Etheridge – Sally asked me to come and look at the chimneys.'

'Oh right – she did warn me – come on in.'

He stepped through the door, and Anna was afforded a brief glimpse of a white van, which was parked half on the verge and half in the driveway. '*J. Etheridge and Son*' was painted on the side of it. Presumably Adam was the son, then.

'Would you like a cup of tea?'

'Tea will be fine, thanks – white, no sugar.'

She filled the kettle and led him through to the furthest fireplace, in the living room.

'So – are you settling in all right?' he asked.

'Fine, thanks,' she laughed. 'Apart from someone pounding on a piano in the middle of the night!'

'A piano?' He looked at her sharply, then at something behind her. She turned, but saw nothing and looked back at him enquiringly.

'Sorry – I thought I saw my mate's van go past,' he shrugged.

'Oh.' She hadn't heard anything. 'I'll go and make the tea, then, and leave you to the chimney.'

When she carried it through, there was no sign of him.

'Mr Etheridge?'

'Adam.' The voice was muffled.

She turned to see his legs in the fireplace, his body hidden from view.

'Adam. Your tea's ready.'

'Thanks.' The next second, he had stooped free and stepped back into the room. Anna froze as he shook his head. No longer wearing the beanie or fleece, a cascade of blond hair fell around his shoulders. 'Damn!' He bent to pick up an elastic hair tie which had fallen on the floor, his T-shirt doing nothing to hide the muscles which rippled through his lean frame. Retrieving it, he pulled his hair back into a pony tail, catching sight of Anna's face as he did so. It was his turn to look puzzled. 'Is there a problem?'

Anna was uncomfortably aware of her heart beating against her ribs. This was ridiculous. She held out the mug of tea. He took it from her, his eyes never leaving her face.

'No. it's just, seeing your hair, reminded me ...' She could be wrong, of course, but decided to take a shot in the dark. 'What were you doing with the goats on Saturday night?'

'The goats?' He shrugged, gaze never wavering. 'Calming them down. I knew they'd be upset by the fireworks.'

'So you're ... what? A goat whisperer, rather than a horse whisperer?'

He laughed. 'I don't limit myself to a particular species.'

'Just good with animals?'

'You could say that. I have to say, I wasn't aware of your presence. I hope I didn't alarm you.'

'No,' she lied. 'But what was it exactly that you were doing with them?' She thought of some esoteric reading that had been thrust on her by a friend. 'You had me going for a moment – I thought you were doing the LBR.'

'LBR?'

'Lesser banishing ritual.'

'I really don't know what you're talking about.' He smiled and shook his head before lowering his gaze and taking a mouthful of tea.

'So you're not Wiccan, then?'

'Wiccan?' His eyebrows shot up. 'I don't think running around naked outdoors would suit me. And if you saw me with the goats, you'll know fine well I wasn't naked.'

'Mmm. I also know fine well that not all Wiccans work naked.'

'Is that so? It's not a subject I've ever studied.'

'Perhaps the Western Mystery Tradition, then?'

'You've completely lost me now. If it's my religion you're after, I was brought up Church of England.' He laughed suddenly. 'Hang on – you saw me doing this sort of thing, right?' His body seemed to flow into a series of beautifully graceful moves. 'I do martial arts, if that's any help.'

'And you thought that would calm the goats?'

He smiled at her in amusement. 'No "thinking" about it – it did.' He took another swallow of tea and set the mug down on the hearth. 'Anyway. I'd best get back to this fireplace.'

'I have to go and see the Misses Webb ...'

'Yes, I know. I'll lock up behind me when I leave. I have a spare key. You can check that's OK with Sally, if you want.'

'No. That's fine.' She stood awkwardly for a second. 'Well. I'll be off, then.'

He nodded and disappeared back inside the chimney as Anna gathered up her things and left.

She walked across the Green, pondering their conversation. How stupid did she feel? He probably thought she was quite mad. *Whatever possessed me to come out with the LBR nonsense?* She smiled wryly to herself, thinking of Professor Roland Featherstone, the friend whose esoteric interests had made her feel so foolish. *Wait till I tell Roly* – he'll *probably think I'm mad, too!*

Taking a deep breath, she lengthened her stride and soon passed the church. *Be logical. It was dark. I was nervous. I could easily have been mistaken. Maybe he* was *just making soothing noises, doing his martial arts stuff.* She kicked at a stone. *Not that anything he just did in the living room looked remotely like what he was doing on Saturday night, mind. The circle, the facing the four directions, arms over his head ... It looked just like the description of the LBR, or something very like it. And why would anyone, anyway,* do *the LBR for a couple of goats?*

An image flashed before her eyes, dismissed before it had time to become fully formed. *Summers, don't you* dare *let Roly's silly ideas take hold! There's no such thing as black magic and sacrificing goats to the devil. It's all a load of superstitious nonsense.*

She thought suddenly of the fact that Adam had a key to April Cottage. *Will he give that back to Sally when he's finished today, or keep it for access if he has to come back? And why does the thought of that make me so uncomfortable? Sally wouldn't give him a key if she didn't trust him ...*

She forced herself to put Adam out of her mind and concentrate on the matter in hand, paying more attention to her surroundings now, not having been to this part of the village before. Sally's directions were, again, easy to follow. Buildings were sparse and the fields and hedges had now given way to woodland. *It should be just around the corner on the left* ... Sure enough, she came across a gate and stile bearing a signpost indicating that this was the way to Broomwood House. She chose to use the gate, laden as she was with the briefcase and camera equipment, being careful to close it behind her. The subtle scent of damp vegetation pervaded her nostrils as she walked along the footpath, trees and chaotic undergrowth bounding her route. Just a few moments later, Broomwood House came into view, a huge, old, double-fronted building with crenellations across the top and diamond-paned windows. A car was parked to one side of it and as she approached, she could see a wider, rutted track leading away behind the house, and a broad driveway sweeping down to what she understood to be the route usually taken if approaching by vehicle. The brass door-knocker was shaped in the likeness of the head of the Green Man. She smiled to herself and rapped it sharply, hearing footsteps descending stairs before it was opened by Sally Arnold.

'Lovely timing! Come on in.'

'Thanks.' She wiped her feet before stepping into the hall. 'Good God!' she breathed, looking around her.

Sally chuckled. 'You ain't see nothing yet! Come on through.'

Anna followed her into the kitchen. 'This is unbelievable – it's just like a time warp!' Her eyes darted between the ancient cooking range and early electric cooker, then to the Belfast sinks and scrubbed table. The only concessions to the present century appeared to be an electric kettle, a toaster and a microwave cooker, which hummed happily, and from which the rich smell of a meaty stew escaped.

'And you've still seen nothing yet! I've made a pot of tea, but if you prefer coffee ...'

'Tea's fine. Good Lord, Sally – I can't get over this.'

'Was that the door, Sally? Are you all right?' A cultured, elderly voice seemed to float down from upstairs. Sally moved to the kitchen door before shouting her reply.

'I'm fine, Miss Alice. Dr Summers has arrived.'

'Oh how lovely! You will bring her up?'

'In a minute, yes.' She turned to Anna, handing her a mug of tea and indicating a silver sugar bowl. Anna shook her head. 'They've been looking forward to seeing you. They're pretty good at present, too. As I said before, they have their good days and their not-so-good days, but they're on fairly good form just now. They were tired today, though – didn't want to get up – so they'll have their lunch in bed.'

'Do you do this for them every day?'

Sally nodded. 'Have done for the last eight months or so. I eat my own lunch here as well, on weekdays – Frank says it's my way of getting more than just an hour for lunch!'

'Their solicitor said you've been a godsend.'

Sally shrugged in embarrassment. 'It's not as if they've any family left and I don't mind doing it. Has Adam been to look at the chimneys?'

The change of subject threw Anna for a second. 'Yes. He was still there when I left – he said you'd given him a spare key and that he'll lock up when he's done.'

'I expect he'll drop it off later, when he's finished.'

The microwave signalled the end of cooking time with a sharp ting and Sally removed the casserole dish from it. Taking plates from the dresser, she began to serve the stew.

'Can I do anything?' Anna asked.

'Slice some bread, if you will – four slices on two plates – nice and thick, like doorsteps, is how they have it with this. Thanks.'

Anna took the wooden lid from a large bread crock and retrieved the loaf within. 'Wow! This looks great!'

'On sale in my shop, if you want some!'

'I'll be round later! Bread knife?'

'In the block over there.'

Sally put everything on to a large tray and headed for the door. 'You have a good look round – take photos or whatever – and I'll take you up to meet them when they've finished their lunch. Oh – and I brought you those papers of Aunt Ida's about April Cottage – in the big envelope on the side, there.'

'Thanks.'

Anna put it in her briefcase and finished her tea before taking out her camera and notebook, aware of voices and laughter coming from the women upstairs. She took general shots of the kitchen from every angle, then moved in to take close-ups of the ancient appliances. Satisfied, she moved back to the hall, taking another couple of shots before opening one of the many doors which led off it. Walking through it, she caught her breath. *Oh my God . . . !* Not only had she walked into another time warp; she was in a different world. Chinese or Japanese. *The Oriental Room*, she wrote in her notebook before starting to take shots. It was like a museum, she thought, yet a happily lived-in one. Most museums, she felt sure, would give their eye teeth to have stuff of this quality. Lacquer work, ceramics, fabrics, weaponry – it was exquisite. How had the Misses Webb come by it? There was far more to photograph in here and she took her time, missing nothing. She tutted to herself as she changed the film. *I should have brought more with me . . .*

Finally closing the door, she opened another one, this time encountering blackness. Disconcerted for a moment, she ran her hand along the wall and flicked on the light switch, finding herself in a different kind of museum this time. She felt almost light-headed as she stared at the magnificent furniture and wall-coverings. Dear God! This had to be early Arts and Crafts Movement. The darkness had been caused by the fact that, at first sight, the room appeared to have four walls and no windows. On closer inspection, however, she found the back wall not to be a wall at all. Full-length sliding panels, papered in the same William Morris wallpaper, drew back to reveal glass doors which, if opened, would lead, down a couple of steps, into the garden at the back of the house. She stood for a moment, breathing the scent of lavender and beeswax. Someone – Sally, no doubt, in recent times – had lovingly looked after this furniture. She felt strangely comforted by the old-fashioned smells and beauty around her. It was here that Sally found her, a few minutes later, busily taking more pictures.

'Sally – this is absolutely marvellous!' She drew the sliding panels shut again, to protect the wood from the sunlight. 'I'd already prepared all sorts of obvious questions for the sisters before I came, but having seen this – well . . .' She laughed and shook her head. 'My head is positively reeling!'

'It's a beautiful place, and it's nice to have someone else here who appreciates it.'

'I'm just amazed – I mean, you said they had a burglary last year – how come all this stuff is still here? It must be worth a fortune.'

'It is. But I reckon it wasn't professional thieves that broke in. Lads, most like. They pinched jewellery, the TV and video, and tore up a few books. It could have been a lot worse, certainly.'

'Were the sisters in at the time?'

'No, thank God. Frank had taken them to a classical concert. The shock though – that was terrible. They used to go out and about a lot – Molly was still driving in her eighties, you know – but after that – the burglary – well . . . they've hardly set foot out of the house since. And that's what's done for their confidence, in my opinion. Still – come up and say hello. I'm really hoping you'll be good for them.' As they approached the foot of the stairs, she lowered her voice and added, 'By the way – don't say anything about the murders at Swifford Maisey – it would only frighten them.' Anna nodded her assent as she continued. 'Normally, I bring in the newspapers for them, but I want to try and keep it under wraps.' Raising her voice, she called out, 'We're on the way up!'

The stairs led to a broad, branched landing with many doors. Sally turned left and knocked at the first door on the right.

'Come in!'

'All finished with your lunch, are you? This is Dr Summers, the lady that's going to talk to you about the old days. Anna, this is the Misses Alice and Molly Webb.'

Anna approached the huge, four-poster bed, her face smiling whilst her mind did further somersaults. *She should have warned me! They're like a cross between Miss Havisham and Charlie and the Chocolate Factory . . .*

The Misses Webb sat side by side in the bed, propped up by many cushions and pillows, and covered by blankets and eider-downs topped with a richly embroidered throw which matched the hangings of the four-poster.

'Do come closer, my dear. I'm Alice and this is my sister, Molly. You must excuse us, not being up at this time of the day, but we were so tired and November is always so miserable, don't you think?' Alice patted the bed and Anna sat on it, shaking their gnarled hands. Alice's hair was grey and she was wearing a lilac-coloured nightgown and bed-jacket, whilst her sister, white-haired, was dressed similarly in blue. Both sisters were wearing glasses, but put aside the magazines they had been reading. 'It's so exciting, having a visitor – we don't often get to see new faces, do we, Molly?'

'No, dear.'

'Well, thank you very much for agreeing to see me ...'

'Our pleasure, my dear! Sally explained to us about your project, and we'll help in any way we can.' Molly nodded as her sister spoke.

'Wonderful!' Anna took out her recording equipment and explained what it was. 'Is it all right if I use this? It will save me having to stop you, if I were taking notes. You can talk away to your heart's content without interruption.'

'That's fine, dear. I'm not sure where the electricity sockets are, though.'

'That's all right – I know.' Sally found one straight away and watched with interest as Anna checked sound levels and stated the date, time and the sisters' names.

Sally looked at her and asked, 'You all set then?'

'Yes, thanks.' Anna turned back to the sisters. 'This is such a wonderful house – I feel privileged to have seen it. And I have so many questions ...'

'We love it, don't we, dear?' Alice spoke and her sister nodded again. 'We were born here, you know. In this very bed, as it happens, though of course we've had several changes of mattress since then. This was our father's house, you see ...'

'Just make sure the catch is dropped, when you leave.' Sally whispered the words in Anna's ear and smiled as she slipped out of the room to return to work.

Chapter Eight

The old summerhouse was no longer in mundane use. Lit now by candlelight, it had been cleansed and dedicated for the evening ritual. The heavy wooden shutters were closed, the stone circle built, Sacred Space and its Guardians invoked.

Four robed figures stood motionless at the quarter-points of the circle, their synchronised breathing the only sound in the silence. Burning incense on the charcoal brazier spiralled upwards, spreading its heavy perfume in an ever increasing haze.

The One, in the North, spoke.

'We Four are the Guardians of the Keepers of the Old Knowledge. Solemn Council is now convened. I call upon The Second to speak the words of Megan Painter's Curse.'

The Second began to intone the words passed down in secret for almost three hundred years:

'Know now thou slay'st an innocent
to cover up thy foul intent and crime;
yet as my soul do flee
let now this curse be laid on thee –
Whoever in the Swiffords will
another innocent to kill,
shall by the hand of their own kin
pay dear in judgement for their sin;
As here these gallows do no good
this curse shall strike first here, in Blood,
at those who instigated sin,
but shall not stop until it win,
in every village overspill

seeking others there to kill,
followed by Earth and then by Water,
in Maisey and Holt, shall come the slaughter,
in Fen by Fire, in Lea by Air,
those who do evil, have a care –
The Judgement comes, the Arm of God,
for burying me in unhallowed sod.'

The words hung in silence before The One spoke again.

'The Petersons were but the first. The next shall come in Swifford Maisey. By Earth. Let the Symbol of our Power be brought forth.'

A large wooden chest, wrapped in hide, was carried to the centre of the circle, where it was placed on the floor. Arm outstretched, The One pointed an elaborately carved wooden staff at the figure in the South.

'The Second – I call you. Kneel with your hand upon the chest.'

Their eyes met and held. The One began the ritual words.

'I call upon you to swear by the vows and penalties of your initiations – the Calling, the Sacrifice, the Commitment and the Source ...'

The procedure was repeated with The Third, in the East, and The Fourth, in the West, before The One went to the centre to be called upon in turn by the other three Guardians.

This part of the Council completed, The One returned to the North before speaking again.

'Drum for me. Raise the Power.'

The others took up bodhrans and beaters. As the rhythm built and the skins sang, The One began to dance, mind, heart, body becoming attuned to the harmonies, to the living resonance between beats, before sinking to the ground and becoming still.

Chapter Nine

Tuesday November 8th

Alice and Molly Webb, elegantly dressed, but with hair still unbrushed, were looking out of their kitchen window and nodded sagely as a huge flock of birds wheeled and turned.

'It will rain within the hour,' Alice told her sister.

'Yes, dear.'

They moved to the kitchen table, where Alice poured tea into fine china cups, whilst Molly buttered toast.

'Did you see the way the silver birch shivered? I don't think the trees like this time of year any more than we do. Still, one mustn't grumble. We're nice and cosy here. Have you taken your tablets, Molly?'

'Oh, no. I'll do it now.' Molly got up and shuffled to the work surface, picking up the egg cup in which Sally Arnold had left her morning medication. Taking a tumbler from the drainer, she filled it with water and swallowed the pills, placing it in the sink to join the mugs from which they had drunk their cocoa the night before.

'I can't understand the newspapers not being delivered again. I shall have to have a word with Sally at lunchtime. One needs to know what is going on in the world.' Alice frowned and tutted under her breath.

'I don't see why. It never changes much.'

'Well, of course it does! It's a different world now to when we were young.'

'Only the fine detail. It's still all wars, famine and violence.' Molly resumed her place at the table.

Her sister looked at her sharply. 'Well, who got out of bed the wrong side this morning? Of course things change! Think of the developments in science, Molly . . .'

'Not all of it good, in my opinion. Atom bombs. Genetic modification. Designer babies.'

'Really, Molly! Whatever is the matter with you?'

'Nothing's the matter with me. I'm tired, that's all. I shouldn't think there's anything wrong with that, at my age. I don't know why we couldn't just have stayed in bed, like yesterday.'

'Idle hands, Molly – idle hands. And you shouldn't be tired. I slept like a log.'

'Exactly. *You* slept like a log, and *you* snore. Kept me awake half the night. I gave up in the end and came downstairs to talk to Mother.'

Alice paused, marmalade knife in hand, and peered at her sister uncertainly, a little stab of alarm fluttering in her chest. She took a deep breath. Best to change the subject.

'I wonder if that nice Dr Summers will be calling on us today? That should cheer you up. I did so enjoy her company yesterday, didn't you?'

Molly's face brightened. 'Oh yes. I do hope so. Such an interesting young woman. It was so nice to see her little boy, too. It seems such a long time since we had a child in the house.'

'Child? What child? She didn't have a child with her!' Alice's glance slipped to her plate, where marmalade had dripped from her knife. Looking back at her sister's blank face, her voice trembled as she said, 'Sometimes, Molly, I worry about you . . .'

Anna sat at the dining-room table, fingers flying over the keyboard of the laptop. Dear God! The transcription would take hours – how many hours, she dreaded to think. But what marvellous stuff! She knew she wouldn't be able to stay on top of it during her time in Swifford Lea, but had nonetheless made a start the previous evening. The Webb sisters, like many very elderly people, were remarkably garrulous once you got them going. She pulled a notepad towards her and scribbled 'more tapes' beneath the already listed, 'more film' of her shopping list. Sitting back, she glanced out of the window and saw Maggie rounding the bend in the road, apparently going home. Glancing at her watch, she pushed back the chair and moved swiftly through the sitting room to open the front door.

'Maggie! You all right?'

Maggie raised her head from the newspaper she was holding and blinked.

'Yes. Well . . . not really.'

'Do you want to come in for a coffee?' Anna held the door wider, making room for Maggie to pass.

'Are you sure? I'm not disturbing you or anything?'

'I wouldn't have asked if you were. Come on in.'

Maggie slumped on the sofa and sighed heavily. 'This is terrible, Anna – have you seen it?' She held out the newspaper.

'No. I haven't been out yet this morning.' Anna took it from her, flinching at the headline which screamed, **MURDER IN SWIFFORD MAISEY**. Silently, she read it, brow furrowing. 'This doesn't make sense, surely?'

'I know. It's not so much what they're saying, as what they're *not* saying, isn't it?'

Anna scanned the article again. There were references to shock and disbelief rippling throughout the tight-knit villages, bloody massacre, the usual stereotypical epithets – sleepy hamlets, virgin countryside, da-de-da – but this – what was this? Anna read it aloud.

'Tight-lipped police are saying nothing at this stage beyond the fact that they are not seeking anyone else in connection with the incident. A more detailed statement will be issued once the post-mortems have been completed and other forensic evidence examined . . .'

Maggie stood up and rolled her neck, breathing deeply. 'Looks to me like they're saying that Seth Peterson blew a gasket and killed Karen, then himself.'

'Good God! Did you know him? I mean, I know you said the daughter went to school with Jack, but – how *is* Jack, by the way?'

Maggie followed as Anna moved through to the kitchen to get coffee on the go.

'Taking it hard, as you'd expect. He didn't go to college yesterday. I shouldn't think many of them did, not from round here. It was bad enough before, thinking some nutter from outside had done it, but this – well, it beggars belief. Yes, I did know Seth. Not intimately, but on and off over the years, especially when the kids were younger. Parent–teacher evenings, and all that. I don't know …' She leaned against the cooker as Anna put the kettle on. 'What the hell makes people do something like this?'

Anna's attempted reply was interrupted by a rap on the kitchen door. She opened it and found Adam Etheridge outside. He peered past her and nodded to Maggie before speaking.

'Sorry – I hope I'm not interrupting anything?'

'No. come on in. Is it the chimneys again?' *Stupid question – what else could it be?*

'Yes. This is Dave, by the way.' Another man entered the kitchen, as dark as Adam was fair. 'Look, I don't know what time you're seeing the Misses Webb today – we could come back later, maybe … ?'

'No, no – you go ahead. Sally needs to get the work done, I know.'

'Tell you what, Anna – why don't we go round to mine instead?' Maggie offered.

'OK.' Anna turned to Adam and indicated the cupboards. 'You know where everything is – help yourselves. The kettle's on. I'll only be next door.'

Picking up her shoulder bag, Anna walked with Maggie the few yards to her house.

'Oh, Maggie – this is lovely!' She looked around the living room in appreciation and was struck by a sudden thought. 'Where's your piano, then?' Maybe now would be the time to have a quiet word. The playing had disturbed her every night so far.

'Piano? We don't have a piano, love – Jack plays guitar. Come on through. I'll put the kettle on.'

Stella Timpson sighed as she read the latest report of the murders in Swifford Maisey. *What a pity! For one glorious moment, I thought the Blessed Rhianna had done me a favour and gone berserk. Damn! I could have been in there! No way Philip could pull this thing off without her. Still. Not to worry. Some gentle intimidation could be in order now. Shouldn't take much to have her cracking up again. I wonder …* Slowly and carefully, she looked through her diary. *Rather full this week, unfortunately. Next week doesn't look too bad, though. I could maybe fit in a day or two to pay a visit then …*

Jack Taylor sat miserably in the college coffee shop. He hardly knew how he'd managed to get through the last lecture. It was like a gaping hole had entered his life and swallowed him up. He raised his head and groaned inwardly as a group of fellow-students entered the room and made a bee-line for his table. *I don't want to talk about it! Why can't they just leave me alone ...*

'Hey, Jack – have you seen this? We just got it from the Student Union.' A newspaper was thrust in front of him. 'Looks like Karen's dad went off his chump, mate.'

'What?' Jack snatched it up and read the article. Looking up, he said, 'That's stupid. I've known them all my life!' He looked round for support, for someone else from the Maiseys. A couple of heads nodded agreement. One, at the back of the group, did not.

Gavin Morgan was, if anything, even paler than the rest of those who had known Karen Peterson outside college as well as in class. He lived in Swifford Fen and, like Jack, had been to school with her. He shivered involuntarily, his legs suddenly weak. No one noticed. They were too busy looking at Jack. Gavin's mind buzzed, groping for clarity through what seemed like treacle. *The newspapers – the police, even – are already half-way to saying it, then. But they've got it wrong, if they think it was Seth. It wasn't any of them. It was ...* His thoughts faltered, trying to find expression for ideas too terrible to articulate. *Curses and that can't be real*, he told himself. *They just* can't. *It's like a horror movie, only worse. At least with films, you* know *it's not real, that it* couldn't *really happen. Just special effects and stuff.*

Sweat broke out on his upper lip. *Oh, God!* he prayed. *Why don't you help me, if you exist? I can't talk to anyone else about it – they'd think I was crazy.* He didn't want to believe it himself. One part of him just *couldn't* believe it. But it seemed as if what the Voice had told him was true ...

Ellie Smith was frantic as she parked her car in a secluded spot and started running through the woods. She'd wanted to get away, to follow up on that last text message from Karen, but when the news had broken, all hell had let loose. She'd been in a state of shock and disbelief, so upset that her mum had taken her away to her Auntie Gina's in Market Eaton until this morning. She hadn't wanted to go, but Mum had said it would all be too much with reporters and CID swarming all over Swifford Maisey. She'd tried to tell them about Karen's last message, wanted to tell the police, even, but no one was listening and she'd overheard the phone calls between Mum and Dad while they were away. Dad knew Ben Carter, who'd found the bodies and he was in a terrible state and had blabbed to Dad over a lot of whisky, even though he wasn't supposed to. She had strained to hear, standing at the top of the stairs, and although she had obviously only heard Mum's side of the conversation, she'd got a pretty good idea of what had happened.

It sounded awful, just awful. Blood everywhere and writing in blood and she didn't want to think about what Karen may have gone through before she died; not Seth either. And then, yesterday, when Mum was speaking even quieter on the phone than before, it had finally hit her that the police weren't looking for anybody else. All the strength had gone out of her and her legs went all trembly and weak and she really thought, for a moment, that she was going to faint, although she'd never fainted in her life, but her head went all funny and she'd gone hot and cold all over.

If only I'd texted her back. If only I'd told somebody at the time. Maybe it would have changed things, made a difference. She thought back to Saturday night. Leaving the pub without a care in the world, pissing off the blokes that had been letching after her, saying goodnight to Maggie and that Dr Summers what had come to talk to the Misses Webb. Telling Pete and Pat she'd see them in the morning for her shift. How could everything have seemed so normal?

She stopped to get her bearings, realising that she'd been running blind, just crashing around in the undergrowth. Her face was wet with tears. They'd even run into her ears, and her nose was all snotty. She stopped, leaning against a tree before sliding to the ground and sitting with her back against it, oblivious to the dampness seeping through her jeans, trying to slow the hammering of her heart and the horrible shivery feeling that had come over her.

Why could such things happen? Why? How could there be a God? She found herself sobbing uncontrollably, great shuddering gasps that shook her whole body so badly that she wondered if you could actually die of grief and anger and pain.

It seemed like ages before the emotional storm subsided. Then, taking more deep, shuddering breaths, she wiped her face on the sleeve of her jacket, ignoring the snail trails she left on it, as she pulled her mobile phone from her pocket. She had saved Karen's message, meaning to text her back, but hadn't. She'd been tired after her shift, decided to ring her in the morning, but by then it was too late.

It's all my fault – I should have tried. I should have asked her to come over to ours for the night. Oh God! And to think I was embarrassed about my mobile going off in the pub, and called her a daft bat! Oh, Karen ... I am SO sorry ...

She cried again, hauling herself to her feet, and brought the text message back up on to the screen. She'd just thought it was daft at the time. Now, with the searing clarity of hindsight, guilt overwhelmed her. Her mind translated the textual shorthand into normal words. Only these weren't normal. '*I don't know how much longer I can stand this. If anything happens, go to our old Woodcutters place. I've left it there. Then you'll know.*'

Ellie flailed her fists at the tree in frustration. *How could I have ignored that? God, if what happened* hadn't *happened, I should at least have worried that she might be in trouble or suicidal or pregnant or something! But I shouldn't have ignored it ...*

Physically steadier now, but her mind still churning, Ellie looked around her. The Woodcutters Cottage place that Karen had mentioned wasn't a cottage at all. When they were little – up till about the end of the first year at secondary school, in fact – they'd had a secret place, a den, where they had solemnly declared themselves to be the only members of the Woodcutters Cottage Club, their own invention, where they'd told stories and played at camping and dreamed of what their lives would be like. Kids' stuff. Only now, Karen no longer had a life.

Ellie squeezed her eyes shut and wiped away more tears, then started jogging along familiar paths, going deeper and deeper into the woods until she came to their place. She stopped, breathing heavily. Now she was here, she felt a strange reluctance to follow through. What had Karen left for her? What good could it do, now that she was dead?

The hollow lay before her, long since overgrown, surrounded by ash and oak. Slowly now, she made her way forward. If Karen *had* left anything, it would be in the old hiding place. They'd used it as kids, to leave secret messages written in simple code. She felt a pang of anxiety. It had rained so heavily on Saturday night, surely a piece of paper would be gone, sodden and illegible? Breathing hard, she pushed herself through the tangle, twigs snapping beneath her feet, brambles clutching at her clothing. *Please don't let me be too late. I need to know ...*

Finally, she was there. She crouched down and pushed aside the obstructing vegetation. The slab was still in place. It was an old, broken paving slab from when Mum and Dad had decided to build a patio, years ago. What a job they'd had carrying it, stopping to drink lemonade along the way, giggling, not a care in the world. They'd dug a hollow beneath it, their hiding place for messages and forbidden magazines they couldn't risk taking home for others to see. They'd dirtied it up, covered it in leaves. Now, it was worn and smooth and covered in moss. Had it been disturbed recently? Ellie couldn't be sure. She lifted it carefully, putting it to one side and caught her breath. Something *was* here! Something wrapped in a plastic bag from a bookshop in Market Eaton. Hands trembling, she unwrapped it. *What ... ?*

It was Karen's diary. She felt her heart lurch. For a moment, her mind reeled at the implications. Maybe now, she'd know, would find out what had been troubling Karen, what had been going on in her family. Perhaps Seth had been drinking or had money troubles or something ... She ran out of ideas. None of them seemed plausible, anyway. She clutched the diary to her chest before stuffing it into her inside jacket pocket. Best get away from here, first. Just in case. She replaced the slab carefully, covering it over with sodden, rotting leaves. Funny how she hadn't noticed the smell before. It was as if she'd been so focused on getting here, and her reasons for doing so, that her senses had been suspended until now. Satisfied, she got up and moved backwards, covering her tracks, just like they'd done as kids.

Only when she got back to her car did she take out the diary and start to read it. *Maybe it will help me to understand. Maybe ...* She skimmed through to begin with, baffled by the ordinariness of the entries.

Bought two CDs.
Hair cut, 10 a.m.
Jack Taylor broke my make-up mirror at college.

She turned the pages faster.

To Gran's for the day – boring, boring, BORING!
Oh my God – I think Stuart Trimble fancies me! NO WAY!

Suddenly she blinked. What was this? A whole page of writing. Lots of pages. Her face froze as she began to read. Her scalp prickled, the hairs on her arms stood on end. Her mouth went dry, her mind numb with disbelief. This couldn't be right. This *couldn't* be true. Not Karen ...

Even with the car windows closed, her anguished cry tore through the stillness around her, sending a pair of wood pigeons into startled, crackling flight.

Chapter Ten

Pete and Pat Barker had been surprised when Ellie turned up at the pub. Even more surprised when she'd pleaded with them to be allowed back to work that very day. They'd been reluctant, out of sympathy and concern for her, telling her not to worry about taking time off, saying it was too soon after her friend's death to think about coming back, but she was having none of it. She couldn't afford to fail. Now she had a plan in mind, she *had* to talk them into it. After reading the diary, it was the only hope she had of gaining justice for Karen.

The greeting Anna received as she arrived to interview the Misses Webb once more was even warmer than the previous day. While they finished their lunch, Sally warned Anna about further measures she'd taken to ensure that they didn't learn about the Peterson tragedy.

'I've told them there's been a problem with the railways and that the national papers aren't getting through, and that the locals have been hit by a strike at the print-works. They seem to have bought the story. I've also taken extra precautions.' She pulled some batteries from her pocket. 'They have an old radio – it doesn't work on the mains – and I've removed these just in case they take it into their heads to tune in for local news.'

'OK. I've got you. I'll make sure I don't let anything slip.' Anna went off to take more photographs until the sisters were ready to see her, this time discovering a vast library, wall to ceiling with books on three sides. She blinked in amazement. There were ladders on each wall for access to the higher shelves, and even an antique cabinet holding cards meticulously cataloguing the contents. It was a bibliophile's dream. She could quite happily have stayed here for the whole afternoon, but was all too soon called back to the Misses Webb who, today, had decided to be interviewed in what Anna thought of as the Arts and Crafts Room.

'How lovely to see you again, my dear!' It was Alice who spoke. Both sisters were seated in armchairs on either side of the fireplace. A hardbacked chair had been pulled up in the middle for Anna to sit on, along with a small, exquisitely inlaid table for her recording equipment. She soon had everything ready and before she knew it, the sisters were chatting happily about how they used to go to school in a pony and trap.

'Most of the village children went in a horse and cart, didn't they, Molly? But Father always sent us separately. I'm not really sure that was such a good thing, but still ...'

'It set us apart, you see. Not that anyone would have dared to call us hoity-toity, but they thought it.'

'Some of them. Not all. And perhaps it was best, in the long run. When we became teachers, later, we had a natural sense of authority with the parents as well as the children.'

'You were teachers?' Anna interjected.

'Oh yes. Didn't you know? We taught everything, to begin with. That's how it was back then. Later, of course, we had our own subjects. I taught English and French, Molly taught crafts – mostly needlework and cookery.'

'And we both taught music, of course.' Molly's face brightened as she said it. 'We've always loved music haven't we, Alice?'

'Oh yes. Do you remember when we taught Daniel Faraday's children privately, in exchange for eggs and poultry?'

'And wasn't it Daniel's daughter that nearly died in the snow-drifts when the village was cut off in the winter of '47? Three weeks, we were cut off! Happened again in '63 and '81, though not for so long, of course ...'

Anna let the tape roll on, enchanted by their stories.

It was closing time at The White Hart and Anna and Maggie made the short walk home together. It had been a subdued evening, largely due to Ellie's sudden return to her waitressing duties. Pat had kept a strict eye out to see that the girl had not been pestered and on the whole, people had avoided talking about the murders in her hearing.

Anna was already thinking ahead to her next meeting with the Misses Webb. She had lots more fascinating stuff down on tape, all of which was throwing up further questions. The sisters had gone off at tangents, talking about everything from old courting rituals and their childhood games, through to village politics, local families, and what they saw as the benefits of a rational, humanistic education. *This could run and run,* Anna realised. *The sisters' memories alone, that is, and then there are other people I need to speak to, as well.* The Misses Webb had talked about village doctors, some now dead, others retired; crime and punishment, along with police officers and judges, again, some now dead, others retired. *I must speak to Philip, find out just what the state of funding is on this. He's going to be over the moon with the potential.*

She was brought out of her reverie by Maggie saying goodnight and with a quick wave, went down the path and let herself into April Cottage.

The Misses Webb were preparing to go to bed. Alice had been downstairs, adding boiling water to the mugs of instant cocoa that Sheila Finney had left ready for them, along with Molly's evening medication. It was bad enough worrying about Molly's osteoporosis, but lately ... Her sister had perked up considerably following Dr Summers' visit, but still Alice shivered, not wanting to dwell on what she felt was an increasing deterioration in Molly's mental faculties. She leaned against the sink and closed her eyes, as the familiar, fluttering fear took hold of her chest again.

Please don't let us have to go into a Home. I couldn't bear it. And what if we were separated? What if Molly had to go and I were left here on my own? We've never been apart. We ... She pulled herself up sharply. Whatever was she thinking of? *Praying?* To what? To whom? Maybe her *own* reasoning faculties were in decline.

'Rational humanism.' She spoke the words aloud, forcing her mind back to its original thoughts. Which were what? Oh yes. The cocoa. Sheila. Sheila popped in every evening to give the place a quick once-over and make sure they were all right. She was Sally Arnold's niece and Alice still thought of her as a nice girl, although she was now married with three children. Carefully, she placed the mugs on a tray in the dumb waiter and sent it on its way upstairs.

Molly wasn't in the bedroom. Alice tutted under her breath, wondering what her sister was doing. She *should* have been getting undressed by now, though that could be a long process, even with Alice's help. She went back to the bedroom door and looked along the corridor. *Oh no* ... The door to Father's study was ajar. Setting her shoulders firmly, Alice walked to it, calling her sister's name.

'Molly! You should be getting ready for bed!'

'Should I? I was just looking ...' Her voice trailed off, and Alice followed her gaze to the photographs on Father's desk. The room had not been disturbed since he died. Except for the burglary, of course. Alice closed her mind to the violation, telling herself that it had been minor, in this room, at least. She moved forward. The desk was large and made of oak, with a beautifully tooled leather top. She allowed her hand to caress it, almost imagining for a moment that the lingering smell of Father's fragrant pipe tobacco was still discernible in this room where he had spent so many hours. No. She mustn't allow herself to be carried away by Molly's silly fancies. She reached out, gently taking her sister's arm to lead her back to their bedroom.

'Come along now. The drinks will be getting cold. And you need to take your tablets.'

'Yes. Yes, of course. Has she photographed it? That nice young woman?'

'Father's study? I don't believe so. Not yet.'

'She should, you know. For posterity. It personifies him, don't you think?'

Later, lying together in bed, Molly struggled to remember what else it was she had been meaning to say to Alice. Her mind swam with images, some startlingly clear, others shrouded in a diaphanous mist. *What was it now ... ? Oh yes!* The mist had parted at last and she could see it quite clearly. *Why ever did I not say something at the time? She couldn't have disagreed with me then.*

Alice, already half-asleep, was startled by the ferocious pinch her sister gave her. 'Molly! What do you think you're doing?'

'Dr Summers – I *told* you she had a little boy with her!'

Heart fluttering, Alice made no reply, but turned on her side and wept silently into her pillow.

In April Cottage, Anna had just turned off the kitchen light and was about to take herself upstairs to bed when she stopped, rooted to the spot. *What was that?* She stood silently, ears straining. There it was again. Her scalp prickled and a chill swept over her body. Footsteps. On the gravel drive outside the kitchen door. How she knew, she couldn't say, but somehow they seemed furtive, skittering. *Oh God . . .* Her mouth went dry as a bone. The next moment, she was barely able to repress a shriek as an insistent tapping came on the kitchen door. *Pete! I must phone Pete!*

'Dr Summers! Dr Summers? Please – it's Ellie!'

Relief flooded through Anna. Switching the light back on, she crossed the room and drew back the lace curtain. Sure enough, Ellie's face, white and pinched, peered back at her, blinking at the light.

'Ellie – what's happened? Come on in.' Anna drew back to allow the girl to pass, firmly closing and locking the door behind her. 'You frightened me to death – I was just about to go to bed!'

'I'm sorry to disturb you, it being late and all, and skulking round the back, but . . .' The girl bit her lip and clutched her canvas bag to her chest. 'I need to talk to you. It's really important.'

'OK. Come on through.' Anna led her into the sitting room, wondering what on earth this could be about. *I hope she's not ill and thinks I'm a medical doctor . . .*

'Can I get you a drink? Tea or coffee?'

The girl shook her head.

'Please – sit down. How can I help?'

Slowly, the girl sat in an armchair by the window, eyes darting around the room. Her face was a picture of indecision. Anna sat on the sofa and waited, mind racing. *What on earth is going on?*

'Oh God – I was so convinced this was the right thing to do, and now I'm not so sure . . .'

'Take your time. You don't have to say anything you don't want to. And – if you've changed your mind about whatever it was, that's fine. I'm not going to hold you prisoner.' Anna smiled, trying to reassure the girl, all the time aware that she had no idea why.

'Look – ' Ellie blurted. 'I'm here because you're an outsider and you're a doctor, aren't you?' She held up her hand as Anna started to speak. 'Not a medical doctor, I know that, but – you're an expert, right? On history and folklore and witchcraft – stuff like that?'

Anna frowned. 'Well – yes and no. It depends on what you mean by "expert", I suppose. I specialise in oral history and folklore. Sometimes that overlaps into so-called witchcraft, but I'm certainly not an expert in that.' The girl's face fell, then brightened again as Anna added, 'I have a friend who is, though.'

'Right.' The girl was silent for a moment, blinking rapidly, her body as taut as a piano wire. 'But do you believe in it? Yourself, like?'

Anna's eyebrows shot up. 'Witchcraft?'

'Well, maybe not witchcraft, but – you know – curses – that sort of thing.'

Anna exhaled noisily and shook her head. 'I'd be lying if I said I did. But that's not to say that I'm right about it, of course, and there are certainly people who *do* believe it, there can be no doubt about that.'

'And do you think they're mad?'

Anna shifted uncomfortably, held in Ellie's intense gaze. 'Well ... I wouldn't say that, necessarily. Mistaken, maybe. Who knows? It's not really something I've given a lot of thought to.'

'But do you believe in God?'

Anna squirmed inwardly. Where on earth was Ellie going with all this stuff? 'Again – it depends what you mean by "God", I suppose. I used to have a vague belief in a Higher Power of some kind but ...'

'But you don't now?'

'Well, no.' The answer felt lame.

'Why not?'

Shit! I wish we'd never started this conversation. 'Well ... it's not so much that I don't believe, as I don't know *what* to believe. I can't make sense of things, I suppose I'm saying.'

'Like tragedies and stuff? You wonder how God can exist when such terrible things happen?'

'Yes. It's what theologians call "The Problem of Evil", I believe.' Anna felt it was time to take the bull by the horns. 'Look, Ellie – I don't mean to be rude, but I don't understand where this is leading – why you're asking me these kinds of questions.'

'This is why.' The girl's eyes stayed on Anna's face as she reached into her bag and pulled out a thick, ring-bound A5-sized book. 'It's Karen's diary. You know – Karen Peterson? The murders. She was my friend.'

'Right. I'm terribly sorry, Ellie. I know what you must be going through ...'

'Do you?' The girl shot her a fierce look.

'Oh yes. Believe me, I do.'

'You may have lost someone. But not like this.' Ellie dropped her eyes and leafed through the pages, finally offering the opened book to Anna, who took it from her with open curiosity. She started to read and gasped.

'Now do you see what I mean?' Ellie's voice was ominous.

'Ellie, you have to take this to the police!' Anna made no attempt to hide her shock. 'How on earth did you get it?'

Briefly, Ellie told her, eyes brimming with tears as she recounted the text message and her journey into the woods.

'Good Lord! You poor girl! But you must take it to the police – you do see that?' Anna realised that her heart was hammering.

'I can't!' The words rose into a wail which propelled the girl from her seat. 'It would be a betrayal, don't you see that? She *trusted* me. She was my friend and I let her down. And now it's too late, and I can't, I can't! It's all my fault! If I'd known, I could have stopped it!' She stood, shaking her head and crying.

Awkwardly, Anna approached her, mind racing. *Good God – I've only read a couple of pages and I'm shocked – what else might be in there? And what can I do?* She put her arms around the girl, trying to straighten out her thoughts as the muffled sobbing finally subsided. The girl pulled away, blowing her nose noisily. Anna exhaled loudly.

'Let me get this straight, Ellie – you feel you can't take the diary to the police because Karen was your friend and you feel you would be betraying her if you did so?'

The girl nodded.

'But I didn't know Karen, so I *could* take it to them – right?'

Again, the girl nodded.

Anna shook her head. 'I'd still have to tell them where I got it from.'

'Couldn't you just say as how you found it somewhere? Aren't you supposed to keep your sources confidential, like priests and journalists and that? Please?'

Anna grimaced. 'They'll still need to talk to you, Ellie. They need to know about Karen's text message.'

The girl stood, shredding the damp tissues in her hands, conflicting emotions swimming across her face. Finally, she spoke.

'How about this, then? I don't want them to know that I come to you with it, see? That would still be an act of betrayal. But if you was to say that I dropped it, getting into my car or summat, and you couldn't catch me, and you come home and read it, like – well, then, I'd have to talk to them but it wouldn't be me who'd betrayed her – right?'

'And would you tell them about the text message and how you went in search of the diary?'

'Yes. I'd have to then, wouldn't I? Because they'd come to me and asked.'

Anna ran a hand through her hair. 'I understand your thinking, Ellie – about not betraying Karen – but why *are* you giving this to me? Why not to someone you know?'

The girl's face was pinched as she fought to hold back tears again.

'Because I don't want anyone else to know. Not people that knew her, like. Not yet, like this. And I want you to stop the evil that overtook her. You or your friend – I don't care. I just want Karen to be all right.'

'What?' Anna felt as if she'd lost the thread. 'How can Karen "be all right", Ellie? What do you mean?'

The girl bit her lip. 'In the afterlife, like – if there is one. I don't want her suffering torment or being punished or going to hell or nothing like that.' She pointed to the diary, lying open on the sofa where Anna had left it. 'You read that and you'll understand what I mean. It was the Voice that done it, see? Because of Megan Painter's curse. You've got to stop it, Dr Summers. It's got to be stopped.'

Fletcher Godfrey was lying alone in the darkness of his bedroom, wishing he hadn't finished off the evening's drinking with a whisky chaser. The Peterson deaths had really got to him. He and Seth had grown up together and what the police were implying was just too awful for words. His stomach felt sour and he knew he'd probably have a bad head tomorrow. He must really have overdone it this time, though, he thought, as he began to drift into sleep. For a moment there, he'd almost imagined he'd heard a strange voice, calling his name . . .

Chapter 11

Darkness. Darkness.

Shadow on shadow.

Hanging, motionless, nothing beneath her feet.

Silence.

Heavy, tangible, almost breathing.

Reaching without touching.

Nothing anywhere.

Panic rising. Where is she?

Breathe, breathe.

Panic again, threatening to overwhelm her.

When she breathes, something seems to be breathing her, feeding on her every breath, growing, burgeoning, rippling through the silence like a wind-borne sigh.

Danger.

Fear.

All senses alert, yet sensing nothing.

No points of reference.

Yet the Thing is growing, coming closer, as if to envelop her. How can she run, with no ground beneath her feet? How can she know where to run when all she sees is darkness?

And then the Thing speaks.

The Voice.

Legs turn to jelly. Bowels twist. Stomach turns.

Cold. So cold.

It snakes, the Voice, a writhing hiss, indistinct, but growing in volume, echoing, echoing ...

She struggles to understand, understanding only that she needs to flee the danger. But how can she flee without sight or reference or ground beneath her feet? Where and what is this nothingness of dark?

Why is she here?

Where is help?

A pounding now in her chest, swishing in her ears, palpitations forcing the rush of blood which dizzies her even further.

Can't breathe. Can't breathe. Oh God. Oh God. GOD HELP ME!

Light comes, bringing a snarl of reaction from the Voice.

Blinking, she peers as the darkness recedes, yet what she sees makes her recoil in terror. A scream rises from her belly but cannot reach her throat, which closes, stricken by sheer, suffocating horror.

She hangs in an Abyss, a chasm between two cliffs of terrifying proportions.

The depths below seem bottomless, swimming before her eyes in increasingly inky blackness.

Above her, blackness again, unremitting, boundless, no pinprick stars, no moon. And the light is so little and she cannot see its source, knows only that she hangs here, and knows not why.

'NO-O-O-O-O-O!' Her scream bounces back from walls of rock, mocking, taunting, leaving her unable to draw further breath.

Suffocation.

Suffocation.

Her head spins, her eyes dim, and images shimmer, colours pulsating, forming, reforming, until she sees a girl without a face, axe in hand, floating towards her.

A mouth appears; vile, twisted, not the girl's mouth but that of the Voice which drives her, and which now begins to chant.

She struggles to recognise the words.

Oh God. The rhyme.

'Lizzie Borden took an axe and gave her mother forty whacks; when she saw what she had done, she gave her father forty-one . . .'

Over and over.

Louder and louder.

And now another assault upon her ears. The sound of a piano playing. Classical music swells, louder, faster, seemingly in an attempt to drown out the obscene rhyme.

But the movement of the faceless girl persists.

Swish . . . swish . . . the axe cuts air, coming closer, closer, until suddenly, shockingly, the figure of the girl is blotted out.

By her husband.
She moans. 'Guy . . .', further words forestalled as the axe appears in his *hand now, and he screams at her, a torrent of invective and abuse, before finally calling, taunting her.*

'Who do you love? What do you love, Rhianna? Your work. Your bloody stupid work. You let her come between us and I warned you what would happen . . .'

The faceless girl, still hidden from view, begins to speak over him, her voice changing to that of the Voice as she chants about vengeance, vengeance, blood sacrifice for the propitiation of sin, and all the time, Guy comes closer, swinging the axe which swishes as it cuts through the air, air which does not deserve the name for this is foul, thick, suffocating; no giver of life.

'You will pay, Rhianna. See how you will pay . . .'

Her heart lurches as he pulls, like a magician pulling a rabbit from a hat, a child from his pocket. Their *child. Jamie.*

Her son, on his toddler's legs, rushes towards her, unaware, beaming, calling, 'Mummy! Mummy!' and Guy, never taking his eyes from her face, swings the axe and chops the child to pieces, sending flesh and blood and bone splattering down upon her in an obscene rainfall of carnage.

'Jamie!' Anna sat bolt upright in bed, soaked in sweat, breath coming in ragged gasps. Her heart was hammering so much, she thought it would burst through her ribs. She stumbled out of bed, groping for the wall, the light switch, standing shivering as the bulb finally lit the room. She leaned against the wall, legs trembling, then, propelled by further urgency, fled along the corridor, stumbling and tripping on the uneven steps before finally reaching the bathroom, where she was agonisingly sick.

She leaned against the toilet, too weak to move, heart still hammering, mouth now dry and sour. She shut her eyes, then flashed them open again, as images from her nightmare threatened to come to life once more behind her eyelids.

Dear God! Dear God! Slowly, she managed to calm her breathing, sitting on the floor until she felt able to stand. Legs unsteady, she moved slowly to the sink, where she splashed cold water on her face and rinsed her mouth. Straightening up, she caught sight of herself in the mirror, where her reflection, stark in the electric light, stared back at her, pale and with black rings beneath the eyes. She flinched. What had she expected to see? Blood? Jamie's blood? She shook her head to clear the image. *For Christ's sake – it was just a dream.*

She stared at herself, anxiety gnawing in the pit of her stomach. There was no blood. It *was* simply a dream. But she had neither looked nor felt this bad since the accident.

Chapter Twelve

Wednesday November 9th

Fletcher Godfrey stared at his reflection. The magnifying mirror, swivel-mounted, was ancient. He'd used it for shaving for more years than he cared to remember. He grunted as he nicked himself, thinking sourly that the result matched his bloodshot eyes. He would have to cut down the drinking. Never a fanciful man, he had been more than a little alarmed by the previous night's experience. He'd heard that alcoholics saw things and, thank God, at least that hadn't happened to him, but still ... Did they hear things first, *then* start seeing things? He'd never come across anything like that.

Besides, he told himself, *that's irrelevant. I'm not an alkie. Just had one too many. Well, a couple of whisky chasers. That could be what did the damage. It's never happened before, and I don't usually drink chasers ...*

Shaving done, he wiped his face on the towel. It had been unnerving, though. Maybe it was a drunken dream. Bit OTT, though, hearing that voice. It had seemed so real. *Daft bugger! Pull yourself together, man!* He checked his reflection one last time, dabbing at the nick. Shame you couldn't still get styptic pencils, and he hated sticking cotton wool on shaving cuts. You just wound up looking like a defrocked Father Christmas.

Anyway, this would never do. He was supposed to be seeing the vicar this afternoon and there was work to be done before they got together and started talking about the funeral. He hoped there wouldn't be any problems. Reverend Fury was a funny bugger, and no mistake, with a name that matched his nature. Real doom and gloom merchant, hard-line conservative when it came to it. Reckoned BSE and CJD and Foot and Mouth were God's punishment on a sinful nation. Like the Plagues of Egypt, he said, designed to bring sinners to their knees and bend their stiff necks to the Divine will.

Christ! If he cuts up awkward about burying Seth ... He wouldn't about Karen, he knew. Innocent victim, she'd be, so that was all right. But if it *were* true that Seth had killed her and then himself ...

Fletcher grimaced. Reverend Fury was bad enough about suicide. Hadn't wanted to bury Eddie Clemens, who'd hanged himself during the last Foot and Mouth outbreak. *Poor bastard!* Stood and cried, he had, when they'd come to shoot his herd. *You can't tell me the man was in his right mind. And what God wouldn't have compassion in a case like that?* Reverend Fury hadn't shared Fletcher's views, however, and it had taken some delicate dealings by the bishop to get Eddie a decent Christian funeral. And Eddie had only killed *himself*, not anybody else – least of all his own daughter.

Squaring his shoulders, Fletcher straightened his tie. *Any nonsense from him and I'll go to the bishop myself. What Seth did was wrong, but he must have been out of his mind to do it.*

Sally Arnold looked up in surprise as Anna approached the counter. They'd barely been open five minutes. 'You're out and about early!'

'Yes. Something unexpected cropped up.' Anna placed her basket on the counter. Sally started ringing up her purchases, taking in, without comment, the make-up which had obviously been applied to cover the younger woman's haggard appearance.

Anna paid for her goods and added, 'I've got a couple of things to post, too,' her face falling as she turned and registered the fact that the post office counter was closed.

'Oh – that doesn't open until nine.'

'Damn. I've got to go out – away from the village, I mean.'

'You're not leaving already?' Sally failed to hide the surprise in her voice.

'No. Oh no – I don't mean the end of the project. I just have to go to see someone.' Anna stood uncertainly, mind racing ahead to what she was going to have to tell the police. Even more to the point, how to find out who the local officer was without arousing suspicion.

Sally noted her hesitation and the small packets in her hand. 'Why don't you leave them with me? I can give them to Frank when he opens and you can settle up with me later.'

'Are you sure? I don't mean to be a nuisance, but I really wanted to get them off first thing.'

'No problem.' Sally took the packets from her. 'Will you not be seeing the Misses Webb today, then?'

Anna blinked in surprise, as if only now becoming fully aware of the conversation. 'Yes. That is, I don't see why not. I might be a little late, though.'

'You can always pick up their key from here, if you need to.'

'Thanks.' She had a sudden flash of inspiration 'Oh – speaking of the Misses Webb reminds me – something they said yesterday – who's the police officer around here?'

Sally's eyebrows rose. 'Police? That would be Janice Mills in Swifford Holt. But if it's something from the Misses Webb's reminiscences – apart from the burglary, that is – it would be before her time. You'd need to talk to Fletcher Godfrey.'

The college cafeteria was already crowded by the time Jack Taylor entered it for his mid-morning break. A group of boys watched him as he crossed the room to the table occupied by the Swiffords contingent, staring openly, then talking behind their hands. Jack ignored them and slid into a seat.

'Are you on for the sleep-over?' he was asked.

'Yes. No problem.' He cleared his throat. 'I – um – I talked to my mum. About funerals. She says there's a book for them. She's going to get a copy so we can see what we're in for.'

'That's good of her, mate. Thanks.'

Jack thought gratefully of his mother's intervention that morning over breakfast. He had looked at her across the breakfast table, wondering how on earth he could start to ask her what he wanted to. It was such a tricky subject.

'Spit it out, Jack, for God's sake!' she'd suddenly said. 'You're eating more of your bottom lip than your toast.' Was it that obvious? She had always seemed to have an unnerving knack of knowing when something was bothering him. He sometimes wondered if mothers were psychic. A flash of half-buried memory had come back to him. How old had he been? Four? He certainly hadn't started school. They'd been in the kitchen, him and Mum, and she was washing up at the sink, her back to him, when she'd suddenly said, 'Don't you dare put that spoon back in the marmalade pot, Jack Taylor, after you've just licked it!' Never even looked round. Just carried on with the dishes. Even now, he could remember the open-mouthed awe he'd felt. He'd asked her how she'd known and, again, without turning round, she'd told him that mothers have eyes in the backs of their heads. He'd believed her for at least another four years, he reckoned, before sussing it out, after overhearing a conversation between her and Sally Arnold, where she'd revealed that the blinds had been open and, being dark outside, she could see his every move reflected in the kitchen window. Anyway, she was on to him now, and he'd cleared his throat.

'We're having a sleep-over at Cassie's place on Saturday night ...'

'Oh yes? Who's we?'

'All of us from college. Who were in the same classes with Karen.'

His mother had nodded. 'And?'

'And ... well ... it's just ...' He took a deep breath. 'It's the funeral, Mum. We all want to go, right? But – we were talking and well ...' He shrugged helplessly. 'Well, none of us has been to one before and – is it going to be awful?' The last words came out in a flurry. This was so stupid. He'd sounded like a little kid.

'Oh, Jack! What can I say, love? It's awful that there's need of one at all, but the service in itself ... no, that's not awful. Or it shouldn't be. They're sad, Jack – what funeral couldn't be? You're there because you've lost someone you care about. But it's ...' she'd seemed to struggle to find the right words. 'It's a really important thing. A rite of passage, I suppose, where you get a chance to say goodbye and – it's a marker. It's designed to help those left behind as well as the ones who've died.'

'Have you been to many?'

'Nan and Grandpa, when you was little. Couple of friends, too – accidents, they was. And my Aunt Caroline – she had cancer. Look – if you're worrying – there's a book with the funeral service in it – in the church. Do you want me to borrow one so you can at least see the kind of thing that will be said?'

He had felt deeply moved. 'Thanks, Mum. I think that would be good.'

An apparent argument brought Jack out of his memory and back to the college cafeteria.

'Still a load of bullshit, though,' someone was saying. 'If there really was a God, Karen and her dad wouldn't be dead, right?'

'Well, God didn't kill them, did he?' a girl protested. 'If her dad went off his head, well . . .' There was an uncomfortable silence.

'It makes you think, though, doesn't it?' Everybody seemed to have an opinion now. 'I mean, you live with your parents for years. Think you know them. Think you can trust them, and then . . .'

'Oi – retards!' The cat-call came from the other side of the room.

'Ignore them.' Jack flushed as he spoke. He knew it was the group who'd stared when he walked in. From Market Eaton, they felt themselves superior to anyone who came in from outside town, particularly the Swiffords group, who were looked on with contempt.

'How's your mate, Karen, then? Any more of you inbreeds been killing each other? Just asking, you know, 'cos it saves us the job.'

Without warning, Gavin Morgan exploded from his seat, knocking it flying.

'Shit!' Jack and the others rose as one, watching in disbelief as Gavin ran right for the centre of the hostile group. Rushing across the room behind him, they were too late to prevent him launching himself at the leader of the group with a swinging right hook.

'Whoa! Whoa! Break it up!' Jack was not physically the biggest of his group, but thrust himself between the two, surprisingly authoritative. He grabbed Gavin by the scruff of the neck, pulling him backwards. 'They're not worth it, Gav! Leave it!'

The atmosphere crackled with barely suppressed violence, supporters of each side jostling into the fray.

'Back off!' Jack commanded.

'What's going on here?' One of the lab technicians, a burly-looking man, strode towards the trouble.

'Nothing. We're just going back to classes.' Jack was trying desperately to defuse the situation.

The man's eyes flickered from Jack and Gavin to the other group.

'About time you were doing the same, then, isn't it?'

The silence was pregnant. Jack's heart was hammering, wondering which way it would go. Finally, the other boy dropped his gaze and shrugged at the tech. 'Yeah. Right.' He looked at the rest of his group. 'Come on – we're out of here.'

They left *en masse*, Jack only letting go of his pent-up breath when the last of them had gone through the door. He turned to the technician.

'Thanks.'

'No problem. But you ...' the man fixed Gavin with a stare '... should know better than to rise to that sort of crap. They're the lowest of the low. Don't let them drag you down to their level.'

Jack felt Gavin stiffen, but, still holding on to him, shook him to stop him answering back. 'Listen to what the man says, Gav. He's right.'

The technician nodded and walked off towards the counter.

'Come on.' Jack indicated the other exit and led the group away. Once outside, he rounded on Gavin.

'What the hell's got into you, man? That could have been some serious shit!'

To everyone's astonishment, Gavin now lunged at Jack, knocking him backwards as he thrust the heel of his hand into Jack's shoulder.

'You don't get it, do you? You just don't get it! It's the Wrath of God, and you worry about pricks like that?!'

He stormed off down the corridor. After watching him until he was out of sight, the others turned to Jack.

'What the fuck was that about?'

'You don't think he's on drugs or something, do you?'

Jack shook his head, eyes still focused on the now empty corridor as if it might hold the answers he was seeking.

'I don't know what to think anymore.'

Sally Arnold had been rushed off her feet. Tim Taylor had brought in his regular minibus of pensioners, collecting them from their homes to take them shopping, as the bus service was virtually non-existent these days. The minibus was a lifeline to them, many unable either to stand for long or to walk for any distance, and certainly not with shopping bags to carry.

She now welcomed the break that came with their departure and popped out to the kitchen to make tea for herself and Frank. It was only as she set down his mug on the post office counter that she remembered her promise to Anna.

'Oh damn! I nearly forgot! Dr Summers was in first thing this morning. I said I'd give these to you for posting.' She held the little packets in her hand, frowning. 'Something's wrong, there, Frank. She was all over the place – completely scattered. And she looked haggard under her make-up.'

'Probably just got Barkered again.'

She shook her head. 'No. Trust me. Something's wrong.'

He held out his hand for the packets.

'Back-up disks for her work,' Sally told him. 'One to her home address, just first-class. The other's first-class recorded delivery. Said she's been a bit "belt and braces" since she lost a load of stuff a couple of years ago.'

'I know the feeling!' Frank grimaced, thinking about his own early efforts to master the IT skills he needed these days. He dealt with the one packet swiftly, then froze. 'Sal!'

'What?'

'Have you seen who this is to?'

His wife moved beside him. 'No. I didn't look. What's wrong?'

Frank said nothing, just holding up the packet with his thumb pointing to the name of the addressee.

Professor Roland Featherstone. Their eyes locked.

Frank's voice was sharp as he asked, 'How the hell does she know him? And why would she be sending anything to him from here?'

Anna let herself back into April Cottage and, after putting the kettle on, slumped into a chair at the dining-room table, head in her hands. She didn't like lying to people, least of all the police. Still, at least it was done now and, she told herself, it hadn't exactly been lying, not by the letter of the law, anyway. She ran a hand through her hair and breathed out noisily. *I told the policewoman that I'd picked up the diary after Ellie dropped it and drove away. And that's the truth.* She grimaced, thinking of how

Ellie had made her act out the pantomime as she'd left the previous evening. *I just didn't tell Janice about the conversation we'd had before that happened ...*

Had she pulled it off, though? The policewoman had seemed to believe her. She had no reason not to, really, and Anna had been ready and willing to make a statement. The rest was up to Ellie. Well, some of it, at least.

She rubbed both hands up and down her face, trying to alleviate tiredness. It didn't work, and all she wound up doing was smearing her make-up. *Damn!* She went into the downstairs bathroom and removed it, shocked by her reflection once again. *Who am I trying to kid? I look like shit.*

She had barely slept last night, firstly due to sitting up and reading Karen Peterson's diary, and secondly, through staying up even later, typing the entries into the computer. She knew she shouldn't have done it, but felt compelled to do so, particularly as she'd promised Ellie that she would ask her friend for help. She'd saved everything to floppy disks, mailing one to herself at home and another to Roly. The third copy was in her briefcase.

Oh God – I need to check that Sally got them off OK. And settle up with her. And phone Roly. She rubbed her face again, trying to get some order into her muddled thoughts. By the time she'd made herself a pot of very strong coffee, she had a plan ready. She could deal with Sally on the way to see the Misses Webb. But first, she needed to make that phone call.

Roly answered on the fourth ring, his beautifully modulated baritone voice a pleasure to her ears.

'Hello, Roly – it's Rhianna.'

'Rhianna! How lovely to hear from you! To what do I owe this pleasure?'

Anna's facial grimace carried into her voice. 'I'm not sure it's going to be a pleasure, Roly. I need to see you. Urgently. Something very bizarre has come up. I need your help. Your professional help.'

'But of course. Anything for you – you know that. Would you care to elaborate?'

Anna hesitated. 'Not over the phone – no. When would it be convenient for me to call on you?'

'Just name the time. I'm hardly overrun with visitors these

days. Which is nice for one's research, but not so good on the social front. This sabbatical is making me feel like a hermit!'

'How about tomorrow, then?'

'Tomorrow is fine.' They arranged a time, then Roly asked, 'Rhianna – just satisfy my curiosity on one thing before you come – in which of my professional capacities are you seeking my advice?'

'Both.' She left him no time to ask further questions, simply breaking the connection.

She sat for a moment before getting up and pacing the dining room. Even now, in daylight, she didn't want to think about the contents of Karen's diary. She would have to print the file off and take it with her tomorrow, in case the floppy hadn't yet arrived. Anna shook her head in frustration. She looked at the clock. If she went to the shop now, she could settle up with Sally and get the key to go and visit the Misses Webb by herself. She had to get on with things, not allow herself to become side-tracked. There was work to be done.

By early evening, she was feeling much better. The sisters had been on fine form, even asking her to photograph them in their late father's study. This had led, in turn, to many stories about his life, with a wealth of photographs, letters and documentation being produced to illustrate it. Anna had marvelled, not only at the sheer volume, but at the sight of the sisters from infancy onwards, the photographs, quite apart from their personal value, being a catalogue of the history of fashion throughout almost a century. When she had commented to this effect, the sisters had sprung an even bigger surprise on her – a visit to the sewing room. Anna had stood open-mouthed. Built-in cupboards were jam-packed with clothes the sisters had worn over the years, and all, since childhood, had been made by Molly.

'I even hand-stitched a suit for Father, once.'

'Goodness, Molly – I never dreamed . . .'

'Yes. Four-buttonhole cuffs, if I remember correctly – and all of them opened. Two buttonholes on the lapel, as well. That's not easy to do on the bias, you know.'

'We gave a lot away, of course,' Alice put in, 'but all our favourite pieces are here. Molly designed them, too – she trained as a bespoke tailor . . .'

'Nine months, that was. Mr Savory was my teacher.'

'This was before she went into teaching,' Alice had added.

'They're beautiful! Did you do everything by hand?'

'Heavens, no! Just the most special things. I've had a variety of sewing machines – look – here's my first.' The old woman opened another cupboard to reveal an ancient treadle model. 'I can't tell you how thrilled I was when I got that.'

Anna had never seen Molly so animated.

'This was the last one I used.' She indicated an electric machine that Anna estimated was about twenty years old. 'I do so miss it, you know. Being able to sew. But between my eyesight and arthritis . . .' She sighed. 'Never mind. Old age comes to us all, and I've had years of enjoyment.' She opened another door, her gnarled hand tripping along the hanging rail. 'Oh, look, Alice – here's the evening gown I made for you during the war!'

'Parachute silk! Do you remember that evening?' Alice turned to Anna. 'We felt quite wicked! Told Father we were going to a classical recital, and sneaked off to something quite, quite different.'

The sisters' faces lit up at the unelaborated memory, a conspiratorial smile passing between the pair. And that had set them off on another string of stories . . .

Anna came out of her reverie and glanced at the clock. It was later than she thought, and darkness had fallen. *What am I doing, sitting without the lights on?* She gave an involuntary shiver as she pressed switches and drew the curtains. *The last thing I need is darkness, after reading that poor girl's diary.* Still, at least Sally and Frank had got her packages off safely and she would be seeing Roly tomorrow, for what it was worth. *At least then, my promise to Ellie will be fulfilled. It will be out of my hands, thank God.* What to do now, though? There were still too many hours until bedtime and she didn't want to be alone. *This is silly. I've got to get over it.* She wasn't sure whether she meant the diary entries or her nightmare, and didn't want to think about either. And how would she sleep tonight? *With the light on, if necessary*, she conceded. *But in the meantime, there'd be no harm in asking Maggie if she wants to go for a drink . . .*

They didn't stay at the pub for long. Anna tried to avoid eye contact with Ellie as much as possible. The girl was looking strained, but appeared to be coping with her duties. Anna wondered if Janice, the policewoman, had spoken to her yet. Lost in thought, she was caught off guard and found herself under Ellie's wordless, beseeching gaze. Uncomfortably, she turned away to listen to Maggie, who had been confiding her concerns about Jack, her son. Anna found herself making suitably sympathetic noises, when there was a sudden silence at the bar. All heads turned.

Pete, sauté pan in hand, had a face like thunder. Several people were backing away from the bar. Anna frowned, trying to place the face of the man who seemed to be the object of his displeasured attention. Oh yes – Dave, wasn't it? The workman who'd come with Adam to look at the fireplaces.

'What did you say?'

Anna shivered at the quiet menace of Pete's voice. Several people now got up from their seats and started backing quietly towards the door.

'Hey – come on – it was just a joke!'

'Well, it was in very poor taste!'

Anna and Maggie glanced at each other. Dave was unsteady on his feet and obviously reading neither Pete's body language nor his words. Quite the contrary. He laughed at him, repeating what he'd said.

'I just said as how it's a good thing the plods know that Seth Peterson done his daughter in, because you'd be hard pressed to give an alibi for the night in question after getting locked out by your lady-wife.' He turned his back on Pete and waved in the direction of the remaining customers. 'Baby-sitting his goats! Can you believe it?'

'And why wouldn't they?' Pete had come out from behind the bar and was quietly allowing the sauté pan to swing in his grasp.

'What? A chap with a temper like you? And access to sharp instruments?' There was a collective indrawing of breath. Anna thought Maggie muttered 'Bleedin' hell!', but wasn't sure.

'Get out of my pub. You're barred.'

'What?'

'You come in here, stinking, after drinking at that shit-pit over the road – we don't need your custom.'

'Who says?' Dave was belligerent now.

'I do. And my word's law in here. Unless you want me to call the other kind.'

'Janice Mills?' Dave spluttered in derision. 'Phone her now, she won't get here till after closing time.'

Chris, the Morris Man leader, tried to clear his throat, Adam's apple bobbing. 'Dave – I – er – I think it would be best if you just went. We don't want any trouble, eh?'

'Fuck off, tosspot!' Dave's arm whipped out sideways to push Chris over. Pete had hold of his wrist before the planned blow had time to find its target.

'Insulting my regulars, now, as well?' Dave buckled under the other man's grip, falling to his knees. Pete still had hold of his wrist. 'You can walk, or you can crawl. Take your pick ...'

The atmosphere soured; many people chose to leave, Anna and Maggie among them. Back at April Cottage, Anna locked the doors and decided to make herself a cup of hot chocolate before going to bed. She shivered, thinking of how she'd been about to go to bed last night, when Ellie had appeared at the kitchen door. Would she come back tonight? Anna fervently hoped not, but steeled herself for the worst.

Oh God! This is stupid! To add to her apprehension images from her nightmare pressed forward. She pushed them firmly back. *It was just a dream. And Karen – well, the poor girl was obviously seriously disturbed. Deluded. Everything here is all right. There's no need to worry.*

Why couldn't she stop, then? And if she was so sure that Karen Peterson was ill – mentally disturbed – then why was she taking the transcript of the diary to Roly Featherstone? *Because I promised Ellie, that's all. And I shouldn't have promised. And I shouldn't have copied the diary, either. Oh hell!*

Distracted and disturbed, she paced the room until her eye fell on a large envelope. The one Sally had given her on Monday. *Ah! The history of April Cottage. That should make for better bedtime reading.* Curling up on the sofa, she opened it, sliding out the contents. Masses of photographs, sepia, black and white and colour, plus newspaper cuttings and documentation, some of it very old. As she leaned over to put her mug down on the coffee table, a cascade of photographs slid to the floor. *Damn!* She reached forward and picked them up. Several were now upside down, and she glanced at a handwritten note on the back of one.

'Aunt Ida', it said, with a date of just a few months ago. Intrigued, Anna turned it over, wondering what the owner of April Cottage had looked like. She caught her breath, staring at the picture in disbelief. There, in this very room – *and beneath my bedroom* – Anna realised as her skin crawled with the shock – Sally Arnold's Aunt Ida was pictured playing a beautiful old piano where the sofa now stood.

Chapter Thirteen

The summerhouse, once more, was no longer in mundane use. The Four had come together in Council yet again and this time, the subject under discussion was Dr Rhianna Summers.

The Fourth spoke. 'She came to see me today, in my official capacity. She brought Karen Peterson's diary with her.'

'What? How the hell did she come by that?' It was The Third who asked the question.

The Fourth smiled briefly. 'Not in the manner she told me, of that I'm sure. Some cock-and-bull story about Ellie Smith dropping it when she got into her car last night.'

The One spoke. 'This is far worse than we'd imagined. I take it she is aware of the contents? She looked dreadful when I saw her this morning. Now, I can understand why.'

'Oh yes. She said she'd found it, read it, and, in light of what she'd read, turned it straight over to me.'

'And what does she make of it?'

'She thinks Karen Peterson may have been suffering from mental illness.'

'Does she now?' The One looked at The Second. 'This might explain the packet she posted today.' The others looked at her in query. 'To Professor Roland Featherstone.'

A hissing of breath ran around the room.

The Third cleared his throat. 'There was something I meant to mention earlier – she's heard Ida's piano.'

The eyes of The One narrowed. 'This is not good. And Molly Webb speaks of seeing a dead child with her.'

'Earthbound?'

'I think not. Molly simply picks up traces at times.'

'Is Dr Summers aware?'

The One thought before replying. 'I think not. All this, and now the diary. What is her connection?'

The Second raised his arm in a gesture the others recognised. 'As we have been talking, I have seen a vision of her. She is on Edge of Sight and Edge of Calling. That is her strength at present, but also her weakness. Madness or Enlightenment. There is no middle way. She is in a very dangerous position.'

'Then to find out the nature of her connection to Roland Featherstone is vital. She could be a powerful enemy.' The One looked at The Second. 'How close to Edge is she?'

The Second's eyes closed. 'She has walked the Abyss for around two years. She cannot sustain that much longer in ignorance. Any time now, she will either fall . . .'

'Mad.'

'. . . or reach safety.'

'Enlightenment. You say she walks the Abyss. On what does she walk?'

The voice of The Second was sombre. 'That, I cannot see. But neither does she know. Yet.'

The One pondered before speaking further. 'Then we must keep her very clearly in our sight . . .'

Chapter Fourteen

Thursday November 10th

Fletcher Godfrey was not amused. It was one thing to think he'd heard a voice after having a few too many; it was something else to hear it again when he hadn't been drinking at all. And he *had* heard a voice – there was no shadow of a doubt. Even now in daylight, the hairs on the back of his neck prickled as he remembered it.

'*Fletcher* . . .'

That was all it had said, but it had said it over and over again. He shivered. What the hell was going on? It challenged everything he'd ever believed in. Or not, as the case may be. He didn't believe in ghoulies and ghosties and things that go bump in the night. Hadn't ever believed in much at all, truth be told. Certainly not supernatural twaddle. The fact that he carried out a lot of unofficial duties for the church didn't enter into the equation. Someone had to help, and he'd been happy to take things on after he'd retired early from his policing duties. A lot of it was outdoors, too – checking security, keeping things neat and tidy. It kept him fit and occupied and he liked being in the open air. He didn't want to be stuck at home, brooding. Thinking. Too much of that could drive a man mad.

He wondered if that was what had happened to Seth. Not being stuck at home, because he wasn't, but the brooding and thinking part. Maybe remembering things that he shouldn't. He set down his mug of tea and stared blindly at it. Christ! What if it were *Seth* who had been calling to him? This time, it wasn't just the hairs on his neck that prickled. *Dear God! That kind of stuff simply can't be!* He shifted uncomfortably. You read about unquiet spirits and such like, but it couldn't be true. Just superstitious nonsense. *I've seen bodies in the morgue. Once you're dead, you're dead. That's it. Finito.*

Pushing back his chair, he stood up and carried his mug to the sink. Best stop this line of thinking before it got properly started. There was the vicar to see. He hadn't managed it yesterday, after all. Not that it was his fault. He'd turned up, but Reverend Fury had sent him away. Said something urgent had come up. He'd tried to stop him seeing into the house, but Fletcher had caught a glimpse of Janice Mills in the corridor behind him. Police business, eh? Probably to do with the Peterson tragedy, though quite what, he couldn't think. Anyway, he'd gone home with an arrangement to meet the vicar later today. He hadn't been looking forward to it, in any case, but after this Voice business ... *Stop it right there! Just bloody get on with things.* Resolutely, he pushed the Voice out of his head and locked the house behind him before going to the shed to get his bicycle.

Anna almost missed the note. It had been pushed through the letterbox in the front door, but had been covered by the local free newspaper. It had no envelope, and the paper looked as if it had been hastily torn from a notebook. She frowned as she read it, heaviness spreading over her once again.

Janice come to see me and I told her everything, like I promised. PLEASE get your friend to help. Ellie.

She sighed, pulling her jacket from the coat-peg. Why the hell did all this have to happen now? She was really enjoying her work with the Misses Webb, but, as if the murders themselves were not bad enough, she had to have got herself involved with Ellie and Karen Peterson's diary. *Oh God! Can nothing in my life be straightforward?*

She had slept fitfully last night, tormented by irrational thoughts after finding the photograph of Sally's Aunt Ida at her piano. How many times had she told herself not to be stupid? That the dead can't play pianos and that the piano was no longer even in the house? Still the fear had persisted. She shook her head and, picking up her car keys, rebuked herself. *Come on, Summers!*

Look at what you're implying – that the house is haunted. That's rubbish, and you know it.

She sat for a moment in the car before starting the engine. There must be a rational explanation, but what? She closed her eyes, searching for an answer. Maggie had no piano and there was no house at the back. What about the pub, then? Was it possible that Pete and Pat had a piano upstairs in their living quarters? She would ask. Just to set her mind at rest. But not now. Right now, she had to whip round to the shop and let Sally know that she would not be visiting the Misses Webb today – something she should have done when she returned their key yesterday afternoon, but had forgotten to do.

Moments later, she had pulled the car up on to the tarmacked surface in front of the shop, being sure to take her briefcase inside with her. She waited while Sally finished serving a customer.

'Sally – I forgot to mention – I shan't be visiting the sisters today.' She swung the briefcase into view. 'I have a load of tapes to drop off back at the university. This job is bigger than I expected. I think it would be best if Philip – my boss – can get someone on to the transcription straight away. There'll be mountains by the time I've finished!'

'Righto. Will you be away long?' Seeing Anna's puzzled look, Sally explained her question. 'It's just that I need to sort out about having the chimney relined now that Adam's removed the obstruction. Best to do anything messy while you're out.'

'Oh, I see. Sure. I shouldn't think I'll be back until late afternoon, if that's any help. But don't mind me, anyway – just do what you have to do.'

Sally smiled as Anna left the shop. 'I'll keep that in mind.'

Gavin Morgan had bunked off from his college classes and wandered into the centre of Market Eaton. His mind was in turmoil. Nobody understood. Nobody. They were offering counselling now, as well. As if that would do any good! What could you do against the Wrath of God? He shivered, despite the temperate weather. Was this what the biblical prophets had felt like? He'd have thought that being privy to Divine information would be a privilege. *Would* have thought. Not now. Now, he knew better. It was a horror, a burden that you couldn't share and that set you apart from your friends. He'd never been religious. Another reason he found it so astonishing – and frightening – that God should choose to talk to him. Why didn't God talk to someone like Reverend Fury? He was a minister, after all.

Gavin felt suddenly sick. He couldn't bear this. He just *couldn't* bear this. If anyone had said, even a couple of weeks ago, that he'd be reading the Bible, he'd have laughed. Not now. He had spent hours, frantically trying to make sense of it all. *Why me? What have I done to deserve this kind of attention? I've hardly ever set foot in a church in my life. I ...* His eye was caught by the open doors of just such a building. He could see into the interior, see the stained glass and a statue and candles. Quickening his step, he walked inside, then stopped, unsure of what to do. He turned to his right and saw the altar. There didn't seem to be anyone here, apart from an old man kneeling at the back and a woman cleaning a brass rail. He held his breath. No – it was all right. They didn't pay him any attention. Awkwardly, he moved forward, head down, before sliding into a pew. Still no one seemed to notice him. His breathing quickened and, mouth dry, he slid forward on to the kneeling rail and began to pray.

It was a shock to Anna to go back to her home. As if, after being away for just a few days, she was viewing it from a different perspective. Slowly, she opened the front door, nose twitching at the staleness that met her within. *God! Any one would think I hadn't opened a window in the last two years. Maybe I didn't.* She blinked and brought herself back to her present purpose. Had the floppy disk she'd posted to herself arrived? She'd brought the spare, in case it hadn't, but it had, sitting on the mat with a couple of bills. Scooping up the lot, she tossed the bills on to the hall table, carrying the disk package through to the living room, where she booted up the computer before opening it. As she waited for the machine to go through its start up procedure, she glanced around her, seeing the room as if through new eyes. She winced as she looked at the photographs. How had she crammed the place with so many? As she took in the faces of her dead husband and son, her heart began to palpitate, not just at seeing them again, but at remembrance of the nightmare she'd had, of Guy's brutal words and Jamie's flying flesh. Feeling faint and nauseous, she sat down, putting her head between her knees. *Dear God! Don't let me crack up again!* Slowly, she managed to bring her breathing back under control and finally stood, knowing she had to take some sort of action. Undecided on what to do first, she opened the word-processing package on her machine, pushed the floppy disk into the 'a' drive and opened it. She stared, uncomprehending for a moment before realising that it was blank. *What on earth? Maybe I picked up the wrong one. Damn!*

Going back to the hall, Anna opened her briefcase and found the spare. That, at least, still had the Karen Peterson diary file, albeit deliberately misnamed, just in case. Just in case *what*, she didn't like to think about. Telling her machine to print two copies, she turned her attention once more to the room. *God – it's filthy! When was the last time I vacuumed or dusted?* Shaking her head, she hesitated only fractionally before gathering up all the photographs in her arms and taking them upstairs to the spare bedroom. Her heart was hammering. *It's not healthy*, she told herself. *One of each. That's all that's needed. They don't all need to be on display.* Her hand hovered. Which to choose? Decision made, she ran back down the stairs, hunting under the kitchen sink for polish and a duster. She bit her lip at the amount of dirt she removed from the mantel shelf. *I never even realised.* Suddenly remembering Philip's recent visit, she flushed to the roots of her hair. *Oh God! What* must *he have thought? And still he gave me this job . . .*

Moments later, the computer switched off and the front door locked behind her, Anna was back in her car, printouts of Karen Peterson's diary firmly in her briefcase, and on her way to meet Roland Featherstone.

Stella Timpson was like a cat on a hot tin roof. She had received a second page of the mysterious manuscript today and was champing at the bit to get to Swifford Lea. Next week had filled up too much to be able to go then, as planned, and unfortunately, the weekend was out of the question. Darling Max wouldn't be happy about it at all. In fact, the less said on the subject to darling Max, the better.

How ironic, though! And how absolutely maddening! Here I

am, closer in geographical proximity than Philip Jackson's bloody institution, and with other connections besides. Had I known anything about this a couple of years ago, I could have seized the initiative and Philip, damn him, would be spitting feathers. More to the point, Rhianna bloody Summers would still be locked away in her mental hell, instead of having all this handed to her on a plate. How can *all this wonderful material be available to her and not me?*

By God, somebody would pay for this! Freshly fired up, Stella checked her diary and cancelled all her tutorials for a week on Monday. She would go then, come hell or high water.

Adam Etheridge surveyed the sitting room of April Cottage carefully. He'd sent Dave Logan away, to do an estimate on an enquiry from Swifford Holt. He was good at his job, which was the reason Adam employed him, but that didn't mean he had to like the man. Everyone else was reeling from the Peterson business, but not Dave. *More like a bloody vulture, crowing over the fact that the two of us did work there a couple of months ago. Yeah. Really good recommendation, that. Do draw people's attention to the connection.* He'd also heard about the man's run-in with Pete Barker at The White Hart the previous evening. He would have to think things over carefully. Dave was becoming a liability.

Adam made an effort to clear his mind. He mustn't allow himself to be distracted from the task at hand. Dr Summers was away for the day – most of it, at any rate, and he'd arranged for Walter to come over later to see about relining the chimney. Right now, however, he had the house to himself and knew what he had to do. Not, however, as a builder.

His intuition had guided him, and drawing the Elhaz rune this morning had confirmed it. After performing a short ritual, he reached into his bag, withdrawing pieces of dried rowan and yew. Most were small. These he placed by windows and doors. The larger bundles, he affixed to the two chimney breasts. Hopefully, Dr Summers wouldn't even notice them, especially not the smaller ones. The big ones ... well, if she said anything, he would say Sally had taken them down, ready for him to work on the chimneys, and he'd simply replaced them. He also hid gold ribbons and small amethyst crystals around the house, along with dried angelica, muttering under his breath as he did so. Ida Wooley's piano had been donated to the village hall after she died, but he paid special attention to the area where it had stood.

This phase of his plan complete, he closed his eyes and breathed deeply. *Right, then. That should take care of things for now. Until we find out exactly what Anna Summers' connection to the Witchfinder General is ...*

Maggie Taylor was cursing herself. How could she have forgotten to get the Order of Service book for Jack? He'd mentioned it again when he came back from college last night and, flustered by her own inefficiency, she'd promised to get it today. *Now!* She told herself. *Do it now, before you forget again.* He'd been awfully quiet, which had worried her, and wasn't amenable to talking things over. All he'd volunteered was that the college was arranging counselling, if they wanted it, for anyone who'd known Karen. She wasn't sure what she thought about that. Trip on a pavement these days, and it seemed that all people were bothered about was suing somebody and getting compensation and claiming post-traumatic stress disorder. She snorted. Poor buggers in the First World War and suchlike were the ones who'd needed help, but what happened – they got shot for cowardice. All that seemed to be happening now was a load of namby-pambying and more lawyers on board the gravy train. Still, this business with the Petersons was bad, and no mistake. It was bad enough somebody Jack's age dying anyway, but the circumstances ... Maybe counselling would help. Often, you needed a space to talk to somebody who *didn't* know the people involved. She had hoped Jack would talk to her, but recognised that mothers – parents, for that matter – might not be the ones you'd open up to in a situation like this.

Putting on her coat, she walked across the Green and headed for the church. To her surprise, it was locked. Reverend Fury was a great believer in keeping it open from morning until dusk, despite thefts from rural churches being on the increase. Not that anyone had tried anything here, mind. Maggie grimaced, thinking of the kind of wrath the vicar would call down on any miscreants who dared try. Fire and brimstone, no doubt. Still, at least he kept the churches in the other Swiffords locked. They were only opened for services, and Fletcher always kept an eye out for vandalism and suchlike. She supposed he made the exception here because the vicarage was next door.

She stood for a moment, undecided as to what to do next. Try the vicar at home, she supposed. Not a prospect she relished. She was saved from putting her thought into action by meeting Madge Tompkiss, who cleaned for Reverend Fury. The older woman's eyebrows shot up in surprise. She couldn't remember seeing Maggie Taylor near the church apart from weddings and funerals, and there weren't many of either, these days.

'Is the Reverend around?' Maggie asked.

'No. Gone over to Maisey to meet Fletcher about the Petersons' funeral arrangements.'

'Right. Thanks.' Maggie walked away, thinking she'd catch him – or, preferably, an open church, later – when, on a sudden impulse, she walked briskly back home and got out her bicycle. It was only a few miles and it was a nice day and it might be a good idea to shift a few of those extra pounds she'd been putting on after over-indulgent meals at The White Hart. What the hell! She wouldn't be away long and could do her work when she came back. And if Fletcher was with him, she shouldn't have to say more than a couple of words to the Reverend himself, either.

By the time she'd cycled just over two miles, Maggie was wishing that she'd made the journey by car instead.

'Blimey, girl! You're not as fit as you thought!' She chided herself aloud. *Whatever possessed me? Bleedin' hell! I'm going to ache in places I didn't know I had, at this rate!* Oh well. Served her right. *And* showed that she needed to do exercise more often. She frowned dubiously, wobbling as she skirted round a dead rabbit. *Not exactly the best time of year for it, is it though? Winter coming on. Then it'll pee down and we'll have gales in the spring. What the hell! If the weather's fine, do it. If it ain't, don't. Simple.* She wondered for a fleeting moment if Anna might like to join her on a bike ride, then dismissed the thought. *Probably too busy with the old girls. Besides, she's so thin, she hardly needs to be burning off any calories. Might do her more harm than good. Shame, though. There's bound to be a couple of spare bikes knocking around somewhere. At Sally and Frank's, maybe. Or even the old girls themselves. I'm sure I used to see Alice on a lovely old sit-up-and-beg model, with a basket on the handlebars.*

Her attention was drawn by a flash of colour some distance ahead. As quickly as she'd noticed it, it disappeared round a bend in the road and it was only as she rounded it and came on to the straight herself that she realised it was Fletcher Godfrey's bicycle. She pedalled furiously, trying to catch him up, but, finding the effort too much, called out to him instead.

'Fletcher! Fletcher! Hold up a minute!'

The man turned in surprise then pulled into the side of the road and dismounted, waiting for her to come alongside.

'Morning, Maggie. What are you doing out this way, then?'

Maggie had to get her breath back before she could reply.

'Looking for the vicar. Well, not exactly. I was looking for an Order of Service book, but the church back home is locked.' Seeing the puzzled look on his face, she grinned. 'No – I haven't got religion. It's for Jack and his mates. None of 'em's been to a funeral before and I thought it might help. You know – give 'em some forewarning of what they're in for.'

Fletcher grimaced and Maggie's face became sober.

'I know what you're thinking, Fletcher. Just the same as me, I bet. I'm pleased I've seen you, actually – I did want to have a word. Do you think he's going to cut up rough? About burying Seth?'

'More than likely, I reckon. You know his views as well as I do.'

'Oh Gawd! It's not what's needed, though, is it? Not for Seth, and not for any of us.'

'Umm.' Fletcher remounted his cycle and looked at Maggie enquiringly. 'You about ready to carry on?'

'Yeah, I reckon. Not too fast, though, eh?'

They cycled together in a companionable silence for some time before Fletcher spoke again.

'I'll try to suss out what his thoughts are. Not that he'll try hiding them, that's for sure. But my hands are tied, Maggie, you know that. I've got no influence with him.'

'What about the bishop?'

He glanced at her darkly. 'Shouldn't think he'll want to get involved, unless it's likely to cause a scandal. We had a performance enough over that last suicide. But yes – I've thought it over. And I will go to the bishop if I have to.'

'Well, if you do, you can tell him from me that it'll cause a scandal and a half if Reverend Fury don't do the decent thing.'

Fletcher shook his head. 'I wish everyone saw it that way. Most people do, of course, but it strikes me there's no reasoning with them as reckons they've got their own personal hot-line to God.'

They were nearing Swifford Maisey now and dropped into single-file to cycle through the village. The church here, rather than being in the centre of the village, was on the far side of it, small and with a stone wall surrounding its carefully tended graveyard.

'I suppose he'll insist on separate graves, then, eh? That's if he's prepared to bury Seth at all. Do you reckon ...'

Maggie's words were drowned by a piercing shriek.

Then another.

And another.

Both she and Fletcher wobbled to a halt and looked at each other, fear mirrored in their eyes. Wordlessly, they set off again, urgency pumping adrenalin to their muscles so that the wheels flew.

'That's coming from the churchyard!' Fletcher glanced at Maggie over his shoulder.

She nodded, too frightened and breathless to comment without slowing down.

Rounding the last curve, the churchyard came into view on their right. Maggie ran into the back of Fletcher's bike as he slammed on his brakes, coming to a sudden halt.

'What the hell's going on there?' he shouted. 'Hold on – we're coming!'

Fletcher roared the words, frightening even Maggie. Without further thought, both he and Maggie ran towards the lych-gate, leaving their bicycles in a tangled heap. Gravel crunched and flew beneath their feet as they entered the churchyard, just in time to catch a glimpse of a figure disappearing round the back of the church. Fletcher started to run after it, giving up when he heard a car engine start, swiftly followed by the sound of the vehicle screaming away. He stood, fists clenched, cursing silently before turning back to Maggie.

She wasn't where he expected her to be. He had assumed that she'd followed him, but she hadn't, her attention having been caught by something else. Even from a distance, Fletcher could tell something was wrong. Terribly wrong. Spurred on again, he ran towards her. She was half-bent over a grave, one hand extended towards it. She stepped aside to let him see, opening her mouth, but no words passing her lips.

For the first time in her life, Maggie Taylor was speechless.

Chapter Fifteen

Anna had to drive around for a while before finding a parking space some streets away from Roland Featherstone's house in Nottingham. Black clouds were rolling in overhead and the air held the brooding clamminess about it that foretells a storm. Taking her raincoat from the back seat of the car, she shrugged it on and pulled it around herself without fastening it, before setting off down the road at a brisk pace, briefcase in hand.

The area was familiar to her from long ago, although it was – how long since she'd last visited? Around three years, she decided. Before the accident. Around the time of Jamie's first birthday. Her face pinched involuntarily at the memory and she pushed it aside.

She had been a student here for many years, first as an undergraduate, then for her Master's before researching her PhD. That was how she'd met Roly. He'd been a lecturer when she was a fresher, and then one of her tutors on the M.Phil. They'd become friends and then ... *Then, he wanted more and I couldn't give it. But he's stuck by me through thick and thin.* Maybe the problem for her was the age difference – he was sixteen years her senior – or maybe it was that the chemistry simply wasn't there. Or hadn't been at the time, at any rate.

It was with some shame that she realised that this was her first visit to him since the accident, although he'd visited her on several occasions. *Before I totally shut him out. Along with everyone else.* She sighed as she turned, at last, into his road. *Some friend I am! And the first time since the accident that I'm in trouble, what do I do – run to him for help. Stop it, Rhianna! It's not me that's asking for help. It's Ellie. And as well as being a friend, he's the best man for the job.*

Moments later, she was enveloped in a hug, breathing in the scent of him. Leather and expensive soap. She closed her eyes against his chest, suddenly glad to feel so protected.

'Rhianna! It's so good to see you!' He held her at arm's length, his brown eyes looking into her face with undisguised scrutiny. 'Well – I'm not sure what to think!' he said at last. 'But where are my manners? Come on through.' He hung her raincoat in the hall and led her into the kitchen. 'Just one or two things to finish off . . .'

'Has the disk arrived?'

'Sorry?'

'The disk – I sent you a floppy – it should have come by recorded delivery.'

'No. I'm afraid not.'

'Not to worry. I thought the post might be unreliable from such an isolated place, so I've brought a printout.' She set her briefcase on the table and opened it.

'Whoa!' Roly held up his hand with a smile. 'I'm more confused than ever! But before we get down to any kind of business, we're going to eat and you're going to relax.'

Anna couldn't help but smile in return. 'If you say so.'

'I do. Sit down. What can I get you while we're waiting?'

'A cup of tea would be wonderful.'

'Not an aperitif?' He raised his eyebrows.

'I wish! But no. It's a long drive back.'

'To this isolated place I know nothing about yet?'

'Exactly.'

He put the kettle on as Anna settled herself at the table. The kitchen was warm and welcoming, always, as she remembered it, the hub of the fine old Georgian house. Bunches of dried herbs and flowers hung from wooden racks suspended from the ceiling. Brass and copper gleamed. And Roly – Roly looked barely a day older than when she'd last seen him. Just over six feet tall, he was still lean and trim, his dark hair speckled with grey now, and, of course, he had those beautiful brown eyes – spaniel eyes, she'd always thought, for some illogical reason. It was just so good to be in familiar surroundings with someone she trusted. It was good to feel *safe* again. Anna felt her shoulders droop and realised she was horribly close to tears.

Roly, acute as ever in sensing her mood, crouched beside her chair and put an arm around her shoulder.

'Hey! Come on – it can't be as bad as that, surely?' He couldn't imagine anything being worse than what she'd been through when Guy and Jamie had been killed. He lifted her face gently and smiled.

'Oh – I'm sorry, Roly. I just feel quite out of my depth and I haven't slept well for the last few nights and – ' She groped unsuccessfully for a tissue in her briefcase. Roly got up and offered her some kitchen towel. She blew her nose and let out a sigh. 'I'm just being silly. We'll talk later, as you said.' She nodded towards the cooker. 'Whatever that is, smells wonderful!'

'Come on!' He took her by the hand and led her through to the dining room where two places were already set at the oval antique table. 'You just sit and recover yourself.' He brought her tea through on a tray, then busied himself in the kitchen.

By the time they'd finished their meal, Anna was fully restored.

'Mmm,' she sighed. 'I've eaten only one meal to match this in the last couple of years, and the man who cooked that is a professional chef!'

'I'm honoured!' Roly grinned.

They looked at each other for a moment, then Anna said, 'I think it's time we got down to business.'

'OK. Let's go up to the study.'

Anna retrieved her briefcase from the kitchen and went up the stairs behind him. The study was a large room, still with the original fireplace, and a solid oak desk with one chair either side of it. All other available space was taken up by books, stacked from floor to ceiling in custom-made shelves. Anyone who didn't know Roly would be boggled by the sheer volume. Anna knew better. The two adjoining rooms formed the library proper. She thought of the library at Broomwood House and smiled. Roly would love it. Her pulse quickened as an idea formed. *Perhaps, if he has time, he would like to see it. I could ...*

'Right then – make yourself comfortable.'

'What is this – *Listen with Mother*?' Anna laughed.

'I'll listen – you talk. I have to confess, I was intrigued by your phone call, to say the least.'

'I never thought I'd be coming to you with something like this. Look – before we begin – I have to ask you to keep everything you hear and see in the strictest confidence. Partly academic and partly – well, legal reasons, I suppose. You'll understand why, when I tell you.'

She fell silent. Roly sat back in his chair, waiting for her to collect her thoughts. *Oh dear. I come all this way and it all seemed so urgent. Where the hell do I start?* She cleared her throat.

'This all began when Philip Jackson came to see me.' Roly nodded his recognition of the name. 'I'd barely been out of the house since – since the accident, as you know,' Anna continued '... and he had a job persuading me, but – well – I wound up taking it. Doing research in a place called Swifford Lea ...'

Roly reached behind himself and pulled a map book from the shelf.

'Let's take a look. That's not anywhere I'm familiar with.'

While he searched for it in the index, Anna's thoughts were racing towards clarification. By the time he'd found it, she had everything in order and began to unfold the facts.

Sally Arnold was approaching the Green, on her way back to the shop, after having lunch with the Misses Webb, when she saw Janice Mills' police vehicle, a Land Rover Discovery, pulling up outside Maggie Taylor's house. She slowed her pace, curious to see what was going on. Both Maggie and Janice climbed out, Janice in order to open the back, from which she took a mangled bicycle. *What on earth ...?* Maggie, normally so ebullient, was pale and dishevelled. And wasn't that Fletcher Godfrey in the front seat? Averting her eyes, Sally continued on her way. *Looks like there's been an accident, then. Still, at least neither of them is hurt ...*

Roly Featherstone had read the printout of Karen Peterson's diary in silence. Slowly, he put it down on the desk in front of him and raised his eyes to Anna's face.

'You took a hell of a risk, copying this.'

'I know. That's why I'm asking you to keep it confidential. What do you think?'

He turned the question back on her. 'What do *you* think?'

Anna sighed and shook her head. 'I don't know what to think, Roly, beyond the fact that the poor girl was suffering from some sort of delusion.'

'Yet you still brought it to me.'

'As I told you – I promised Karen's friend, Ellie. She's worried about her prospects in the afterlife.'

'Bit out of your field, eh?'

'Exactly. That's why I want your opinion – wearing both your hats, please.' She tried to smile, but it felt as if her muscles weren't co-operating.

'Academic expert on witchcraft, and amateur psychic researcher.'

'Precisely. So . . .' she tried again '. . . what do you think?'

He sat for a moment, eyes closed, before replying.

'I think we need to find out more about Megan Painter's curse.' He stood up and headed for the door. 'Come on – nothing's springing to mind, so we'll have to take a look next door.'

Anna followed him into the first of his library rooms. Moving to a card index, he ran through it swiftly.

'Curses ... curses ...' He turned to her in disappointment. 'Nothing here, I'm afraid.'

'So there isn't one.'

"Not necessarily. Sometimes these things are highly localised. Kept under wraps.'

'But you usually manage to sniff them out.'

'Usually, yes. But in this instance . . .' He sat down, the pair of them falling temporarily silent.

'Well,' Anna said at last. 'I think this backs up my idea that Karen was sick – delusional.'

'Quite possibly,' Roly agreed. 'But I think we need to investigate further. If it is a very localised thing, it may have been passed on orally. Probably in a bogeyman context. Or woman, in this case.'

Anna smiled. 'It was Old Tommo round our way. He died when my grandparents were little. An eccentric who owned a timber yard and slept in a coffin therein! Frightened the pants off my grandad when he was a little boy and sneaked into the yard at night for a dare. Rose up out of the coffin like Dracula and chased him off. Not that Grandad needed much chasing – he probably set an unrecognised world record for sprinting, I should think!'

Roly laughed. 'Megan Painter aside, though – what was this Voice Karen talked about?' He started to head down the stairs, Anna following him.

'Just that!' she retorted. 'A voice in her head. It's like people believing that God told them to kill a rock star, or the President, or their grandmother. Isn't it some kind of mental illness?'

'Nine times out of ten – yes. But this is certainly interesting.' Roly was making a fresh pot of tea.

'You don't believe it's real?!'

'I'm not saying that, but I'm not discounting it. I know you don't believe in the supernatural, Rhianna, but you've brought it to me because you know I'm at least open to the idea. With my academic hat on, it's interesting. With my psychical research hat on, I want to understand how and what the girl was reacting to. You know your sociology, Rhianna, and, God knows, I know the sociology of religion. It's fascinating the way the group mind can work – or the individual mind, in cases like this. People want something to believe in, but nine times out of ten, they can't be bothered to think for themselves. Want someone else to work it out for them and tell them what's so. It ultimately comes down to an abnegation of personal responsibility – let the leader decide – whether that leader is Stalin, the Pope or somebody like Jim Jones or David Koresh. And that gives power to the ones they put on a pedestal. Their word is law, because their word is God's word.' He pulled down a biscuit tin from a shelf, along with a plate on which he laid out a selection. 'On the other hand, of course, in the less hierarchical types of sects or cults, the set-up attracts those who are powerless or marginalised in modern society. In the world, they're nobody. In their group, they can be a prophet or speak in tongues. They have their own hot-line to God without the mediation of a leader, and that validates them, gives them a sense of self-worth, makes them feel they're important after all – in the divine plan, if not the cultural one. I'm a natural sceptic, Rhianna, but I'm open to the possibility that there's something in it – that's where my psychical research hat comes in to play. Even there, a great deal is down to psychology and the power of suggestion. Sometimes we're asking the wrong question if we ask, do curses work? Perhaps, more accurately, we should be asking *why* they work. Believe me, anything can work if someone believes it enough. You've read anthropology – read stories of things like the aboriginal pointing of the bone. Would it work if the intended victim didn't know? Almost certainly not. God – I could go on for hours – I'm sorry. Look – these old ladies you're working with . . .'

'The Misses Webb – yes?'

'Why don't you ask them about local legends? Don't necessarily come straight out with Megan Painter's curse, specifically – how would you know about it? But throw out the bait. You need to keep your back covered, as far as having illicit information is concerned.'

'Yes. But ...' Anna was busy thinking. 'I could say I'd been to visit you – as a friend, of course. And you'd just happened to say something like, "Oh – the Swiffords? There's a curse associated with that area, did you know?" I'll think of something.'

'Just be careful, that's all.'

'I will. And you will hide the printout carefully in the meantime? And the disk, when it arrives?'

'Of course. How many other copies are there?'

'Two. The one I printed this from, and the one I sent myself, but that was blank.'

'Blank? Rhianna ...'

'I must have picked up the wrong one – don't worry – I'll check through the disks back at April Cottage, find it, and scrub it. *And* make sure there's no record on any hard drives.'

'That's not what I was thinking of, actually.' He leaned back in his chair, giving her a long look. 'If there *is* some kind of evil force at work, it could have caused the disk to scramble.'

Anna made no attempt to hide her scepticism. 'You don't seriously believe that!'

'Just indulge me, will you?' He frowned. 'Is there anything else I should know about? Has anything else happened around you that might be construed as being out of the ordinary?' He saw the hesitation in her face. 'Rhianna – what?'

'Oh, it's – look, there must be a perfectly rational explanation – I just haven't found it yet.' She found herself wilting under his gaze and told him, hesitantly, about hearing the piano, and the photograph she'd found.

Roly brought down the legs of his chair with a crash, his excitement bubbling over. 'Good God, Rhianna! That's a classic scenario! When did this woman die?'

Anna shrugged. 'I'm not sure, exactly. It's not the sort of thing one feels able to ask. Sally Arnold just said "recently" in her letter.'

'Sally Arnold?'

'Yes. Sally and Frank. They run the local shop and post office. Ida was her aunt.' She saw the look on Roly's face and felt a tremor of confusion. 'What's so important?'

'You posted the disks from the Arnolds' post office?' Anna nodded. 'And one's blank and one has not yet arrived. Back upstairs,' Roly told her. 'I think we need to talk through a few more things. And I need the names of people you know in the Swiffords.'

'Don't tell me – ' she laughed. 'There's a black magic coven, and I'm right in the middle of it!'

'Don't even joke about it, Rhianna!'

'Come on, Roly – didn't you say that some of these weirdos refer to you as the Witchfinder General? And didn't I once hear you famously say that you had yet to find a so-called modern witch with genuine power! "Bicker and bitchcraft" was the phrase you used, if my memory serves me! I'll be OK if you're on my side, right?'

She laughed, realising, too late, that she'd never seen him looking so serious, and tried to defuse the tension.

'Look, it's probably nothing. I just came to you about the diary, remember, and that wasn't even off my own bat! I'm sure half this other stuff is just me being over-tired and over-imaginative.'

'There's more?' He looked at her sharply.

Oh shit! Why did I ever have to open my mouth? 'Well,' she offered reluctantly, wishing they could get off the subject, 'I suppose you'll want to know about Adam Etheridge and the goats?'

Roly Featherstone's heart was hammering. What the hell had she got herself into . . . ?

Anna set off on the long drive back to Swifford Lea much later than she had planned. Once off the motorway and on to country roads, the swathe of her headlights seemed to symbolise the cutting of her rational mind through the jumble of feelings clamouring for attention following her meeting with Roly. *Chalk and cheese. I'm the Scully to his Mulder, yet we're both trying to make sense of the same things in our own ways.* True, he wasn't saying – in so many words, at least – that he believed Karen Peterson's experiences to be real, but he was willing to look at them from a perspective which, to her, was simply not available. The business of the piano and Adam's ritual with the goats had worried him.

'He could be a solitary practitioner of some sort, but it's more than likely that he belongs to a group,' he had told her.

Practitioner of what? What kind of group? He hadn't been specific, but, along with the business of Karen's diary, Anna knew he had to be thinking in terms of what he would call 'the black arts'. Anna snorted as she changed down to take a bend. To be fair, though, and as she had reminded him, even Roly had said that much of what passed for so-called witchcraft these days – black or white – was nothing more than mumbo-jumbo, credulous people believing they had access to supposed occult power. That didn't make the black side of things any less dangerous, of course. Twisted people of any kind could and did do terrible things the world over. But believing they were 'tapped in' to evil forces or the devil – well ... They may believe it. Anna did not. There was more than enough evil in the human heart without creating outside agencies for it.

She shuddered. No matter how much education or science or civilisation advanced, it seemed only to be a veneer, varying in thickness, perhaps, but under which a persistently primitive undercurrent lay surprisingly close to the surface. Hadn't she herself come across this, time and time again, in her studies over the years? Even now, there were people who believed that birth-marks and certain malformations in babies were caused by shocks during pregnancy. The Human Genome Project had yet to make its mark, it seemed, along with modern advances in medicine and nutrition.

She tried to shake off her feeling of unease. *Be positive! At least you've discharged your duties as far as the diary is concerned. Roly has it, and will give it some thought. That should be enough to set Ellie's mind at rest.* But not Roly's, she knew. *If only I hadn't told him about Adam or the piano! He's going to be checking up on me, wanting to know of any further developments.* She shook her head, irritated with herself, as she crested the hill that would soon lead down into the village. *Don't be ridiculous! There won't* be *any further developments. Poor Karen ... poor father! But it's over. There is no 'Voice'.*

She frowned, thinking of the diary entries, thinking of the impact the news would make back in the Swiffords. Since that last, terse, police statement, everyone had assumed that Seth Peterson had killed his daughter. What would the reaction be once people realised it was the other way around? The police were bound to make another statement before long, now they had the diary. And weren't the funerals due to be held soon? She swore under her breath, thinking of Maggie's son and Karen's other friends. How on earth would they be able to come to terms with that knowledge? She wondered just how much information the police would release. What would be worse for those who'd known the girl? The fact that she'd killed her father and then herself, or the fact that she believed she was forced into doing it by some 'Voice' that told her she was the Arm of God and that it was her duty and privilege to do so? A killer. And crazy. Did that make it better or worse? She didn't know, and right then, didn't want to. *It's not my business. I just want to get in, relax and have an early night. And NO* – she spoke the word aloud – *I am NOT going to think about pianos or nightmares or anything else. I'll perhaps go into Market Eaton at the weekend and see if I can't pick up some herbal remedies. There's bound to be something gentle and non-addictive to help me sleep. It's just being away from home for the first time in so long. I'm out of my comfort zone and psychologically vulnerable, that's all. Like I said to Roly – I'm over-tired and over-imaginative. I'm sure I can take steps to sort that out.*

She turned carefully into the parking space of April Cottage. *Yes – going to Market Eaton is a good idea. I can get some of my films developed, too. They'll be nice to show the sisters.* She got out of the car and stretched. *Well – I've been a good girl all day – maybe it's time to have a drink. Nice glass of wine should help me sleep.* She pulled her briefcase from the passenger seat and locked the car, walking to the front of the cottage with the thought in mind of asking Maggie if she'd like to join her, but her neighbour's house was in darkness. *Perhaps she's already at the pub. Funny she didn't leave her lights on, though.* She wondered for a second if she should turn on the lights in April Cottage before continuing on her way, but decided against it. *I shan't be long. Just one quick glass.*

The pub seemed even more jam-packed than before and Anna had to elbow her way to the bar.

'On your own then tonight, eh?' She recognised the man who spoke as Chris, the leader of the Morris Men, who looked slightly the worse for wear.

'Well, she would be, wouldn't she?' his companion put in. 'Maggie being otherwise engaged.'

'Sorry?' Anna's attention had been distracted by Pat, who, having observed her battle to the bar, had a glass of red wine at the ready.

Chris shrugged. 'Whether with Fletcher or Janice, we don't know. Either way, I shouldn't think she's enjoying it. Horrible business.'

Anna groped in her half-opened briefcase for money and handed over a note. She turned back to the men, frowning.

'What is?'

'Exactly! She don't know, do she? She'm 'aven't been 'ere today, so I 'eard.' The other man nodded sagely.

'Strewth! You missed all the excitement, then!' Chris shook his head and lowered his voice. 'Not that we want any more of that sort, I can tell you! The Petersons was bad enough.'

Anna felt a knot of apprehension form in her stomach.

'What sort are we talking about?' Her mouth had gone dry and she sipped her wine nervously.

'God! He'll keep you here all night before he gets round to it!' Pat leaned across the bar to speak to her. 'It was dreadful. Maggie and Fletcher were over in Swifford Maisey this morning. They found the vicar dead. He'd been buried alive.'

Chapter Sixteen

Friday November 11th

Anna stood under the shower and marvelled. How had she slept so well, after the previous day's events? *Maybe*, she mused, *you get to a stage where you simply switch off*. And she hadn't heard the piano again, either. Counting her blessings, she finished her ablutions, dressed and made herself a hasty breakfast before deciding what to do next. She half-wondered about phoning Roly with the news about the vicar, but decided against it – for the time being, at least. *No point until I know more about what happened*. The people in the pub hadn't been too clear about it and she had forced herself not to ask too many questions, for fear of arousing suspicion or appearing ghoulish. *It's odd, certainly, as well as being awful. But only because of the timing, given the Peterson business. No one in the pub thought it could be anything but an accident – the sides of a grave caving in on him – but then, they hadn't spoken to either Maggie or Fletcher Godfrey*.

She went through to the living room, collecting her camera equipment, then stopped suddenly. What was different? She looked around, frowning. Something *felt* different, but she couldn't put her finger on it. She shrugged her shoulders and checked her camera gear. *Come on, Summers – don't let all this death and talk of curses get at you. This is a lovely cottage and there's nothing to be afraid of. If I hadn't heard the piano and seen the photograph, I would never have worried at all. But that could be – and logically,* is *– a case of adding two and two and making five. Still ...*

She wondered if there was some way she could find out more about Sally's Aunt Ida and when she'd died – Roly seemed to think her 'recent' demise might be significant and had asked for more detail. She stood, trying to put her thoughts in order. *First things first. If I'm going to go into Market Eaton with films for developing, I could use up more of what I've got here this morning on village shots. So that's number one on the list. And if I can talk to Maggie – well, maybe I can kill two birds with one stone there. Try and find out a bit more about what happened to the vicar* and *get information about Aunt Ida. The latter, at least, shouldn't be too difficult. They were neighbours for God knows how many years. Maybe even* three *birds with one stone – come right out and ask her who, around here, has a piano. OK. And when I've done that – then I can phone Roly.*

Plan of action devised, she locked the door of April Cottage and set out across the Green.

Fletcher Godfrey's hands were unsteady as he drew water to fill the kettle. *Jesus Christ! Jesus Christ!* He shook his head angrily. This was no time to be calling on God. If it hadn't helped the vicar, what the hell chance did *he* stand? His head swam and he found himself trembling. He slumped at the kitchen table, breathing hard to fight off the feeling of nausea that threatened to overwhelm him. God! It would have been bad enough last night anyway, trying to sleep, after the business with the vicar. The same images that had appeared behind his closed eyelids then, shimmered in front of his open eyes now. *Oh Christ!* He shook his head to disperse them. He'd never forget it as long as he lived, that look on Maggie Taylor's face, and then seeing what had struck her speechless. It had been difficult, to say the least, trying to sleep. What with that, and remembering what they'd found in the church afterwards. But even that hadn't been the worst of it. Oh no. He shuddered violently. He had to have dreamed it. He *had* to. He was shockingly aware of tears beginning to run down his cheeks. *Christ! All those years on the Force and I never cried once, and now ...* He stood up and kicked the chair over in anger and frustration, then tipped over the table as well, before thumping the wall over and over again. This couldn't be happening to him! It *couldn't!* It was bad enough hearing that bloody Voice to begin with, but at least it had only said his name. Even – just even – at a pinch – he might have come round to thinking it was Seth and that it's not the end when you die after all. But last night – well. It had said a damned sight more than just his name. Blood-curdling stuff. Unbelievable. No bloody way was that Seth, and that was for sure. He shook his head and leaned over the sink, skin crawling as he relived the experience. He had sat up in bed in disbelief, horror and bewilderment washing over him till he'd well nigh wet himself. And then he'd pulled himself together. Shouted at it, out loud. Told it to bugger off, it was just a figment of his imagination.

Then it had been the worst.

Because *then*, it had answered him back ...

Anna was standing in a previously unexplored part of the village, on a narrow footpath bordered by overhanging trees, when she heard it. *What on earth?* She snapped the back of the camera shut. She had been changing the film, which was the only reason she'd stopped. She listened again, senses heightened. There it was again. The sound of muffled sobbing, away to her right.

She felt a twinge of guilt. What if it was Ellie? She had meant to have a quick word with the girl in The White Hart last night, simply to say that Roly was now in possession of the relevant information, but what between the crush at the bar and the whole place being abuzz with the news of Reverend Fury's death, she hadn't managed it. She'd been half-surprised that Ellie hadn't turned up at the cottage again. *Oh damn! I suppose I ought to go and have a word. Try to reassure her.*

Following the direction of the sound, she made her way along the path until she came to a break in the hedge. Peering through, she saw no one to begin with, but the sound of crying was more distinct here, definitely closer. Turning sideways, she pushed her way through the gap, holding the camera above her head for safety, almost falling as she emerged into an overgrown field.

'Damn!' She swore loudly as she clutched the camera to her chest and struggled to keep her balance. Immediately, there was movement, and, to her astonishment, Maggie Taylor got up from the log upon which she'd been sitting, hurriedly dabbing at her face with a crumpled tissue.

'Maggie! God – I'm sorry. I didn't mean to disturb you. Are you all right?' Anna winced at the inanity of her own question. Of course the woman wasn't all right – she was dishevelled and her face was streaked black with tears where her mascara had run. 'I'm sorry – that's such an appallingly stupid question. Oh hell – do you want me to bugger off and leave you alone?'

'No.' Maggie fished in the pocket of her sheepskin jacket and pulled out a further wad of tissues, blowing her nose noisily and wiping her face. 'Don't tell me – I bet I look like a bloody racoon!'

'Well – yes – rather.'

'Oh God!' Maggie shook her head and sank back on to the log. 'Come and sit down, Anna – I won't bite.'

By the time Anna had joined her, Maggie was crying again, head in her hands. Awkwardly, Anna placed an arm around her shoulders, feeling terrible when this seemed to release even more tears, rather than stemming the flow. She sat helplessly until, at last, the emotional storm seemed to pass.

'Thanks, Anna. I needed that.' Maggie mopped her face again.

'I take it this is to do with yesterday? I was in the pub last night and they said there'd been an accident and the vicar was dead ...'

'Accident?' Maggie's look was fierce. 'That was no bleedin' accident! Not that I'm supposed to talk about it yet, but I expect it'll be all over the papers by later today. Good God, Anna – I don't ever want to see nothing like that again – ever! It was like some bleedin' horror film!'

Anna's body tingled. *Oh no* ... She tried to say something, but Maggie cut her off, launching into how she and Fletcher had come to be in Swifford Maisey. It seemed that the floodgates had been opened, and all Anna could do was sit and listen as the story poured forth. When she got to the part where they had first heard the screaming woman, Maggie could contain herself no longer and jumped up, pacing back and forth across an area of withered grass in front of the log. She lit a cigarette, hands trembling.

'Don't tell Jack. He thinks I've stopped. I *had* stopped until yesterday. This woman, screaming – it shook us rigid. Ran into the back of Fletcher's bike, I did, and he was roaring like a bull, saying we was coming to help, and we went running through the lych-gate ...' Maggie paused and turned to stare Anna right in the face. 'I don't know what possessed me. Why I didn't just follow Fletcher or go round the other side of the church to try and find her ... He may be older then me, but he's a bloody sight fitter – faster all round. And me legs was killing me, truth be told. Anyway – he was running hell for leather, and what do I do? I glances over to where the sound seemed to have been coming from – to start with, I mean – and there's this pile of earth, right?' Her voice caught, and she struggled to go on, face working. 'I walks over. Walks. And I keep thinking, that can't really be what it looks like. It's me eyes playing me up or something. Only it wasn't.' She blinked hard, trying to stem a fresh flow of tears. 'It was a hand, Anna. A hand and a forearm, sticking up through the earth. And I sort of fell down on me knees, looking at it, and then Fletcher was with me and then . . .'

It took quite some time for Maggie to compose herself enough to tell Anna of their desperate scrabbling in the earth and the terrible uncovering of the vicar's dead body.

'His mouth was full of earth. He'd suffocated, we reckon. God – the look on his face! Fletcher cleared it away, tried to revive him, but we both knew it was no good. Jesus, Anna!' Maggie shuddered. 'Never mind Jack going for counselling – it'll be me at this rate. I just can't seem to get the sight of it out of my head. Stunned, we was. I can't begin to tell you. And Fletcher – old habits die hard, I expect, him being the ex-local bobby – he says – eventually, when either of us could speak – he says, "We'll have to phone Janice, Maggie" – she's the police here now – and I just gives him me mobile and lets him get on with it. And we was so shook up and all, and the church door was open and, honest to God, I don't know about Fletcher, but I thought me legs was going to give way. So we went to sit in the church, like, till Janice arrived and – oh my God, Anna, it was terrible. Not as bad as actually finding the vicar, of course – I can't imagine what would be, and I don't want to – but you don't expect it in a church, do you? Not anywhere else, come to that.'

'What, Maggie? What was in the church?' Anna's mouth had gone familiarly dry again as she waited for the woman's answer.

'It was – you 'aven't been in the church in Swifford Maisey, have you? 'Course you 'aven't – it's what they call a late medieval church – all whitewashed inside – well, limewash, I think it was originally – to cover up wall paintings and such during the Reformation.'

Anna nodded.

'I couldn't believe it. Neither of us could. We must have looked like a right pair of goldfish, mouths hanging open, you know, just

– just speechless. There was writing all over the walls – looked like it was in blood – oh, shit, I hope not.' She shook her head again, then forced herself to refocus. 'Writing,' she repeated. 'All about the Wrath of God and some bleedin' curse from 1732.'

Pete Barker was singing to himself as he drove through the countryside towards Swifford Holt and George Lewis, his favourite pig farmer. Beautiful meat, George reared, and no mistake. Oh, what he could do with that succulent pork! Had he not been driving, he would have closed his eyes to savour the thought of the creations he had in mind. All those subtleties that lesser chefs would miss, and so simple, so delicious, so … He frowned, seeing rubber on the road in front of him. Christ, somebody had been ramping it up to leave marks like that! Bloody idiots! He hoped they weren't going to get a sudden influx of boy racers. He chuckled to himself and smiled. Round here? They'd kill themselves, as likely as not, on these roads. Twists and turns you wouldn't believe. Serve the buggers right if they did – just so long as they didn't take anyone else with them. Boy racers? No. They were in it for an audience. It was all ego and testosterone-driven. That was why they raced round the inner ring-roads of cities. Cocking a snook at authority in general and the police in particular.

Thinking of the police brought Janice Mills to mind. Bloody hell, that woman had had more on her plate in the last week than would normally have happened around here in years. Not that they'd had murders at all, as far as he knew. He'd heard all sorts of tales from the locals since the Peterson tragedy, all of it trivial in comparison. And now the vicar! Pete had seen him – from a distance – but had never met him. Not a popular man, by all accounts, but even so … And poor old Maggie, finding him. It didn't occur to him to feel sorry for Fletcher Godfrey. Fletcher was an ex-copper, so he'd probably come across similar stuff before, even if not here. Well, maybe not similar, but he was an ex-copper and a man and what the hell – he'd cope. Maggie, on the other hand, was friendly and excitable and she'd been brilliant from the first day he and Pat had set foot in the village. He didn't like to think of her being upset. Still, accidents happen, though it seemed a horrible way for someone to die. He wriggled his shoulders to rid himself of the thought. Buried alive! Terrible. Probably digging a grave, ready for one of the poor Petersons, and the sides caved in or something. No way was that ever going to happen to him. *Bugger that! I'm going to be cremated. That way, at least if there's been some horrible mistake and I* am *still alive – God forbid – it'll all be over in a flash. Flash in a pan! Kind of fitting for a chef, eh?* He chuckled at his own joke, and brought his mind back to the order he was taking over to George Lewis, then to his own herb and vegetable garden. Only the best would do. Fresh – none of this frozen nonsense. Organic, as far as possible, too. *Real* food. Most people nowadays had never tasted it. Wouldn't have a clue.

'I'm on a mission from God!' He paraphrased the Blues Brothers out loud. 'You are what you eat. And Christ knows what that makes most of the population ...'

He changed down, ready for the snake-like double-bend that would take him round on to the cliff road. There *was* actually a slightly quicker route he could have taken, but it was a beautiful day and he loved the smell of the sea.

'Bloody hell!' He spoke aloud again, braking as he did so. Rubber was visible on the road again, the tracks this time leading directly to the edge of the cliff.

'Oh, Christ!' He brought the car to a halt and scrambled out, unclipping his mobile from its hand-free fitting and taking it with him. Slowly, he walked towards the spot where the tracks disappeared, heart sinking as he noted the flattened marker poles, lying with their reflective eyes turned now towards the sky. 'Oh Christ!' he muttered again, this time more as a prayer for himself as he neared the edge. Only his family knew that he wasn't very good when it came to heights.

Forcing himself to breathe slowly and steadily, he inched his way forward. It was no good. He could feel his legs trembling already, and his palms were slick with sweat. *Shit! Get a grip, man! This is serious!* He backed away, closed his eyes and breathed deeply again, before lowering himself to his knees and finally flattening himself out on his stomach. *Right. Do it. You can't fall, because you're not standing. Do it, man! Do it!*

Inching forward again, he gritted his teeth, tension in every muscle as he fought to overcome his fear. At last, he was at the edge, heart hammering, head swimming. *You silly bugger! You can't faint, lying down!* With a supreme act of will, he forced himself to look over it, eyes widening with shock.

Shit, shit, SHIT! He scrabbled backwards, panting, gasping for breath, and rolled over on to his back, closing his eyes against the whirling sky and gulping in air so hard, it hurt. *Oh my God!* Forcing himself to sit up, he punched Janice Mills' number into his phone.

'Come on – come ON!' He almost screamed at it as he waited for his call to be diverted to her mobile. At last he heard her voice, and struggled to his feet.

'Janice – it's Pete Barker. I'm out on the cliff road going into Swifford Holt. There's been an accident – a car's gone over the edge. And there's a woman's body lying on the rocks ...'

Chapter Seventeen

Roland Featherstone sat back in his chair and pinched the bridge of his nose. He had been examining, in depth, the copy of Karen Peterson's diary which Rhianna had given to him yesterday and sat, lost in thought, for some time. This was quite extraordinary. The girl had not burned with zeal, believing herself to be the Arm of God; quite the contrary – she had fought against 'the calling' with every resource she possessed. Those resources, were, however, puny and limited by her age and lack of exposure to religious belief or systems of spirituality. How she had fought, though! The academic shook his head and gave a nod of respect to the dead girl. What on earth had been going on? Was she mentally ill? Could such a shocking breakdown have occurred so suddenly, seemingly without warning? An acute onset of split personality, perhaps? He wished he could ask the advice of one of his colleagues in Psychology, but unless and until the business was made public, he couldn't do that without compromising Rhianna as his source.

He read certain entries again. She had been incredulous, to begin with, then worried that she was hearing things which, to her mind, meant going mad. And once the Voice had got going, she had decided to fight, rather than take things lying down. He glanced at the page in front of him. The entry was for September 10th.

I been and bought a Bible today. I can't believe all that stuff the Voice tells me is right. I felt depressed after I started reading it, though, 'cos there is *loads and loads of stuff about blood and sacrifices and all that.*

She had read quickly and commented, just a couple of days later:

I can't get my head round this. The New Testament is different. It's like the Voice is talking to me from the Old Testament, without taking account of the New one and Jesus. I'm praying to Jesus to help me. I'd talk to Reverend Fury, if I could, but he's horrible. Perhaps I'm just scared that he'll back up the Voice, and where would that leave me? Besides, I couldn't tell him why *I want to know the things I do, because he'd think I'm mad and tell Dad and then I'd more as like get locked away. I don't know what to do.*

This hadn't held her up for long, however. She had been to see a Unitarian minister in Market Eaton.

... she was really helpful. I didn't tell her the truth, of course – well, not all of it, and though I feel a bit bad about that, at least I found out stuff without her thinking I was mad. I just said as how it confuses me, all this talk about retribution and blood sacrifices and the sins of the fathers being visited upon their children unto the third and fourth generation, and stuff, and I told her it frightens me and she said there's no reason to be frightened because Jesus done away with all that through wrapping everything up in himself and making the supreme sacrifice. She's given me stuff to read and invited me to some services. I feel bad because I won't be able to go, not being able to drive yet and the buses are crap around here on Sundays, but at least maybe now I can tell this Voice that it's wrong and why *it's wrong, and see if that does any good.*

It hadn't. The Voice had confused the girl further, with talk of the New Covenant only applying to those who believed, and saying that the full weight of the Old Law would be heaped upon those responsible for wickedness, for by their wickedness they had shown that they did not believe. *And the wages of sin is death*, it had told her, and even Karen Peterson now knew that that was a quote from the New Testament. She had continued her prayers and reading, however, and, besides talking to the Unitarian minister again, had taken the further step of going into the Catholic church.

They'd just finished the Mass, apparently, but there were still people inside – leaving, like, but there was a lady with a stall with cards and statues and stuff. I didn't know what half of it was, but she was friendly, like, so I said I wanted to buy something nice for a Catholic friend, and asked her what all the things were for. I wound up buying a rosary, because it's got Jesus on the cross, and I bought a little crucifix to wear round my neck, and I even took some Holy Water. She didn't charge me for that, and perhaps if I sprinkle it round the house and specially in my room, the Voice will go away.

It hadn't. Still the girl had battled with it, trying reason and prayers and her precious Holy Water, all to no avail. Roland Featherstone grimaced as he read one of the following entries. This had taken her into a whole new realm of experience.

I was wandering round in my lunch break from College, and found this little bookshop in one of the back alleys where I've never been before. 'Seekers', it's called, and some of the books are new and some are second-hand, and this particular one, well, the title just jumped at me off the shelf, like, so I bought it.

That book had been Dion Fortune's *Psychic Self-Defence. Old hat,* Roland Featherstone thought, *to someone like me. But a revelation to Karen.* She'd started performing the Qabalistic Lesser Banishing Ritual, morning and evening. *The one in there is the beginner's variety – adepts and initiates know much more powerful forms, but still, it should have worked. The very fact that it didn't is surely indicative that the girl was waging war within herself. Ditto for all the other stuff she did.* She'd bought other books, too, and tried everything from circles of salt to burning black candles in a 'cauldron' of water in an attempt to banish curses. And the Voice had laughed at her.

So – what's the verdict? He tapped the table absently. Most likely, she had, indeed, gone mad. There was still, however, from the look of some of the things the Voice was saying, a remote – a very remote – but nonetheless niggling possibility that she had come into contact with something very real, very evil. And incredibly powerful . . .

Anna and Maggie were making their way slowly back to the centre of the village. Maggie had calmed down considerably by now and thanked Anna profusely for her listening ear.

'I'm just glad you feel better.'

'I do, believe me. It was just so good, getting it off my chest. God – you won't say anything, will you? I wasn't supposed to let on, and there's no way I could have told anyone in the village.'

'Not even Jack?'

'Especially not Jack. He's got enough on his plate, as it is. Oh God!' Maggie stopped dead. 'Who's going to do the funeral now? The Petersons', I mean? Bloody hell – there's the Remembrance Service on Sunday, as well.'

'Not your problem, Maggie. Let the church authorities work it out.'

'It's awful, isn't it? Part of me is just relieved that it won't be Reverend Fury, but I wouldn't have wished the man dead. You never met him, of course. Real High Church but sort of fire and brimstone fundamentalist as well. I was worried sick about the effect he'd have on all them kids, truth be told.'

Anna was thinking over the things she'd heard and decided to chance a question.

'Any idea who the screaming woman was, Maggie? Has she come forward or anything?'

Maggie shook her head. 'No idea, Anna. We never got a look at her. Christ! The way she was screaming, we thought she was being raped or murdered. It was her we was expecting to find, not the vicar.'

'You don't think maybe *she* ...'

Maggie threw her a frightened glance. 'Killed him? Oh God – I don't know. I don't even want to think about it. But – and I bet we're right in the shit for destroying the evidence – when I found the vicar ... well, somebody had been jumping up and down on that grave, by the look of it. Loads of footprints, and it looked like a woman's shoes – court shoes, or something, with them little heels. We mucked it all up, dragging the vicar out. But what else could we do? We was hoping – you know ...'

'Dear God! Could it have been an hysterical reaction to finding him there herself, do you think?' Anna's flesh crept at the thought.

'I don't know, Anna. Different people react in different ways, don't they?' Maggie bit her lip. 'I couldn't speak at all when I found the vicar. Fletcher swore – and he was sick, after he'd given him the kiss of life.' Maggie's face took on a pinched look. 'I expect all them same things has gone through Janice's mind, even though it'll be out of her hands by now. I don't know – talk about "it never rains but it pours", eh?'

They were back on the main road now, and the village shop was coming up on their right. As they neared it, Sally Arnold came out through the door and fell into step beside them.

'Morning!' She glanced at Maggie's face. 'You all right, love?'

'Yes, thanks – Anna's been looking after me. You off to the sisters?'

'Yes.'

Maggie turned to Anna. 'Oh God – have I held you up?'

'It's not a problem – I'll just whip into the house and collect my recording equipment.'

'I might as well wait for you, then.' Sally crossed over the road with the two women as they approached the little row of buildings. She touched Maggie's arm lightly as they reached the gate. 'You look like you could use a lie-down.'

'Chance would be a fine thing! I've done bugger-all this morning, besides upsetting myself about yesterday – I've got to get some work done.'

'Well don't be too hard on yourself. Look ...' Sally's smile included both women '... why don't the pair of you come over to me and Frank for a meal tomorrow evening? You ...' she looked specifically at Maggie '... have had a shock and need to let up. And you ...' she turned to Anna '... must wonder what kind of God-forsaken place you've landed up in.'

Maggie smiled. 'It's all her fault, really,' she told Sally, nodding towards Anna. 'None of this lot started till she arrived. Your middle name's not Jonah, is it, Anna?'

'Bloody hell, I hope not!' Anna didn't appreciate the joke.

'Bring Jack, if he wants to come,' Sally continued.

'Tomorrow? That's Saturday, isn't it? Bleedin' hell, I'm losing track of what day it is, now. No. I mean, yes, we'd love to come, wouldn't we, Anna? But Jack will be away – there's a load of 'em from college having a sleep-over.'

'Fine. Just the two of you, then. Quarter-to-nine all right? I know it's a bit late, but with not shutting the shop until eight ...'

'That'll be fine. We'll be there. I'll perhaps see you later, Anna. Come round for a cuppa this evening?'

'Sure.'

Maggie disappeared into her house and Sally and Anna walked the last few paces to April Cottage.

'I'm sorry,' Sally said. 'Poor Maggie was obviously so wound up, she never gave you a chance to answer for yourself. Is tomorrow all right?'

'Yes; it's fine. Thanks for the invitation. Shan't be a sec.' Anna shot into April Cottage, quickly gathering together the things she needed for her visit to the Misses Webb, whilst Sally waited outside. Maybe now, she'd get a chance to ask a few questions about Aunt Ida. The cottage locked behind her once more, the two women set off across the Green.

'I thought you usually visit the sisters by car, to save time on your lunch break?'

'Only if I'm delivering stuff. Wastes petrol, otherwise. Couldn't have done, today, anyway – the car's in for its MOT. Bad business about the vicar, eh?'

Is she trying to pump me for information I might have just picked up from Maggie? 'Yes,' Anna agreed. 'Rotten for Maggie and Fletcher, too. Must have been a hell of a shock.'

'Met Fletcher yet, have you?'

'No.'

'Just wondered. You asking about the police and all, the other day.'

Oh God! When I was saddled with the diary and didn't want to arouse suspicion ... 'Mmm. Thanks for the information. Yes, I shall need to speak to him at some point, but right now hardly seems to be an appropriate time.'

'Not to worry.' They were walking down the lane which held the stile giving pedestrian access to Broomwood House. Sally pointed to a cottage set back from the road some distance away. 'When you do get round to it, that's where he lives.'

'Thanks. I was looking through your Aunt Ida's papers the other evening, by the way. They're fascinating, Sally. Did she live in April Cottage all her life?'

Sally shook her head as she clambered over the stile, Anna following her.

'Moved there after she got married. Uncle Stan died ... oh,

must be going on fifteen years ago, I reckon. Loved it there, she did.'

'Was her passing very recent? I just wondered, with your saying that the cottage was going to be put up for sale.'

Was it Anna's imagination, or did Sally's look augur disapproval of her question? At any rate, the woman answered it.

'Middle of September, it was. Very unexpected. She had a stroke.'

'I'm very sorry. Were you very close?'

'Indeed we were. She brought me up after my parents died. Never had children of her own. Her and Uncle Stan were everything to me.'

Anna felt a strong flush of embarrassment. 'I'm sorry – I didn't mean to pry. So – ' she stared at Sally, reddening further as realisation dawned. 'So April Cottage was *your* home, too?'

'That's right. I only moved out when I married Frank.'

'Well, the papers you lent me are marvellous. Would it be OK to copy them? As a history of one particular dwelling?'

'This'd be used for your academic study, right?'

'Yes.'

'Then I don't see why not. Well – here we are.' They had reached Broomwood House. 'Let's see what the sisters are up to today, shall we?'

It was only as she was walking back to April Cottage, over three hours later, that Anna realised she'd forgotten to ask about local bogeymen and curses. The sisters had been full of life today, with a wealth of stories about their father and their travels. They had taken two foreign holidays a year for well over half a century, each one faithfully recorded in diaries and photograph albums. Anna smiled to herself. They had kept everything, from the letters they had written to book accommodation, to flight tickets, boat tickets, trinkets and other mementoes purchased during their stays. She really would have to talk to Philip. *No more thinking about it – do it. Arrange to see him next week.* The sisters were so incredibly well organised – they were an utter godsend for research purposes. She had been astonished to be shown original scraps of paper, on which Molly had drafted letters, in English, along with handwritten copies of the French translations Alice had sent to hotel managers with whom they had become familiar over the years.

Some were touching, showing, as they did, the gradual decline in their father's health. *Could you please provide us with a ground-floor room for Father this year, as he is no longer able to cope with stairs?* she remembered.

Poor old boy! Anna negotiated the stile with ease, having left her recording equipment behind. The sisters had been happy for her to leave it in the library. She would need now only to take fresh tapes with her each day. *I must ask about their mother, though. They've never really mentioned her, much.* Preoccupied as she was to get home and make a list in order to get herself better organised, she almost walked straight in front of a car coming down the lane, headed for the centre of the village.

'Bloody hell, Anna! Watch where you're going, woman! I've had enough bloody frights today as it is!' Pete Barker's face was thunderous as he wound down the window to yell at her.

'Sorry, Pete – my fault entirely.' She had jumped back, heart hammering, and it was only as she took in his appearance that the full impact of his words hit her. 'What else has been scaring you, then?'

He shook his head. 'There's been an accident over at Holt. A car went over the cliff.'

'Oh dear. Anybody hurt?'

'Just a bit. There was a dead woman on the rocks.'

'Oh God – how awful! When was this?'

'This morning. Well, that's when I found it. Don't know when it went over, mind.'

'You didn't see it happen, then?'

'No, thank God. Let's hope it's right what they say, eh?'

'Sorry?'

'About everything happening in threes – the Petersons – the vicar – now this. That should be an end to it, right?'

'Let's hope so,' she agreed, as he continued on his way.

Later that afternoon, lists made and with her thoughts more in order, Anna phoned Roly. 'Hi! Thought I'd phone and check if the disk arrived.'

'It did. And like the one you posted, it was blank.'

'Oh bugger! I forgot to check through the blank ones here. It's probably my fault. I'll do it later and call you, OK?'

'OK. So – how are things progressing?'

'Well ... there's more bad news, I'm afraid.' She gave him

Maggie's account of finding the vicar, and the graffiti in the church.

'This is quite extraordinary!' Roly paused before asking, 'You're sure there was an explicit reference to Megan Painter's curse?'

Anna thought carefully. 'I don't think she was named. At least, Maggie didn't say so. Just referred to "the curse of 1732".'

'Well, at least it may bring it out into the open. Give you more reason for asking questions.'

'Hold your horses! I'm not going to be asking around, willy-nilly! Just the sisters, when the opportunity is right. They don't even know about the Petersons yet, let alone this latest episode.'

'How come? Surely the place must be buzzing?'

'Yes, but they don't leave the house. And Sally stopped their newspapers – doesn't want them being frightened.'

'Sally being this village shop person you mentioned?'

'That's right.'

'And to whom you gave the disks for posting?'

'Yes. Oh come on, Roly – you surely don't think *she* has anything to do with this?'

'You can't be too careful, Rhianna. Did you find out any more about her aunt?'

Anna told him of their conversation just that morning.

'I don't like this at all,' he told her. 'You're staying in what used to be her home ...'

'Roly! I think you're seeing Reds under the beds. And I haven't heard the piano again.'

'Just keep me up to date with developments, will you? And take care of yourself.'

'You'll be asking me to do the LBR myself, next!' Anna protested, thinking of Karen Peterson's references to it.

'It might not be such a bad idea, you know. I wish I'd shown you ...'

'Stop it! And it didn't do Karen much good, did it?'

'According to you, that's because the Voice was in her own head.'

'Precisely. What the hell else could it be?'

Roland Featherstone didn't like to tell her.

She wouldn't believe him if he did.

*

Later, at Maggie's, Anna asked her if she'd heard about Pete Barker's experience.

'No! I expect they've been busy at the pub. I've been avoiding it since – you know – finding the vicar. Didn't want to get asked about it.' She frowned suddenly. ''Ere – you don't think ... ?'

Anna didn't have time to ask what. Maggie had picked up the phone and was soon speaking to Pete Barker himself. Anna, of course, could only hear Maggie's side of the conversation, which was largely taken up with commiseration with Pete on the shock he'd had.

'I know. It's awful, isn't it? I was just saying to Anna, I've not been in the pub myself because of not wanting to get asked about the vicar ... Yes. Yes. 'Course I will. Anna? She's here now, and really sorry for nearly chucking herself under your wheels.' Maggie winked at Anna, who smiled back from her seat on the sofa. 'Well, that'd be a bit drastic! What else has anybody got to talk about? I'm just not ready yet.'

There was the sound of Maggie's letterbox snapping, followed by a soft thud. Anna mouthed, 'Shall I get that?' and Maggie nodded, listening to Pete. Anna went into the small lobby and picked up what turned out to be the local newspaper. Unfolding it, she gasped at the headline.

Curse at work in Swiffords?
Death and desecration – are Satanists to blame?

Taking it into the living room, she held it up so that Maggie could see it.

'Oh my Gawd! Pete – have you seen the paper? No? Anna's just picked mine up.' She read it to him, then listened, nodding. 'I wasn't supposed to say nothing. Neither was Fletcher, and I can't imagine for a minute that he'd have talked to a journalist. What? Yes. I'll bring Anna with me, shall I? Sure. We'll see you later, then.'

Hanging up the phone, she took the paper from Anna and read the whole article.

'Well – this'll put the cat among the pigeons, and no mistake.' She tapped a paragraph and passed it over for Anna to read. 'This was why I wanted to talk to Pete.'

Following the suspicious death of Reverend Stephen Fury in Swifford Maisey yesterday, police are appealing for witnesses to come forward. They particularly want to speak to a woman heard screaming in the churchyard around the time his body was discovered.

'She could hold vital evidence,' a police spokesperson said, 'and we are appealing for her to come forward so that she can be eliminated from our enquiries.'

'You think the woman who went over the cliff could be the woman in the churchyard?' Anna asked. 'That's a bit of a long shot, Maggie.'

'I'm not so sure, and we can but ask. I'd best give Fletcher a ring. Warn him about this, and ask if he wants to come with us tonight.' She picked up the phone and, glancing at a piece of paper on the wall, began to press numbers.

'I thought you didn't want to be seen in the pub?'

'I don't. Not that it'll make much difference now, with this lot splashed all over the front page. But we're not going to the pub as such. Pete's going to lock up on the dot. We'll go round the back after chucking-out time, and then we're going upstairs to their flat. Just after eleven o'clock. Hope that's not too late for you?' Raising her finger to her lip, she indicated that her call had been answered. 'Hello, Fletcher – it's Maggie ...'

Chapter Eighteen

Saturday November 12th

Anna drove to Market Eaton on automatic pilot, her mind filled with thoughts of last night's meeting with Pete Barker and its aftermath. It had just been she and Maggie who had gone in the end, Fletcher Godfrey having declined the invitation in no uncertain terms.

'I've never known him be so rude,' Maggie had exclaimed, her feathers unexpectedly ruffled. 'Perhaps finding the vicar got to him more than he's letting on – being an ex-policeman, you don't expect it, do you? Still, he's only human, after all.'

So they had walked the short distance together, cutting across the fields at the back of the cottages and skulking by the private back door entrance leading to Pete and Pat's flat until they were let in as Ellie and Aaron, the pot-wash, left. Anna had managed to hang back, catching Ellie's beseeching glance, and had run after her, calling, 'Ellie – I think you dropped this!', in a bizarre re-run of their pantomime of a few nights earlier. Alone in the dark, she had pretended to hand something over, assuring the girl that Karen Peterson's diary had been passed to Roly. Ellie's relief had been palpable, and she had squeezed Anna's hand before saying 'thanks'.

Once inside, Anna had followed the others to Pete and Pat's simply and beautifully furnished living room, where, almost without preamble, the conversation had turned to the newspaper article.

'Jesus, Maggie! What the hell is going on? I feel like we're living in the middle of *The Rocky Horror Show*, only for real!' Pete exclaimed.

'I dunno, I really don't. But how did the newspaper get hold of it? The writing about the curse? Neither me nor Fletcher's talked to anybody about it.' She had studiously avoided Anna's eye as she'd said this.

'They probably had somebody out there, sniffing around. You know what some of these hacks are like.' Pat had shrugged.

'Yes, but I didn't think the local ones was like that. At least they haven't put what it actually said, mind, which is just as well.'

Everyone looked at her expectantly, but she had shaken her head firmly.

'More than my life's worth. I know *you* wouldn't say anything, but ...'

'No need to apologise – we understand,' Pete had assured her. 'It's a bad business, though.'

Anna had sworn inwardly, startled that Maggie had not shared everything with her. *Damn! That information could have been crucial to Roly. Still, at least the curse in general has been aired.* She had cleared her throat.

'Does anyone know anything about this curse, though? What did the paper say – 1732?'

Pete and Pat had shaken their heads. Only in the village for a year, they had never heard anything about it. Maggie had chewed her lip, thinking.

'No,' she said finally. 'Can't say I've ever come across it. Do you think there might be something in the library?'

'I'm going in to Market Eaton in the morning – I could stop off and have a look.' Anna had intended doing so anyway, but wasn't about to say so.

'Right. But what about this talk of Satanists? I don't like that at all.' Maggie had looked thoroughly alarmed.

'What a load of bollocks!' Pete had snorted his derision. 'Sells papers, that's all. You've lived here twenty years, Maggie – don't you think you would have noticed any strange goings-on?'

Maggie had pulled a face. 'I'm sure you're right. But it's going to stir things up good and proper, isn't it? Makes us sound like a load of thick weirdos.'

'What about you, though, Pete?' Anna had put in, anxious to find out if the car crash had any connection. 'You've had a pretty unpleasant experience yourself.'

He had shrugged. 'Not as bad as Maggie's, that's for sure. And at least this was just an accident. She must have been driving like a maniac, mind.' He told them about the rubber on the road and his discovery of the wreckage, editing out only his fear of heights.

'Poor Janice looked frazzled when she got there. What with the Petersons and the vicar, she's had more than a bellyful this last week. Anyway, she'd called the air ambulance and all that, but it was obvious to both of us that the woman was dead – her neck was all wrong. We just didn't know if there was anybody else trapped inside the car.' Pete shrugged. 'There wasn't.'

'But we don't know who the dead woman was?' Maggie had prompted.

'No. Shouldn't take long, though. They'll run the licence plates through the DVLA, won't they? She might have had ID on her, anyway – credit cards in a handbag or something.' Pete paused, light dawning as he looked at Maggie's expression. 'Hold on – what it said in the paper – about a woman in the churchyard – you're not thinking ...'

'I know it sounds ghoulish, and I'm sorry. It's just that – oh, Anna's right, I'm sure – it's a ridiculous long shot – but, well – it had crossed my mind – yes. What with the timing and all, it just seems a bit too bloody coincidental for my liking.'

'Bloody hell!' Pete's eyebrows had shot up to almost meet his receding hairline.

'There's no logical reason,' Maggie had admitted. 'It's just the timing, like I said. We heard her screech away in a car, and I suppose I'm just putting two and two together and making five.'

They had pondered that for a moment in silence, before finishing their drinks and leaving, everyone feeling rather flat.

Once back at April Cottage, Anna's sleep had been uneasy. Her senses seemed to be heightened, making her aware of every creak and groan of beam and floorboard in the cottage, as well as every sound outside, of which there seemed to be many, from the hooting of owls to the rustling of trees. She had felt thoroughly out of sorts when she had got up, a feeling not helped by having to leave a message on Roly's answerphone when she had tried to phone him. She limited it to her name, saying simply that she would try him again later.

What would I have told him anyway? It's all speculation. Still, at least I can do something positive now. Get the films developed, buy more – tapes, too – and have a look in the library. She didn't hold out much hope on the latter. If Roly himself had no reference to the curse, there was more than likely none to be found. Still, he'd be digging for information, too, so hopefully, between them, they should come up with something.

Fletcher Godfrey was also in his car that morning, but was headed in a different direction. He looked haggard, and had barely been able to keep his breakfast down. What the hell was going on? Maggie Taylor's phone call yesterday evening had rankled him, but his rudeness to her rankled even more. He'd told her that he wasn't running round like a thief in the night, and Pete Barker's discovery was none of their business and no, he bloody well *didn't* think it had anything to do with the business in Swifford Maisey. Why should it? He'd gone on to warn her about speaking about the graffiti in the church and had been mad as hell when she'd told him that the newspapers already had hold of it and what they'd come up with as a result. It wasn't like him to be rude or lose his temper, and however shaken he'd been by recent events, that didn't give him an excuse. He'd have to apologise, of course, and the sooner the better, but right now, he had other things on his mind.

He'd heard the Voice again last night. Taunting him.

'*You don't see it, yet, do you, Fletcher? The pattern. But you will ...*'

Enough to give anyone the heebie-jeebies. Made him wish he'd gone to see Pete Barker after all. *At least I wouldn't have been alone in the house.* The thought did not comfort him. He suspected that the Voice would have been waiting for him, whatever time he'd come home.

This morning, though, light on what it had said was beginning to dawn, and it had made him ill. Unlike Anna, he had been listening to the local radio station when he got up, and he had turned towards the machine, incredulous, as he had heard the news report.

'Police have today revealed the identity of the woman killed when her car went over the cliffs in Swifford Holt yesterday. The dead woman was named as Emily Parsons ...'

He hadn't listened to the rest. Emily Parsons! Em! For God's sake! It couldn't be ... He had had to sit down to steady himself. *Dear God, no!* The Petersons had been a tragedy, but a one-off. The vicar didn't make sense. But Em ... Two out of the three had connections with him, and one connection in particular. But it couldn't be *that*. No one knew. They'd all sworn ...

He'd gone hot and cold, then. *Could* it have been Em in the churchyard? He hadn't seen her for God knows how long. She'd become a virtual recluse after Henry had died. And it *still* didn't make sense. Why would Em be in the graveyard? Fletcher's thoughts took a crazy turn. What if *she* had killed the vicar? Utterly ridiculous. Reverend Fury was not a small man, and to get him into a half-dug grave, then smother him with earth, would have taken more than the average woman's strength. And why *should* Em have done it? No reason. None at all. And if she *was* the woman in the graveyard – well – she'd been screaming, hadn't she? His – and no doubt Maggie's – first thought had been that the screaming woman was being attacked. The dead vicar was the last thing they'd expected to find.

Back to Em, then. Em's car had gone off the cliff, and that was an accident, surely? But still ... if his thoughts on the connection *were* right – not that they could be, of course – but if they were, then what if she'd left evidence behind? Confessed to anything? *Why would she? I haven't. And Seth can't have done, or Janice would have been hauling me in by now, at the very least to ask me about the incident and at worst – if Seth implicated me ...* Fletcher did not allow himself to think the sentence through to its logical conclusion. Stubbornly, he told himself that it all had to be a horrible coincidence – especially as the vicar didn't fit. But two of the others dead within the week ... It didn't bear thinking about.

Abruptly, he pulled the car over to the side of the road. What was he thinking about? Heading for Em's house in Swifford Holt. What if Janice were there? Or family, come to that matter? Em and Henry had had three children. All grown now, of course, and long gone from the village. No work in these parts, on the whole, and house prices creeping up. But where had they gone? Would they be likely to be here yet? And what the hell would he say if anybody asked him what he was doing there? *Paying my respects, that's what. To an empty house?* His own thoughts mocked him. *I should have got a bunch of flowers. People do that all the time, these days. Leave bunches of flowers, when there's been an accident.* His thoughts mocked him again. *At the scene of the accident, you prat! You'd have to leave them at the edge of the cliff, not on the bloody doorstep.* He thumped the steering wheel in frustration. It was all irrelevant, anyway. He didn't have any flowers. He had no excuse. Should he turn back, or should he go on? If the latter, what would he do when he got there? What had he been *thinking* of doing?

Checking, he acknowledged. Checking that she hadn't dropped him and Mike Morgan in it. They were the only two left, now. He wondered, for a moment, if he should talk to Mike. *And say what? That you're hearing a Voice? Jesus! This whole thing is crazy! We all kept our word. We did what was right – what was best. Nobody else knows. Nobody. Even the Bloody* Voice *hasn't said anything about* that! *It* has *to be coincidence. Surely the vicar proves it? He just doesn't fit.*

Fletcher Godfrey raised his head and looked at the road in front of him. Should he go on, or should he go home? Slowly, he drove to the next passing point before turning the car round and heading back to Swifford Lea, fear flickering in his stomach like captive spiders.

Jack Taylor had jumped straight in the shower after coming home from his job at the egg factory and was now rummaging in the kitchen for brunch.

'Jack!' Maggie slapped her son's wrist. 'Don't you *dare* drink that juice straight from the carton!'

'Sorry,' he mumbled, opening a cupboard to lift down a glass. 'Is my sleeping bag clean?'

'Did you wash it last time you used it?'

'Oh. I don't remember.'

'That's a "no", then. You'd better dig it out and put it in the machine, hadn't you?'

'But, Mum ...'

'No "buts", Jack Taylor – you've got more buts than a billy-goat! And just to remind you – slavery was abolished in 1833. You're a big boy now – you can do it yourself!'

He flung toast on to a plate and stamped off upstairs.

'Don't you go trailing crumbs all through the house, either!' Maggie called after him.

God! Get off his back, woman! She chided herself as soon as the words were out of her mouth. *You're the one with the problem, not him.* The problem was the sleep-over. She was worrying that they might get up to no good. They almost certainly would. That meant 'have a drink', she acknowledged, which wasn't so bad, providing they didn't overdo it. But they were upset about Karen and she wondered, as she had so often before, if drugs were going to be available. Hopefully not. Surely not, if Cassie's parents were there. But *were* they going to be there, or were they away? She cursed herself for not having thought to ask. If she did so now, Jack would moan that she was treating him like a baby. Besides, even if they *were* there, how would they know, short of the kids smoking pot and stinking the place out? Frisk them for pills?

'Who'd be a parent?' she muttered darkly. Whatever you did, you were wrong. Whatever happened to the sunny-natured child you'd brought into the world? Once they hit adolescence, it was like they turned into aliens. She shook her head and poured another cup of coffee. It wasn't just Jack and the sleep-over she was worrying about. She was more grateful than she cared to admit for the invitation to Sally and Frank's this evening. *That's* where the real problem lay. Maggie didn't want to spend the night at home alone.

Anna was killing time. She'd bought everything she needed, checked the library, to no avail, and was waiting to pick up the films she'd put in for developing and printing. It would have been cheaper to collect them next week, but she'd asked for the four-hour service, for two reasons. One, she wanted to be able to show the photographs to Philip when she went to see him on Monday, and two, she hoped that showing them to Sally Arnold this evening would in some way make up for the gaffe she felt she'd committed with reference to her Aunt Ida. Sally had been very good to her – to the study – by facilitating access to the Misses Webb and providing the use of April Cottage. Anna felt guilty at having upset her, and however unwitting the offence she'd caused, she wanted to make up for it.

Thinking of the evening ahead put another train of thought in action. *I take it this evening is informal, so no worries about what to wear. I ought to buy a bottle of wine, though.* She set off through the unfamiliar streets, looking for an off-licence. If all else failed, there was bound to be a supermarket here, but it would be nice to find somewhere with a specialist selection. Market Eaton was a beautiful town, bisected by a wide river and with its main streets and large central square filled with predominantly Queen Anne architecture. As she climbed the hill to the top part of the town, Anna was fascinated by winding alleyways and unexpected ornamentation meeting her at every turn. *Might be nice to come here for a few days' break in the summer*, she mused. *Must be lovely then, down by the river. Lots to explore ...*

Impulsively, she set off down an alleyway lined with ancient-looking shops, their brightly painted frontages showing a variety of styles; bulging lead-paned bay windows competed with more modern counterparts. *Never get built, these days – the planners would want everything to look uniform.* Hand-crafted jewellery, teddy bears and heavenly scented herbal remedies were among the things which vied for her attention. Hold on – what was this? Anna's pulse rate moved up a notch as she came to 'Seekers', a bookshop. Wasn't this the one that Karen Peterson had been to? The one where she'd bought books on magic and self-protection? Without even thinking about it, Anna pushed the door open and went inside.

It wasn't at all what she'd expected. Somehow, she'd had an image in her mind of a dark interior and the mouldy smell of old books. She couldn't have been more wrong. It was brightly lit and the scent of a joss-stick filled the air with the fragrance of light, summery flowers.

'Can I help you?' A tall young man rose, smiling, from behind a desk in the corner, where he had been reading a magazine.

'I'd just like to browse, if that's OK.' Anna smiled in return.

'Help yourself. Are you a student of esoterica? That's mostly what we stock.'

'Folklore is more my line, but I have an interest.'

'Yes, you'd get a fair bit of overlap, I expect. You'll find folklore on that wall.'

Anna followed the direction of his arm and scanned the shelves, plucking out a volume. 'Oh – you have a couple of mine!'

'Really?' The young man came over to join her. 'Dr Rhianna Summers? I'm Dave Riley – you wouldn't like to sign them for me, would you?'

'Sure.' Anna scrambled in her bag for a pen and obliged, knowing that signed copies could command a higher price.

'So what brings you to these parts?' Dave asked.

'A new research project, actually. Over in the Swiffords.'

Dave pulled a face. 'You picked a bad time for that. Have you heard about what's been going on?'

Anna happily feigned ignorance. He seemed the talkative type, and she might get more out of him that way.

'No, sorry. I've only just arrived. Do enlighten me.'

He shook his head. 'Really bad business. A father and daughter killed, and a few days later, the vicar was found dead – buried alive.'

'How awful!'

'Yes, and that's not the worst of it.' He leaned closer and dropped his voice. 'The girl that died, she was in here, buying books, just a couple of months before it happened.'

'No! You think there's a connection?'

'Well, I wouldn't have done, but this thing with the vicar, see – there was stuff on the walls of the church – painted, sprayed – I don't know – and they're reckoning there's some black magic stuff going on round there. Maybe the girl got wind of it. Tried to protect herself, you know?'

'Good Lord!'

'Makes you think, doesn't it? I mean, it's interesting to read about in a theoretical sense,' he waved an arm around the shop, 'but stuff actually happening – well, that's a different ball-game entirely.'

'You surprise me,' Anna told him. 'Having a shop like this – I would have thought you'd have been a believer.'

'Oh, I am. In the good stuff. Changing yourself and your environment. Serving the planet. But *black* magic – hell, that's always been Dennis Wheatley fiction to me.'

'Isn't it the same as anything else, though? You know, things being neutral in themselves, but it comes down to how you use it? Like splitting the atom.' Anna played devil's advocate.

'Maybe. I just don't like thinking about it, though. Demons. Causing harm to others. That's not my scene at all. That's what I told the police, too.'

'The police?'

'Yes. They came round asking questions – knew she'd been here, I don't know how. Terrible, isn't it?'

Anna nodded her agreement. 'So what did she buy?'

Dave moved across the room and took several volumes from the shelves.

'These.' He showed her the collection. 'I told them, if they think anything like this is involved, they ought to get an expert in. somebody like Roland Featherstone.'

Anna's eyebrows shot up.

'He's first-class – knows more than anybody in the country on this kind of stuff,' Dave continued, mistaking her surprise for ignorance.

'Really?' Anna chose not to disillusion him.

'Really. Sound guy. If I was in CID – especially with this vicar business happening – that's who I'd ask about it.'

'Well, thanks. For warning me, I mean. Seems like I'd best be on my guard, eh? But you've never heard about black covens around here before?'

'Absolutely not.' Dave shook his head for added emphasis. 'You sure you don't want to take some of these?' He indicated the books Karen Peterson had bought. 'Just to be on the safe side?'

It was precisely the excuse Anna needed. 'Thanks. Maybe I will.'

Moments later, she was outside the shop with her purchases under her arm.

Fletcher Godfrey had devised a plan. Once again on his way to Emily Parsons' house, this time, he had his battered bicycle in the back of the car and could legitimately say he was going over to see a mate to find out if it could be fixed, or whether it needed dumping. Not that he needed to ask, of course – that frame could never be put right and still be safe, but it was a passable enough story should he be asked to explain what he was doing over this way. Even better, he could say that he realised that the bike was irreparable and he was offering it to Phil for spares for the bike shop. Yes. That would do nicely. And at a push, he could even say he'd decided to pop in and visit Em as he was passing. No one could prove he'd heard the news that she was dead, and he'd known the woman for donkey's years. *Besides, why should anybody be suspicious of me, anyway? Good, solid citizen. Ex-local copper. I'm getting fired up over nothing.*

It wasn't until he was almost there that he came across Janice. She had obviously taken a different route, coming via Maisey by the look of it, turning into the road from the right of him by Blake's Elm Barn. *Damn! Damn, damn, damn! If I'd stuck to my guns this morning, I'd have been here before her.* Fletcher moistened his lips, realising that his mouth had gone dry. *Don't be so bloody stupid. It was an accident. And Em would never have dropped any of us in it.*

As he had foreseen, Janice indicated left and pulled over in front of Em's cottage, which stood alone just after the long bend in the road. *Bugger!* Oh well – there was nothing else for it. Play it friendly. He pulled into the side of the road and wound down his window.

'Hello there, Janice – what brings you out this way?'

The policewoman looked tired, but was nonetheless immaculate, her blond hair pulled back in a bun.

'More bad news, I'm afraid. How about you, Fletcher?'

Thank God he'd thought of a cover story! He tipped his thumb towards the boot and trotted it out, uncomfortably aware of his heart beating against his ribs.

'What do you mean, "more bad news", though?' he added. 'I'd have thought we'd had enough this last week to last us a lifetime.'

'You and me both.' She narrowed her eyes and looked at him with renewed interest. 'Oh, bugger. I take it you haven't heard, then? Emily Parsons?'

'Em?' He looked from Janice to the house and turning off the engine, got out of the car. 'What the hell's happened?'

Janice shook her head and told him about the accident.

'Em? My God – I'd heard about the car, of course, but I never realised ... Bloody hell ...'

'I'm going to have to get into the house to find details of her next-of-kin. You knew her quite well, I take it?'

'We used to go dancing together – her and Henry and me and my Pamela. Oh, Christ! What an awful thing for the boys.' He still referred to her sons that way even though they were long since grown men.

'You don't know where they are, I suppose?'

Fletcher shook his head. 'Lost track, I'm afraid. To tell the truth, I haven't seen much of Em since Henry died. She got a bit reclusive.'

'So I've heard. Oh well ...' Janice strode round the back of the cottage. 'No keys with her, so ...'

Fletcher followed her, picking up the milk that was still sitting on the front doorstep.

'You shouldn't have to break in, with any luck,' he told her. 'She always used to keep a spare key under the third stepping stone in the path. I was always telling her off about it, but things were different then.' He put the milk on the wooden table outside the back door and lifted the stone. 'Yes – still here.' He gave it to Janice and followed her once more as she returned to the front of the cottage, thinking desperately of a way to ensure he didn't have to leave immediately.

'Any idea what caused the crash?' He hung back from the door as Janice tried to open it.

'Too soon to say,' she said, as he knew she would, 'but it looks like she was going like a bat out of hell.' She fiddled with the key and frowned.

'Here – let me – always was awkward at the best of times, and with the damp ...' He moved to the door, jiggled the key free and reinserted it. 'Doesn't sound like Em – speeding.' He spoke with his back to Janice, concentrating on what he was doing. There! The key had run in, smooth as silk this time.

'Well, there's not many women of her age drive like Schumacher but ...' Janice's voice stopped as Fletcher pushed open the door. Something about the set of his shoulders, the way he suddenly seemed to freeze. 'Fletcher? You all right?' Something about his unnatural stillness made her skin crawl.

'Shit! Shit! Oh bloody SHIT!' Fletcher Godfrey backed out of the cottage so fast, Janice had to grab him to stop him falling over.

Chapter Nineteen

Anna and Maggie walked together across the Green, each carrying a bottle of wine. A cold wind had whipped up and cloud was building in the dark sky. Maggie pulled her coat around her and shivered as she pulled her mobile from a pocket.

'Jack? It's Mum. You all right? Good. Listen, I'm going to Frank and Sally's this evening – couldn't remember if I'd told you. Anyway, I've got the mobile with me if you need me, OK? Yes. I know you probably won't, but I'm just letting you know. Have a good time.' She ended the call and shook her head. 'He'll be deaf by the morning if they keep playing music that loud all night.'

Anna laughed and followed Maggie along the side of the shop to a gate set in the wall. Going through it, they entered a long garden, following the path past a summerhouse and vegetable patch to the back door, which Frank opened as they approached.

'Thought I heard the gate – come on in!'

They stepped into a large kitchen where Sally greeted them cheerfully, a green apron wrapped around her as she busied herself with final preparations for the meal.

'It's nearly ready – can I get you a drink?'

'Lovely! We've brought offerings, too,' said Maggie, indicating the bottles she and Anna had brought with them.

'Thank you very much! Will you do the honours, Frank, and take the girls upstairs?'

Anna and Maggie were seated in the upstairs living room, sipping wine, when Sally started bringing in the food.

'You could do with a dumb waiter, like the Misses Webb!' Anna observed, as Frank descended the stairs to fetch further dishes.

'Oh, don't I wish! I don't know why we've never done it, thinking about it! Right then – help yourselves!'

Inevitably, as the meal progressed, conversation turned to recent events and the lurid newspaper article.

'I don't know what this place is coming to – Anna must think she's come to a madhouse,' Maggie said.

'And do you?' Frank smiled as he asked the question.

'I don't know what to make of it, I'm sure. Have you heard about this curse the paper was on about?'

Sally and Frank glanced at each other before Frank replied. 'Not a sausage. And we're born and bred here.'

'1732? That's what the newspaper said, right? I'll try and do some digging in the Records Office.' Anna spoke to save Maggie having to admit she'd seen the date in Swifford Maisey church, but needn't have bothered.

'Yes, and that's the weird thing – now it's out in the open – though God knows it wasn't me, and I'm sure it wasn't Fletcher, neither – it was painted on the walls of the church when we found the vicar.'

'The curse?' Sally looked incredulous.

'Well, not in itself. At least, I think not. Just a load of stuff about vengeance and the Arm of God reaching down the centuries.' Maggie frowned in concentration. ' "As the sins of 1732 was punished, so are the sinners now being punished." Something like that. There was a lot of it, to be honest, and it was horrible, and – I don't know – I thought I'd got it firmly in my head, but now – it's like I've blanked it out.'

'Probably the shock. It must have been awful,' Sally sympathised.

'You're not wrong. But I don't understand it for the life of me. All this talk about Satanists ...'

'Anything to sell newspapers, eh?' Frank snorted.

'That's what Pete Barker said when he saw it.'

'Do you think they'll try to tie in the accident on the cliffs?' Anna asked.

'To the curse? I don't see how.' Frank looked at Maggie. 'Did you know Emily Parsons?'

'Is that who it was? I'm not sure. The name rings a bell, but I can't put a face to her.'

'I shouldn't think you did,' Sally put in. 'Lived in Holt. She was more Fletcher's age, and her kids are long gone from around here.'

'What a performance, eh? No crime or nasty goings-on for God knows how long, and all this happens in a week. But that curse business – who'd want to kill a vicar? I mean – not that I'm religious, myself – but why would he be referred to as a sinner – that stuff in the church? Makes no sense, does it?'

'Why should it? It's not as if curses are real, is it? You'd think there'd be more logic in this day and age.' Anna hesitated.

'But?' Frank prompted.

'Well – I was in Market Eaton earlier today – which reminds me, Sally – I've brought the photographs to show you – but while I was there, I came across one of those alternative bookshops ...'

'Alternative?' Maggie looked puzzled.

'Specialist, then. This one carried what the owner called esoterica, along with some folklore and New Age stuff. The folklore was what interested me. Anyway – the owner said he'd had the police around about Jack and Ellie's friend – Karen Peterson, was it?'

'Karen? The police? Whatever for?' Maggie nodded as Frank offered to refill her glass.

'Well, that's the funny thing – apparently, she bought a load of books on magic and psychic self-protection a few months ago.'

'Why in God's name would she do that?'

Anna shrugged. 'Beats me. It does seem strange, though, given this reference to a curse.'

'Oh Gawd! The police will be calling in Ghostbusters if things go on like this!' Maggie rolled her eyes.

'It's not unheard of,' Anna told her. 'A friend of mine has been used by the police a couple of times where occult activity has been suspected. As a consultant.'

'What? Psychic, is she?'

'No!' Anna laughed. 'And it's a he. Roland Featherstone. He's an academic and an expert on witchcraft.'

'Good God! That's a funny sort of friend to have, Anna.'

'Not really. He was one of my tutors, years ago. Not that I'm into witchcraft, you understand, but there are areas of overlap.'

'Now where have I come across that name?' Sally frowned.

'He's written several books and advised on TV programmes,' Anna offered.

'No. It's not the sort of stuff we'd be into, is it, Frank?'

'Hardly.'

'Oh – it could have been my packets!' Anna realised.

'What?'

'The packets I left for you to give to Frank when the post office opened, the other day. My belt and braces computer disks?'

'Oh right!' Sally looked as if light had just dawned. 'That must be it, then. Anyone for pudding?'

Jack Taylor was impressed. He'd been to Cassie's house before, of course, which was huge, but had never been inside the barn conversion. Cassie's mum was an artist and her dad was a TV producer, so they were really cool kinds of people, but this ... Well, this was something else. They'd converted the barn a while back and let it out for weekends and stuff. Not that there was a load of tourism in these parts, but they seemed to do pretty nicely out of it. Probably all their artistic connections. But it wasn't being let this weekend, and it had been turned over to them for their party. How cool was that? They'd been given a kind of mini-lecture beforehand, which was understandable enough – respect for the property, no drugs, not too much to drink, and no sex on the premises. Jack had chuckled to himself at the latter. With the amount of land they'd got, people could sneak off to a hundred places and not get caught. Bit nippy, mind, and it looked like it was going to rain, but what the hell? Anyway, he knew where he'd rather be – right here, in the kind of warmth and luxury he'd always dreamed of.

The building was vast. The entrance door was a wooden, stable-type affair – you could have all of it open or just the bottom or top. To the left was a big double bedroom with en-suite bath, and straight ahead was a kitchen that had everything, including a dishwasher. That was something his mum had always wanted but had never bought. But off to the right was the living area, and it was fantastic. A huge, high room, it had a wood-burning stove, four sofas, a dining table and coffee table, and the kind of TV and music centre that made Jack drool. You could crank it up as loud as you liked, here, and not disturb a soul. The furniture had been pushed back against the walls to create a dance floor, already heaving with bodies. Wooden stairs led up to a little galleried sleeping area on the left, while past that, were three further bedrooms and a bathroom. Cassie's mum had decorated the furniture with stencils and special washes and stuff, and the whole thing was brilliant. All the boys were crashing over here – there was even a Z-bed and at least one of the sofas pulled out to sleep on – while the girls were sleeping in the main house. *One day, I'm going to have a place like this.* Jack promised himself. *Only my barn conversion will be a recording studio.*

Masses of food had already been spread across the dining table and the smell of cooking was wafting through the barn. Everybody had chipped in and a couple of the girls had been to the supermarket in Market Eaton and bought in loads of stuff. The boys – those who were old enough – had bought an assortment of booze.

'Cool or what?' Jack had to shout to make himself heard above the pounding music.

'Too right! You still at the egg factory?' Wesley Turner's face was already flushed with alcohol.

Jack grinned. 'Last shift this morning. I'm starting at a garden centre next week.'

'How did you manage that? You know bugger-all about plants, don't you?'

'Yeah. Bugger-all about fish, either.'

'Fish?'

'That's what I thought! "What do you know about tropical fish?" they asked me.'

'So what did you say?'

Jack shrugged and grinned. 'That they swim.'

'And you still got the job? Jammy bastard! Better pay, is it?' Like everyone else at college, Wesley was concerned with making enough from weekend work to run a car, or have driving lessons or just have a life outside study.

'Better everything, mate.'

Wesley looked round. 'Everybody here now?'

Jack ran faces through his head before replying. 'More or less. Just the Harrison twins and Gavin Morgan still to come, I think.'

'They picking him up?' Gavin still hadn't passed his test, but both Harrison boys could drive.

'Yeah. Let's hope he'll unwind a bit, eh?'

The two boys looked at each other. Since his outburst at college, Gavin seemed more and more withdrawn and none of them really knew quite what to do about it.

Jack shrugged. 'If he can't chill here, he's beyond redemption. Ai-eee, mama!' His eyes followed Tessa Clearwell as she snaked her way through the throng. 'Don't you just love women . . .?'

'Given the chance, man; given the chance!'

Gavin forgotten, the boys pushed through the crowd and followed in her wake.

Fletcher Godfrey was a nervous wreck. Since getting home, he'd had the TV on full blast, desperate not to be alone with his thoughts. Desperate not to think about what he had seen at Em's. *Jesus Christ! Everything's turning into a madhouse!* He went through to the kitchen to make tea and nearly jumped out of his skin when a face appeared at the window. The kettle clattered into the sink and he swore liberally before yanking open the kitchen door.

'For Christ's sake, Mike! Can't you knock?'

Mike Morgan laughed. 'I have been. For about the past five minutes! You trying to deafen yourself, or what?'

Fletcher beckoned him inside and walked through to the living room, where he switched off the TV, his thoughts racing.

'Sorry. I must have nodded off and sat on the remote or something. This is an unexpected pleasure, I must say. What can I do for you?'

Mike pulled a bottle of Scotch from inside his jacket. 'Yes, I'm sorry, Fletcher. I know we've not had a drink in a while, and I know it might be a bad time for you, what with the vicar and all, but – well – I need your help. Off the record.'

Fletcher attempted a chuckle. 'I've been off the Force for years, Mike, you know that.' He looked at his friend speculatively. 'Take the weight off.' He indicated a chair, and went to get glasses. What the hell could Mike want? His head swam as the thought occurred to him that maybe Mike had been hearing the Voice, too. *Don't be so fucking stupid. Get a grip, man.*

He placed the glasses on the coffee table and let Mike do the honours.

'Cheers!' They toasted each other and Mike sat, twirling the glass between his hands.

'I – um – I'm not sure about this, Fletcher. Didn't want to take it to Janice because she might be all gung-ho and feel she had to make it official. I just need your advice, really. It's Gavin.'

'Gavin?' Fletcher felt a curious sense of relief. At least it wasn't anything to do with the deaths, then.

'Yes. I – um – I think he might be taking drugs.'

'Shit! I'm sorry to hear that, Mike. Not that he'd be the first, even round here. I'm afraid it's everywhere these days.'

Mike took a deep drink, exhaling noisily through his nose before he spoke again.

'What am I going to do? I don't know how to handle it, you know. He's always been such a good kid – just the normal scrapes. Nothing you nor I didn't get up to. And now this.'

'What is "this", exactly? And does Rosie know?'

'We've talked about it. She noticed it first, I'm ashamed to say. She's as worried as I am. More so, probably, being his mum.'

Fletcher leaned forward and topped up Mike's glass. 'So what makes you think he's using drugs?'

'Complete change in his personality. Mood swings – Christ, he never so much as cracks his face, these days. Locks himself in his room for hours on end. Won't talk. Not eating properly. Need I go on?'

'Well, drugs would fit, with no shadow of a doubt. But I have to say, Mike, so does adolescence. It's worse for them now than it's ever been. Peer pressure. Performance pressure. You name it. Also ...' He chose his words carefully. 'There's Karen, of course.'

The men's eyes locked. Mike looked away first.

'I know what you're saying, and I would have thought the same, but it's not just since then, Fletcher. We'd noticed it before. It's definitely been worse since, mind.'

'Hardly surprising. Still – have you checked his room?'

'Earlier tonight. Oh, I know we should have done it before, but it seemed like an invasion of his privacy. You don't want to believe your kid's doing something like that. Anyway. Yes. We looked tonight – he's out at a sleep-over. And his room's clean, so far as I can tell. Of drugs, I mean.' Mike allowed himself the first hint of a smile. 'Plenty of dirty socks and mugs under the bed with mould in. Rosie nearly had a fit. Wanted to take 'em downstairs and wash 'em, but I said no, leave 'em where they are, otherwise he'll know we've been in.'

'Mmm. Still – if he's out for the night, he could have taken any drugs with him. You do know what you're looking for, I take it?'

'I know what resin and grass look like, and there was no sign. No aerosols, either – he uses a solid stick deodorant and gel on his hair, not spray. And no sign of tablets.'

Fletcher nodded. 'The simplest thing, you know, would be to talk to him.'

Mike sighed. 'I knew you'd say that. And I know you're right. It's just that if we do, it's going to blow years of trust. How would you have felt if your parents had thought you were taking drugs?'

'Astonished! No – I know what you mean. But the important thing is to make sure he knows you're asking out of concern for him. If he's got a problem – drugs or not – you want to help. Above all, keep your temper when he loses his – because he more than likely will do, and that's no indication of guilt, either. It's a bugger, Mike, isn't it? Either way, you're dropping yourself in it.'

'Yeah. Well.' Mike picked up the bottle and offered it to Fletcher, who nodded. 'Anyway, enough of my troubles – how are you? Must have been a shock, finding the vicar. I don't know what the hell's going on around here. Seth. The vicar. And now Emily Parsons. At least she was an accident, though, thank God.'

Oh no, she wasn't. Fletcher kept the knowledge to himself and took a deep draught of Scotch to stop himself thinking any further on it. *Thank Christ I didn't get in there earlier today, after all, though. No way I could have kept what was in there under my hat. Christ! I would probably have pissed myself. Or thrown up. Forensic would have loved that, eh?* He imagined himself trying to explain what he'd been doing there, and shuddered. At least with Janice on hand, he was covered.

'You all right?' Mike asked.

'Sure.' Fletcher gasped as the Scotch bit his throat again. 'Just went down the wrong way, that's all.'

*

It was turned midnight when Anna and Maggie made their way back across the Green to go home. Both slightly tipsy, it had taken Anna a while to realise that Maggie's disinclination to go into her house was not just down to garrulousness.

'Are you OK?'

'Yes. No. I'm just being silly.' Maggie's laugh was forced. 'I know it's stupid at my age, but what with everything that's going on – well, I'm scared to sleep in the house alone.'

'That's not silly! Oh, Maggie, you should have said! Why don't you spend the night with me? It won't take two ticks to make up a spare bed.'

Maggie had taken no further persuading, though she did put her foot down about not troubling Anna to quite that extent.

'The sofa will be fine, honestly. Just chuck me a duvet or a couple of blankets.'

And so it was that she awoke several hours later with a thick head and a bladder that felt like it was about to burst. *Oh Gawd! Serve me bleedin' right.* She padded silently across the darkened living room, feeling her way through the unfamiliar territory to the corridor that led off to the dining room on the right, and the downstairs bathroom straight ahead. Putting on the light, she allowed herself a sigh of deep pleasure as she sat on the toilet and put her bladder to rights. She glanced at her watch. Ten-to-three. She washed her hands in cold water and splashed some on her face. *Oh God, but I need a fag!* Jack would have been horrified to know she had started smoking again, especially after all the lectures she had given him. She'd done so well, too, but finding Reverend Fury . . . She felt even more guilty about the way she had driven to Market Eaton to buy cigarettes, just to make sure no one in the village knew. Anna had caught her with one in the field, of course, but Anna wouldn't split on her. She'd stop again. Of course she would. This was just a temporary crutch until things calmed down a bit and she'd got her head back together. But right now, she needed a cigarette.

April Cottage had always been non-smoking as far as she knew. Stan and Ida had never smoked, and nor did Sally and Frank. *Bleedin' hell woman! Just go back to bed. Don't think about it.* She was thinking about it, though. More to the point, she was craving it. Just the one, of course. Leaving the bathroom light on, she crept back to the living room to find her bag. It was no good.

The illumination didn't stretch that far, even though she'd left the door open. Slipping her feet into her shoes, she fumbled in the dark, eventually managing to retrieve her cigarette packet and a box of matches. *I really ought to buy a lighter. It would be a dead give-away if Jack heard matches rattling. God! What's wrong with me? Of course I don't need a lighter. Smokers have lighters and I'm not really a smoker anymore. And I won't be smoking that long. Just for a few more days. A couple of weeks at the most. Then I'll pack it in. Again. For good.*

She made her way back to the bathroom. She was wearing a pair of pyjamas that Anna had lent her, but knew it would be cold outside, and there was no other place for it. She looked behind the bathroom door. No dressing gown. Well, of course there wouldn't be. Anna no doubt kept her clothes upstairs. *Bugger!* She went through to the kitchen, fumbling for the light above the hob so that she could see without advertising the fact that she was up and about. *As if anybody would notice at this time of night! The whole bloody place is fast asleep. As it should be.* For a split second, the thought popped into her head that maybe someone or some*thing was* out there, watching, but she pushed it firmly out again. *Don't be ridiculous.* She spied a coat on the hooks by the back door. That should do it. Putting it on, she carefully undid the bolts. Good. They didn't squeak. The key was where Ida had always kept it, on a hook beneath the kitchen cupboards. *Right then. Shut it behind me, nip round the back, have a quick fag, and back to bed. Bob's your uncle, and nobody any the wiser.*

Seconds later, she was leaning against the wall as the nicotine hit her bloodstream, giving her a head-rush. *Oh God, that's good.* She closed her eyes and continued to smoke. It had been raining and she pulled the coat around her, a defence against the creeping sense of dampness that seemed to pervade the air and rise through the soles of her feet. *Not long now. Soon be back inside, snug under that duvet.* She wondered what to do about the coat. It would smell, she knew. Cigarette smoke always clung to fabrics. *There'll be air-freshener in the bathroom. I could give it a quick squirt. Myself, too, come to that. Maybe ...*

She froze. The hair on her head seemed to be crawling towards her crown. *What the hell was that noise?* She swallowed convulsively, wishing her mouth were not so dry. *Just an animal. Don't be so stupid. Shit!* Whatever that sound was, it was not an animal.

Not unless something very large, heavy and two-footed could be classed as such. Heart thumping, Maggie started to back along the wall. *Hang on a minute* ... Was that light she'd glimpsed? In the air, on the other side of the fence? But the other side of the fence was *her* house.

Legs unsteady, she moved silently towards it. Could she find a crack or a knot-hole big enough to see through? Indeed she could. Not clearly, but with enough of an angle to let her see that somebody's legs were disappearing through her kitchen window ...

Chapter Twenty

Anna barely had time to think. One moment she was sound asleep; the next, Maggie had woken her by a combination of shaking her shoulder and whispering urgently in her ear.

'Anna! Somebody's just broken into my house!'

'What!' Anna was out of bed in a shot, and heading for the light switch.

'No!' Maggie hissed. 'We don't want 'em knowing we've sussed 'em!'

Anna pulled on her dressing gown, thrust her feet into slippers. 'Have you phoned Pete?'

'I'll do it now you're awake. If I can find me bleedin' mobile ...'

'Use mine.' Anna retrieved it from the bedside table, where it was plugged in for recharging, handing her a torch from the drawer. 'But how do you know? About the break-in?'

Maggie punched in Pete's number, giving Anna a potted story about having heard a noise when she went to the bathroom and going outside to investigate.

'Maggie! You could have been attacked!'

'Well, I wasn't! Hello – Pete? ...'

Moments later, they were huddled by the kitchen door, awaiting his arrival.

'Right.' The big chef's face was grim. 'Pat's called the police. In the meantime – one for you ... and one for you.' He handed each of the women a heavy-bottomed saucepan.

'What's this for?' Maggie's voice was edgy. 'I've no intention of making breakfast for 'em.'

'Better than hitting them with your handbag.' Pete bared his teeth. 'Come on. Have you got your keys, Maggie?'

'Yes.'

They crept along the front path to Maggie's house.

'We're not going in, surely?' Anna asked. 'What if they're armed?'

'If they're armed, we run like hell. If they're not – we stop the bastards. There's too much of this stuff goes on. Time for the Empire to strike back.'

'Pete – death isn't the only potential problem here. You don't want to wind up like Tony Martin – in jail for defending your property.'

'You can go back if you want.'

Anna shook her head and sighed, exasperated. Two eight-stone women, even led by Genghis Khan, did not, in her opinion, make up an adequate defence force against an unknown number of housebreakers. Her nerves already stretched, the mental image this conjured up had her on the verge of inappropriate laughter. She bit it back, as another thought crept its way into her head. Maggie would have been at home alone, tonight. Anyone would know that Jack was away. And Maggie had found the vicar and seen the curse graffiti in the church. What if . . . ?

'Right.' Pete's voice cut in as they huddled together at Maggie's open gate. 'You say he went in the back window, Maggie?'

'Yes. The back door is bolted, as well as locked.'

They looked at the house. No lights. No tell-tale torch-beams. They were joined by a breathless Pat, also wielding a saucepan.

'Looks like a pyjama party!' she whispered. 'I've phoned Janice. The call was diverted, though.'

'What – even on her mobile?'

Pat nodded. 'I left a message.'

'Jesus!'

'This may not be such a good idea if help isn't on the way,' Anna pointed out.

'We've got all the help we need. Come on.'

Pete led the way down the garden path and stepped aside when he reached the front door, holding the torch to allow Maggie to use her key. Once open, he signalled to the others to wait, while he stepped inside. Anna's nerves were at screaming pitch as the waiting went on. Finger on lips, he came back to the door, signalling the others to follow him. Once inside, they made their way cautiously across the living room in the direction of Maggie's kitchen, following the light from Pete's torch. He shone the beam into the Belfast sink, then on to the draining board. Muddy footprints were evident. Casting the beam wider, they were able to see where the intruder had crossed the floor to the mat by the back door.

'OK. Looks like he's a big bugger. But it looks like there's only one.'

A burglar who wipes his feet? Anna thought. *This is crazy.*

They stood, listening, senses acute, heightened by fear.

Silence.

More silence. Anna felt as if she wanted to scream. Anything to stop this interminable absence of sound. Ah! There was a collective in-catching of breath as a noise was heard. Not a creak. Not a movement of mortar or the settling of a beam. It was undeniably the sound of footsteps upstairs.

'Right! Let's go!' Pete flicked on the kitchen light, checking that the door was still bolted, then ran into the living room, calling to Maggie to switch on the lights there, too.

Blinking in the brightness, the group gathered at the bottom of the stairs as Pete called out in a voice loud enough to wake the dead.

'OK, sunshine. There's four of us, we're armed, and the police are on their way. Come on down ...'

Molly Webb was used to darkness. She knew every inch of this house, and seldom switched on lights during her nocturnal wanderings. Alice was snoring again and it had disturbed her and besides, there was so much on her mind, and she had to get it sorted out. Oh dear. *What* did she have to get sorted out? Now she came to think about it, she couldn't remember. She paused in the upstairs corridor, one hand against the wall, the other on her walking stick, as she tried to make sense of the jumbled imagery that vied for attention in her head. Robert? Was it to do with him, then? Oh dear.

Dubiously, she carried on until she reached her own bedroom, the room she never slept in anymore, although she couldn't for the life of her remember why. Here, at least, she did put on the light. She'd need to see what she was doing if she wanted to find the photograph of Robert. *But do I? Why do I? Oh dear. Perhaps it will come to me when I find it ...*

She rummaged through the chest of drawers. Why wasn't it there? *Ah – now that, I do remember. Because Alice threatened to burn it. So I hid it away, nice and safe.* She straightened up, frowning. *But where did I hide it? Where would Alice not look for it? Of course ...*

She set off down the corridor once more. *How strange that Alice would show no compunction about going through my underwear drawers, yet would never dream of entering my professional domain. How ironic. Professionalism. That's what some of the arguments were about. That's what ruined my life, in the end. All because of Alice and Mother.*

Pushing open the door of the sewing room, she turned on the light and limped across to the linen dresser with its extra long drawers. *Now which bolt did I conceal it in?* She stood for a long moment, eyes closed, sliding, sliding, through fragments and mists until memory cleared. The tartan. How logical. Robert Strachan. Pronounced the proper way, with the hard 'ch'. None of that Sassenach nonsense where they turned it into 'Strawn'. Wasn't that what he had told her when they'd first been introduced? A Scot, and proud of it.

She pulled open the third drawer down. Its runners were still smooth, kept so by repeated rubbings with beeswax. And there it was. Molly's eyes misted as she gazed at it, remembering the kilt he'd worn, how dashing he'd looked. Carefully, she reached inside, her fingers separating the folds until she felt the touch of leather. Yes. Yes. She clutched it to her bosom, hobbling painfully to the centre of the room, where she was able to sit down at the worktable. Only then did she allow herself to look at it, the photograph in a leather frame that had held her hopes, her dreams and finally, the cold and bitter ashes of her heart's ruined desire.

Molly was unaware of the tears that fell as she gazed sightlessly at the picture. She only knew she could no longer see properly, and wasn't that something to do with what she'd come here for? Oh dear. The house sighed around her, stirring and settling in its sleep. The house slept every night, unlike her, and sometimes, Mother. *Oh Mother! You were so advanced in many ways. So liberated. Approved of women's suffrage. Encouraged us to take up professions. And Father, too. It was just in that one area. Marriage. Alice had to marry first. She was the elder sister and I could not marry before Alice. But Alice never wanted to marry, not after Jeremy Westwood-Smith. We never told you about the pact. Never told a soul. We were both in love with him, you see, but we put our love for each other first. I wouldn't hurt her and she wouldn't hurt me, but I wish I had. I didn't think ahead. Never expected to love again, and when I did – well, Alice wasn't married and I couldn't be allowed until she was. But she never loved any man but Jeremy. Apart from Father, of course, which was quite different. Love for one's parents is not the same as …* Her thoughts faltered. *My goodness. My goodness. And I tried to make them understand. It's the twentieth century, I told them, and women have the vote and we can work – unless we're married, of course. But they didn't see. Wouldn't let me. And when Robert said he was going away to Canada, and proposed to me, well of course, I thought he was coming back. Of course I did.*

Molly rose unsteadily to her feet. *Now* she remembered what she had come here for. Back to the linen chest. A different drawer, this time. A hidden drawer. *Why didn't I hide the photograph there? Nobody knows about this drawer but me, and it would have been even more appropriate than the tartan.* Was it still there, the bolt of fabric, so fine, so precious? Yes. Oh yes. Lovingly, her fingers stroked it, held it to her face, breathing in the delicate scent of roses and jasmine. *Now* she remembered, and now she knew what to do and what she had to do in order to do it. She would tell Sally, next time she saw her. Oh dear. She might forget by then. Best write a note, perhaps, to remind her. Whether she meant to remind herself or Sally, she couldn't now remember, but did it anyway, handwriting laboured and uneven due to the arthritis in her hands. Finally, everything in her domain returned to normal, and with the light switched firmly off, she made her way slowly back to bed.

Fletcher Godfrey woke up in a sweat. Good God! It was as bad as when Pamela had been going through the menopause. Sheets, pyjamas – it was rolling off him. His breathing was laboured and he felt thoroughly sick. Nothing to do with the Scotch, either. He'd only had a couple, even if Mike Morgan hadn't left till gone midnight. No. This was the nightmare.

He shivered as he made his way to the bathroom for a pee. He leaned one hand against the wall and closed his eyes. *Sweet Christ! No – don't think of Jesus.* He shuddered as images of the crucifixion came to mind. Only it wasn't Jesus on the cross, it was a lamb. *For fuck's sake!* He shook his head angrily. Didn't the church talk about Jesus as the Lamb of God? He wished he could say it had been his subconscious mind at work, producing religious imagery, but it wasn't. He knew what he'd seen when he'd opened Em's front door. Glimpsed it before he'd stumbled backwards, reeling with shock, homed in on it even as Janice had caught him, and stared at it, open-mouthed as she'd helped him up. Somebody – some sicko bastard – had hung a crucified sheep in Emily Parsons' living room.

For one awful moment, he wondered if what he had felt in bed was sweat, after all. *Of course it was! Look at you, man! Not a spot of blood on you. Get a grip, for Christ's sake.* He didn't want to go back to bed. What the hell time was it, anyway? He went back to the bedroom, to the cabinet on which stood the reading lamp, alarm clock and his watch. Half-past three. Shit! What a god-awful time of night to be awake. Too early to get up, but he wouldn't settle yet, not for a while, at least. A cup of tea, maybe? Or another shot of Scotch. That might settle his nerves. Bloody hell! The nightmare would have been bad enough anyway, but the thought that it had been real – in Em's living room – made his body hair rise. Had she seen it? Was that what had sent her screaming to her death along that cliff-top road in the car?

He went downstairs, poured himself a stiff drink – Mike had left the bottle with him – then went through to the kitchen and put the kettle on anyway. Who said it had to be one or the other, Scotch *or* tea? He'd have both.

'*Fletcher …*'

He froze.

'*Have you got it yet, Fletcher? Cracked the code? Put the pieces of the puzzle together?*' The Voice mocked him. '*Shall I tell you? Spell it out in words of one syllable? No. That would be far too easy. I'll leave you to guess. For a* little *while longer …*'

'Jack.' The boy's name was chorused as he descended the stairs of his house, trembling with fear. Maggie went ballistic, yelling at him about how he was supposed to have been at the sleep-over and what the hell did he think he was doing, climbing in through the bloody back window when he had a perfectly good set of keys, or had he lost them? And why the HELL hadn't he phoned to let her know that he was coming home? And where the bleeding hell was his CAR? If she'd seen the car, she would have known it was him, and now look – all these people disturbed AND the police called and oh my Gawd . . .

It was Pete who put a restraining hand on her arm, stemming the verbal diatribe. In the silence, everyone looked at Jack, *really* looked, for the first time since he'd appeared and all the pent-up fright had mixed with relief and anger in his mother's outburst. Fully dressed, he was white as a sheet, yet his face was puffy and his eyes were red, and in them was an expression that turned Anna's blood to ice.

'Oh my Gawd, Jack – what's wrong?' Maggie spoke for all of them.

The boy shook his head, stumbling down the last couple of steps and wandering over to the sofa, where he collapsed with his head in his arms. Pat shot a look from him to Maggie.

'I'll put the kettle on, shall I? And phone the police and tell them they're not needed?'

It was Pete who nodded. Maggie was kneeling in front of her son.

'Listen, Jack – whatever it is – look, I'm sorry I flew off the handle, but we were scared stiff, thinking you was a burglar. Have you had an accident? Is that what it is?'

Mutely, he shook his head. Maggie took one of his hands in hers, rubbing it like a baby's back.

'I didn't want to wake you,' he said at last. 'That's why I climbed in through the kitchen. I knew you'd hear the key if I came in the front, sleeping above the door. I didn't want to disturb you.'

'All right, Jack. All right. It's OK now.'

'Where's the car, Jack?' Pete spoke quietly. 'How did you get home without it?'

'The car's fine. I could've driven, except I'd had too much to drink. Cassie's dad dropped me home. And some of the others. The police will want to talk to us tomorrow.'

Pete and Anna shot each other a look of concern. Maggie swallowed hard.

'What is it, Jack? If you're in trouble, I need to know. Is it – is it drugs?'

The boy laughed, a harsh, barking sound without a shred of humour.

'I wish it was, Mum. God, how I wish it was! Anything would be better than this.'

Maggie glanced uncertainly at Pete and Anna. Pat came back into the room, with teapot and mugs on a tray. She set it on the floor and glanced from Pete to Maggie.

'Do you want us to go?'

Maggie shook her head. 'No. If you don't mind.'

'Of course not. Here – I'll pour.' Pat did so, running back to the kitchen for milk and sugar.

'Take your time, son,' Maggie told Jack.

When he spoke again, his voice was low, head still down. 'I can't believe how it happened. The way it started. It was so *stupid*!'

'What was, Jack?'

'The argument.' He lifted his eyes to hers. 'Holly Sykes was being really bitchy to Jade Morrison. About Jade being *poor*, can you believe the cheek of it? And I said, "What makes you so special, then?", and she starts on about how *she's* got this, and *she's* got that, and how Jade's got nothing, and what tossers her parents are because they're thick – which they're not, by the way. Just because you're not Brain of Britain, doesn't mean you're a useless human being. And Jade's dad's really handy, you know, and . . .'

'Where's this leading, Jack?' Maggie prompted gently.

He blinked hard. 'The whole place had gone quiet. I ripped into Holly, saying *she* hadn't got a thing. Everything she'd bragged about was her parents', not hers, and how dare she? And that was when Gavin started.'

'Gavin?'

'Gavin Morgan. You know – from Swifford Fen?' He shook his head. 'He started laughing. It was horrible. Ugly. Demented. I don't know how to describe it. And then – when he managed to draw breath – he started yelling at us – all of us – telling us how stupid we are, and how predictable and how materialistic. We thought he'd had too much to drink, you know? And I told him to shut up, and he wouldn't, and I yelled at him to stop, and listen to me, and he grabbed me by the throat and screamed – right in my face – almost *spitting* at me. And he screamed, "No – YOU listen – ALL of you listen!", and he pushed me away. And he jumped on the table and started . . .'

Jack shook his head again, his gaze now taking in everyone present.

'You wouldn't *believe* what he was saying. The stuff he was coming out with. All about the Wrath of God and judgement and – Jesus, Mum – he must have been off his head! He was talking about a Voice. A Voice that spoke to him. Like it was God or something. And he said that Karen had heard it and that what it told her was true, and he knew, because it was speaking to him as well. I was getting really worried, then, and told Cassie to go and get her dad. Quietly, you know? So Gavin wouldn't notice. So she slipped out. And Gavin was screaming about how we're all sinners and God's going to get us. And Andy Harvey got bolloxed with him, then, and pulled at his legs and told him to shut up – he was scaring the girls. The girls? Christ! He was scaring the crap out of all of us! And Gavin fell off the table because of Andy grabbing his legs, and he and Andy had this scrap – it was over in a flash, but Gavin kicked the shit out of him, and I pulled him off, and . . .'

Jack's hands were beginning to shake. Pete took the mug from him and put two spoons of sugar into it before handing it back.

'Take your time, Jack. Take your time,' he told him.

Jack took several deep swallows before he spoke again.

'We fell against the table, and he grabbed a knife. A big one, with a black handle, like you use.' He looked at Pete as he said it. Everyone but Jack was now holding their breath.

'He pulled it on me. Threatened me with it. Told me to back off.' He gave a mirthless chuckle. 'I backed off, all right. We all did. A lot of the others had backed right out of the barn, by now. But Gavin – he ran for the stairs. I thought he was going to lock himself in a bedroom and slash his wrists or something. So I started moving towards him. Slowly. Talking to him, trying to calm him down, you know? Only he wouldn't. He started screaming that we had to listen. That Karen and her dad had died because of the sins of the fathers. That Reverend Fury had died because he was a – a whited something – mouthing the right words, but didn't understand the true judgement of God. And he was planning to bury Seth in unhallowed ground, and he didn't have the right to. I didn't understand it. And he said – he said that Emily Parsons killed the vicar as an act of righteousness, but that she had to die, too, because she was another one who was paying for sins. It was crazy. The whole thing was crazy. And all the time, he's going backwards up the stairs – Christ – it was the barn conversion – there's this gallery thing? And then – oh shit – and then he got to the top and he jumped on the ledge. And he was yelling about how his family would be next, how they were going to burn. BURN! Can you believe that? And he said it was all true because this Voice had told him so, and it was all to do with the curse. And THEN ...'

Jack wiped his hand across his face, as if trying to remould his features. He bit his lip and fought to hold back tears.

'And then, it was like he'd suddenly woken up from a bad dream. And he's teetering on the ledge, right? Still with the knife. And the ledge is like only this wide ...' Jack measured a short distance between his hands. 'And it's – Christ, I don't know – twenty metres high off the ground? And Gavin kind of blinked. And smiled. And he just launched himself off. Like he could fly. Only he couldn't. And there was this big ... fountain ... arc thing of blood ... and everybody screaming, and I just couldn't stop him – I couldn't grab him. He's dead, Mum.'

Chapter Twenty-one

Sunday November 13th

Alice Webb had never been the kind of person who hovered between wakefulness and sleeping. She was either awake or asleep, with no in-between, just as if someone had flicked a switch. So it was with her usual sense of relaxed alertness that she opened her eyes. She did not consciously expect anything when she awoke, being simply grateful to still be alive, but had grown used, over the years, to what she would see. If she was lying on her back, the ceiling, of course, and if on her left side, the ladder-backed chair and the wall. If on her right side, however, she expected to see her sister, and beyond her, the dressing table and finally, the chest of drawers beneath the window. It was with more than a little surprise, therefore, that Alice's eye fell upon something out of place, something that should not have been there. She blinked, and drew in her breath. Could she be dreaming still, and merely have imagined that she had woken up? But why would she dream of this? From what foggy depths of memory had this image been dredged?

With a tingling sense of unreality, she slipped from the bed, pausing only to pick up her glasses from the chair before approaching the dressing table. Molly was still asleep, and was one of those people for whom the transition from one state to another was a gradual one, with movement, stretching of limbs and a considerable amount of moaning before the fully sleeping or waking state was finally achieved. She was, at present, still oblivious to the vibrant world of consciousness around her.

Alice thought fleetingly of Rip Van Winkle before manoeuvring her glasses on to her nose and looking at The Object more closely.

'Oh.' The cry was almost silent. She stood, shoulders slumping, eyelids blinking rapidly as if to check – or deny – that the photograph was really there. Robert Strachan. Alice reached out her hand as if to touch it, but drew back at the last moment, closing her eyes, a pained expression on her face. Was it shock she was feeling or was it guilt? Memories flooded back. How he had charmed Molly! Sweet-talked her with Robert Burns' poetry. Alice shook her head as a line intruded, unbidden, the Edinburgh accent still clear to her after almost sixty years. *Poor wee cowering timorous beastie ...*

This remembering wouldn't do. She had done what she thought best at the time, and she stood by that. Here they were, she and her sister, still together. And together, they had nursed, first Father, then Mother. *I could never have managed on my own. Molly had to be made to understand*. She flinched at the lie. Molly had never understood because Molly had never been given the choice. That would have been fatal. It was far better that she didn't know. But where had the photograph come from? *I thought it had been destroyed years ago. Thought she'd got over it. She was always too soft. That's why I threatened to burn it. That's why I did what I did with the letters*. It was with troubled mind and uneasy conscience that Alice Webb put on her dressing gown and made her way downstairs.

Anna was gritty-eyed and her body felt reluctant to move, as if she were somehow trying to wade through treacle. She rolled over and groaned, knowing she had to face the day, but not yet knowing how. It had been almost 5 a.m. when she'd left Maggie's, but, despite going to bed shortly thereafter, her mind had recoiled from sleep, too preoccupied by Jack's account of the party to allow her to slip into the all too possible horrors of unconscious imagery. She felt leaden, wanting only to rest. She may well have drifted off again, had it not been for the plaintive notes of a bugle floating into her head.

What the ... ? Oh God – oh shit! She sat up abruptly. Today was Sunday. Remembrance Sunday. Cursing herself for having forgotten, for not having set the alarm, for missing the service, she jumped out of bed. *Damn, damn, damn! I meant to be there. To photograph the wreath-laying ceremony. Oh ... BUGGER!*

Thoroughly out of sorts now, she went downstairs and filled the kettle. This was not a good start to the day. *Calm down, Summers. Given everything that's been going on, it would probably have seemed insensitive to take photographs. Intrusive. At least I can get pictures of the wreaths, later. Oh God ...* She wondered if news would yet have filtered through about the boy's death at the party. Hell's teeth! She would have to tell Roly about this! God knows what he'd make of the boy's rantings but ... *What do* I *make of them?* She shuddered, thinking of what Jack had said, unable – unwilling – to take in the implications. The sooner she could speak to Roly, the better. She tried his number, frustrated to be connected to his answering machine again. Where the hell was he? What could she most usefully do? After some thought and a couple of slices of toast, she made up her mind.

She was seated at the dining table, putting information into the laptop when the tapping came at the door. She closed the file before getting up to answer it. Whoever it was, she didn't think it wise to let them see that she had been trying to record Jack's account of events leading up to the boy's death.

Her caller was Maggie, smartly and sombrely dressed. Her make-up was impeccable, but did little to hide the drawn look etched into her features.

'Maggie – I didn't think you'd be up yet! Come on in. How's Jack?'

'Still sleeping, I hope. We sat up until God knows what time. Me, I had to be up for the Remembrance Day Service – I'm on the parish council.'

'Come on through. Coffee?'

'About a gallon of it. Through an intravenous drip, if you've got one.'

'I'll find the biggest mug I can.'

Seated in the living room, Maggie began to talk. 'I felt such a hypocrite out there today, Anna. Not the religious thing, though I've never been religious, as I think I've said before. But Jack ...' The mug wobbled in her hands, and she put it down on the table.

'Jack? I don't understand.'

'What kind of mother am I? All I could think of after I packed him off to bed this morning was the fact that he went through all that trauma last night and comes home, to sneak in like a thief, because he's worried about waking me up. Good God! Am I such an ogre? If that had been me, I'd have come home screaming blue murder. But he couldn't talk to me.'

Anna shook her head. 'That's not necessarily the case, Maggie. Shock can be a funny thing – and Jack was deeply shocked – quite rightly, too. I think it's more likely that he was so overwhelmed by the experience that he didn't *want* to talk about it. More that he was unable to, rather than you not being available for him.'

'I dunno. God! I've got to pull myself together. He'll be needing to talk to the police, and I've got to support him all I can. I dunno ...' she repeated. 'I was thinking – once he's done that – of taking him away for a few days. It's bad enough round here, anyway, with all this curse stuff, but once this lot hits the papers – well, I don't know about you, but I wouldn't be surprised if we get overrun with reporters. Television, even.'

Anna grimaced. She suspected that Maggie was right. The Swiffords would more than likely be a hotbed of media attention. So much depended on how the situation was handled, but, given that Gavin Morgan's death had been so public, she couldn't see any way to lessen the impact. She wondered sourly if any witnesses would jump on the bandwagon, giving exclusive interviews to the press in return for payment.

'Look – I'm sorry.' Maggie's voice broke through her thoughts. 'I didn't mean to come round here and moan. I came to thank you for last night. Being so supportive, and all.'

'Me? I did nothing. Pete was the real hero.'

'Well, I just appreciate it, that's all. But I'd best get going and let you get on with whatever you're doing.' Maggie stood up to leave. As she reached the kitchen door, she turned. 'Oh, bugger! We was going to have lunch at the pub again, wasn't we? I can't face it, Anna, I'm sorry. And Jack needs me.'

'Don't worry about it. And if there's anything I can do – anything at all – just let me know, OK?'

'Thanks.' Impulsively, Maggie leaned forward and kissed her cheek. 'Thanks, Anna. You take care, now.'

Anna closed the door and sighed. What a mess! And in practical terms, what was she going to do about lunch? She didn't fancy going to The White Hart alone, but had only very basic supplies in the house at present. She looked at the kitchen clock. The shop would be shutting soon, too. Oh damn!

Her mobile rang, startling her with its peal in the quietness. In her scramble to answer it, she didn't look at the display to see who was calling.

'Rhianna!'

'Roly!' Relief washed through her. 'I've been trying to get hold of you – the most awful thing has happened ...'

'I know. I'm on the case, so to speak. We need to talk. If I drive into Swifford Lea, how do I find you?'

'But that's miles! ...'

'Hardly. I'm in Market Eaton.'

Anna's spirits soared. 'If you set off now, you can meet me at The White Hart for lunch.' Maggie's booking wouldn't be wasted, after all.

Fletcher Godfrey walked across the Green, heading in the direction of his house. How he'd dragged himself out of bed for the Memorial Service, he didn't know. He felt rough as old boots, and his best efforts at sprucing himself up this morning had done little to disguise the fact. Still, it hadn't been the kind of occasion where people paid much attention to him, thank God. He certainly wasn't in the mood to be sociable, and had welcomed a set order of service and prayers. He'd shown his face, and that was all that was required of him. He'd nearly lost it, come the 'Last Post', mind. Evocative at the best of times, the notes seemed to have wormed their way through his usual stiff upper lip to the point where he'd great difficulty in restraining himself. His face had been working and twitching away something rotten, and he'd kept his eyes studiously on the ground, afraid that someone might notice. It was the closest he'd come to breaking down since his wife had died, and the thought of showing that degree of lack of control in public had shaken him.

He was half-way home before he realised he didn't want to be there. The house seemed tainted now, with nightmares and, above all, with that bloody Voice. Fletcher closed his eyes as he tried to face the awful possibility that he might be going mad. He felt overwhelmed, as if for one terrible moment he was teetering on the brink of some precipice into which he might fall, with devastating consequences. How could you be normal one minute and mad the next? How did that happen? And why, in God's name, should it happen to him? He felt as if the ground had been pulled from beneath his feet. There was no stability any more. If you couldn't trust your own mind, your own reasoning faculties, what the hell *could* you trust? He'd always imagined that madness afflicted only fanciful sorts, airy-fairy weak people; artistic types, perhaps, with too much imagination for their own good. Well, that wasn't him, was it? He'd always been stolid, down-to-earth – had prided himself on that fact. Nobody pulled the wool over Fletcher Godfrey's eyes.

He stopped, the thought of wool bringing back images of his nightmare. Worse still, of the scene in Emily Parsons' cottage, which had inspired it. Who the hell could have done such a thing? More to the point, perhaps – *why*? For only the slightest instant did he toy with the idea that Emily herself might have done it. Why would she? And the logistics of it . . . He shook his head. Not Em. He couldn't believe that. Christ! Nothing made sense any more. He tried to put the incident out of his mind, but found himself coming back to it, like a tongue persistently probing at something caught in a tooth. He may be retired, but his old police instincts were running a thousand scenarios through his head, picking up on every little detail that wasn't right. Apart from all the big things, there were basic issues. Inconsistencies. Why, for instance, when her body had been found, had she not had her house keys on her? The house was locked, so where were they? In the car? They'd be found. In the sea? Not a chance. But logically, they should have been either on the key-ring with the car keys, or in her handbag or a pocket. He'd ask Janice, maybe. No harm in it. It was just niggling him, that's all. *Making a mountain out of a bloody molehill.*

Anxiety gnawed at him. SOCOs would be going over Em's place with a fine-toothed comb. Quite apart from the horror of the crucified sheep, what else might they find? *Back to that again, eh?* It was stupid even to think of it. Em had never breathed a word. None of them had. So why would any of them put it in writing? There was no evidence to connect them with it, and it was years ago. Why rock the boat? *We got away with it. Nobody suspected a thing.*

It wasn't working. However much he tried to convince himself otherwise, doubt remained. What might they find at Em's that would link her and him – and the others – to it? He refused to think of it as a crime. It had been justice. Of course it had. Of course it had. He knew the thoughts that were waiting to chase into his head, and beat them off before they could become explicit. He wanted to laugh, right here in the lane. He had a picture of himself as a kid, with hands over his ears going 'La-la-la-la-la', at the top of his voice, to stop another kid saying something he didn't want to hear. Another sign of his impending madness?

He had to face it. He had to prepare for the slim possibility that there might be something at Em's that would bring Janice to his door in her official capacity. New copper coming to question the old copper. He had to hold his nerve. His stomach rumbled and he realised he hadn't eaten breakfast. Old jokes came to his mind about the condemned man eating a hearty meal. They suddenly weren't funny, anymore. He stood and looked at his house. He didn't want to be in there alone. Not now. Not yet. He rubbed his chin, noting the unevenness of his shave. Scraped the razor over his face in too much of a hurry, this morning. Ought to buy new blades, too. Scratching himself to shit. *Bugger it! Damn, blast and fucking bugger it!* He patted his jacket pocket, confirming that his wallet was there. He hadn't wanted to be sociable earlier, but now was a different story. Now, he didn't want to be on his own, and he didn't want to be at home. Nothing else for it, then. He'd check out Pete's cooking at The White Hart.

Anna was waiting in the car park of the pub when Roly drew up, his face breaking into a smile when he saw her.

'Rhianna!' He climbed out of the car and hugged her. 'I can't tell you how good it is to see a normal face!'

'That bad?' She pulled herself away to hold him at arm's length and take a good look at him. His skin was tinged with the pallor of tiredness, but his eyes were strangely bright, as if his mind were working overtime.

He shook his head. 'You don't want to know. Not yet, anyway. Let's enjoy our lunch before we get down to more serious talk.' He put his arm around her and together, they walked the short distance to the back of the pub. 'But what about you?' he asked, giving her shoulder a gentle squeeze. 'You look as if you've hardly slept.'

'Got it in one. I didn't.' Anna hesitated as they reached the door. 'Have you heard about last night's occurrence?'

'The Morgan boy? Yes. I take it that's what you were referring to on the phone. But how do you know?'

'I'll tell you about it later. I don't know if the news has broken here yet, so I think we'd better keep stumm and act dumb if any reference is made. OK?'

'Of course. It's what I would have suggested myself.' He pulled open the door and followed her inside.

They were eating dessert when it happened. Up until then, everything had seemed normal. The pub was busy and people were chatting amiably. Anna had run her eye over the crowd and spotted what she had come to think of as all the usual faces. *Except one*, she noted to herself. Ellie appeared to be absent again, and the familiar knot made itself felt in her stomach. *Oh hell – she was probably at the party last night.*

Her thoughts were cut off by the sounds of a commotion outside. Glancing out of the window to her left, Anna let out an involuntary cry.

'What . . . ?' Roly followed her gaze. Below them, on the pavement at the front of the building, an extraordinary performance was taking place. It seemed like an exaggerated mime to begin with; a grim-faced woman with a broom appeared to be wrestling with a man who had hold of her around the waist. Breaking free, she laid into him with the broom before applying it to another, older man.

'DON'T you try and manhandle me! I'll kill the bastards! I swear to God I'll kill them!' She screamed the words as the true objects of her wrath ran amok.

'Ohhh shit!' Anna rose from her seat. 'The goats!' She meant only to enlighten Roly, but it seemed, by the time they had got downstairs, that the entire pub had taken her words for a rallying cry, a crush of people spilling out on to the pavement to view the pandemonium.

'What the HELL do you think you're doing to my goats?' Pat yelled, as she ran around, desperately trying to catch Hetty and Joe.

'Butchering the bastards! Have you SEEN my garden? What's left of it?' The woman was incandescent with rage.

'Now then, Carol – calm down!'

The older man who had been hit with the broom had managed to get himself between her and the goats, which now made a dash for the back of the pub, followed by several of the regulars.

'Just stay out of it, Fletcher – this is none of your business!'

'It's my business, Carol, when you assault me with a broom.'

'And it's MY business when you assault my goats! How dare you!' Pat darted towards Carol and was herself caught a resounding *thwack* just as Pete burst through one of the kitchen doors.

'What the fuck . . . ?' In an instant, he grabbed Carol and had her down on the ground, immobilised. The man Carol had wrestled with earlier now snatched up the dropped broom and started laying into Pete.

'How DARE you manhandle my wife!'

With a howl, Pat launched herself at her husband's assailant. *Bill*, Anna remembered, now the marital connection had been made known. *Bill and Carol. The firework people.*

Fists had now started flying, arms and legs flailing. Anna saw a look pass between Roly and Fletcher, then they waded in to the mêlée to try and break it up. The crowd was baying and cat-calling and the scent of fear and sweat and excitement seemed to fill the air. How could things descend to this? The next moment, pounding footsteps heralded the arrival of Frank Arnold and Adam Etheridge. Frank's roar was enough to stop everyone in their tracks. Finally separated, accusations flew, insults were hurled and minor scuffling carried on until Bill and Carol finally stormed off home to call the police.

'The nerve of it! When she started it and hit my goats and hit Fletcher! There ought to be a law against it!' Pat was shaking with temper.

'There is.' Fletcher's voice was dry, his breathing laboured. He glanced at Roly. 'Thanks for chipping in there.' He held out his hand. 'Fletcher Godfrey.'

'Roland Featherstone.' They shook hands and Fletcher turned to Adam and Frank.

'It's a good thing you two waded in. We couldn't have handled the four of them on our own.'

Roly smiled and held out his hand again. Adam glanced at Anna before nodding at Roly, ignoring his hand and saying, 'I'd best help Pat with the goats.'

Frank was busy dusting down Pete's back. He, too, gave Roly a nod before saying to Pete, 'Miss Fennimore phoned in a panic.' He inclined his head in the direction of a cottage opposite the pub. 'I'd best go and calm her down, I think.'

The crowd was dispersing now and Roly looked from Anna to the pub. 'Do you want to go back and finish your dessert?'

'No.' She shook her head. 'How about we go and check on the goats, then retire back to mine for coffee and conversation?'

'Sounds good. Are the natives always this hostile?' His boyish grin and tousled hair took Anna back to her student days and she smiled.

'They haven't been so far. But then, things are hardly normal at present, are they?'

She led the way to the goats' field where Adam was finding it easier to calm the animals than to calm Pat, who was still furious.

'Good God! We would have quite happily paid the bill for damage to their garden, but did you SEE the bloody woman? Attacking poor, defenceless animals!'

Roly looked around, taking in the landscape, before raising an eyebrow at Anna. She nodded her assent. They'd had more than enough histrionics for one afternoon. Best leave them to it.

Chapter Twenty-two

Alice Webb had said nothing to her sister about the appearance of Robert Strachan's photograph. Molly herself had made no reference to it, either, although she had been a great deal more animated than she had been for a very long time. Almost back to her old self, in fact. Certainly a great deal more lucid than she had been of late. Alice had listened in astonishment as Molly had made a series of suggestions and requests, having to concede that they were all good and practical.

'It's too quiet in this house, Alice. We may not be able to play much ourselves, these days, but I do think we should have music. That little old portable radio doesn't seem to be working – we don't even get to hear the news. Why can't we get some sort of music system with a radio built in? I've seen them advertised.' Molly had handed over cuttings from magazines to illustrate her point. 'I'm sure there must be something that would be simple enough for us to operate. And what about a new television set? I know we said we wouldn't bother after the last one was stolen, but there are some wonderful things on show nowadays. Packages you can get – yes, I believe that's what they're called. You subscribe, and there are marvellous things – gardening and history and science and things from the old days that we used to like watching. Miss Marple. Poirot. All those series. *Dad's Army*, too – do you remember how we used to laugh at that?'

Alice, nonplussed, had to agree that she did, and looked at the further advertisements which Molly offered.

'And while we're at it – don't you think it's about time we got our eyes tested again? I don't know about you, dear, but I'm having to hold things further and further away to read properly and at the rate I'm going, my arms won't be long enough, soon. What do you think?'

'Well, I – I have to admit that it all sounds very ... very ... Well, yes – why not? We could talk to Sally about it tomorrow.'

Molly frowned. 'I don't think we should bother her, you know. Between looking after us and running the shop, I'm sure she must be rushed off her feet. And whilst we might need her to take us to the optician, it did occur to me that young Mr Michaels might be more appropriate to deal with the purchasing of things. Having power to write cheques for us and such like. What about telephoning him in the morning? Being young, too, I expect he's more up-to-date with all this modern gadgetry.'

'I think that's a very good idea, Molly. I shall make a little note to myself to remind me to do it,' Alice said. And she did.

As they walked back along the path on the way to April Cottage, Roly asked Anna if Adam was the man she'd seen with the goats on her arrival in the village.

'Yes. The one you thought might be a solitary practitioner of some kind.' She shrugged. 'He seems pleasant enough to me.'

'You can't always judge a book by its cover, Rhianna – you know that.'

'Yes, I do, but his story of martial arts seems borne out by local talk about him. And had I not seen what I did, there would be no grounds for suspecting him of anything.'

'But you *did* see, and there's still the business of the blank disks to be explained.'

'Damn! I'd forgotten all about them. There would still be no connection to Adam, though, but I'll check that out straight away.'

Anna dug in her pocket for her keys and opened the door of April Cottage. Roly hung back, admiring the building.

'Come on in – it's even better inside!' she smiled.

He grinned and stepped over the threshold, his eyes taking in the surroundings.

'Very nice.' He stood for a moment, eyes closed. 'No more trouble with ghostly pianos?'

Anna gave an embarrassed shrug. 'Not a tinkle. I probably just imagined it.'

'I don't think so.' He opened his eyes and seemed to shake

himself. 'Right – let's swap notes and get down to business. I could use a coffee first, though.'

'Of course. I'm sorry – I'll go and put the kettle on.' She disappeared in the direction of the kitchen, leaving Roly in the living room.

The moment she was out of sight, he crossed to the fireplace and examined the broom and yew on the chimney-breast. Swiftly, he crossed to the window. Sure enough, just as he had expected, smaller, unobtrusive pieces were in evidence there, too. *Well, well! Someone's taking no chances with Rhianna.* He had little time for further exploration before she was back, calling him through to the dining room.

'My laptop and printer are through here.'

Roly joined her at the table. She poured coffee for both of them.

'So – are you really on the case?' She was sorting through disks and, discarding some, put one into the floppy drive and opened it.

'Cases, plural. But yes, as consultant on the occult elements involved.'

Anna pulled a face, blowing out air. 'Jack said the Morgan boy was ranting about a Voice and the judgement of God before he took a dive. Just like the stuff in Karen's diary.' She took out the floppy and inserted another one.

'Jack?'

Anna explained and Roly listened, his face grave.

'I've only heard the bare bones of it from the police so far,' he told her. 'Tomorrow, I get to look at the evidence.'

'What evidence?'

'Apart from the SOCO stuff, there should be actual video footage of what occurred.' He placed his hand over Anna's and squeezed. 'Kids being kids, at a party like that, several of them had taken video gear with them. It won't be pleasant viewing, of course, but it can't be any worse than the Peterson deaths.'

'Oh – look – here's the disk!' Anna broke in. 'I must have posted a blank one to you after all.' Her voice was relieved. Swiftly, she inserted the next one from the pile. 'And here's the other!' She smiled. 'So – no occult interference involved – just me being distracted!'

'That doesn't change the Peterson case, though, does it? People are dead – there's no mistake about that.' He paused, his face tightening at the recollection of the evidence he'd seen. 'Now that was sheer carnage.' He took the disks from Anna and slipped them into his pocket. 'Why don't I keep these for now?'

'OK,' she shrugged. 'But I thought there would have been another police statement about the Petersons by now. About how Karen did it, rather than Seth.'

Roly's eyebrows shot up. 'That's just it, though, Rhianna. Karen Peterson didn't kill her father ...'

Sometime later, Anna pushed back her chair and began to pace the dining room, brow furrowed in concentration.

'Let me get this straight.' She turned to Roly. 'It looked like Karen *had* killed her dad – as you and I suspected after reading her diary. And the police were thinking the same thing – *especially* after reading her diary – but the post-mortem ...'

'... threw up the interesting fact that Karen and her father were killed by a right-handed person. And Karen Peterson was left-handed. And there was curse graffiti all over the house.'

'Good God!' Anna sat down and stared at Roly. 'And the vicar ...'

'... was definitely not an accident. And curse graffiti again.'

'What about the woman who went over the cliff?'

'Emily Parsons? Curse graffiti there, too. Forensics are having a field-day at her place. Rhianna ... you trusted me with Karen's diary – I'm trusting you, now. I shouldn't be telling you any of this, but – ' He took a deep breath. 'When the police went into her house after the accident, the first thing they found was a crucified sheep.'

'What?!' Anna looked stunned. 'And with what Jack said last night – about the Morgan boy – him hearing the Voice, too – what the hell is going on, Roly?'

'I don't know, Rhianna. Not yet. But I think you and I need to do all we can to help the police find out.'

Fletcher Godfrey sat nursing a pint of best bitter in Pete Barker's living room. The pub was closed, Pat was still with the goats and Pete was in the bathroom, cleaning up a cut above his right eyebrow.

'Thanks again, Fletcher.' Pete walked in, looking scrubbed and shiny, but his face bore a scowl, reflecting his thoughts on the incident that had marred his day.

'You're welcome. Ugly business.'

Pete made a harrumphing sound. 'As if Janice hasn't had enough on her plate. Murders and accidents going on all round and that pair of prats next door can't keep their tempers over a couple of goats.'

Fletcher frowned, the policeman in him picking up on Pete's use of the plural. 'Emily's accident, you mean? In the car?'

'That and Gavin Morgan.'

'Gavin?' The older man felt as if his blood had turned to ice.

'You haven't heard? Last night, at some sleep-over party. Dead. Rumour has it he went off his chump and took a dive over a balcony.'

'Jesus Christ!' Fletcher's hand shook as he put his pint on the coffee table.

'Are you all right? You've gone white as a sheet.'

'Jesus Christ!' Fletcher repeated. He stood up. 'I have to go, Pete. I know the family well.' He looked sick to his stomach. 'Thanks for the pint.'

'Come and have another when you're feeling better.'

Wordlessly, Fletcher left, his mind elsewhere.

He vomited into a hedgerow on the way home, standing on trembling legs, chest heaving, skin clammy, as he thought about what Pete Barker had said. *Why? Why?* It sounded like the lad was on drugs, after all, then. What the hell must Mike and Rosie be going through? It didn't bear thinking about. *Christ! If only they'd searched his room earlier. Confronted him about it.* He closed his eyes and spat. No good thinking like that. More than likely it wouldn't have changed anything, anyway. Gavin would probably have denied it all and there may well have been nothing to find in the house. Druggies could be devious. Came with the habit. Living at home, and all, his stash was almost certainly elsewhere, if not on him.

Arriving home, he slammed the front door behind him, walking straight through to the kitchen to get the whisky bottle. The amber liquid burned his throat, but settled his stomach. The same could not be said for his nerves. It felt like the whole bloody world had suddenly erupted into madness. He'd have to phone them. Mike and Rosie. But what could he say? What the hell could *anyone* say that would make one jot of difference? Their son was dead. His ears picked up the sound of a car pulling up outside, the heavy clunk of its door. Now what?

'Sorry to bother you on a Sunday afternoon, Fletcher. Can I have a word?'

Janice. Janice bloody Mills. P-O-L-I-C-E. Was this how people used to feel about him?

'Come on in.' He stepped aside to let her pass, suddenly embarrassed by the glass in his hand. 'It's about the goats, is it? And the fight?' *Please, God, don't let it be about anything else. Not that business – that connection . . .*

She turned weary eyes on him. 'Haven't got round to that, yet. I suppose I can kill two birds with one stone, though, while I'm here, if you know anything about it.'

'What's the other bird then?' He waved her to a chair before sitting himself, draining the glass and setting it on the floor beside him. 'Sorry about this, by the way. I just heard about Gavin Morgan. Unbelievable. Mike – his dad – was round here just last night.'

'You know them well?'

'Since way before Gavin was born. I was best man at their wedding.'

'I'm sorry.' Janice knew it was inadequate, but there was nothing more appropriate to say.

'Aren't we all? What the hell is going on, Janice, eh? Can you tell me that?'

'No.' She shook her head and sighed. 'I only wish I knew. That's why I came to see you, as a matter of fact.'

Fletcher's gaze was level, but he felt his heart-rate increase. 'Me? How can I help? I'm as baffled as the next man. Market Eaton CID are on the cases, aren't they? Let them try and sort it out.' He was as surprised as Janice at the bitterness in his voice.

'I expected better than that from you,' she told him.

'Did you?' He ran a hand through his hair. 'Maybe I'm just fed up with other people's expectations. I'm retired. I'm not Sherlock Holmes and I'm not bloody God, if there is such a thing – which I very much doubt, given what's going on round here at present.'

'I'm sorry.' Janice stood up. 'I'll come back another time. About the goats, anyway.'

'No, no!' Fletcher pushed himself to his feet and stood facing her. 'It's me that should be sorry. Look, I'll go and put the kettle on, shall I? You ask whatever questions you want. If I can help, I will. I just feel right now that I don't have answers for anything.

That doesn't excuse my behaviour – I've no need to take it out on you and God knows, if anyone knows you have a job to do, it should be me.'

'Like you said, Fletcher – it's CID's baby, but it's a monstrous one. I just wanted to pick your brains. You know this patch better than anyone.'

'I used to. At least, I thought I did. But this . . .' He ran his hand over his face. 'Let's start again, shall we? I'll go and make that cup of tea.'

Chapter Twenty-three

'Roland Featherstone is here, then?' The flames from the brazier threw giant shadows on the walls of the summerhouse as The One asked the question.

The Fourth nodded as she spoke. 'Yes. He got embroiled in a fight over the Barkers' goats. Quite the hero, according to Fletcher Godfrey.'

'As always. He was here to see Dr Summers?'

'It would appear so.'

The Third signalled his intention to speak. 'They were together when I was calming the animals down, back in the field. And they left together – to go back to April Cottage, by the look of it.'

The One hissed. 'I cannot bear the thought of that man setting foot in there. You put protection in place?'

'Yes. But if she invited him in, I've no doubt it's undone.'

'Then you'll have to go back.'

The Third nodded his assent.

'I don't understand the woman.' The Second's voice was low. 'She shows no sign of his contamination and yet they seem to be friends.'

'Does she know or does she not?'

'If she does, she must be powerful indeed to cloak herself in innocence so well.'

'Beyond the cradle there is no innocence – only varying degrees of ignorance or naiveté. You have had no further visions of her?'

'None.' The Second shook his head, his shadow monstrous compared to the others.

There was silence, as The One digested everything that had been discussed in the Council. Finally, she spoke.

'His being here – on our territory – has upped the stakes considerably.'

'We cannot stop now. Death by Fire is coming.'

'You are right. We cannot stop. We are called.' She thought for a moment. 'We are fighting on more than one front, now, though. We must plan carefully.'

Giving the signal for the drumming to begin, as the rhythm rose, she started her whirling dance once more.

Chapter Twenty-four

Monday November 14th

The nightmare had returned. Anna stood, face upturned to the fine needles of water in the shower, trying to erase its memory from her mind. She closed her eyes and let it wash over her, willing it to obliterate the violent, Technicolour imagery. *So much colour in so much darkness*. She shuddered and turned away, pouring shower gel on to a sponge. The mere thought of that abyss terrified her. The Thing coming closer, invisible, disguised by darkness, yet she knew it was there, knew it was evil with a certainty that had made her skin crawl. Sounds, hissing, writhing, echoing all around her, yet she could make no sense of them, hear no words. Suffocation, suffocation. Fighting to breathe in an atmosphere that was heavy, leaden and sour as an ancient, rotted blanket. Rising terror, bursting through her chest into panic as she fell, then stopped, fell, then stopped, like a lurching lift, out of control. The piano again, fierce, discordant, pounding, its notes somehow lifting her, yet still there was nothing beneath her feet. Pinprick light. Confusion. No girl with an axe, this time. Thank God. But a voice. Not the Voice, like before, but Roly's, calling out to her.

'Rhianna! Rhianna! Come to me! This way!'

But the music screamed into a crescendo of sound, drowning him out, and suddenly, in front of her, Adam Etheridge, holding out his hand, mute, his eyes calling her to him as clearly as Roly's voice.

'Rhianna! Don't trust him! Look – look!'

And as she had looked, Adam had turned into a grotesque creature, cloven-footed, horned of head and she had screamed, backed away, only to fall again into the very pit she was trying to escape.

Anna shook her head viciously in a final, successful attempt to banish the dream. Pushing open the door of the shower cubicle, she wrapped herself in her terry robe, tied a towel in a turban round her head and walked down the corridor towards her bedroom. *What?* She paused, unsure whether she had heard anything or not. Pushing the towel away from her ears, she listened. Oh damn! It was the door. She ran to the bedroom window, fumbled with the lock, then had it open and looked below her. Her view of the front door, to her right, was obscured by shrubs, but as she looked to her left, she saw Adam Etheridge's van pulled up near the back entrance.

'Adam?'

A second passed, and he appeared below her. 'Sorry to be so early – did I get you out of bed?'

'No, no – I was in the shower. I'll be right down.'

Pushing her feet into slippers, she ran downstairs to let him in, refusing to allow her self to be influenced by the grotesque imaginings of her dream. Pulling open the kitchen door, she stood awkwardly, struck, for some illogical reason, by the extraordinarily electric blue shade of his eyes. *So much colour in so much darkness ...*

'Are you going to ask me in or send me away until later?' Adam's smile seemed like an intimate caress.

'I'm sorry – of course not. Come in, I mean. I do apologise – I didn't sleep well, and overslept and ... Just come in, and I'll put the kettle on and make myself decent.'

He stepped inside. Almost imperceptibly, his shoulders seemed to rise. Anna had a fleeting impression of him as a dog on point, then, as quickly as she had noticed it, it was gone. *Oh God! Perhaps he's embarrassed at me being half-undressed.*

'The kettle's on now. I won't be a minute – go on through.'

He nodded his acknowledgement and she ran back upstairs, throwing on her clothes and roughly towel-drying her hair in record time. Back in the kitchen, she made the tea, only to realise that she was out of milk. She groaned inwardly, remembering, too late, yesterday's problem with supplies before Roly had phoned. *We must have finished the milk when he came back here for coffee and to talk about the cases. Oh bugger!* Walking through to the sitting room, she found Adam rummaging in a bag of tools.

'I'm sorry – I'll have to pop to the shop for milk.' A sudden thought struck her and she looked around. 'No Dave today?'

'No.' His tone was terse. 'One of the reasons I'm so early. Being on my own, I have to allow more time for the jobs.'

'Is he sick?'

'That's one way of putting it.'

Who got out of bed the wrong side this morning, then? She frowned as she turned away. He'd seemed all right when he arrived. Oh well. Grabbing her purse as she passed through the kitchen, she set off for the shop. Never mind Adam and his moods, but she was dying for a cup of tea herself.

Even from some distance away, she was surprised to see a queue outside the store. Glancing at her watch, she reassured herself that she hadn't got the time wrong. It should have been open almost an hour ago. What on earth was going on? She smiled at Maggie, who was pacing restlessly in front of the building.

'I thought I was the only one who'd overslept this morning!'

'Overslept? If only!' Maggie cocked her head and indicated a hand-printed sign inside the shop door. 'There's been an accident.'

'Oh God!' Anna felt the colour draining from her face. 'Not another . . .'

'No – nothing like that, but bad enough.'

Before she had time to explain further, Anna moved closer to read for herself.

SALLY FELL DOWN THE STAIRS DURING THE NIGHT AND IS IN HOSPITAL IN MARKET EATON. MAVIS BLEDSOE WILL OPEN THE SHOP AT 9 A.M. APOLOGIES FOR ANY INCONVENIENCE. FRANK.

'Hell's bells! That doesn't sound good.'

'Them stairs are lethal. Well – you commented on 'em yourself, didn't you, when we was round there the other night?'

Back at April Cottage, Adam Etheridge got straight to work. Not on the fireplace, but on undoing what Roland Featherstone had done to counter his own measures, and on putting in place something rather stronger than he'd used last time. Handy, Anna being out of milk. How long would she be at the shop? He grimaced. A lot longer than she anticipated, he hoped. Frank had told him it wouldn't be open until nine, but she didn't know that and hopefully, by that time, there should be quite a queue. There was, however, the risk, albeit slight, that she might come straight back, deferring her shopping until things quietened down. He hoped not. Frowning, he realised he'd have to make a decision. No time for a full-blown ritual, then. Just the preliminaries.

Frank Arnold unfolded himself, with difficulty, from his car, just as a fresh-faced older woman came trotting up to the shop.

'That's Mavis,' Maggie informed Anna.

'Like buses, isn't it? You wait ages for one, then two turn up at once,' someone in the queue commented. 'How's Sally, Frank?'

'She's all right, thanks. Broken leg and concussion, but – she's all right.'

'Thank God for that! You look like you haven't had a wink of sleep, man.' Mavis moved to the door and unlocked the shop.

'You're not wrong. Still, at least she's settled now.' Frank turned to the group. 'Come on in. We'll have you served as quickly as possible.'

'Don't you go worrying about us. You look like you need a cuppa – want me to put the kettle on?' Maggie asked.

'Thanks, love. That would go down a treat.'

Maggie followed Mavis through to the back of the shop and the lights went on. Anna put her hand on Frank's arm as he headed for the counter.

'Frank – the Misses Webb. Do you want me to sort out lunch for them?'

'Oh Lord! Yes, please – would you mind?'

'Not at all. Do you want me to take the keys now?'

'That's a good idea – I'll just get them.'

He disappeared through the rear door just as Mavis, now wearing an overall, came back into the shop and turned on the till. An instant queue formed, ready for her attention. Anna picked up a basket and started collecting what she needed. *Hell – I was out of just about everything yesterday.* Frank was back at her side before she'd finished, pressing the keys to Broomwood House into her hand.

'We really appreciate this – thanks very much.'

'No problem. Do you know if there's food in the house, or shall I get something for them now?'

'No, no – no need for that. Sally makes meals and freezes them. You know their kitchen? Well, there's a door at the back – if you go through there ...' he took back the bunch of keys and held one up '... this is the key for it – you'll find two doors opposite. One's the downstairs lavatory. It's the other one you need – the freezer's in there. Everything's labelled with what it is and how long it needs in the microwave. You need to keep that door locked, though. And mind the step. That's why we keep it locked – don't want the old girls taking a tumble.'

Anna nodded. 'I'm really sorry about Sally.'

Frank blinked. 'Yes. Thanks.'

Maggie appeared with a mug of tea. 'Come on, Frank – get this down you. Then if you've any sense, you'll get your head down – you look done in. How long will they keep Sally in hospital? Do you know?'

'A day or two for observation, that's what they said. The break's clean and been plastered – it's the concussion they're keeping an eye on.'

'Right. Well, you mind you get your head down – don't want you nodding off at the wheel when you go to see her.'

He struck the palm of his hand against his forehead. 'Oh damn!'

'What?' Maggie asked.

'How stupid can you get? I've asked my niece to come in and do the last few hours in the shop so I can go and visit – it'll be too long for Mavis, otherwise.'

'So what's the problem?'

'She makes tea for the Misses Webb, that's what. What the hell's the matter with me that I didn't think of that?'

'Tiredness and worry, I should think. You really do need to rest, Frank.'

'Maggie's right,' Anna told him. 'And it's *not* a problem. Just tell me what the routine is for their tea, and I'll do it.'

'I can't put you to all that trouble!'

'It's no trouble. Honestly.'

'If you're sure ...'

'I'm sure. Now then, you drink you tea and tell me what to do ...'

Stella Timpson was sitting absolutely still. Her previous anger and jealousy had been replaced by icy-cool reflection, her thoughts now completely focused on the situation at hand. *There has to be a way for me to turn this thing to my own advantage. What? How? Think, woman! The Blessed Rhianna – a hermit for the past couple of years, from what I've heard – turns up in the Swiffords at Philip Jackson's instigation and – wait.* Why *did Philip choose her in the first place? He knew the risks – her mental state and all that – so why* her? She closed her eyes to aid concentration, dredging up facts and figures. *I wouldn't put it past him to be feeling magnanimous – trying a bit of rehabilitation. He always did like her. But Philip Jackson runs a tight ship. He has a department with a budget, all the usual constraints. Above all, he's a pragmatist. So why take a risk on the Blessed Rhianna unless he had to? Why would he have to? A gender issue? He has only male assistants on board. Could that be it? Something in the remit specified that a woman was needed?* She shook her head, frustrated. *Don't get sidelined. He chose her, for whatever reasons. And the hermit comes out of retirement and straight away, murders happen. Could she? Could she really have done it? It would fit – she loses her own family, goes off her head and removes other people's.* Regretfully, she shook her head again. *No. Much as I'd like to, I can't believe it. It might, however, be worth sowing doubt in the appropriate minds. If she were taken in for questioning, say, that might be interesting. Either she cracks up again, or it gives adverse publicity to Philip's project. A major embarrassment. That could work.* Her eyes snapped open and she scribbled on an A4 pad.

Right. One possible tactic. Let's find others. Stella frowned now, thinking about her anonymous note, the two document extracts she'd received. *Who sent them and why? Someone else in Philip's department who considers the Blessed Rhianna a risk? Any way in through that?* She allowed her mind to float with the possibility and drew a blank, feeling again the flutterings of resentment that her enemy had such juicy information at this particular time. *She's doubtless picking up Brownie points even now, showing the stuff to the police. She* is *showing it to the police?* A grim half-smile tugged at the corners of her mouth. *Would I, if our positions were reversed? Alas, yes. Think of the wonderful publicity it would generate, once this killing business is over. Publicity. Would the Blessed Rhianna* want *that? She's been low profile for so long ... Possibly. To regain entry and acceptance in the academic community. But possibly not. Not if she's unstable, still. She might not like it. Might not cope with it. Liberal conscience, however. She wouldn't conceal anything that might help solve the crimes. But is* Philip *sure of that? Just how much faith* does *he have in his protégée? Can I undermine it? Oh yes. That's certainly worth a go. Divide and conquer. Let's start on him. Soften him up before I go to town on her.* Smiling broadly now, she reached for the telephone.

Anna rushed through the door of April Cottage, hefted her carrier bag on to a work surface and pulled out the container of milk, flicking the switch of the kettle back on as she did so.

'Sorry I took so long!' she called. 'Sally's had an accident. Did you know?'

A second passed before Adam came into the kitchen, carrying a large, heavy flashlight. Once again, the beanie and fleece had been removed so that he was wearing only a T-shirt and jeans. 'What's happened?'

Anna explained, adding that she would be on meal duty for the Misses Webb.

'Good thing they've got used to you.'

'Yes. So I might be out rather longer than planned. Do you have the spare key?'

Adam shook his head. 'I'll pick it up later.'

Anna handed him a mug of tea. 'How's the chimney coming?'

'Fine. Sally had all the estimates and she's given the go-ahead. Saves having to drop the asking price, which she'd have to do if the buyer had to get the work done themselves.'

'What exactly is the problem?'

He inclined his head. 'Come and see.'

She followed him through to the dining room. He put down his mug and stepped towards the fireplace, motioning her to join him. Anna stooped to walk into it, gasping in astonishment as he snapped on the beam of the flashlight and directed it up the chimney.

'God! I didn't realise it was so big!'

'Oh, quite something these original ones are. See up there?' He waved the light and manoeuvred himself behind her to give her an unimpeded view.

'What am I looking for?'

'First of all, a blackened beam.' He put his free hand on her shoulder and angled her body. 'There – see?'

She did see. She was also acutely conscious of his closeness to her, smelling the cleanness of his clothes and the tang of soap.

'But what's a beam doing up there? Won't it catch fire?'

'That's what the Inspector's worried about. Not that it has done for the last God knows how many years, but it's got to come out.'

'You said the first thing. What else?'

She heard him chuckle, a low, throaty sound. 'Unbelievable, this is. Take a look.' He swung the beam further up.

'What?' Anna strained to see.

Adam pressed close behind her, stepping her forward, toward the wall. She felt suddenly light-headed, feeling the outline of his every muscle against her back and legs.

'Right up there. What does that look like to you?'

She stared in disbelief. 'No! It can't be surely?'

'That's what I thought, when I saw it.'

'I'm not seeing things, am I?' She half-turned towards him, her shoulder pressing into his chest. 'It looks like a door.'

'That's because it is.'

'But where does it go? And why the hell would anyone put a door in a chimney?' She felt him shrug.

'*How* they put a door up a chimney is what interests me. And rather more to the point, is how I'm going to get it out.' He chuckled again and stepped away from her. She felt him move out of the fireplace and followed suit.

'It's bizarre,' Anna said.

'It certainly is.' He picked up his mug and took a deep swallow of tea.

'And what about the other chimney? In the sitting room?'

'They're joined, you see. Back to back, but not straight on, and . . .' His explanation was cut off by the sound of the front door bell. Anna excused herself and went to answer it.

She came back into the room with Janice Mills. 'It's for you,' she told Adam. He raised his eyebrows as he nodded in greeting to the policewoman.

'Don't tell me – it's about the goats. I heard Carol and Bill were making a complaint.'

'I'm afraid not.' She glanced at Anna and flushed slightly. Turning back to face him, she said, 'I'm sorry, Adam, but I have to ask you to accompany me to Market Eaton to help in an ongoing enquiry.'

Philip Jackson put down the phone and closed his eyes. Jesus Christ! He knew Stella Timpson was a shit-stirring bitch, but this had to take the biscuit. *And she has the gall to talk about Rhianna being off her head!* He breathed deeply and tapped one foot impatiently against the back of the other. Sighing, he pulled the desk blotter toward him, where he had scribbled down the stuff she'd read out to him. This has to be a hoax, surely? There was no way Rhianna would not have told him about something like this. *Stay calm*, he told himself, rerunning their conversation through his mind. He hadn't wanted to talk to Stella, of course, but she'd insisted, telling Debbie, the administrator, that if Philip didn't want to talk to her, she'd have to phone the police directly. That threat, besides alarming him – completely irrationally, of course – had certainly piqued his interest. What she'd had to say, however, didn't make the slightest sense.

'Well, Philip – you must be feeling really pleased with yourself. Assisting the police with this terrible business in the Swiffords.'

He'd frowned, half looking at the telephone receiver in a futile attempt to check that he'd heard her correctly. What the hell was she talking about? He'd played it cool, both from habit and simply because, not knowing the facts, he was running blind.

'And how might I be doing that?'

'The documentation, Philip. About the curse.'

'I really don't know what you're talking about.' He really ought to make a recording of that sentence. It was one he seemed to use a lot with her.

Disconcertingly, she had laughed then. Not her usual forced effort, either. She had sounded, for once, genuinely amused.

'Of course, I understand that you've probably been sworn to secrecy for the duration and I would have loved to have been able to help myself, but having only the first two pages – you really need to tighten up on security, by the way.'

'Stella – '

He could almost see the grin when she spoke next. Like some Frankensteinian Cheshire Cat.

' "A most shameful and wicked episode in the Year of Our Lord 1732 . . ." '

'I beg your pardon?'

'I never thought I'd live to hear you beg, Philip!'

She had paused, and Philip had snatched up his pen, praying that she would repeat what she'd said. She had. With additions.

' "A most shameful and wicked episode in the Year of Our Lord 1732 and how it came to be unearthed . . ." '

He had bluffed, of course. Declined to comment, as she no doubt expected him to, but looking at the words now, he realised that his palms were sweating. Surely to God, if Rhianna had this, she would have come running? And what had Stella meant by regretting the fact that only two pages were in her own possession? Abruptly, he stood up, rubbing both hands through his hair as if massaging shampoo. There had to be more. Stella assumed he knew about it – *had* it. *But I don't. I bloody well don't.* And any talk of lapses in departmental security were bullshit. Sure, Stella had found out about the Swiffords project, but it wasn't exactly secret and Philip would have laid money that that had been down to Ted Bridges, stirring the pot. *He has his eye on my job. That's no secret, either. He's like a bloody vulture, just waiting for me to cock up so he can seize his opportunity. But he can't have sent Stella this document because I don't have it. Which means, if it* does *exist – and let's not discount a hoax at this stage; that would be right up Stella's street – but if it* does *exist, it means Rhianna has it and is keeping it under wraps.* Philip's skin turned clammy. Stella had echoed his thoughts in her parting shot.

'I do hope – for your sake, you understand – that you're bluffing, Philip, when you admit no knowledge of this document. I'd hate to think that I have it and the Blessed Rhianna has it and you don't. Why ever would your protégée do that, after all . . . ?'

Adam Etheridge waited until they had cleared Swifford Lea before turning to the policewoman to ask, 'What's going on, Jan?'

Janice looked in her rear-view mirror before replying. 'I'm sorry, Adam. The investigating officers have had a tip-off that you've been working in the houses of every victim during the past few months.'

'What! And that makes me a suspect, does it? Good God Almighty!'

'Just routine follow-up. They have to do it.'

'Right.' His face was flushed and his jaw tightened. 'This has got to be Dave.'

Janice glanced at him, eyebrows raised.

'I had to sack him. It's his way of getting back at me.'

'Anonymous tip-offs are often malicious.'

'Stupid sod. Yes, I have worked in all the victims' houses – as he's been all too loose in talking about recently. But so has he. By shooting his mouth off, he's putting himself in the frame, as well.'

Janice smiled. 'Then, once you've told them that, they'll be having words with him, too.'

Adam took little comfort from her reply. 'This is not what I need right now. Not what *we* need. Featherstone's been doing his stuff in April Cottage. I could hardly bloody breathe in there. I wanted to counter what he's done while Anna's over with the Misses Webb.'

'It's Anna now, is it?' Janice's eyebrows were becoming over-exercised. 'Watch yourself, Adam. She's in the enemies' camp – don't you forget that.'

'That's just it, though, Jan – I don't believe she is. I touched her this morning. Got the feel of her. She's still in no-man's land. It's not too late. We can bring her over to our side.'

'Adam . . .'

'It would have been the perfect opportunity – to do a working while she's out. I've done the preliminaries, but we're going to have to go full out on it. She'll be gone for longer than usual with the Misses Webb today – she's doing their lunch – tea as well, come to that – with Sal being out of action.'

'Neat. The story's been accepted, then.'

'No reason why it shouldn't be. Frank put a sign up, saying she fell downstairs. What a performance, though. Something else we don't need, eh?'

'Too right. What exactly happened? Frank's message to me was a bit garbled.'

'I'm not surprised. They were out, scouting the perimeter round the Morgan place, getting ready to do the business, when Sal caught her foot in a root or something and fell headlong on to a rock. Out cold, she was. Frank nearly had a fit when he found her lying there.'

'It could have been really nasty if they'd been found in the vicinity.' Janice shook her head. 'Be a bit difficult, explaining what they were doing prowling around the area, to say the least.'

'You're not wrong. It's a good thing Frank's as big as he is. He was able to assess the damage and carry her to the car on his own.'

'How the hell did he explain it to the hospital? If she was supposed to have fallen down the stairs in the middle of the night, she'd have had her nightclothes on, surely?'

'It was too bloody close for comfort, that's for sure. He brushed the leaves off her and said she'd sat up, reading, and must have woken up, gone downstairs to check the kitchen lights or get a glass of water – you know the kind of thing. Said he heard a yell and a series of bumps and ran out of the bedroom to find her crumpled at the bottom of the stairs.'

'Shit! I just hope Sal backs it up. They could suspect a case of domestic violence, otherwise.'

'She'd come round by the time they got there. Groggy, and her leg was playing merry hell, but she got the gist.'

'What are we going to do with Sal out of action, though? We can't stop now.' Janice changed down as she approached the roundabout which led to the centre of Market Eaton.

Adam's face was grim. 'We try again tonight, without her.'

Chapter Twenty-five

Fletcher Godfrey was Pete Barker's first customer of the day.

'Come back for that drink, eh? What can I get you?'

'A stiff one. Double whisky.'

'You all right?' Pete was alarmed by the pallor of the older man's face as he approached the bar.

'No. Can't say as I am.' Fletcher parked his behind on a bar stool. 'Just been over to see Mike and Rosie Morgan.'

'Say no more.' Pete shoved a glass under the optic.

'What can you say, in a situation like that? Nothing. Not a bloody thing that makes one jot of difference.'

'There you go.' Pete put the glass in front of him. 'And thanks again for your help yesterday.'

'Janice taken your statement, has she?'

'Yes. Doesn't compare to this business of the lad, though. Christ! If me and Pat ever have kids ...' He looked at Fletcher. 'Got any of your own?'

'Two. Son's a photographer in London. Daughter's a teacher in Sheffield. Sarah's married. Ian's not.'

Pete nodded. 'We've only been married two years. Lived together before that, but we want to get the business going, get ourselves settled before we start a family.'

'Sensible.' Fletcher seemed to be staring into the bottom of his glass as if it were a crystal ball and he was waiting for it to produce information. He looked up suddenly. 'Sorry. If you don't mind, Pete, I'm going to take this over there –' he gestured to the far corner of the room '– and sit quiet for a bit.'

'Sure. Take care, eh?'

'I will.'

He found the seat he wanted and sat nursing his glass. *Jesus! That's got to be one of the hardest things I've ever done. Talking to Mike and Rosie.* He closed his eyes, pained by the memory, by the sheer rawness of their grief and the total inadequacy he had felt in the face of it. Rosie was still almost numb with shock. Her eyes, red-rimmed and dark-circled, had seemed huge, her skin puffy and colourless. She seemed dazed, her movements slow and clumsy, barely able to respond to his awkward condolences. She'd excused herself and headed for the stairs after barely a couple of minutes.

'A lie-down might be the best thing for her,' Fletcher had observed.

Mike, wild-eyed, had looked at him despairingly. 'I wish she would. She's not slept, you know. Not a wink, since Gavin ... She's not lying down. She just sits in his room, clutching one of his sweaters and crying, rocking backwards and forwards. I don't know what to do, Fletcher. I just don't know what to do.'

'Has she seen a doctor?'

Mike had nodded. 'He said he'd rather not give her sleeping pills and stuff. Said it's better if she just gets it out. What the fuck does he know? It's not his son that's dead, is it?'

'Jesus, Mike – I don't know what to say. I can't begin to imagine ... I'm just so sorry.'

'It's too late, isn't it? Maybe if I'd talked to you before, or we'd searched his room, confronted him earlier ...'

The man's anguish had been so palpable, it had pierced Fletcher to the core.

'Hindsight's a terrible thing, Mike, and totally useless. You did what you thought was best, and you couldn't have done different and – '

'– and it wasn't fucking good enough and it was too fucking late and Gavin is DEAD!'

Mike had broken down then, into great exploding sobs, the like of which Fletcher hoped never to witness again. He had stood helplessly while Mike staggered around the room, bending double under the weight of it all. Finally, he had straightened up and looked at Fletcher, his eyes haunted.

'Maybe it's punishment. It's the only thing I can think of that makes any sense.'

Fletcher's heart had hammered. 'Jesus, Mike! You can't really think that?'

'You got any better suggestions?'

'Gavin's death was an accident, man! A terrible, terrible accident. You can't blame yourself ...'

'Don't tell me what I can and can't do, Fletcher! It's not your kid that's lying in the fucking mortuary!' Mike had rounded on him then, his train of thought spinning out of control. 'And what about Em? And Seth and Karen? Christ!'

'Slow down, Mike! That's not logical, and you know it! Where would the vicar fit into that scenario? And don't forget – me, you and Rosie are still here. It's random, man – random acts of violence, and the only reason you're putting them together is because of ... well – because of something that happened years ago. Something that the facts don't fit, when you examine them closely.'

Fletcher took a gulp of his whisky. *Christ! I was trying to convince myself, as much as Mike. More so, maybe.* Thank God, Mike had calmed down a bit, then. His shoulders had suddenly slumped, as if he'd somehow caved in on himself, and he'd turned to Fletcher with a look of unutterable weariness on his face.

'You're right. I'm sorry, Fletcher. I know you're right – in here –' He'd tapped his head with a forefinger. Moving his hand to his chest, he continued. 'It's here that's getting at me. Guilty conscience, eh? After all this time ...'

'It's understandable, in the circumstances. God knows – you wouldn't wish it on your worst enemy. But no guilt, Mike. No guilt. Think of the consequences if we hadn't acted.'

Mike had slumped into a chair. 'Thanks, Fletcher. I needed that. Thank you.'

And so Fletcher had left him, thanking his lucky stars that he had never shared with the others what he had later discovered ...

'Have you seen the paper?' An excited voice in the bar brought him back to the present. Fletcher looked up as Pete called, 'What?' in response to the question. A group of regulars had come in for their lunchtime pints.

'The police – they're saying now that someone outside the family did the Petersons in.'

'What?' The paper was snatched from the bearer of the news and the small group of men huddled round it.

'Bloody hell!' It was Chris, the Morris Men leader who spoke. 'Fine time to be changing their tune, isn't it? The bastard will be well away by now, and here we all were, thinking poor old Seth had gone off his head.'

'What's happened then?' Pete strained over the bar to see.

Chris shook his head. 'Don't know, exactly.' He craned his neck over another man's shoulders. 'Something about "discoveries made in the light of new forensic evidence". That throws it wide open again, then.'

'Maybe. Maybe not.' It was old Ben Pritchard who spoke. Must be pushing eighty, if he was a day.

'What's that meant to mean, Ben?' Pete humoured him.

'Lil Calthorpe seen young Janice picking someone up this morning.'

'Go on with you! They wouldn't send Janice for a suspected murderer! They'd need two plods for that, surely? And send the CID bods. Am I right, Fletcher?'

All eyes swivelled to the corner. Fletcher rose slowly and walked over to the bar, signalling Pete that he wanted a refill.

'That would depend. On a lot of considerations. Who are we talking about, anyway? Or don't you know?'

'Oh, I knows, all right.' Ben accepted another half and raised his glass, taking a sip and wiping froth from his upper lip before he continued. 'Young Adam Etheridge, is who.'

'Adam? Probably just got a job for him to do. Making safe at Seth's or Emily's.'

'Then he'd go in his van, wouldn't he? I'm assuming he keeps the tools of his trade in it?' Ben shook his head. 'At April Cottage, he were. Janice went in, brought him out and got him into her car. Drove off that way.' The old man waved his arm. Several pairs of eyebrows were raised. 'Can't get to Em's nor Seth's on that road, now, can ye? Last I looked, it still only goes to Market Eaton.'

'Shit!' Someone muttered under their breath.

'No need to add two and two together and make five,' Fletcher pointed out. 'Probably some entirely innocent explanation. Adam's never been in trouble.'

'Up till now,' someone put in darkly.

'More than likely that git Dave, stirring up trouble,' Pete said.

'Oh aye? And how would he be doing that?' Ben asked.

'He was bragging about the fact that he and Adam had done work in the houses.'

'There you are, then!' someone said.

'There you are, what?' Pete laughed. 'He also pointed out that I don't have a cast-iron alibi for the night the Petersons were killed. Doesn't mean I did it. Nor Adam, either.'

'Quite right,' Fletcher put in. 'And by bringing attention to the building work, Dave would be putting himself in the frame, too.'

'So why did Janice pick up Adam?' Chris persisted.

'We don't know. So it's pointless to speculate.' Fletcher had heard this kind of rumour all too often before.

'Dave's been causing a fair bit of trouble lately. Some of you must have seen him in here, when I barred him. And from what I've heard,' Pete added, 'Adam sacked him. Stands to reason he'd badmouth the man after that.'

'Then why have the police picked him up? That's what I want to know,' Ben asked.

'They'd have to,' Fletcher told him. 'All leads have to be followed up.'

'No smoke without fire, that's what I say.' The old man shook his head above his glass.

'That's rubbish, Ben Pritchard, and you're old enough to know better!' Fletcher's voice was sharp.

'I'm old enough to know it ain't strictly true that he's never been in trouble, either, which you seem to have forgotten even though you're younger than me and were the village policeman at the time!' the old man shot back.

'What are you going on about? Good God, you don't mean ...'

'Oh yes, I do! Him and Gideon Claybourne and Edward Miller ...'

'They were kids. It was a lot of fuss over nothing, as well you know. And don't tell me that *you* never went scrumping – or even poaching – when you were younger.'

'You think about it, though – he's the only one of 'em left in the village *and* he does all that martial arts stuff *and* he wasn't man enough to keep his wife.'

A snigger ran through the group.

'What the hell's that got to do with anything?' Pete, as a newcomer, was rapidly losing track of the argument.

'Ah, but I see what you're getting at!' Chris chimed in. He

turned to the others. 'I read a lot of "True Crime" books. There's often a link with macho types and sexual inadequacy, and that, in turn, can lead to feelings of alienation and repressed violence. He could even be –' He glanced around and lowered his voice '– a latent homosexual.'

'I've never heard such a cock and bull story in all my life!' Fletcher slammed down his glass in disgust. 'Just what are we saying here? You go following that train of twisted logic and you might as well say that all martial artists are murderers, all homosexuals are murderers . . .'

'What about paedophiles, then?'

'Good God Almighty! The vast majority of paedophiles are heterosexuals!'

'And you know that for a fact, do you?' Old Ben was having none of it.

'The statistics bear me out.' Fletcher glanced across the group to Pete, who was shaking his head at the course of the conversation. 'And let me reiterate – Adam Etheridge is a good, hardworking man who's never been in trouble with the law, and – if my judgement is right – like as not, never will be.'

A couple of the men shifted uncomfortably on their bar stools. After a second's silence, one of them said, 'He's meant to be looking at our conservatory roof next week.'

'Christ! I'd think again about that, if I was you. Just till he's in the clear, like . . .'

'I've heard enough of this shit,' Fletcher spat. 'I'm going home.'

Anna let herself into the Misses Webbs' house and called out, to let them know she had arrived. Much to her surprise, Alice, followed by Molly, came into the hall from the Oriental Room to greet her.

'Good morning, my dear. And how are you today?'

'Very well, thank you.'

Alice peered beyond her, towards the front door, and looked at her quizzically.

'No Sally today? We didn't hear the car, did we?'

'No,' Molly replied.

Both sisters were dressed and looking very smart in old-fashioned suits, their hair brushed, the only incongruity in their appearance being slippers rather than shoes.

'I'm afraid Sally's out of action. She had an accident during the night.' Not wanting to alarm them unduly, Anna made as light of the event as she could, reassuring the sisters that Sally was recovering well. 'I'm afraid you have me for chief cook and bottle-washer today!' she finished.

'How very kind of you! But such a shame about poor Sally. We must write a letter. Will you take it for us?'

'Of course.'

A frown crossed Alice's face. 'So she won't be able to come tomorrow, either?'

'I'm afraid not. It will be me again, I expect. Is that a problem?'

'Oh no, dear. Not at all. It's just that we're having a visitor tomorrow and might perhaps need an extra place for lunch.' Alice turned to her sister. 'I do think we should at least offer him lunch, dear, don't you?'

'Quite so.'

'I'm sure that can be accommodated.' Picking up on Alice's use of 'him' and bearing in mind what Sally had told her and Philip of the sisters' aversion to men, Anna felt she had to ask who they were expecting.

'Our solicitor, dear. Such a very nice man, and always so helpful. There are one or two matters to be discussed.'

'Right. Well, I'll make a note, then – one extra for lunch tomorrow.'

'You're so kind!'

'Not at all. Now then – I'd better get started on today's! Where would you like to eat?'

'Oh, in the dining room, I think, don't you, Molly?'

'That would be very nice, yes, Alice.'

'I'll get on with it, then. Shall I make a cup of tea for starters?' Anna knew the old women were very fond of tea and always ready for a cup.

'How lovely. We'll take that in the music room, I think. Come along, Molly. We don't want to get under Dr Summers' feet, do we now? It is Dr Summers, isn't it? Sometimes I fear I muddle up people's names.'

'Not today,' Anna laughed. 'You're quite right.'

Leaving the sisters to it, she went through to the kitchen, trying to remember where Sally kept everything. Cutlery and crockery were no problem, and it didn't take her long to find table mats. Going through to the dining room – to her, the Arts and Crafts Room – she was assailed by an intense wave of heat when she opened the door. Alarmed, she reached for the light switch and stepped through to find the sliding wall closed and an ancient electric heater glowing with both bars on. It was worse than a sauna, she thought, and probably doing the furniture no good at all. Swiftly, she moved across the room, opened the sliding wall and sought to open the French doors behind it. Locked. That, at least, was sensible, but where was the key? Glancing round, her eye swept along the mantel shelf, arrested by something metallic behind the clock. She had found it. Picking it up, she bent to switch off the fire. *They must have been in here yesterday evening and gone to bed, leaving it on. All night. Dear God . . .* She shook her head at the frayed condition of the flex and the heat of the plug when she removed it. *I wonder . . .* Glancing over her shoulder, she decided to remove the thing from the room altogether. The sooner she could get Frank to repair or replace it, the better. Best let it cool, first, though. She unlocked the French doors and threw them open, marvelling at the patio and garden. What a wonderful view. She paused momentarily, then set the table and, closing the door to the room behind her, went back to the kitchen to finish making the tea, taking it on a tray to the music room.

Alice was seated at the piano, beautifully straight-backed as she ran her fingers over the keys. She smiled as Anna laid down the tray on an occasional table.

'We used to have such fun, playing. Mother was very good, wasn't she, Molly?' Without waiting for her sister to reply, she continued, 'I should think it needs tuning again, though. Can you remember when we last had it tuned, Molly?'

Her sister shook her head. 'I thought Mr Gladstone died.'

'He did, dear. But then we had young Mr Winters.' She turned to Anna. 'Blind, you know. Piano tuners often are. Their hearing compensates, I expect. Oh.'

Her sudden stop took Anna aback. 'Is something wrong?'

'Well, yes. That was something we wanted to ask Sally today. To make appointments for us to have our eyes tested and get new spectacles. Preferably this week. And Molly's denture is broken . . .'

'And I need the chiropodist. Though she comes here. But opticians don't do home visits, to they?'

Anna knew that Sally would be unable to drive while her leg was in plaster and that Frank would have his hands full between looking after her and running the shop.

'I could take you to the optician myself,' she offered. 'Is there someone you see regularly?'

'Mr Baker in Market Eaton. We've been going there for years, haven't we, dear?'

Molly nodded. 'But what about my denture? And the chiropodist?'

'Well, I'm sure Dr Summers could call the chiropodist – such a nice young woman, she is. Her name is Melody and I think we have her card by the telephone. Dear me, I could have called her myself after I spoke to our solicitor this morning. How very remiss of me.'

'Don't worry – I'll see to it. But your denture ...' She turned to Molly. 'Are you unable to eat comfortably? I'm thinking about what I should do for your lunch.'

'Oh no, dear. It's my other set that's broken. The one I have in is fine. I just thought that if we were going to get our eyes tested, I could get the denture repaired at the same time.'

'Very sensible.' Anna smiled. 'Leave it with me.'

Stopping off to close the dining-room windows – she wanted only to clear the overheating, not freeze the sisters – Anna followed Frank's instructions with regard to lunch and, whilst it was cooking, made the necessary phone calls, finding the chiropodist's card where Alice said it was, but having to look up the optician in the phone book. Finding the denture repair laboratory necessitated a trawl through the Yellow Pages, but by the time the sisters had eaten their lunch, she had arranged everything to her satisfaction and their pleasure.

'How very efficient you are, my dear! Thank you so much. I shall make a little note so that we don't forget.'

'I've written it down for you. Everything's set for Thursday.' Anna handed over the piece of paper.

'We shall look forward to that. It seems such a long time since we've had an outing.'

'Too long, if you ask me,' Molly put in.

'Well, I didn't. But you're quite right. I wonder if our library tickets are still operative? Or even if I can find them.' She frowned. 'I'm sure it will come to me. Do you think we could go to the library as well? On Thursday?'

'I'm sure we can. Now then –' Anna was interrupted by the peal of her mobile phone, clipped into the breast pocket of her jacket. 'Do excuse me!'

Alice and Molly watched with open curiosity as she answered it.

'Roly! How lovely to hear from you!' The sisters' manner of speaking was infectious, she realised with a smile. 'Are you all right? I thought you'd be up to your ears.'

'I am!' The warmth of her greeting surprised him and gave him renewed hope. 'But that doesn't mean I don't have time for you! I was rather hoping we could meet up this evening. Have dinner at my hotel – hopefully without the locals fighting! At least they don't have goats here.'

Anna laughed. 'That sounds just the ticket.'

'Are you sure you don't mind driving over here?'

'Of course not. What time?'

'Seven-thirty for eight?'

'I'll be there.'

She ended the call and the sisters glanced at each other.

'Is that one of those mobile telephones, dear?'

'Indeed it is. Wonderful things.'

'So we've heard. May we look? We've never seen one before, have we?'

Molly shook her head as Alice held out her hand. Anna handed it over.

'It's so small! Is it true that the signals are bounced off satellites, orbiting the earth?'

'I believe so.'

'But how is it powered?'

'By a rechargeable battery. Here, let me show you.' As Anna reached to take it back, it rang, startling Alice almost into dropping it. 'See – press this button and say hello.'

Cautiously, Alice did so, saying, much to Anna's amusement, 'Doctor Summers' mobile telephone. Miss Alice Webb speaking.'

Anna gestured to her, reminding her to hold it against her ear. Alice listened for a moment, then, handing it back, said 'It's for you, dear. Professor Philip Jackson.'

Chapter Twenty-six

Tuesday November 15th

Anna drove steadily south, thinking, for the moment, of anything but her reason for doing so. It didn't work for long because, even in going over her dinner with Roly the previous evening, the subject had come up.

She had met Roly at his Market Eaton hotel, originally a fifteenth-century coaching inn. With its huge, original fireplaces and exposed timbers, it had exuded a warm welcome, backed up by friendly staff and good service. They had had a drink in the bar before their meal and Roly had looked taller than ever beneath the low ceiling, smartly but casually dressed in slacks and cashmere sweater. His face had lit up when she'd arrived, but Anna had noticed immediately the dark circles beneath his eyes.

'Bad?' she'd murmured as he hugged her.

'Not exactly family entertainment. Let's not talk about it for now. Later, perhaps, but not here. Too public.'

She'd nodded and they'd taken a seat, sinking into sumptuous red leather chairs to look at the menu. Choices made, Roly had asked her how her own day had been.

'Rather busier than anticipated!' She told him about Sally's accident and the extra duties she had undertaken in looking after the Misses Webb.

'Gives you more time with them, though. How's it going?'

'Very well. They're on extremely good form at the moment, but I shan't get much time with them over the next couple of days, I'm afraid. They're seeing their solicitor tomorrow, and I have to go and see Philip. The only way I can do that, while sorting out their meals, is to do their lunch tomorrow, leave their tea ready and drive home. I'll stay overnight, see Philip first thing on Wednesday morning and belt back in time for their lunch again.'

'Good God! Can't someone else sort them out?'

Anna had shrugged. 'I was happy to offer, at least until some more permanent arrangements can be made once Sally's out of hospital. It's just having to see Philip that's put the fly in the ointment, logistically speaking.'

'Put him off. Can't it wait a day or two? I would have thought he'd welcome you being able to spend more time with the old girls.'

'Quite.' She'd hesitated then, before blurting out, 'I think something's wrong, Roly.'

'What do you mean?'

'I don't know. That's the problem. He phoned me on my mobile when I was with the sisters at lunchtime. I can't put my finger on it.'

She'd thought again about their conversation. Philip had asked, as was to be expected, what Roly had – how were things progressing? She had been enthusiastic in her reply but, quite abruptly, Philip had said that he had to see her as soon as possible.

'Oh Lord, Philip – don't say there's a problem with the funding! This is so much bigger than you can have imagined and the sisters are an absolute mine of information.'

'No – nothing like that. But I do need to see you, Rhianna. Can you come in tomorrow? And bring what you've got so far?'

She had felt decidedly uneasy then. For one awful second, she had wondered if he was going to give her the sack. Totally irrational, of course – why on earth would he do such a thing? There was certainly no reason that she could think of. Swiftly, she had explained the new situation now that Sally was temporarily unable to look after the sisters, but still, Philip had been insistent, forcing her to make the arrangement she had just explained to Roly.

She had looked at him as they went through to the hotel restaurant, and grimaced. 'I've never known Philip quite like this.'

Roly had squeezed her hand. 'It could be, you know, that he's worried about you being alone in the Swiffords with all this shit happening. I know I am.'

'You don't think he's going to pull the plug on the research?'

'I have to say that, in his place, I would. At least until the situation is over.'

'But the sisters could be dead by then! They're in their nineties, for God's sake! While they appear healthy enough in many ways – well – I could just turn up one day and find that one or other – or both, God forbid! – had simply died in their sleep!'

'There's no point worrying about it,' he had pointed out. 'Neither of us can second-guess Philip's reasoning. You'll just have to wait until you see him.'

He was right, she knew, but it didn't make things any easier. She was involved with the project now; involved, too, with the sisters, and wanted to get on with things as swiftly as possible. Still, the evening had progressed well enough. The meal had been lovely, though the hotel chef certainly could not match Pete Barker's cuisine.

Afterwards, they had taken a walk through the streets of the market town, Roly, keeping his voice low and an eye cocked for possible eavesdroppers, bringing her up to date on the investigation.

'I've seen video footage of Gavin Morgan's death – you know several of the kids had camcorders? Awful. Absolutely appalling. The poor boy was obviously terrified by this "Voice". It even told him that his parents would burn in hell.'

'But why?'

'Some heinous supposed crime. God knows what. None of it makes any sense, does it? They're running tests on the body, of course, toxicology amongst them, but – who knows? And there's certainly nothing on record – of his parents having any brushes with the law. They even got your Mrs Plod to talk to the guy who was the police officer before her – held the post for years. If there'd been even a whiff, he should have known. Nothing. Ditto for Emily Parsons and the vicar – unless you count being disliked, in the latter case.' Roly had frowned in concentration. 'It's this bloody curse that seems to be the link. That and the Voice.'

He had stopped then and turned to her, ticking off points on his fingers.

'One – Karen heard the Voice. She and her father dead – butchered. And curse graffiti all over the house. Two – no evidence that the vicar heard the Voice and he was suffocated. No blood, but again, curse graffiti, this time in the church where the funeral service for the Petersons was due to be held. Three – Emily Parsons. Crazy ramblings in a notebook that indicate that she was hearing the Voice. Car over cliff – accident or suicide? And found in her house – curse graffiti *and* a crucified sheep. There's been an interesting development linking her and the vicar, though. Her phone records show that she called him the night before he was found. Nothing in his diary, so there was a lot of speculation about that. Then lo and behold, his housekeeper came forward. Seems she found a slip of paper – behind the telephone table or something – with Emily's name, a time and the church scribbled on it. She confirms it was the vicar's handwriting, so it seems as though they'd arranged to meet there.'

'Why?' Anna had mused.

'If we knew the answer to that, things might be a whole lot clearer. God – I've lost count of the numbers now!' Roly laughed, an incongruous sound given the topics under discussion.

'Four, I think.'

'Four, then. Gavin Morgan heard the Voice and, to put it bluntly, it looks as if it drove the kid off his head. Though whether the fall alone would have killed him is another matter. Bloody unfortunate – on all counts – that he caught himself with the knife as he fell.' He had shaken his head. 'It's so bloody frustrating! If we could have had Gavin alive, questioned him about the Voice ...'

'Talking of questioning,' Anna had said, 'Adam Etheridge got hauled in today – I assume, to do with this investigation.'

'The goat man? How are they, by the way?'

'Recovering. Pete's keeping them indoors at night – there's a suitable outbuilding. Just until things calm down a bit.'

Roly had nodded, asking. 'How did you come to hear about it? Adam Etheridge, I mean?'

'He was working in April Cottage when Janice Mills came to collect him.' Anna had explained what had happened.

'And you wonder why Philip might want you out of there?'

'But Philip doesn't know!' Anna had protested.

'You take my point, though? Good God, Rhianna – you don't want to be anywhere near the man, let alone having him under the same roof!'

'But why was he picked up anyway?'

'They've picked several people up, to be honest. Anyone who's worked in all the victims' homes – builders, plumbers, fire alarm people – you name it.'

'So there is still no actual evidence, then?'

'They've been hauled in, in an attempt to find it. Rhianna – trust me on this, will you? Just – stay out of his way as much as possible.' He had gripped her by the shoulders then and drawn her close. 'I really couldn't bear it if anything happened to you.'

Before she had known what was happening, he had kissed her.

Making a stop at a petrol station, Anna tried to put Roly and the kiss out of her mind. She had been shocked by the intensity of it, shocked, too, by her own reaction. She had, after all, kissed him back. *What the hell came over me? I love Roly – as a friend. I like, trust him, but there's never been a sexual attraction. For him, yes. But not for me. Not until now.*

Oh God. This was getting complicated. On all fronts. *First of all, I don't want to think about Philip's reasons for calling me in. Now I don't want to think about the business with Roly. What the hell* can *I think about?!* She suddenly smiled to herself. *The Misses Webb. At least they're a safe enough subject.* She had got so many memories from them yesterday, including the most hair-raising accounts of traveling dentistry without anaesthetic. Not that it had been inflicted on them, of course, but still ... And stories of what they'd termed tinkers and gypsies and travelling salesmen; mop fairs and wake fairs and circuses. Fabulous stuff. *If only I'd had time to transcribe more, before seeing Philip. He* has *to see reason. He can't pull me off this now.*

Today had also been a delight, with them, even if no interviewing had been involved. They were so looking forward to seeing their solicitor and had dressed in their finest clothes, skittish as schoolgirls. Anna had prepared an extra lunch, as requested, and had left the house when he had arrived, getting a smile and a firm handshake as he asked how she was getting on. She had explained to him, as well as to the sisters, that their tea was all prepared and under cover, part in the larder, part in the fridge. *Well*, she thought as she changed lanes, ready for her motorway exit. *Hopefully, they've all had a good time.*

A momentary silence fell as Adam Etheridge walked into The White Hart. Keeping his eyes straight ahead, he moved to the bar as the murmur of conversation started up again in his wake. Pete

Barker had noted the reaction, his mouth forming a grim line as his eyes swept over his clientele.

'Thanks for coming, Adam. What can I get you?'

'Pint of best, please, Pete.'

Pete pulled the pint and handed it over, smiling. He prided himself on the way he kept his cask ales. None of that namby-pamby chemical bollocks in his establishment. Turning, he raised the flap and joined Adam on the other side of the bar, gesturing towards the back door of the pub.

'Bring it with you and I'll show you.'

Adam nodded and followed him outside. Sunset was approaching and the sky was swathed in washes of pink and yellow light. Crossing the car park, they took the path to the goats' field, stopping short at three old barns on the right-hand side, two of which stood quite close together while the third was some distance away.

Adam took a couple of slow mouthfuls of his pint, savouring the taste before he spoke. 'Are you serious about this?'

'Too bloody right,' Pete told him. 'Bloody taxman's crucifying us for living over the pub. I'm buggered if I'm having that. Bastards! Pat and I have talked it over. Talked to the bank, as well. We were planning on turning all of these into cottage-style guest-suites. Had some preliminary drawings done and all that. Now, we've decided to go ahead with these two, but that one –' Pete pointed to the third. 'That one, my son, we want to turn into our home.'

Adam raised his eyebrows. 'You're looking at a fair bit of cash, Pete. And what about planning permission?'

'We already have outline consent for the original proposal. We're putting in now for the alteration. I don't foresee any problems, to be honest. They've been banging on for a while about selectively targeted tourism, and although we haven't been here long, we've built up a good reputation. What with getting the stars and being in the *Good Food Guide* and what have you, they know we wouldn't do anything tacky or attract what might be termed "undesirables".'

Adam looked at him dubiously. 'I know what you mean and I would have agreed with you, up till the past couple of weeks. But now – we're becoming famous for all the wrong reasons. What's going on here will either put people off altogether, or simply attract ghouls.'

'True,' Pete conceded. 'But by the time we get everything up and running, it should all be over, please God. Not exactly going to be a five-minute job, this, is it? So – while we'll have to hang fire on our own place until it's been through the appropriate channels, I don't see why we can't get the ball rolling on the guest accommodation. What do you think?'

Adam looked at him levelly. 'You sure you don't want to ask someone else?'

'You telling me you can't do it?'

'No. No, I'm not. But some of the work, obviously, would need to be sub-contracted, and while I've got plenty of lads who usually work with me on jobs like this, well – I'm not sure they'd be so keen, just at present.'

'Tell me something, Adam.' It was Pete's turn to look the other man in the eye. 'You been going round killing people?'

'No, I bloody haven't!' Adam's face flushed.

'Well, then. I want you to do it. Can I set things in motion so you can give me a quote?'

'Why are you asking me, Pete? Or is that a daft question, given that I've suddenly got a crop of cancellations and deferrals?'

'It was always my intention to ask you. Nothing's happened to change that.'

'You know I got hoiked in by the police today/'

'Is there anybody round here that *doesn't* know?' Pete shrugged.

'Little Miss Professor, eh?'

'What?'

'Dr Summers. Spreading the word.'

'You couldn't be more wrong, mate. I do know who set the tongues wagging, as it happens, but it wasn't her. Anyway. You've told me you've done nothing wrong. Your word's good enough for me.'

'And Pat?'

'And Pat. So will you do it, Adam?'

The builder's eyes ranged over the barns as he downed more of his pint, nodding slowly. Finally, he held out his right hand.

'Providing I can get the labour, you've got yourself a deal.'

'Good man!' Pete clasped his hand, slapped him on the back with his other one, and together, they walked back to the pub.

*

Alice and Molly Webb were in their kitchen, preparing to have a late tea.

'My goodness, Dr Summers has done us proud! I do so love salmon and cucumber sandwiches, don't you, Molly?'

'Indeed I do, Alice! So nicely presented, too. And what's that?' Molly's view was partially obscured as her sister peered inside the fridge.

'Salad, Molly. Well, I never. We don't usually have salad with our sandwiches, do we? What did she leave in the pantry, then?'

'Oh Alice! Jelly and fruit cocktail! *And* –' Molly turned to her sister, beaming. 'French fancies! I *love* French fancies, Alice!'

Alice smiled in return as she set things on the kitchen table. 'That young woman is spoiling us! Not that Sally and her niece don't look after us well, of course. They do. Oh my, yes. But it's so nice, having a new face around. And she has the time to talk to us, too.'

'I'm so looking forward to Thursday. New glasses! That will be wonderful.'

'Molly!' Alice was scandalised as her sister took a bite of a French fancy.

'Well, who said you have to have the savoury things first, anyway? It's just a custom. It all goes down the same way.'

Alice blinked, seeing in Molly's face the exact impish expression she'd had as a somewhat naughty child.

'Whatever would Mother or Father say?'

Molly shrugged. 'What they don't know, can't hurt them.'

'Molly! Whatever's got into you?'

'Fun, Alice,' her sister beamed. 'You should try it sometime. It doesn't kill you, you know.'

'Well, really!' Alice turned her back and completed the setting out of the food, affording Molly the opportunity to devour another cake. They sat down and began, officially, this time, to eat.

'Well, haven't we had a lovely day? It was so nice of young Mr Michaels to come over, wasn't it?'

'Mmm. He's looking very like his father, don't you think?'

'Quite so.' Alice paused. 'I think he's losing his hair earlier, though. Receding at quite a pace, by the look of it.'

'It's their hormones, you know,' Molly observed sagely.

'I beg your pardon?'

'Hormones. Testosterone or is it tostesterone? Some such name. Male pattern baldness. Father told me about it.'

'He did? Well.' Alice cleared her throat and decided to change the subject. She wasn't sure that male hormones were a suitable subject while they were eating. 'So nice that he's put everything in hand so quickly.'

'Father?' Molly looked puzzled.

'No, dear – Mr Michaels. I really wasn't expecting that.'

'Oh – I see what you mean. Yes.' The impish twinkle was back in her eye. 'I've found it all terribly exciting. I just hope we remember everything.'

'The cable people are coming on Thursday, whilst we're on our visit to Market Eaton. He's going to supervise it all himself, with poor Sally being incapacitated and dear Dr Summers acting as our chauffeuse.'

'Well, I know that, Alice. That wasn't what I meant at all. What I meant was ...' Molly dripped jelly from her spoon as she spoke, her hand quivering '... that I hope we remember the operating instructions. The booklet looked rather complicated. And the print was small.'

'Do watch what you're doing, dear – you're dripping.'

'I am?' Molly looked down and tutted. 'So I am. I do apologise. Yes. What was I saying? Oh yes – the instructions.'

'There's no need to worry, Molly. Mr Michaels has very kindly handwritten a résumé of what we need to know. In very large block capitals.'

'Oh dear. Is his handwriting very bad, then?'

Alice rolled her eyes. 'Why on earth should it be bad?'

'Well, doctors are notorious, aren't they? Do you remember when Bernard Johnson misread Dr Harrington's prescription for Mrs Riley? The poor woman nearly died.'

'Molly. This has nothing to do with that. Mr Michaels wrote in large block capitals simply to allow us to read easily.'

'Oh, I see. Until we get our new glasses. How thoughtful.' Polishing off her jelly, Molly lifted the cake platter with both hands, offering it to her sister.

'No thank you, dear. I'm perfectly replete.'

'Oh good! Can we do it now, then?'

'Do what?'

'Oh Alice! We've waited hours! Please? Can we?'

'Really, Molly! Stop squirming in your seat like that. You look just the way you did when you were little and about to wet your drawers! You're not going to, are you?' The question was asked on a note of alarm.

'Well, of course I'm not! I do take care with my pads, you know.' Molly had struggled to her feet, unwilling to wait a moment longer. 'You can do what you like, Alice, but I'm going to do it now!' She shuffled off out of the kitchen, leaving her sister to follow.

Alice's sigh was half-hearted. She, too, was secretly keen to get down to it. As she walked into the music room – this was where they'd decided to have it – she shook her head at the sight of Molly struggling to read the instructions.

'Here – let me do it. You sit yourself down.'

'Like *Listen with Mother*. "Are you sitting comfortably? Then I'll begin ..." '

Alice glanced at the clock on the mantel shelf, then back at their new appliance. Just the normal channels, for now, but the special package business from Thursday. She frowned in concentration as she pointed the remote control at the screen as if it were an overblown magic wand. Had she got it right? Mr Michaels had demonstrated it several times. Yes! How wonderful! The magic wide screen television sprang into colourful glory just as the presenter smiled and said, '... and now, over to our studios for all your regional and local news ...'

Chapter Twenty-seven

Silence. Darkness. The village was still, sleeping beneath a waxing moon that blinked intermittently when gaps between the banks of scudding clouds gave it fleeting sight.

The black-clad figure hugged the shadows, following the contours of hedges and walls like cling film, breathing tightly controlled, mind filled with the goal towards which such measured movement led.

Away from the watery street lights, few and far between, shaded torch beam aided the silent tread of rubber-soled shoes. Not far, now. Not far. And yet, paradoxically, this last lap was where the greatest danger lay.

Discovery could not be contemplated. There could be no excuses offered for a presence that should not be here, could only, by such stealth, have malice in mind.

A pause in progress. Eyes and ears straining to the limit to assess potential danger.

Nothing.

Nothing.

On again, heart-rate faster now.

So near.

So close.

Another pause.

Motive revisited. *Yes. Yes. It has to be done.*

Ultra caution now. The slightest sound could signal to those who cared. *Don't think about the possibility of interception. If it happens, it will be dealt with.*

And now, at last, the goal came into view. Breath was held before the final approach. Despite the cold, the air was heavy with anticipation and thin lines of sweat trickled between shoulder blades, followed the curve of the ribs.

As expected, the door was padlocked. Easy work for the bolt cropper. The snapping of the steel cracked through the night like a gunshot and breath was held again, waiting for reaction.

None came, either from without or within.

The door was eased open and heightened hearing detected reaction within to the slight creaking of hinges.

Now! Now!

Movement, so long controlled and restrained, was at last unleashed.

Into swiftness.

Sureness.

And fatal outcome.

Chapter Twenty-eight

Wednesday November 16th

Anna was up ridiculously early given that she had had such a late night. Since Philip's phone call, she had spent every spare moment transcribing tapes of her interviews with the Misses Webb and last night, back at home once more, had worked into the early hours, preparing a report. So much for letting someone at the university do the tapes later! But she had the bit between her teeth and was preparing to fight him every inch of the way should he seriously be considering pulling her out of the project.

She had struggled out of bed in the early morning darkness to check and recheck everything she had prepared. *It will have to do,* she told herself. *God knows, it should be more than enough.* The nagging doubt and fear had now been replaced by fire in her belly. *Even if he sacks me, he can't* make *me leave. If push comes to shove, I'll bloody well stay and continue the interviewing off my own bat and with my own funds. We can't lose all this wonderful information. If Philip took me away and the sisters died, what they know would be lost for ever, and that's just too awful to contemplate.*

Right. Time to make a move. Come on, Summers – you can do it. Go in there, power-dressed, organised, articulate, enthusiastic. Let's give him a taste of Rhianna Summers at her finest.

Back in Swifford Lea, Pete Barker was marching up the path that led from the goats' field to the main road. From head to toe, his body was one barely controlled network of fury. Striding past the front of the pub, he pushed open the gate of the house next door and in a couple of steps, was down the path and leaning on the doorbell.

Bill Davenport was understandably annoyed by the unrelieved ringing of the bell and, muttering darkly about how it sounded like an out of season wasp on steroids, flung open the door ready to give the offending caller a piece of his mind. He never got the chance.

Pete Barker lifted him clean off the floor, hands around his neck, and slammed him against the wall before he had time to utter a sound. Carol, Bill's wife, who had followed him into the hallway, was stopped in her tracks by the naked rage in Pete's face.

Jutting his chin until his nose was barely a whisker away from Bill's, he virtually spat at the man. 'Just tell me one thing, you bastard – what have you done with ... ?'

Backing away, Carol shouted, 'I'm calling the police!'

'Save yourself the bother,' Pete told her as he let her husband drop to the floor. 'I've already done it.'

Fletcher Godfrey was deep in thought as he walked along Folly Lane on his way to the shop. He had hardly slept a wink last night. The bloody Voice was back. He shook his head, then glanced around to see if anyone had observed him doing so. He was lucky; the lane was deserted. *God Almighty! I'll be talking to myself next.* He took a deep breath, which propelled him into a coughing fit. The air was cold. He shivered, adjusting the scarf around his neck. *Had* he heard a Voice? Could he honestly be one hundred per cent certain he hadn't dreamed it? If his life could be neatly isolated and compartmentalised from everything that was going on around him, he would have answered and said there was every likelihood that it was his slumbering imagination that had produced it, but his life, like Life in general, would not be so easily manoeuvred. He had seen the papers. Heard the talk. Other people had apparently been hearing voices, too. Was it the same Voice?

How the hell am I supposed to know the answer to that? And does it even matter? The point is, I am *hearing a bloody Voice. What it is, God only knows. Pull yourself together! How many years were you a policeman? Ask the right questions! What are the possibilities?* He turned the corner on to the main road. *One: I'm going mad. The Voice is a figment of my imagination, indicating that my mental processes are disturbed. Two: There really* is *a*

Voice, external to my mind. If that's *the case, what does it tell me?* He allowed his mind to float. *Either someone is playing a very sick joke – but how? Or* ... His mind balked at the only other possibility he could think of. *If I'm* not *mad, and if there isn't a rational, human explanation behind all this – a human agency – then that just leaves the unthinkable. It's supernatural. A ghost. A demon. Good God! How can I even* think *such rubbish! Define 'ghost'. Define 'demon'. I can't. and the reason I can't, is that they don't bloody exist.* Life was coming to a pretty pass, when it was easier to think he was going mad ...

'Mind out, Fletcher!'

He had been so engrossed in his own thoughts that he hadn't been looking where he was going.

'Oh – sorry, Maggie. How are you?'

Maggie winced, but managed to laugh. She had just left the shop and set down her carrier bag. 'Apart from you stepping on my feet, fine! Just back from leaving Jack with my sister in London. Thought a break would do him good. Done me good, too, truth be told, but I had to get back – I've got work piling up like you wouldn't believe. Still – it'll be easier to get on with, not having Jack here to worry about.'

'Yes. Well, I shan't hold you up, then.'

'Right. Awful about Sally breaking her leg, eh? And what about Emily Parsons and the vicar?'

'What about Emily and the vicar?' Fletcher's mind snapped into gear.

'You haven't heard? Apparently she'd made an appointment to meet him that morning – when we found him. At the church. I just heard about it inside.' She jerked her head towards the shop. 'I heard about the trouble with Carol and Bill, over the goats, too. I'll bloody give 'em a piece of my mind, and no mistake.'

'Now then, Maggie – let Janice deal with it.'

She shot him an ominous glance before bending to pick up her bag.

'There's dealing with it – and dealing with it.'

Fletcher was alert to what underlay the ambiguity of her statement.

'Maggie ...' he began, but was wasting his breath. She just turned and walked away, waving to him without looking back.

Fletcher walked into the shop, his mind in a turmoil, but had no time to settle into what was bothering him. Animated discussions were taking place, not only about the latest gossip, but also about the non-delivery of newspapers. Frank Arnold, normally so unruffled, was on the verge of losing his temper.

'Yes, I agree it's an inconvenience,' he told an irate customer. 'but think of it from the parents' point of view – would you want *your* kid out on a bike, delivering papers – in the dark, with some bloody homicidal maniac on the loose?'

'No, I would not. But nonetheless, I pay to have my newspapers delivered – why don't you do it yourself?'

Frank rolled his eyes and did a mental count from one to five to stop himself exploding.

'With Sal in hospital and the shop to run? I see – you'd sooner have your newspaper delivered, but the shop shut, would you?'

The customer opened his mouth, ready with a retort, but Fletcher stepped into the breach.

'What's the problem?' he asked, addressing the question to Frank.

'David Blake's parents have forbidden him to deliver the newspapers until someone is apprehended over the murders. We only deliver in Swifford Lea, as you know, and he's never missed a day, but . . .'

'BUT we still want our papers!'

Fletcher looked at the complainer with distaste. Some people had no sense of perspective. He turned back to Frank. 'Is his round made up?' he asked.

'Yes.' Frank indicated a fluorescent orange bag standing by the counter.

Fletcher smiled. 'Lend me a bike and I'll do it. Janice ran over mine, remember.' As he went through to the back with Frank to collect a list of who had what delivered, he added, under his breath, 'And Moaning Maurice back there can bloody well have his last . . .'

Maggie had hammered on Bill and Carol's front door, to no avail. Frustrated, she went home and unpacked her shopping before making herself a quick cup of coffee. *What a bloody performance! Can't turn my back for five minutes*. She sorted through the post, then booted up the computer and checked her e-mails. *God! The deadline's looming on that Italian job. Come on, girl – get yourself together!* It was no good. She couldn't settle. Pushing back her chair, she sighed as she headed for the door. *Just a quick visit. Just to make sure they're all right and give 'em a carrot or something. Put my mind at rest, then I'll come home and work like stink.* She thought about giving Anna a knock. Apparently she'd witnessed the incident with Carol and Bill and some man that was with her had helped Fletcher break up the fight. She frowned, realising that she hadn't seen Anna's car. Maybe she was out, then. Besides, if she *were* in, they'd only wind up talking and then she would lose more time from dealing with her backlog. *Yes, but I can work as late as I like. Sit up all night, if need be.* She wavered. *No. I'll nip down and see Hetty and Joe by myself, come back, WORK, and* then *go and see Anna later. Maybe teatime-ish. Perhaps arrange to go for a drink. Right then. And to save time, I'll go the back way.*

She left her house by the back door, following the garden path to its boundary with the field behind. With practised ease, she pushed her way through a spindly section of the hedge and turned right, striding behind the backs of the houses towards the goats' enclosure. Still some distance away, her eyes became aware of two things at the same time. One: the goats were not in the field; two: Janice Mason's police vehicle was parked over by the outbuildings. Breaking into a trot, her stomach knotted with foreboding as she covered the intervening ground.

'Sorry, Maggie – you can't come any closer.' Janice Mills held up her hand in warning.

'Why not? What's happened?'

She hadn't noticed Adam Etheridge squatting on the ground rolling a cigarette, but he stood up now and shook his head.

'Not Hetty and Joe! No! Oh no! What's happened?'

Adam stepped towards her as Janice said, 'I'm sorry, Maggie.'

'Oh my God ...' Maggie started to shake and before she knew it, was in floods of tears.

Adam put his arm around her shoulder and she turned and clung to him, sobbing into his shirt-front. Over her head, Adam and Janice exchanged a long look.

'BLOODY Bill and Carol! How COULD they! Are they dead or have they just turned them loose? Why won't you TELL me?' Pulling herself free, Maggie stamped her foot in fury.

'Maggie – don't go jumping the gun. There's no evidence to ...'

'No evidence? Isn't it obvious?'

'No.' Janice spoke sharply. 'Don't go making things worse, Maggie. And don't go taking the law into your own hands. We don't know who did it at this stage, but we'll be talking to people. Including Bill and Carol. Just let me do my job, all right?'

Maggie fought to regain control of herself, saying nothing. Janice nodded almost imperceptibly at Adam.

'Adam – you've got work to do in April Cottage, I believe. Why don't you take Maggie home while I finish sealing the area off? Best take her back the way she came. Save fouling things up any further.'

'OK. Come on, Maggie.' Linking his arm through hers, he led her back across the field.

Roly Featherstone was trying to concentrate on the task in hand, 'trying' being the operative word. He knew Rhianna would be seeing Philip this morning. What would happen? What did he *want* to happen? He pushed away the papers on the desk in front of him and tipped back his chair. On the one hand, he wanted Rhianna away from the Swiffords, away from the terrible things that were going on in the vicinity; on the other hand, he wanted to keep her near to him. Things had turned in his favour, he felt sure. He smiled wryly and shook his head. *I'm getting soft in my old age.* Two misnomers in one sentence. One; he wasn't old. Old was seventy or more, and men older than that had fathered children, even before the advent of Viagra. And two? Well, he certainly didn't need Viagra. Soft was quite the opposite of the way Rhianna made him feel. He closed his eyes, growing hard as he thought of Monday evening, remembering their kiss. Remembering, above all, the way she had responded to it. No more resistance. He had tried and failed to interest her in anything other than a platonic relationship when they had first met. When she had married ... Dear God, he thought he had lost her for ever. But now – now he was in the running again. He could leave nothing to chance this time. *Had* left nothing to chance ...

Roly let down the legs of the chair with a thump. *Come on, man – concentrate! People are dying. We need to know why and how and who's responsible. Who or what ...*

Anna had difficulty finding a space in the visitors' car park. It felt decidedly odd to be back on campus after so long away. She took a deep breath as she locked the car, scanning the view in front of her. What did she expect? Nothing could change here. On the other, modern sites, perhaps, but this was the original building, now listed, and nothing could be done to change its outward appearance.

She walked across the car park, heading for Reception. She would have to sign in and obtain a sticker for her car unless she wanted it clamped. The grey, ivy-covered walls looked dull in the flat early morning sunlight, diffused, as it was, by an almost total covering of fat, dirty-coloured cloud. The rain was a steady drizzle, reflecting the dampening of her spirits on seeing the university again. *It's a good thing Philip didn't ask me back here to talk about the Swiffords project. I would never have taken it on, if he had.* She swung her briefcase from one hand to the other before she reached the gate-house. *Steady, Summers! Don't let it get to you.* She smiled as she turned right and began to walk down the long corridor with its drab walls concealed, for the most part, by notice-boards crammed with information. *So much for the paperless office. Never in a million years. Not in academia, at any rate. Oh – and they still haven't fixed the leaking roof, then.* She skirted round the bucket, strategically placed to catch the drips, which was surrounded by yellow signs warning of potential danger. And here she was. Reception. To which all visitors must report.

It was strange to think of herself as a visitor, after so many years here. Strange, but not – what was the word she was looking for? Not uncomfortable. *I'd rather be a visitor than an inmate.* She stopped herself short. What an odd term to have used! As if the place were a prison. *But that's precisely what it had become, by the time I cracked up. It wasn't just Guy and Jamie's deaths that caused that – oh no. It had been a long time coming, and the accident – what happened to them – just precipitated the inevitable. I should have got out long before I did. So why didn't I?* The answer to that question brought her back to Guy and Jamie once more, but she pushed them out of her mind, forcing herself to deal with why she was here this morning, and nothing else.

Moments later, her precious parking pass displayed on the dashboard, and an identity badge pinned to her coat, she was crossing the quadrangle to get to Philip's department. She'd survived this far. She could handle the rest. Bernice, the receptionist, had recognised her and greeted her warmly, commenting on how well she looked.

'You did the sensible thing – got out. It's worse than it ever was, Dr Summers. You wouldn't believe the cuts. How we manage, God only knows.'

'It's stalwarts like you that keep this place going,' Anna had replied.

'Maybe so. But even we stalwarts can't keep going indefinitely.'

Maybe the cloud of depression wasn't simply down to the weather and her own unhappy memories, after all. She came to the end of a corridor, stopped in front of a door and pulled her thoughts together.

'Come!' Philip's voice rang out in answer to her knock.

Taking a deep breath, she fixed a smile on her face and stepped inside.

'Rhianna!' Philip crossed the room and indicated a chair. 'You're looking well – much better than last time I saw you, if you don't mind me saying so.'

'Not at all. You're not the only one.' Anna sat down. 'So why the summons, Philip?' She had decided earlier to take the initiative.

'Summons? I wouldn't put it quite like that. I just thought – with all these dreadful things going on – well ... I just wanted us to liaise, so to speak. You're the one at the sharp end in all this. I need to know how you're doing.'

'With the project or the murders?'

'Both. It must be pretty scary, I would have thought. I don't want you feeling that you have to stick it out. No one could have foreseen these circumstances and I would quite understand if you'd sooner take a break and resume work once an arrest has been made.'

'And have the Misses Webb die quietly in their sleep in the meantime? Oh no, Philip. I think not.' Anna reached into her briefcase and brought out two folders. She handed over the first. 'A report of the work I've done so far. Obviously, I'm concentrating on the sisters first, as you asked, due to their age, but the potential is enormous. I'd really like to know more about the scope of your brief. And here ...' She handed over the second folder '... just to whet your appetite, is a mere fraction of what I've already done. I have a pile of tapes with me, too, that are going to take hours to transcribe. And believe me, Philip, we've barely scratched the surface.'

Philip looked in astonishment at the sheafs of paperwork. By God, Rhianna really had the bit between her teeth. And this might be precisely the opening he was looking for.

'Any major surprises?'

'Like what?'

Philip gave an embarrassed shrug. 'Well – with these murders and all – some clue to the Swiffords Curse, as I believe the tabloids are calling it.'

Anna shook her head. 'Unfortunately not, to date, though I do have an avenue to pursue.' She gave herself a mental kick. *I must ask the Misses Webb. If anyone's heard of it, they would have.*

'Rhianna –' Philip cleared his throat. He had to take the bull by the horns – there was far too much at stake, here. People's lives, as well as the reputation of his department. Not to mention his own reputation, of course. 'Rhianna –' He tried again. 'You wouldn't – how can I put this? You wouldn't hold anything back, would you? Perhaps because you weren't sure yet. Apart from our own interest in matters, if there were anything that could help the police investigation, for instance ...'

Anna looked at him blankly. 'If I had anything that could possibly have bearing on the cases, Philip, I'd give it to the police like a shot.' *And already have*, she added to herself, thinking of Karen Peterson's diary. 'Off the record, by the way – Roly Featherstone's been brought in as an adviser on the so-called occult aspects of what's been happening.' The two men had known each other for years, and Anna trusted Philip with the information.

'Good luck to him. He'll need a strong stomach, from what I've read so far. Look, Rhianna ...' Philip had made his decision. 'I'm going to level with you, and I expect, in return, that you are going to be absolutely honest with me.' He reached for the piece of paper to which he had transferred the words Stella Timpson had read over the phone to him. He read them aloud.

'*A most shameful and wicked episode in the Year of Our Lord 1732 and how it came to be unearthed on All Hallows Eve, 1888, in the village of Swifford Lea, as sworn by my own hand this day. A tale so fantastical that, had it been told to me by any person else, I should have believed them unbalanced of mind. Indeed, I am barely able to believe the veracity of my own senses, having always counted myself a man of both rational mind and superior intellect. How much more, then, is doubt bestirred when the fact of the matter is, that it was a dream that led to me to the unearthing of such hitherto buried deeds; a mere phantasm of the night. And yet the fact remains. What I dreamed was true, for upon waking I was compelled by the overwhelming reality and anguish of him who spoke to me to go and seek what he told me of in the place which, in such dream, he did show to me.*'

Philip stopped and looked at Rhianna, who was leaning forward, open-mouthed. She blinked and flapped her hand, impatience giving it flight.

'Well, go on!'

'You haven't heard or read this before?'

'Good God, Philip – no! Where did you get it?'

'What would you say to Stella Timpson?'

'Stella! But where – I don't understand . . .'

'Neither do I. She – apparently – believes we have it and have passed it on to the police. But if neither you nor I are in possession of it . . .'

'. . . then where and how did she get hold of it?' Anna finished the sentence for him, adrenalin coursing through her system. Stella bloody Timpson! This had to be a joke. 'It could be a hoax . . .' Her voice sounded doubtful, even to herself.

'My first thought,' Philip acknowledged. 'However, I don't believe we can take that risk. Because if it *isn't* . . .'

Anna nodded. 'The police have to be told about it.' She stood up and paced in a tight circle. 'Buggeration! Stella, for Christ's sake!'

'I know. So. You don't have it. I don't have it. I have to call the police.'

'Oh God! She could be sitting on an absolute bombshell!'

'Possibly more of a damp squib – always assuming it *isn't* a hoax. She says she has – what were her words?' Philip frowned in concentration. 'Yes. She said she has only the first two pages. Laughed about security here – obviously thought there was a leak.'

Anna chewed her lower lip. 'Someone wanting me off the project?'

'It's not impossible – not everyone has the faith in you that I do, after two years in the wilderness, so to speak. But it wouldn't be one of my direct team, I can assure you, and besides – we don't *have* the bloody document to leak.'

'Shit. She's going to lap it up. Either way, she wins.'

‘I don’t follow you.’

Anna sat down again and leaned towards Philip. ‘If it’s a hoax, she makes us look stupid. And if it’s not – well – she’s got one up on us, and we’re still none the wiser. What the hell is she playing at, Philip?’

They locked eyes before Philip shook his head. ‘I only wish I knew ...’

Fletcher Godfrey had enjoyed delivering the newspapers. It kept his mind off other, more serious business. For the most part, at any rate. The business of Emily and the vicar was bothering him. He would have to find out more, if he could, and providing he could do so without arousing suspicion. In his heart, however, he felt sick, suspecting that he knew all too well why Emily may have arranged to meet Reverend Fury. There could surely be only one reason, especially if she’d been hearing that bloody Voice. To unburden herself. At least, though – he clung to the faintest glimmer of hope – at least that might mean that she’d put nothing in writing. That she wanted to talk about it, perhaps. And the vicar was High Church enough that he’d have listened to her confession.

Fletcher wondered if she same sort of rules applied as to Catholic confession, but doubted it. A Catholic priest couldn’t have told the police about anything heard under the seal of the confessional –he knew that much from his own days on the Force. *Moot point, anyway. Whatever she did or didn’t tell him, neither of them lived to tell the tale. And nothing’s been found written down, otherwise Janice would be hauling me in. Still doesn’t begin to explain their deaths, though, does it?*

Only partly reassured, he turned left and thought about the last paper in his bag. Moaning Maurice’s. True to his word, he had left it till last, even though his route had taken him past the man’s house quite early in the round. *Bitch, bitch, whinge, whinge. Some folk are never happy unless they’ve got summat to moan about. People murdered in their beds, and all they’re bothered about is their sodding newspaper.* He dismounted and decided to take the short cut through the graveyard. Frank’s bike was a smasher – he might look at getting one of these himself. Amazing what a difference a few extra gears made. The saddle, though – he wouldn’t want one quite like Frank’s. Bit too razor-sharp on the old balls for his liking.

He propped the bike inside the wall while he shut the gate, then wheeled it along the path. *Right then. Let's get this over with. I'm more than ready for a nice mug of tea.* His feet crunched over gravel until he made a left turn, following a path of hard-packed earth which led through some of the earlier, table top tombs. *What the . . . ?* He stopped. Something was sitting on one of the graves – not the table tops, but the standard type with headstones, to his right. His peripheral vision had caught it, registering something amiss. He turned now, to get a better look. A dog? A cat? What the hell was it? And what was it that didn't seem right?

He moved four steps closer before his brain made sense of the optical data being fed to it, and when it did, Fletcher wished it hadn't.

Not a dog.

Not a cat.

Not moving.

A decapitated goat's head.

Chapter Twenty-nine

Anna drove back to Swifford Lea with mixed emotions. Part of her was exultant that the meeting with Philip had gone so well. Not only did he *not* want to pull her off the Swiffords project; he had also stated, explicitly, that he had every faith in her. *I'm not slipping. I* can *still produce the goods*. On the other hand, the business of Stella Timpson's interference bothered her greatly. *That bloody woman's been a thorn in my side for years, and the minute I'm back in the field, she strikes again. It's bad enough anyway, but if this alleged document is a hoax – some publicity stunt on her part – I'll bloody well kill the bitch.*

Still. The project was safe and her part in it was safe. Right now, that was all that mattered. Philip had given her the third degree about her personal safety, but she had quickly set his mind at rest. As she had pointed out, Swifford Lea itself had been untouched by the violence visited upon its sister villages and whilst she was living on her own, so to speak, so were an awful lot of other people – Maggie and Fletcher, for instance. She had also reassured him that contingency plans were in place and told him of Pete Barker's prompt reaction to the false alarm at Maggie's house. She had a land line as well as a mobile and was in the very heart of the village. All the incidents had taken place in isolated areas. From what she had gathered, the Petersons' home stood alone, as did Emily Parsons'. Emily, in any case, hadn't been killed there and her death, at least, was more likely to have been suicide than murder.

Anna frowned, thinking about what Roly had told her about the inside of Emily Parsons' house. How did the crucified sheep and more curse graffiti fit that theory? If Emily had been driven mad by the Voice, could she have daubed the walls herself? Crucified the sheep herself? How big was the sheep, she wondered? Right up until her postgraduate days, she had visited a friend's smallholding every summer and knew that different breeds came in different sizes. *I wouldn't like to try to get hold of one. Then again, I'm not a countrywoman, born and bred, and what was it Becky used to say about shearing sheep . . . ?*

Her mind drifted away in an effort to visualise the Herefordshire countryside she had so loved. Offa's Dyke, bold beneath the sky, in shades of brown and green, squat cottages nestling on its slopes like shrubs clinging close, swinging across the ridge-back rock. Some days had seen haze hanging, hiding detail while cockcrow and bird song rose and fell, harmonies intertwining above the murmur of breeze through bough. In the middle distance, trees and hedges wearing subtle shades of green, had painted a palette riotously rich in colour. Snapshot memories came to her now – dotted houses, cars, a bonfire, curling smoke coiling like a yawn. The bleat of lambs beneath hanging apple blossom. Gates and fences, peeping rooftops, patchwork pointers in the landscape. Raindrops, scattering dust, tapping at the panes of the conservatory in which she had taken shelter . . .

God! How I loved it there. Even toyed with the idea of living in the country myself. She reflected for a moment on how different her life might have been, had she done so. Surprised by the emotive strength of her memories, she realised that they, perhaps, were underpinning the attachment she was beginning to feel to Swifford Lea. *And what would I do with myself all day? How would I earn my living?* Thinking of the lyrical language that had somehow accompanied her mind's journey into the past, she told herself firmly that poets probably starve unless they have another source of income. *Besides, I'm not a writer. Not of stories or poetry, anyway. But books. Non-fiction. I had so many ideas in mind. What if . . . ?*

Shaking her head impatiently, she pulled herself firmly from the reverie into which she had fallen, switching back to what had propelled her there in the first place. *Smallholding. Becky. What did she say about shearing sheep? That was it – the secret, apparently, is in holding them firmly and flipping them on to their backs. They become docile. If Emily Parsons was used to them, it may not have been such a problem after all. So yes – it's at least feasible that Emily could have crucified the sheep. But the vicar? Could she have killed him? Back to square one ...*

She sighed and made a mental note to ask Roly more about the situation when she next spoke to him. That, in turn, had her running Monday evening through her mind again. How had *that* boundary been so suddenly crossed? After all these years, to move from plain and simple friendship to a far from platonic kiss ... Was this what people meant when they spoke of there being no such thing as true friendship between a man and a woman? She had never believed that, had always cultivated male as well as female friends. But Roly! Nothing had happened for years. Why now, then?

People change. Their lives change. Relationships are bound to change unless they're simply outgrown. But do I want *this kind of change in this particular relationship?* She tried to think the question through, but felt that she was wading through mud. Nothing seemed clear. *Except*, she told herself, *that the last thing I would want, would be to lead Roly up the garden path. I can't let that kind of thing happen again, except by conscious decision on my part.* She recognised her vulnerability. Maybe it was natural, coming out of the pain and withdrawal following the accident, that she should find strength and support in someone she'd known for so long, and yet it shocked her far more than her equally unexpected attraction to Adam Etheridge. She flushed, remembering the powerful physical reaction she'd had to him, especially when they'd been together in the fireplace, and shook her head in wonder. Why, after that – even though she wasn't going to pursue it, of course – why, after such a strong reaction to Adam, should she have kissed Roly?

Maybe I'm just a coward ... She glanced at the dashboard's digital clock, firmly closing her mind against further exploration of the subject. She should be back in Swifford Lea in plenty of time to sort out lunch for the Misses Webb. And with fresh stocks of tapes and film, she was itching to get back to work. That, at least, had to be a good thing and a healthy sign. *My interest in my subject has been sparked again. I've broken out of my self-imposed exile. Take it steady. Think carefully about what I want to do. Academia itself still feels wrong for me. But this – research – and being out and about once more – that feels good. So I need to give myself time to think about what I want to come next. Make no rash decisions.*

As she crested the hill that signalled for her the crossing of the boundary back into the Swiffords, Anna felt better than she had done in a very long time.

Fletcher Godfrey and Janice Mills sat in the kitchen of his house, nursing mugs of strong tea. Janice shook her head when Fletcher offered the whisky bottle, watching as he slopped a liberal measure into his own.

'I never understood people being driven to drink,' he told her, 'but I'm beginning to, now.'

'I've seen some things, Fletcher, but whisky in tea – ugh!' Janice shuddered.

'Yes, well – better than drinking it neat at this time of day.'

'There's several million Scots would disagree with you.'

Fletcher merely grunted before taking a gulp. He grimaced. 'And they'd be right. Jesus, Janice! What the hell is going on? I've lived here all my life. Thought I knew these villages. Thought I knew these people. And now, look! The whole situation is plain out of control.'

'It's amazing what folk get riled up about, Fletcher – you know that as well as me. Leylandii. Wind chimes. Now goats. I didn't think things would go this far, I have to say – even if Carol was threatening to kill them on Sunday.'

Fletcher ran his hand over his face. 'I can't believe it. I know the woman's a law unto herself. Right harridan, from all accounts, and upset just about everybody in the village one way or another since they moved here, but still – it's so extreme.'

'I know,' Janice acknowledged. 'But she's been at war with the Barkers since they arrived – and that was before they got the goats.'

'I hear they're denying everything and threatening to sue Pete for assault.'

'Yes. And no witnesses, this time. Not for him, at any rate. Carol's backing Bill's account of how Pete grabbed him by the throat.'

'But to kill with such savagery! It sounds daft, I know, what with them only being goats, but it was as bad as finding the vicar. And at least he wasn't bloody decapitated.' Fletcher stared speculatively at Janice for a moment. 'You don't think ... I mean, Christ knows what they used to behead the goats with, but the Petersons ... same sort of thing, wasn't it? An axe or something?'

'I know what you're getting at, Fletcher, and it's obviously crossed my mind. CID's, as well. They'll be giving them a right old grilling, and no mistake. But the goats – well, I don't condone it for one moment, but I can understand it insofar as it's been a long-running feud and the goats decimated their garden on Sunday. I can see the motive, is what I mean. But the Petersons?' She shook her head. 'I shouldn't think Bill and Carol ever even met them. Possibly never even heard of them, the Petersons not living here in Lea. So what would be the motive there?'

'Don't ask me. Seems to be far too much motiveless crime, these days. But yes, I take your point,' Fletcher conceded. 'And to be honest, can you see Bill and Carol behaving normally – normal for them, I mean – if they'd bloodbathed Seth and Karen?'

'No, I can't. Then again, I can't see them behaving normally after killing the goats, either. Not that they've had a chance – in public, I mean – with Pete finding what was left of them this morning. They're certainly protesting their innocence loud and clear down at the cop shop, though. Having said that, mind, I don't see who else could have done it. Who else would have wanted to.'

'You don't think it's the same bugger that killed the Petersons, then? Aside from the method, I mean, there's this curse business and what had crossed my mind was animal sacrifice. That's supposedly done in black magic rituals, isn't it?'

'So I've heard. But on the face of it – no. There was no graffiti, for a start. Neither in the outbuilding, where Pete found the goats' bodies, nor in the church or graveyard, where you found the heads.'

'I thought I was seeing things, to begin with. And when I got up close ...' Fletcher wrinkled his face in disgust. 'It was only when I ran to the bushes to be sick that I found the other one.'

'Sitting on the bench.'

'Aye. For all the world, looking as if it was gazing out over the gravestones.'

'You're not having a good time of it, are you?' Janice's words were more a statement than a question.

'No, I'm not. And neither are you. But it's small fry, isn't it, for us? The ones who are really having the hard time are them as has been winding up dead.'

Janice stood up and made ready to leave. 'Well, thanks for your help and thanks for the tea. Both much appreciated.'

'Any time, lass, you know that. Though I'd prefer to find no more dead bodies, human or otherwise.'

'You and me both.' Walking to the door between the kitchen and living room, Janice stopped and looked at what appeared to be fresh damage to the surrounding wall and frame. 'What happened here?'

'Oh ...' Fletcher gave an embarrassed shrug. 'I'm afraid I lost my rag a bit when I got home. Shock of it all, I suppose. Wound up taking it out on my surroundings.'

Janice pursed her lips. 'Well, I'm sure you can fix it yourself, but it you're feeling charitable, you might bear Adam Etheridge in mind.'

'Still losing work, is he?'

'Yes.'

Fletcher accompanied Janice to the front door. 'I'll never understand human nature.'

'I don't know anybody that does.' Janice got into her car and drove away.

Anna banged the Green Man knocker and inserted the key to the door of the Misses Webb's house. Immediately she opened it, her ears were assailed by noise. *What on earth ... ?*

Realising that it would be pointless to shout, she listened for a moment, before following the sound to its source. Puzzlement turned to shock when she pushed open the door of the Oriental Room to find the sisters, their backs towards her, sitting in front of a music centre which was thrusting out classical music at high volume. Just as she stepped forward, Alice turned and, seeing her, clutched her hand to her chest.

'I'm sorry if I made you jump –' It was pointless trying to compete with a full orchestra.

Fixing her with an icy stare, Alice picked up a remote control unit from the arm of the chair and pointed it carefully at the sound system, pressing a button with exaggerated care. The sound stopped.

'I'm sorry if I made you jump –' Anna tried again.

'Were you part of the conspiracy, too?' Alice's voice was bitter with accusation.

'I'm sorry? What conspiracy?'

Molly had turned and looked at Anna, her expression puzzled and full of trepidation. Alice swept out of the room, leaving Anna to follow in her wake.

'Alice, I . . .' Anna stopped dead in her tracks. Alice had come to a halt in the Arts and Crafts Room. Right in front of a wide-screen TV.

'Can you imagine the shock when we turned on this contraption to listen to the news last night?'

Anna opened her mouth and shut it again, mind working overtime. Where in God's name had they got the equipment from?

'I expect poor Mr Michaels thought we already knew. But we didn't. And that, I suspect, was down to Mrs Sally Arnold, who, if I have my way, will never set foot in this house again.'

Molly had followed Anna and now, leaning heavily on her walking frame, hovered in the doorway uncertainly.

'But who will look after us, Alice?' Molly's voice trembled.

'We shall look after ourselves, if necessary. Besides, I shall advertise for help. We used to have help, years ago. When Mother and Father ran the house. You remember, Molly – we had a housekeeper and a maid and a gardener.'

Molly looked uncertainly from her sister to Anna and back again. 'I'm not sure people work as servants any more, dear.'

'You've never been sure of anything, Molly Webb. That's your trouble. So –' Alice's eye was turned on Anna once again. 'I asked you a question, young woman. Were you part of this conspiracy of silence?'

Anna let out her breath. 'I don't believe it was a conspiracy, Alice. Certainly not in the way you might think. Sally merely thought . . .'

'Sally didn't think at all!'

'She thought you might be unduly alarmed by reading reports of the recent violence in the area and . . .'

'Recent violence?' Alice, ramrod straight, was trembling, whether from anger or fear, Anna wasn't sure. 'Dr Summers – from what we have managed to piece together, it seems that our vicinity is become akin to . . . akin to . . .' she struggled for the comparison '. . . The Bronx! Massacres. Murderers on the loose!

We could have been murdered in our beds!' Her voice rose to rival thunder.

Anna glanced at Molly, who was blinking away tears and nodding unhappily.

'Ladies,' she said, 'why don't you sit down and make yourselves comfortable, and I'll go and make a nice pot of tea. I think we need to talk about this properly. And I shall do my very best to set your minds at rest.'

Alice glared at her before turning and moving stiffly to one of the upholstered chairs. Molly shuffled forward, looking at Anna beseechingly.

'She's awful when she gets like this,' she whispered. 'She can be rather a bully, you know.'

Anna gave her arm a squeeze, then slipped past her and headed for the kitchen. *Oh SHIT! Of all the things to happen. How the hell am I going to calm them down?*

She worked swiftly and, having found an old hostess trolley at the back of the walk-in larder, wheeled it through to the sisters, laden with sandwiches, soup and tea, everything laid out on the best china. Hidden away on the bottom shelf under a napkin were Battenburg and ginger cakes.

'Would you like trays on your laps?'

'Certainly not. We shall sit at the table in a civilised fashion. The world may be going to hell in a hand basket around us, but our manners and customs are not. Come along, Molly.' Alice put her hand under her sister's elbow and helped her to her feet. Anna quickly transferred the meal to the dining table as the sisters made their way towards it.

'Well, do sit down! You're making the place look untidy,' Alice ordered, indicating a seat at the table.

Anna did as she was told, waiting until the sisters had begun to eat before attempting to smooth ruffled feathers.

'Would you please let me put things to you from Sally's perspective?' she asked.

'You may try.' Alice wasn't giving an inch.

'Look – when the Petersons were found dead, it was originally suspected that Seth Peterson had had a brainstorm and killed his daughter. It wasn't . . .'

'Tommyrot!' Alice scoffed.

'I beg your pardon?'

'Absolute tommyrot! If I'd heard that when it happened, I should have said that whoever forwarded that theory was the one having the brainstorm.'

'Why?'

'Why?' Alice repeated the question as if speaking to a recalcitrant child. 'They were butchered, were they not? As in, there was blood all over the place?'

Anna nodded, not wishing to embroider the detail.

'There you are, then – tommyrot! Seth Peterson was, I believe, the only person I have ever known who passed out at the sight of blood. Always did, right from infancy. So much as a pinprick of blood on his finger – or on anyone else's, for that matter, and he simply keeled over. So that would have put paid to that theory.'

Anna chewed her lip. 'That's very interesting. But the point is, that *was* one of the theories to begin with, and that aside, Sally didn't want you worrying that there was a murderer on the loose.'

'But there is, isn't there?' Alice persisted.

'Well, yes. But no one knew that to begin with.'

Alice shook her head. 'I would never have believed Sally Arnold to be so treacherous!'

'Treachery really doesn't come into it. She did what she thought was best at the time, to shield you from the shock.'

Before Alice had time to reply, Molly cut in. 'You can change the name of a place, but it doesn't do any good, you know.'

'I'm sorry?' Anna turned to her in surprise.

'The Peterson place. Crossways Cottage, they called it, but it used to be called The Gallows House. What good could come of living in a place like that?' The old woman shuddered. 'I wouldn't want to live in a place like that, would you? Especially not after Megan Painter's curse.'

'Balderdash!' Alice's voice was scathing. 'You've always been far too impressionable, Molly. It's all a nonsense.'

Anna's heart raced with excitement. 'What is this Megan Painter's curse?'

'Well, that's where she was hanged, of course. And uttered her curse.'

Alice snorted but Anna ignored her, excitement rising.

'The Peterson house? You're telling me *that's* where this woman died?'

'Megan Painter. That's what I just said. Except it was called

The Gallows House back then.' Molly seemed affronted by Anna's stupidity.

'But how do you know that? And do you know when it happened?'

Alice interrupted, waving her hand in a gesture of dismissal. 'It's just one of those things one learned as a child. And, if one had any sense, dismissed as the utter nonsense it is.'

'Yes, but I thought – with talk of brainstorms and all ...' Molly began.

'Well, you know what thought did!' Alice snapped. Turning to Anna, she asked, 'Would you mind fetching more hot water for the teapot?'

'Of course.' Anna stood up and left the room.

Alice waited a second before hissing at Molly, 'Whatever's the matter with you? She doesn't want to hear about that nonsense!'

'Yes, she did!' Molly protested. 'And I was only wondering if Marcus Beardsmore's account might be helpful.'

'Don't you dare!' Alice warned. 'We don't want *that* skeleton dragged out of the cupboard!'

When Anna returned, the subject of Megan Painter was closed and Molly made no further conversation at all.

Adam Etheridge looked round as he heard a car slow down on the road behind him, flushing slightly as he realised that Anna – Dr Summers – was winding down the window to speak to him.

'Hello, Adam – what's happened here?' She gestured to Bill and Carol's front window, which he was in the process of boarding up.

'Someone put a brick through it.'

'When? Why?'

He moved down the path and stepping on to the verge, where she had pulled up, bent to speak to her.

'When? No one knows for sure. But it was all right this morning. Why? Well ... you've been away, of course. Only just got back, have you?'

'A couple of hours ago. I went straight to the Misses Webb.'

'So you don't know, then.'

'What don't I know?' His roundabout manner was irritating her.

'About the goats.' He told her, being careful not to accuse Bill and Carol directly.

'Oh my God!' Anna stared at him blankly for a second, before shaking her head. 'I know she said on Sunday that she was going to kill them, but I never thought she was serious!'

'Well, somebody did,' Adam said, nodding at the damage.

'And no one saw who broke their window? In broad daylight?'

'Apparently not.'

'What did she do – poison them?'

Adam gave her a strange look before shaking his head. 'Chopped their heads off.'

'What?! Jesus, that's sick!'

'Quite. So was Pete, when he found their bodies this morning.' Adam stepped back from the car, wanting to change the subject. 'Maggie's back, by the way – she was looking for you.'

'God, I bet it's hit her hard! Pete and Pat, too, of course. I'll pop in and see her.'

'Might be best to leave it for a bit. She's not home at the moment, anyway – she's with Pat, at the pub. Pete and Bill and Carol are all over at Market Eaton, being questioned by the police.'

'God, what a mess!'

'Yes. Anyway – I've got work to do.'

'Right. Thanks for telling me, anyway.' As Adam walked back down the path, Anna called, 'Do you want a cup of tea, by the way? When you've finished?'

He turned and looked at her. 'Much obliged. I'll be round in a few minutes, then, if that's all right with you.'

It had taken Frank Arnold a while to manoeuvre his wife into the back seat of the car, but at last, he had her settled. He placed a Royal Stuart tartan rug over her legs before putting the crutches she'd been issued with into the rear foot well.

'You all right, Sal?' He adjusted the cushions behind her back.

'Thanks, Frank, yes.' Sally lifted the rug to look at the plaster cast, embellished with blue and red stripes. 'What a performance, eh?'

Frank checked that the rear doors were locked before getting into the driver's seat. 'Well, at least it's not as boring as the plain white ones they used to put on. And the most important thing is, you're all right.'

'You must be run off your feet, though, and I'm not going to be much use while this thing's on.'

'Don't you worry. We'll manage. Mavis is doing a grand job, helping out, and Fletcher's taken over the paper round for the duration.' He pulled out of the hospital car park and headed for the centre of Market Eaton, where he could pick up the road to Swifford Lea.

Sally listened in silence as Frank brought her up to date with what was happening, furrowing her brow in concentration before asking questions.

'We have to finish it off, Frank; the sooner, the better.'

'I know.' He slowed to a crawl in the marketplace, buses disgorging passengers, shoppers cutting through the traffic willy-nilly. 'They really ought to sort out this congestion. Getting bloody ridiculous.'

'I thought they were going to put traffic lights in at the junctions with Hope Street and Chance Street.'

'So they said. But it's still all talk at present.'

Frank swore as a cyclist almost scraped the side of his car, weaving in and out of the traffic. 'Bloody idiot!' He watched as the man dismounted at the kerb and wheeled his cycle through a knot of pedestrians. Suddenly, he stiffened, like a dog on point. Sally sensed it immediately.

'What, Frank?'

She twisted round awkwardly, trying to see out of the near side window behind her head. The cyclist now forgotten, Frank's attention was fully focused on a man coming out of a shop, carrying a large basket of artificial flowers.

'The Witchfinder General,' Frank spat. 'Roland bloody Featherstone.'

Chapter Thirty

By the time Anna returned to Broomwood House to make tea for the Misses Webb, they appeared to be in a much better frame of mind.

'I have been thinking on what you said earlier,' Alice told her, 'and whilst I still believe Sally was quite wrong, I do believe I can understand her motivation.'

'I'm pleased to hear that,' Anna smiled. 'She really was only doing what she thought was in your own best interests and trying to protect you.'

'Yes. Well. You'd better come on through. And you don't need to make a meal for us, after all – Sheila is here.'

Anna turned in surprise as a woman of around her own age came into the hall. The sisters disappeared into the Arts and Crafts Room.

'You must be Dr Summers,' the woman smiled. 'I'm Sheila Finney – Sally Arnold's niece. Uncle Frank picked her up from the hospital a little while ago, so I'm back on duty with the sisters, so to speak. Will you have a bite to eat with the old girls? Their invitation, I might add. I gather you had a bit of a performance with them earlier. Dear Lord, I nearly died when I came in and found they'd got a new telly and all!'

'That makes two of us!'

'Well, if you can get them chatting and keep their minds off the murders, all to the good.'

'I'll do my best,' Anna promised, as she went through to join them at the dining table. 'It's so nice of you to ask me for tea.'

'Our pleasure, my dear, and the least we can do considering what transpired at lunchtime.' Alice coughed discreetly. 'I fear I was rather rude.'

'Not at all. Your reaction was quite understandable, given the circumstances.'

'It's so nice to have someone else here at a mealtime,' Molly told Anna. 'To eat with us, I mean. It's been such a long time – just the two of us. We so used to enjoy company, didn't we, Alice?'

'We used to enjoy a lot of things, dear.'

Anna used this turn of the conversation to remind the sisters of their promised excursion into Market Eaton the following morning, asking if they still wanted to go.

'Oh my goodness, yes!' Alice's face lit up in anticipation. 'I'd forgotten all about that. How delightful! What time do we need to set out?'

'We shall need to leave no later than 9 a.m. to get you there in time for your optician's appointment.'

'I must write that down and put the note by our bed, so that we don't forget.' Alice frowned. 'Didn't I write that down before? I'm sure I did, but I don't remember where I put it.'

'Don't worry.' Anna pulled an A4 pad from her briefcase. 'I'll do it now.'

'In nice big letters, dear, if you don't mind. Hopefully, we shall be able to use smaller ones after getting our new spectacles.'

'Oh, I can't wait!' Molly breathed.

As Anna wrote the note, Sheila knocked and came into the room to clear the table, knocking over the salt pot as she did so. Anna watched as she scooped up the grains and threw them over her left shoulder.

'I'll bring in the Hoover, don't worry! Sorry – I know it's just a superstition, but still ...' She smiled and gave an embarrassed shrug as she left.

'Funny things, superstitions,' Anna observed.

'Never had time for them myself.' Alice's tone was brisk. 'But Molly knows lots of them, don't you, dear?'

Molly nodded, turning to Anna. 'Would that sort of thing interest you? For your project? We can talk now, if you like.'

'Absolutely!' Anna got up. 'I'll just go and get the recording equipment.'

Molly was a mine of information. It was unlucky, she said, to replace one's chair neatly under the table after eating one's first meal in someone's home; elder should never be cut, but myrtle, placed on the chimney stack, would protect a house from lightning. Similarly, mistletoe tied to the head of the bed would protect one from nightmares, whilst holly should be planted close to a house to protect against enchantment or trouble from witches. Dogs were able to see the Angel of Death, which is why they howled as an omen, whereas to meet a frog in the street foretold the unexpected arrival of money.

'You do know about eating geese?' Molly asked.

'Being lucky to eat goose on Michaelmas Day?'

'Ah – you do! Eat a goose on Michaelmas Day and you shall have plenty during the coming year.'

'But do you know *why* it's supposed to be lucky?' Anna pressed.

'Well, of course! Good Queen Bess was eating goose when she was told of Drake's victory over the Spanish!'

'Correct!' Anna laughed.

The old woman smiled to herself, then leaned forward. 'I know lots of love lore, too, you know.'

'Oh, really, Molly!' Alice rolled her eyes. 'There's nonsense and there's frou-frou nonsense!' She stood up. 'I shall go and listen to some music if you're going to spout further drivel!' She turned to Anna. 'We have a rather fine recording of Renaissance works by Susato Danserye. 1551, you know, and I'm told these compact discs don't scratch the way gramophone records used to.' With a toss of her head, she left the room.

'Oh dear ...' Anna looked at Molly.

'Oh, don't mind her! She gets in a huff, you know. Never got over her inamorato, and I think it's made her bitter. What's that phrase in the Bible?' She thought for a moment. 'Ah, yes – I think it hardened her heart. Such a shame, you know.'

'I'm sure.'

'But love lore is such fun, my dear. Shall I tell you what I know? Spells and all? And flowers, my dear – the language of love and courtship – all in code, of course. I know there are some fairly standard collections, but here in the Swiffords ... Oh yes, I can tell you what flowers a young man should present if he wishes to court you. And the flowers you would give him in return to indicate yes or no.' Molly's eyes twinkled, as she began to talk ...

Stella Timpson was in a foul mood as she drove home, made even worse by the fact that she triggered a speed camera on the way. How in God's name had her provocation of Philip Jackson backfired so badly? *The little shit! I didn't have a clue that he was bluffing when I dangled that bloody part-document in front of him.* She certainly did now. The police had turned up – in her office, for God's sake – and given her a thorough grilling about it. Even then, she had thought that her moment of glory had come. Helping the investigation into the Swiffords situation. Egg all over Philip's face because she had information that he and his useless researcher didn't. But no. Even that possibility had been snatched away from her. A bloody gagging order, no less. Everything ultra-confidential because of the delicacy and seriousness of the situation. The police were sure she would understand. And they had taken everything away, in plastic bags, *and* taken her fingerprints to be able to eliminate them when it came to the forensic examination. The fact that she had already transferred the information to a file in her computer was of little comfort.

'Ha!' She snorted out loud, still seething at the insult. *So. Philip didn't have the document and neither did the Blessed Rhianna. Which raises further questions ...* She allowed her thoughts to run on. *No one in Philip's department could leak a document he didn't have. So who* did *send it to me and why?* Her one small consolation in the matter had been that the police questioning had allowed her to cast aspersions on Rhianna Summers' reputation. *In confidence, of course.* She allowed herself a smile. *Unstable. Incompetent. And I'm not the only one that thinks that, she had pointed out, given the tenor of the letter that accompanied the first document extract. Oh yes. If that cow thinks she can just come strolling back into academia and cross swords with me, she can bloody well think again.*

Still. Back to the letters. She should have realised from the start that they may not have come from Philip's department – the evidence had been staring her in the face. She had automatically checked the envelopes when she'd received them, and what she'd seen had made no sense at all – even less, now. She had been so eager to believe . . . but no – the damn things had been postmarked in Market Eaton. Which raised the interesting possibility that they had been posted in the Swiffords themselves . . .

Anna's mobile rang as she walked towards the village shop after leaving the Misses Webb.

'Roly! How are you?'

'Fine. But how are *you*? I've been thinking about you – about the meeting with Philip, how did it go?'

'Very well. But some quite odd things have come up – oh God! Where to start?' Anna's brain kicked into overdrive, trying to remember everything that had happened. 'Stella Timpson's been sticking her oar in and it looks as if she may have information pertinent to what's going on. Then – have you heard about the goats? And Molly Webb just told me that the Petersons' place used to be called The Gallows House, and that's where Megan Painter died!'

'Whoa! Whoa! I think we'd better meet. Why don't I come over later? We obviously need to talk at some length, by the sound of it.'

'I think that's a good idea.' Anna laughed, embarrassed by the rush of words that had spilled out in her eagerness to tell Roly what she knew. 'At least I can slow down and get my thoughts in order by then!'

'Fine. I'll be with you at eight. Tell you what – why don't I book a table at The White Hart?'

'I'm not sure they'll be serving food tonight ...' Anna's voice was dubious, thinking about Pete being taken to Market Eaton.

'Leave it with me. Got to go – see you later!'

Putting her mobile away, Anna quickly covered the last few yards to the shop. Walking inside, she made her way straight to the counter and asked Mavis if Frank was around.

'He's with Sally, upstairs.'

'Could you ask him if I could have a word, please? It's about the Misses Webb.'

'Oh dear. Are they all right?'

'They're fine now, but I do need to tell Frank and Sally what's been happening.'

Moments later, upstairs in their living room, Anna realised they'd already got the gist from Sally's niece. Sally was sitting sideways on the sofa, legs outstretched and with her crutches propped nearby.

'I'm so sorry,' Anna began. 'I had no idea that the solicitor had turned up with a TV and music centre in his boot. I just assumed they wanted to talk business with him.'

'There's little you could have done anyway,' Frank conceded.

'Well – had I known, I could have asked him to stall them or something.'

Sally, her face pale against the colourful upholstery, pulled a face. 'Sheila says they gave you a really hard time.'

Anna shook her head. 'It wasn't that bad. They were most cross with you, I'm afraid. Thought it was all a conspiracy. But I had a long talk with them and they seem a lot calmer, now. And I'm taking them to Market Eaton tomorrow to get new glasses and have Molly's spare denture repaired. The solicitor is apparently coming over while we're out to supervise cable TV installation.'

'Perhaps as well if you pop over and have a word with him, Frank,' Sally told her husband.

The big man nodded. 'We're going to have to make alternative arrangements for their lunch while Sal's out of action. They don't mind me, but it could get tricky, what with the shop and looking after Sal.'

'It must be a nightmare, with these stairs.'

'It is,' Sally grimaced. 'I feel like a proper baby, having to be carried up and down. There's no way I'd dare try on these crutches.'

'I don't mind doing their lunches while I'm here. I mean, I'm going to see them every day, anyway, so it's no trouble.'

'Are you sure? I mean, it's not exactly what you came here for, is it?' Frank said.

'All part of the job. Anyway, I'll leave you to it.' Anna turned to go, then turned back as a thought struck her. 'Oh, by the way – you've lived here all your lives, haven't you? It's just that Molly Webb said something at lunchtime – about the Peterson place being where someone called Megan Painter died. And that there's a Megan Painter's curse. Did you know that?'

Sally and Frank exchanged a startled glance. 'No. However did she come to hear that?' Sally struggled to sit up straighter and Frank placed an extra cushion behind her back.

'I'm not sure.' Anna shook her head. 'I got the impression that Alice didn't like her talking about it – she said something about it being simply one of those things you heard as a child, but it might be important – you know, with all this curse stuff being bandied about. I just wondered if it were true, and if the police should be told.'

'I've never heard anybody else in the village talk about it, have you, Frank?' Her husband shook his head. 'And the sisters wouldn't take kindly to having the police round, asking questions.'

'Janice Mason's a woman, though,' Anna pointed out. 'They might be all right with her.'

'Maybe. Still ...' Frank stroked his beard. 'Perhaps if you probed gently?'

'I'll try, certainly. Though I'd best get Molly on her own, I think. Well – let's try again – I *will* leave you to it, this time!'

Frank walked down the stairs with her. 'I have to get back to the shop. Mavis needs to be getting home now. Oh – have you heard about the goats, by the way/'

'Yes. Adam told me – he was boarding up Bill and Carol's window.'

'I bet poor Fletcher's wishing he'd never taken on the paper round. Still, if it hadn't been him, it would have been someone else.'

'Fletcher? What's he got to do with it?' Puzzlement showed on Anna's face.

Frank explained about the goats' heads.

'Bloody hell!' She didn't know what to say.

Frank let her out of the back door and told her he'd let her know the result of his talk with the solicitor the following day. He watched her walk down the path, then ran quickly back upstairs to his wife.

'What do you make of that?'

Sally looked at him for a long moment, considering her reply.

'It's never been public knowledge. Nobody else should know about the connection between the Peterson place and Megan Painter. And nobody should know about Megan Painter's curse. *Nobody*, other than one of us. I simply don't understand it. And what the *hell* is Dr Summers' part in all this?' She struggled to her feet, hopping on one leg until she was safely balanced between her crutches.

'What do you want to do, Sal?'

'Keep an even closer eye on her, that's what. Especially since the Witchfinder General is so close. And a Council meeting tonight, Frank. We have to get a move on.'

Anna had only just taken off her coat and put the kettle on when there was a tap at the kitchen door.

'Maggie! Come on in. How are you? And how's Jack?'

'Jack's fine. Staying with my sister till Friday night. Wants to be back for his Saturday job. I think he's right, really – I mean, life does have to go on, doesn't it, and I think it'll be good for him to get back into some sort of routine. Like me coming back so I can get on with work. Gives you some structure and takes your mind off all the shit that's going on. But, that aside – well, I wouldn't mind putting the rest of Bill and Carol's windows through. Just for starters.' Her face was grim.

'I know. It's just awful. Isn't it?' Anna shook her head. 'I couldn't believe it when Adam told me.'

'He's not having the best of times, either, is he?' Maggie observed. 'I saw him earlier – came round looking for you and he was in here, working. Said you was away until lunchtime-ish. Nothing horrible for you, I hope?'

'No. Just dropping stuff back at university. Do you want coffee? I was just making some.'

'Lovely – thanks. The day I turn down a cup of coffee, I'll be either ill or dead.' Maggie sat at the kitchen counter as Anna warmed the cafetière. 'I just can't believe what's been going on while I've been away. Pat's distraught about the goats. Me, too, to be honest.' Her face darkened as she thought about Bill and Carol. 'Evil bitch! Just let me get my hands on her, that's all . . .'

'It's just going to escalate things further, though, isn't it? If you do?'

'Escalate? I'd like to run 'em out of the village!' Maggie looked at Anna and groaned. 'I know, I know! I can see that look in your eyes! Everybody's telling me to calm down. Even Adam, bless him. What a load of wimps, eh?'

Anna poured the coffee. 'I don't follow you.'

'Haven't you heard? People cancelling work he was supposed to do, fobbing him off? All because he got interviewed by the police?' Maggie reached for the sugar bowl. 'He's worked his socks off, building up the business with his dad, and when his wife cleared out . . .'

'I didn't realise he was married.' Anna felt stupid for saying it, remembering the warmth, the electricity that had passed through her when she had stood with him inside the dining-room fireplace. And this afternoon, when he called round for a mug of tea . . . The recollection of his eyes on her, their depths as blue as a Greek ocean ... *Don't even think it, Summers*, she warned herself. *He's not for you. Different worlds, and if he* is *involved in something weird* ... Maggie's surprised voice brought her out of her reverie.

'No reason why you should. And he isn't any more. She run off. Left him for ... someone else. Doesn't go down well in a place like this.' Maggie kept on stirring her mug as if her anger could be vented by doing so. 'Oh, they're used to it with incomers, of course, but the Swiffords born and bred, they're a different breed. This may be the twenty-first century, but they still tend to marry for keeps. It was difficult for him. Especially ... well, never mind, eh?' She finally stopped stirring and set the spoon aside. 'I'm just bloody pissed off that he's going through the mill again.'

'I think everyone is, from the sound of it.' Anna sighed.

''Ere – what you doing later?' Maggie asked.

'I have a friend coming round,' Anna told her. 'That's a point – you don't know whether food's off or on at The White Hart tonight, do you? He was talking about booking a table, but with Pete ...'

'Oh, it's on,' Maggie assured her. 'Pete's been back a while. No sign of the goat-slayers yet, though. Just as well for them, in my opinion. The less we see of them, the better. I don't know how they can hold their heads up.' She finished her coffee and stood up. 'I'd better leave you to it, if you've got company coming.'

Anna walked with her the short distance to the door. 'Well, if you're in the pub later, come and join us for a drink. Oh, and Maggie ...'

'Yes?'

'If you're nervous about being in the house on your own until Jack comes back, the offer of the spare room still stands.'

'God! I hadn't even thought about it, what with the goats and all.' Maggie slapped her forehead. 'Are you sure?'

'Of course. It's only for a couple of nights and kills two birds with one stone, doesn't it? If you sleep here, neither of us is alone.'

'Sure I won't be cramping your style or anything?' Maggie grinned. 'You did say it was a male friend coming later?'

'"Friend" being the operative word!' Anna laughed. 'It's not that kind of relationship.' *Or it wasn't*, she told herself, thinking again of Monday night. *I can't let anything develop between me and Roly. It would ruin a perfectly good friendship*. She was suddenly glad that she'd asked Maggie to stay. It would give her an excuse if things did get heavy. 'He'll be here at eight,' she told Maggie, 'so if you want to bring some things over before then . . .'

'My washing kit and stuff? I'll whip and fetch them now. Then I can be out of your way. And thanks, Anna – I really appreciate it.' Maggie beamed a broad smile before walking briskly down the path.

Anna, closing the door behind her, turned and glanced at the kitchen clock. It might be best if she tried to marshal her thoughts in preparation for Roly, as promised. *Stella. Her so-called document. The goats. What Molly said about the Petersons' house . . .* She went through to the dining room, where her laptop sat on the table and booted it up. *Let's get it down in writing. That always makes things easier . . .*

At eight o'clock sharp, she was startled by the ring of the doorbell. Good God! Where had the time gone? Flustered, she went to answer it. *Hell! I'm nowhere near ready! I haven't even had a shower!*

'Rhianna!' Roly's voice was warm, but Anna stepped back in surprise, unable to see him through the huge dried flower arrangement he was carrying.

'Roly! Come in! I'm so sorry – I was so engrossed with what I was doing . . .'

He stepped inside and, lowering the flowers, smiled and leaned forward to kiss her cheek.

'These are for you. To celebrate the success of your meeting with Philip.'

'Oh, Roly! You shouldn't have! Thank you!' Anna felt her face flush and, picking them up, looked around for somewhere to display them.

'I thought dried ones would be best – you can take them home with you when you're finished here.'

'Thank you!' Anna repeated, finally deciding to place them in the open hearth of the sitting room. 'I completely lost track of the time. I never even heard your car.'

'That's because I parked at The White Hart. The table's booked for nine, by the way. I thought that would give us time to talk privately about the latest developments.'

Anna nodded. 'Good. There's such a lot to tell you. Oh, Lord – and only an hour, too! I really need to shower and change . . .'

'Why don't you do that now? If we can't fit everything in, I can always come back here later.'

'OK. I'll be as quick as I can. Help yourself to tea or coffee – all fairly obvious in the kitchen.'

'I will.' He started to cross towards it, but as soon as he heard her footsteps overhead, turned back to the sitting room, closing his eyes and breathing hard. *Dear God! Someone had been at it again! The atmosphere was barely breathable.* He had to get rid of this influence and quickly, before Rhianna was sucked in to the workings of the other side. He heard the thump of Rhianna's shoes hitting the bedroom floor, shortly followed by her light footsteps and the sound of water gurgling through pipes. Good. She was unlikely to come downstairs and disturb him. But he didn't have long.

I won't need long ... Mouth set in a determined line, he moved to the centre of the room and began his work.

All in all, Roly was feeling happier by the time they had left for The White Hart. He had had time to counteract the magical working that had been put in place before Rhianna had come downstairs, and was aware that his rather more permanent tactics, so carefully pre-organised, would now have a chance to work. The pub was packed, people thronging the bar and heated debate taking place about the killing of the goats. Roly shook his head and glanced at Rhianna as he ordered their drinks. They had discussed the matter themselves before leaving April Cottage.

'I don't understand it,' she had said. 'Maybe I'm just not that raw when it comes to hatred. I mean, if I were Carol, yes, I'd get steamed up, and I can just about get my head around her killing them, but well – maybe I'm just too squeamish. I think I would have poisoned them.'

'Quite. Which is just one of the reasons I don't believe she did it,' Roly had told her.

'But who, then?' Rhianna had asked.

'I think it's rather more serious than a neighbourly feud ...' he had begun.

'Connected to the murders? But how? Why?'

'You have to understand, Rhianna – however alien it is to your own way of thinking – that people into the dark side of the occult use blood as a tool. To raise power.'

'That's disgusting!'

'They wouldn't share your view. Life and power is in the blood. It has to be fresh, however, and there are those who would also add that, the younger the victim – animal or human – the more power can be obtained. And goats, of course, have long been associated with the devil.'

Rhianna had sat back and nodded. 'I've seen pictures of the devil represented as a goat or goat-like figure.'

'Quite. And the heads being severed and left in the graveyard – well, it's another challenge to the church. A direct one. And that would tie in, too, with the vicar's missing cassock.'

'What?' Rhianna had leaned forward, her damp hair giving her face an endearingly elfin look.

'Not public knowledge, so don't repeat it,' Roly had warned. 'Reverend Fury was old school High Church. Always wore his cassock. His housekeeper confirmed that he was wearing it when he left the vicarage on the morning of his death. When his body was recovered, however, it was missing. He was in mufti, so to speak.'

'But why would anyone remove his cassock?'

'For ritual use. Desecration.'

'Black masses and the like?'

'That's about the size of it.'

'What do the police make of it?'

'They're bearing it in mind, of course.' Roly had paused, making a sound of exasperation. 'But going back to the goats – I just wish there were some way I could prove it, get it out into the open. From what you've told me, vigilante action is likely to escalate against Bill and Carol Davenport, with feeling in the community running so high. It might not be just their windows at risk, next time.'

'I know,' Rhianna had grimaced. 'And they weren't exactly popular, even before the trouble with the goats. It's all so ... so – I don't know – *mediaeval*, somehow.'

Roly knew that she had difficulty with the entire concept of the supernatural and had stressed once again, that the reality of it – or otherwise – was not the main issue. 'It's what these people *believe* that matters,' he had told her. 'And that, I know you can understand. Think of the Flat Earth Society; Galileo being persecuted because he believed the earth went round the sun at a time when our planet was considered the centre of the universe; the

Inquisition burning the bodies of heretics in order to save their souls. It's the mind-set that's the issue here.'

Rhianna had nodded her agreement. They had gone on to examine Stella Timpson's unexpected finger in the pie, Roly assuring her that he would be looking into it simply because it appeared to have bearing from the point of view of Megan Painter's curse. His interest had been most aroused, however, by what she had to tell him concerning Molly Webb's comments earlier in the day.

'... and you say the Arnolds claim never to have heard of this connection between the Peterson house and the place of Megan Painter's execution?'

'Apparently not. It may well be pure hearsay. I'm inclined to think it may be the old bogeyman routine at work,' Rhianna had said.

'Then there must be others who were told the tale!' Roly had leaned across the table in excitement, squeezing her hand. 'And,' he had continued, 'you must question Molly further. It would be far better for you to do so than have formal police involvement – at this stage, at least.'

'I know, and I did try.' Rhianna's face had betrayed her frustration. 'After Alice shut her up, I had time alone with her – she was regaling me with all kinds of superstitions, particularly as regards love lore and spells through which to see visions or have dreams of your future partner – you know the sort of stuff. Most of it, I'd heard before, of course, but there were one or two things that I think are definitely local. I couldn't stop her in full flow, but just as the opportunity arose to get back to the subject, Alice reappeared, telling her that they had to have an early night in preparation for their day out tomorrow.' Rhianna had rolled her eyes at the recollection. 'I could have screamed! Sod's law, isn't it?'

Roly had nodded, adding, 'Still, you must try again as soon as possible. I think, however, that I should at least raise the matter with the investigating team.'

Rhianna, unhappily, had agreed. 'You will stress how important it is that a female officer is used if they do think it necessary to question the sisters? Preferably Janice Mills. At least they know her, so it wouldn't be yet another strange face to take on board. They've been quite rattled by the shock of everything and at their age ...'

'Of course. In any case, as you say, it may not even be true.'

'But if someone *believes* it is ... if they used it as some kind of stage-management ... But how did they know?'

'We'll get to the bottom of it, Rhianna,' Roly assured her. 'We have to.' He had squeezed her hand again, willing her to believe him.

'I know. I know everyone's working overtime on these cases. But can you crack it before this bastard strikes again?'

Not a good note, perhaps, on which to have left the house. And now, the pub was alive with argument and threats of retribution. At least upstairs, in the restaurant, the atmosphere was more civilised. As they descended to the bar again after their meal, Roly touched Rhianna's shoulder.

'You know, things could get pretty ugly when the Davenports get back. If you want me to stay the night ...'

'Thanks, Roly, but I'll be fine.' She flashed a smile at him over her shoulder. 'Maggie Taylor's staying over until her son comes back from London. Oh – speak of the devil – there she is – let me introduce you ...'

Chapter Thirty-one

Dead of night. Frost crept over the ground, its hoary breath leaving a creeping silver trail in its wake as it slithered over the slumbering landscape.

April Cottage stood blank-eyed before him, black and silent beneath a satin, star-sprinkled sky, surrounded by uneasy silence.

Eyes accustomed to the darkness now, his coat was no defence against the curling fingers of cold that swirled up through the ground to seep into his limbs, stiffening muscle and chilling bone. He resisted the urge to move. Concentration was all.

Will.

Visualisation.

Power.

A tug of war was taking place, himself at one end, the enemy at the other; representatives of opposing forces.

Darkness. And light.

But this was no game. The stakes were far too high.

In between them, dangerously unaware of the battle being fought, was the prize each sought to win.

Rhianna Summers.

Chapter Thirty-two

Breath.

Deep.

Slow.

Delicious.

Incense breathing its way into her lungs, suffusing her body with weightlessness.

Her mind with clarity.

Her heart with love.

Hanging, hanging, hanging …

Drifting.

Sensual.

Sensuous.

Leaden limbs coming alive, tingling.

Pheromones. Lightning coursing down to the depths of her, waking her, shaking her with its electric charge until her vagina was wet, vulva glistening, ready, ready, aching with the wanting, the heat of desire burgeoning, unbearable, aching for release.

Yes . . . Yes . . . Oh God . . . Please . . . Yes . . . Please . . . Now . . .

Faint.

In the background.

A note. More notes.

Music.

'*Don't listen. Don't let them fool you. Trust me, my love …*'

Still it persists.

Memory stirs.

The Chasm. The Abyss.

Danger. *Danger!*

'Sshhh! No. They can't touch you now. I'm here. You are safe with me . . .'

Faint.

In the background.

Sight. Unclear.

A figure, calling, calling, calling her name . . .

It echoes, bouncing, doubling, beseeching.

Fading . . .

I have to . . . what do I have to do?

'Nothing, my love. Nothing, but be safe. With me.'

Chapter Thirty-three

Thursday November 17th

There's a little green urinal to the north of Waterloo ... *What?* Anna shook her head beneath the spray of the shower and grinned. She hadn't heard that parody since her undergraduate days. It seemed to be running through her head like a litany since she'd opened her eyes this morning. Oh well. At least she'd had a good night's sleep.

As she dressed, she frowned slightly, trying to catch the recollection of a dream which teetered tantalisingly on the edge of memory. No. It had gone. She turned to go downstairs, then caught herself. The flowers! Roly had come back to the house with her and Maggie for a quick coffee last night and, just as he was leaving, had picked up the dried flower arrangement.

'Might be an idea to keep it in your bedroom during the night. That's when most falls of soot happen, and with work on the chimney going on ...'

So here they were. Should she take them back downstairs? No, she decided. They looked so beautiful on the antique pine chest of drawers, she'd leave them where they were. It had been good to see Roly again. His presence had somehow seemed ... what? Like a cloak wrapped round her. Protective. She felt warmed inside by the thought. *I could do far worse than to marry Roly. He knows me. Likes me. Respects me – even if we do disagree on some things*. Marry *Roly?!* She pulled herself up with a jolt. Whatever was she thinking of? Talk about trying to run before you can walk!

Her thoughts were not the only thing that had run away with her, she decided, as she almost missed her footing on the stairs.

Watch out! Don't want to do a Sally! She put the kettle on, slotted bread into the toaster, as Maggie bustled into the kitchen behind her, dressed and ready to go.

'Sure you don't want breakfast?' Anna asked. 'A cup of coffee at least?'

'No. I'm fine, really. Got plenty of stuff at home. Have a good day with the old girls, and I'll see you later.'

Half an hour later, Anna pulled up in front of Broomwood House ready to collect the Misses Webb. Would they be up? What if they'd overslept, or forgotten? She needn't have worried. They were raring to go, excited as children by the prospect of their day's outing.

'Oh, this brings back memories, doesn't it, Molly?' Alice, resplendent in a tweed suit, silk blouse and a hat looking as if it dated from the 1950s, could barely contain her delight. 'We used to motor all over Britain, you know! I don't expect you've seen our car?'

'I didn't know you still had one.' Anna was thrown by the remark and sincerely hoped they were not expecting her to take them in some clapped-out old banger.

'It doesn't work any more.' Alice shook her head sadly. 'Such a shame. But Frank Arnold keeps it cleaned and polished as a new pin. Come – I'll show you.'

Leaving Molly behind, Anna followed Alice round the side of the house to an old, gabled garage attached to the main building. Alice produced a huge bunch of keys from her handbag and unlocked the double doors.

'Here we are.' She reached for a switch and the dark interior was flooded with light.

Anna blinked and looked at the shape in front of her, hidden beneath a cover.

'Shall I?' Anna offered and Alice nodded, moving back out of her way. Rolling back the material, Anna gasped as the car was revealed. *Oh my God! Some old banger ... !*

'Isn't she a beauty?' Pride shone from Alice's face, vibrated in her voice as she moved forward to stroke the bonnet lovingly. 'I can't tell you the pleasure we had from her! Jessica – that's what we called her. And the miles we did! She never let us down. Not once, although we were, of course, members of the Automobile Association.'

'Oh, my word!' Anna ran her hand over the bonnet. 'She's a Jaguar, isn't she?'

'Indeed she is. The XK150. We went to Cornwall every year. And to the Scottish Highlands. In between times, we visited everywhere from the Lake District to the Lincolnshire fens. And the coast of Northumbria – my dear, it's simply magnificent! Have you been?'

Anna shook her head.

'Oh, you must! We have lots of photographs. Yes. Dear Jessica! We were so sorry to have to give up motoring. It wouldn't be safe, I'm afraid. We were reluctant, but, well, to tell the truth, the day we parked her in Market Eaton and couldn't find her again ...' Alice shook her head sadly. 'But never mind. You can be our chauffeuse today.'

'I'm afraid I have nothing as wonderful as Jessica,' Anna confessed as she replaced the cover, 'but I'll do my best ...'

Maggie was checking her e-mails when a thunderous hammering started on her door. *What the ... ?* She moved swiftly to answer it, irritated by its relentless persistence.

'All right! I'm coming! Bleedin' hell!'

She yanked it open and came face to face with Carol Davenport.

'You fucking bitch!' Carol, red-faced and eyes bulging, waved a plastic bag in front of Maggie's face.

'What the hell are you talking about?' Maggie's shoulders shot up round her ears as she faced up to her foe.

'This!' Carol moved the bag under Maggie's nose, opening it to release a malodorous waft of its contents.

'Ughh!' Maggie took an involuntary step backwards as the fumes assailed her nostrils.

'How low can you stoop, you poison dwarf? Isn't it enough that some bastard put our windows out? Shit through my letterbox? I'll show you shit ... !' With a flick of her wrists, Carol ejected the contents of the bag straight into Maggie's startled face.

Roly Featherstone walked to the Incident Room, looking fully focused, but with his thoughts elsewhere. How was Rhianna this morning? It would have been so much better if he could have stayed the night, but still, at least she hadn't been alone, even if

Maggie Taylor's presence had forced him to change his plan of action somewhat. His mouth compressed into a taut line.

It was war. All-out war, now.

He wouldn't let them take her from him.

A flurry of activity further down the corridor alerted him to trouble. His mouth suddenly dry, adrenalin began to race as he wondered what the hell had happened in the Swiffords this time . . .

Fletcher Godfrey's heart was heavy as he thought on Mike Morgan's late night phone call and the request he'd made, wanting him to read at Gavin's funeral. He didn't know if he'd manage it. *I'll have to. I just bloody have to. I can't let them down, at a time like this.*

He leaned the bike against the wall of the shop and walked round to the front. Perhaps, after picking up his bits of shopping, he'd go home for a cup of coffee, before driving over to see them. Gavin's body had been released and they'd been to Market Eaton to discuss arrangements with the undertaker. Clarence and Gregg, they were using. Good people. They'd done Pamela's funeral.

As he pushed his way to the front of the shop, there was a startled jangling of the bell behind him as someone flew through the door. All heads turned. It was Chris, the Morris Men leader, sweating and stricken-faced.

'Dear God! Dear God!' He gestured wildly as he lost the attempt to speak coherently.

Frank Arnold vaulted over the counter and gripped the man by his shoulders.

'What is it, Chris? What's happened?'

Chris blinked rapidly, face working as he fought to speak.

'It's the Morgans. Mike and Rosie. They're dead. Their car blew up.'

Anna sat in the darkened optician's consulting room as Molly's eyes were tested. *There's a little green urinal to the north of Waterloo . . .* God! That bloody skit was still with her. She brought her attention back to the examination going on.

'. . . which is clearest now, Miss Webb? The red or the green?'

'The green.'

Another lens was slotted into place. 'And now?'

'Still the green, thank you.'

The optician made further adjustments, asked more questions. Finally, she switched on the overhead light and handed Molly a plasticised card carrying various sizes of typescript.

'Oh! OH!' Molly's face broke into a glorious, beatific smile. 'I can SEE! I can read even this tiny writing!' Her hand shook as she handed back the card. Anna stepped forward and helped her from the seat.

Molly gripped the optician's hand. 'I can't tell you what this means to me! I'll be able to complete my project now! Oh, it's more than I could ever have hoped for!'

Smiling, Anna helped her back to the reception area and, making sure she was safely seated in the folding wheelchair they were using for the day's outing, took Alice through to the examination room for her turn.

Adam Etheridge steered his van off the road and pulled up on the verge by Fletcher Godfrey's house. He smiled wryly to himself as he walked up the path. Another stalwart making work for him. He knew he was being asked to do nothing that Fletcher couldn't have repaired himself, but still, it was the thought that counted, and he was glad of it. He'd been working the other side of Market Eaton all morning, where word of mouth had not yet spread rumours concerning his questioning by the police. Hopefully, it would all blow over, but in the meantime, there were too many folk around here claiming that there was no smoke without fire.

He knocked on the door and stood expectantly, holdall in hand. After a moment, he knocked again. Still no reply. Surely he hadn't got the time wrong? He looked at his watch. No, he hadn't. Putting the holdall on the ground, he walked round the side of the house. The car was still here, but the bike Fletcher had been lent by Frank Arnold wasn't. Oh well. If he'd gone off somewhere, he shouldn't be too long. Give him a few minutes, then.

Squatting on his haunches in the front porch, he rolled a cigarette and smoked it. When Fletcher had still not arrived by the time he'd finished it, he walked back to the van and dug out his thermos flask, pouring himself a cup of black coffee. He was a tea drinker, really, but no matter what anyone said, tea tasted bloody awful from a flask. He took his time over it and, wiping the cup with a piece of kitchen towel, screwed it back on. He peered down the road, frowning. Not like Fletcher to be late. And he really was late, now.

Startled by a squawking sound, Adam turned to see two crows tumbling and flapping as they fought viciously over Fletcher's roof. His eyes narrowing, he looked down the road again, thinking of how such a sight was reputed to mean a death in the house. Where the hell had Fletcher got to?

Anna and the Misses Webb were having lunch in style.

'All the trimmings, my dear – we shan't stint on a thing. Our treat.' Alice smiled as she passed a menu to Anna.

What a morning they'd had! Anna had taken the sisters for coffee and Danish pastries earlier, whilst they'd waited for their new spectacles to be made.

'Just over an hour? Are you sure? It used to take ages, didn't it, Alice?' Molly had been incredulous when told. 'Oh, how marvellous!'

After that, the weather being fine, if cool, Anna had cheerfully acquiesced to their request to visit the shops, happily pushing Molly in her wheelchair.

'I do hope it's not too much for you, my dear,' Molly had said.

'Not at all. You're light as a feather. I shall just have to be careful not to tip you out when we have roads to cross or steps to contend with.'

'Rear wheels down first, dear – that's the thing!' Alice had ordered.

Now, awaiting their food in the restaurant, Anna marvelled at the amount of bags they'd collected. The sisters had had quite a spree, buying new bed linen as well as new clothes. Anna had quietly checked their position with the solicitor when they'd alerted her to what they had in mind. He had laughed, telling her that they could spend what they liked; money was not an issue.

'Just make sure you fill in their cheque stubs for them. And if they've forgotten their cheque books, or their guarantee cards have expired, just give me a shout. I can arrange for things to be done on my account, and they can reimburse me later.'

They hadn't forgotten their cheque books and their cards were in order, but the fun had only just started. Time after time, the sisters would begin to write out cheques, only to look at Anna quizzically part way through the exercise and ask, 'Do remind me again, dear – what am I signing for?' It had turned into quite a game, but one that had made them very happy.

Molly, too, had insisted on visiting a fabrics and haberdashery store, buying all sorts of bits and pieces, some of which she refused to let Anna or her sister see.

'Just indulge me, will you?' she had asked.

In the end, Anna had left her there with a friendly salesperson, arranging to go back for her twenty minutes later.

'Twenty minutes! Whatever do you need that long for?' Alice had protested, but when Anna suggested that the two of them could go to the library in the meantime and renew the sisters' registration, Alice had gone along quite happily, especially once Anna had pointed out that she would be able to borrow music as well as books.

The greatest fun came as they made their way back to the car after lunch.

'Oh do let's look and see what's on at the Playhouse! There might be something we can come and watch.' Molly had pointed to it as she spoke.

'Yes, but how would we get here, dear? Frank has Sally to look after, don't forget,' Alice objected.

'Oh.' Molly's face was crestfallen, but Anna quickly assured the sisters that she would be happy to bring them, so over the road they'd gone.

'*Having a Ball* – that sounds fun! The balls we used to attend, Molly, what?' Alice's face was alight with memories again.

'I don't think it's quite the same sort of thing ...' Anna suppressed a giggle as they moved towards a poster showing a man in a pair of boxer shorts.

'Really? Well, what is it?'

Anna explained that the Alan Bleasdale play was set in a vasectomy clinic and featured full frontal male nudity.

'And it's a comedy, you say?' Alice asked.

'Well, it must be if it features full frontal naked men.' Molly's voice was droll.

Alice and Anna turned to her in amazement.

'Whatever do you mean?' Alice demanded.

'Oh, nothing. Just that Aunt Adelaide once told me that they look rather like turkey giblets. Men's rude bits. Or was it the turkey neck ... ?'

Anna burst out laughing as Alice's eyebrows were raised and Molly flushed under her sister's gaze.

'Is that a fact?' Alice looked at Anna.

'I beg your pardon?'

'Well, you've been married, haven't you? So you must have seen ...' It was Alice's turn to flush slightly.

'Umm ... sort of, I suppose. But only ...' Anna faltered, wondering quite how to phrase things.

'Only when not erect, you mean?' Alice's composure had been regained.

'Quite.' Anna cleared her throat and quickly pushed Molly further along the front of the theatre, where other productions were being advertised.

'Oh look – they're doing musicals, too! And the town hall has a classical concert coming soon.'

Alice ran her eye down the list of events. 'These new glasses are wonderful.' She turned to her sister. 'Do you need the lavatory before we go home, dear?'

'Oh – yes – that might be a good idea, I suppose.'

'There's a public convenience just around the corner. Perhaps if you'd take her, Anna dear, and I shall get the tickets. I know Molly's tastes.'

Anna nodded. 'Are you sure you'll remember what you're signing for?'

'Oh, yes.' Alice walked away briskly, muttering under her breath once Anna was out of earshot. 'Turkey giblets. Turkey giblets ...'

Fletcher Godfrey's eyes were blinded by tears as he pedalled out of the village. His mind numb with shock, he could only repeat, over and over again in his head, *Oh my God . . . ! Oh my God . . . ! It's my fault. It's all my fault. I could have stopped it.* Should *have stopped it. What in God's name possessed me – us – to do what we did?*

He pedalled until he was breathless, eventually pulling into the verge at the side of the road, where he mopped his face and blew his nose. Where the hell was he? He looked around him, his skin going clammy as he took in the landscape markers that answered his question for him. *Jesus Christ! Go on – rub it in, why don't you!* He hesitated, heart beating hard against his ribs.

The sensible thing to do would be to turn back. Ride on, even. Anything other than stay here. But he couldn't help himself.

Slowly, he dismounted, bumping the bike over grass until he came to the first tree, against which he propped it. Illogically, it seemed to him, his heart-rate had slowed now. It didn't seem right. Surely, being here, knowing what he did – *remembering* what they all did – it should have done the opposite. He breathed deeply through his nose. *Sod it! It's years ago. There are no bloody ghosts, and I'll bloody well prove it ...*

Hesitantly at first, then with increasing confidence, his footsteps carried him forward. The trees, straggly and sparsely spaced to begin with, now became stronger, older, thicker. Before he knew it, he was pushing and crashing his way through undergrowth until, at last, there it was.

He stopped, chest heaving, vision swimming. Jesus Christ! It was still here. The Hanging Tree. Overcome by a flood of memories, conflicting emotions threatened to overwhelm him as it seemed that time itself stretched and warped and wrapped itself around him until he fell, gasping, to his knees. Burning pain seemed to explode across his chest as shame and horror roared in his ears, hammered in his heart and coursed like acid through his veins. Vainly, he tried to fight it, close himself off from the onslaught. *I could have stopped it! Right here, that night. But I didn't. Because I thought we were right. RIGHT, goddamit!*

Chapter Thirty-four

Molly Webb breathed a sigh of relief. Alice was sound asleep. Silently, she eased herself out of bed, frustrated by how long it took to put on her new dressing gown and slippers. What a day they'd had! And at last – at last – she had what she needed to complete her project. Hugging her excitement to her, she made her way laboriously across the room, willing Alice to stay asleep and herself to make no noise that might waken her.

She stood on the landing, pulling the bedroom door closed before switching on the light. The excitement was bubbling now, agitating for expression, but she controlled it, telling herself it was no use trying to hurry because there was no getting away from the fact that whilst the spirit was more than willing, the flesh was weak. It was such a *nuisance*, growing old. She still felt the same inside as she had at – oh, twenty-five – but her body was a different matter. It wouldn't do what she wanted anymore, at least not in a hurry, and some things, well – she could no longer bend down or run or even walk terribly well, unaided. But her eyes – ah, there was the beauty of it! Even though they had deteriorated, the new spectacles were a miracle, a dream come true. With one pair firmly on her face and her close work pair in her pocket, she felt like a new woman. Anything was possible now. The project was no longer a fantasy, a dream in her head incapable of completion due to physical infirmity. Now, *now*, she could give it life.

Entering her work room, she switched on the light and made her way to the chest. On top of it, lay the bags containing the things she had bought from the material shop. Swapping her spectacles, she sorted through them, checking before she began that she had everything she needed. *Yes. Yes. Now these, I shan't need until later, but for tonight ...* Carefully, she moved to the table, setting out the items she had selected. Pins. Chalk. Her best shears. And, of course, the pattern. Time was, she could have worked without one, but this project was too special, the situation forcing secrecy and compromise.

Satisfied, she went back and opened the drawer that had held her dreams for so many years. *More than half a century*, she realised in a moment of clarity that caused her no little astonishment. *My, my! Where does the time go, and why does it become so fleet, the older we get?* Shaking her head, she removed the material and limped back to the worktable. *So beautiful! Still, so beautiful!* She buried her face in its folds, transported by the scent back to the heady days when her heart had leaped and flourished and burned with hope and promise.

She breathed deeply, eyes wet, composing herself before attempting the task. *There can be no mistake. Not after so many years.* Sculptors, she knew, talked of releasing that which was hidden, awaiting discovery, in the stone or wood. So it was for her, even if, on this most numinous of occasions, she had to be helped by a paper pattern. She laid out the fabric, smoothing it, shaking her head with the sheer wonder of its appearance as it seemed almost to transmit light as her fingers moved over it, transforming them, in her mind, from the knotted and gnarled lumps they had become, to the strong and straight hands that had worked so giftedly in her earlier life. She worked steadily to pin the pattern, so utterly absorbed that any concept of time became irrelevant. When she had finished, she blinked, stepping back to look critically at what she had done.

Yes. Yes. It was perfect. In her mind's eye, the finished garment was already clear as a bell. Her fingers would not fail her now. With that image of beauty kept bright before her, she picked up the shears and began to cut out the wedding gown.

With no sound in the summerhouse save that of breathing, even the candles seemed to flicker and sway in rhythm to the synchronised breathing of The Four.

Death by Fire had struck in Swifford Fen. Mike and Rosie Morgan roasted and blasted in their car. Only one Element was left to unleash its vengeance.

Air.

In Swifford Lea.

*

Anna moaned in her sleep as the dream came again.

Breath.

Deep.

Slow.

Delicious.

Incense breathing its way into her lungs, suffusing her body with weightlessness.

Her mind with clarity.

Her heart with love.

Hanging, hanging, hanging ...

Drifting.

Sensual.

Sensuous.

Leaden limbs coming alive, tingling.

Pheromones. Lightning coursing down to the depths of her, flash after flash, till her vagina was wet, vulva glistening, ready, ready, aching with the wanting, the heat of desire burgeoning, unbearable, aching for release.

Yes ... Yes ... Oh God ... Please ... Yes ... Please ... Now ...

Faint.

In the background.

Music.

'*Don't listen. Don't let them fool you ...*' Breath, warm in her ear, on her neck, caressing her breasts, first one, then the other, before it whispers between her thighs, '*Open for me ... open ... open ...*'

She is drowning in desire, but still, the music persists, faint, so faint now that it seems no more than the imaginings of a sigh.

Memory stirs, sluggish, resisted.

The Chasm.

The Abyss.

Danger.

Danger!

In the background.

Sight.

Unclear.

A figure, calling, calling, calling her name ...

It echoes, bouncing, beseeching.

Fading ...

I have to ... What do I have to do?

Heavy. So heavy.

She turns.

In the centre of the bridgeless chasm sits a golden retriever with a green tie around its neck …

Fletcher Godfrey awoke, startled, heart pounding in the darkness. He had dreamed. A terrible dream, of Mike and Rosie Morgan burning alive in their car. Still vivid in his mind, the heat seemed to swamp him. How the hell had it happened? Remembering the raw, naked grief that had ripped them apart with Gavin's death, he wondered – God forgive him – if maybe they just couldn't face it, had made a suicide pact. What a way to go, though. Burned alive …

Next moment, another kind of fear quickened his breathing, prickled his scalp, turned blood to ice in his veins as his name was called, over and over and over again.

'Shut up! For Christ's sake – shut up!'

'*You speak of Christ? You, who have the devil for your father? But no brethren now, Fletcher, eh? None left. Do you know the curse? Megan Painter's curse?*'

Fletcher felt the blackness would suffocate him as the Voice began to intone the words. Silence hung, thick and stifling as the litany was completed.

'*Think not that you can escape.*

Seth Peterson – Blood.

Reverend Fury – Earth.

Emily Parsons – Water.

Mike Morgan – Fire.'

Mind reeling, Fletcher's breath came in swift, shallow gasps. Silence again. Oh God. Oh God. Had it gone? The Voice?

When it came again, Fletcher let out a strangled cry.

'*What is that binds you and Seth Peterson and the others together? What SIN is it? Surely you have not forgotten? An INNOCENT died at your hands, and you've FORGOTTEN?! Oh no, Fletcher. The souls of the corrupt have risen as the smoke of incense, being a sacrifice pleasing before the Lord. Judgement has been unleashed and is almost completed. Almost. For only you remain …*'

Chapter Thirty-five

Friday November 18th

There's a little green urinal to the north of Waterloo ... The parody ran through Anna's head along with a picture of a dog in a green tie as she saw Maggie to the door of April Cottage. *What the hell is wrong with me? Nothing! I'm feeling fine. I'm* ...

'I'll see you later then,' Maggie called, waving as she reached the road.

'OK. And take care!'

'Don't you worry!' Maggie stared contemptuously at Bill and Carol's empty house, make-up failing to conceal the black eye that had been inflicted upon her the previous morning. 'They won't be back for a while, if they know what's good for them.'

Closing the door, Anna went back to her breakfast. The village had been agog with the story of how Carol had thrown shit in Maggie's face, and the fight which had ensued. Both of them had been carted off to Market Eaton; both had been bailed to appear in court at a later date. It wasn't looking good for Carol, that much was sure. Several people had been passing at the time she had chosen to confront Maggie and had backed up the latter's story of how Carol had started it and how Maggie had simply been defending herself. So soon after the beheading of the goats, feelings had gone beyond boiling point. Rumour had it that Janice Mills had quietly suggested that they leave the village for their own safety, whilst the investigation continued. Some were surprised that they had taken the advice; all were relieved; and Janice was now left with a wall of silence following the destruction of every one of their remaining windows once they'd gone.

Anna closed her eyes as a wave of lethargy swept over her. *This is ridiculous! I slept like a log – I think – yet my head feels full of cotton wool.* Telling herself that this simply wouldn't do, she pulled herself together and prepared to leave for the Records Office in Market Eaton.

He was here again.

The Hanging Tree.

This time, by design, rather than accident.

Fletcher Godfrey walked towards it, face pale, eyes dark-shadowed and with grizzled grey stubble still on his chin. He opened his overcoat, pulling, from a poacher's pocket on the inside, a sawn-off shotgun. Breathing hard, he sat down on a log, setting the shotgun beside him. For several moments, he didn't stir, body still, but mind racing, before fumbling in his trouser pocket, eventually withdrawing a packet of cigarettes and a box of matches. He'd given it up years ago. Pamela had never liked it; said it worried her, him smoking – what if he died of lung cancer? Well, she – who'd never smoked in her life – was dead and here he was. Something had to get you sometime. What did it matter now?

He lit up and coughed, unused to it any more, the nicotine giving him a head rush that, even sitting, made his legs feel like water. Never mind the legs, he thought. His bowels had turned to water after last night's visitation. And here he was. Back here. The Hanging Tree.

He hadn't wanted to believe the truth when he'd found it. Had clutched at straws, refusing to accept that he and the others had got it wrong. *How the mind twists and turns, trying to justify its own failures; trying to shirk responsibility.* He shook his head, ground the cigarette butt beneath his heel and lit another, coughing again, not caring, as he sifted through memories that had poisoned his heart, memories that he had carried alone and would die with him.

Slowly, he shifted his gaze.

Looked at the shotgun.

Picked it up.

Reached into his pocket for cartridges.

Loaded it.

*

Anna jumped back in shock as she opened the door to Broomwood House.

'Molly! You made me jump!'

'Oh dear – I didn't mean to.'

Anna took in the old woman's worried expression. 'Is everything all right?'

Molly shook her head. 'I was waiting for you. It's Alice. I can't get any sense out of her today. She's upstairs. Still in bed.'

'Why don't you sit down and make yourself comfortable while I go up and see her?' Anna helped Molly into the Music Room before turning and running up the stairs. *Oh Lord! What if she's had a fall? What if she's dead . . . ?* Mouth dry, she pushed open the bedroom door.

Alice was sitting up in bed, clutching a large teddy bear.

'Good morning – have you come to visit us? How lovely! Your face seems familiar, but I'm afraid I've forgotten your name.'

'It's Anna. Dr Anna Summers. We went to Market Eaton together yesterday.'

'Did we?' Alice looked puzzled. 'I'm afraid I'm feeling a little upset today.'

Anna heard the clunk and hum of the stair lift. Molly hadn't settled after all. 'Oh dear,' she said, sitting on the edge of the bed and taking Alice's hand in her own. 'Aren't you feeling well?'

'It's not me. It's Mother. She has these funny turns, you know, and . . .'

'Don't be silly, Alice!' Molly limped into the room. 'Mother isn't . . . with us any more.'

'Isn't she?' Alice stared at her sister, round-eyed.

'Of course not, dear. And it's *you* who isn't well!'

'Aren't I? Oh dear.' Alice looked first at her sister, then at Anna. Turning back to Molly, she asked, 'What's wrong with me, then?'

'You drank too much cocoa. It's not good for you. I've told you that before.' Molly eased her way to the nearest chair and sat down gratefully.

Alice sat frowning for a moment, then, a smile splitting her face, walked the teddy bear up and down the counterpane of the bed.

'We always wanted a bear when we were little, but never had one, did we, Molly? And Sally bought Bear for us and he's so sweet . . .'

She waved his arms at Anna, squeezing him in the middle to produce a squeak which she claimed was his voice, going on to interpret what he had to say.

'Bears are so comforting. They fit so beautifully into one's shoulder or bosom. He really likes you, Anna. Don't you, Bear?' She nodded the animal's head.

'Right.' Anna stood up and smiled briskly. 'Come on, Molly – you come down with me and we'll sort out a nice cup of tea and some lunch. Alice, you stay where you are, and I'll bring it up for you presently.'

'Thank you, my dear. That's so kind. Isn't that kind, Molly? I'm so tired, you know. I really don't think I could get up today.'

Molly safely seated downstairs once more, Anna phoned Sally Arnold to let her know the position.

'Perhaps she overdid it yesterday. In Market Eaton. They seemed so happy ...'

'Oh, don't go blaming yourself. These things happen, at their age, I'm afraid,' Sally reassured her.

'Should I call the doctor, do you think?'

Sally thought for a moment. 'No. Not as long as there's no sign of a stroke. I don't think it's worth bothering him with at this stage. I'll get my niece to check them at tea time and we'll take it from there. Alice could be right as rain by then. Stranger things have happened, believe me.'

Anna put down the phone. *Right. What's best to do next? Besides make lunch? Let me see ...*

She served Alice first, making sure she was able to feed herself, then went back downstairs and helped Molly towards the dining room. She stopped as they came to the telephone table in the hall.

'Molly – do you see here?' She pointed to a large notice she had pinned to the cork board above the phone.

'Yes, dear. These new spectacles are wonderful, you know.'

'Right. That's my phone number. My mobile phone, so you can get me at any time of the day or night. I don't want you to worry at all. If you need me, for whatever reason, you just call – OK?'

'Well, if you're sure, dear ... but what's the number 2 doing below it?'

'I am sure. And the number is the short cut I've programmed into your phone. So, you can either phone the whole number or you can simply press 2 and it will come straight through to me. Have you got that?'

Molly looked dubious.

'Here – just lift the receiver and press 2.'

Molly did so, and within seconds, Anna's mobile was ringing. Molly's face lit up.

'How very clever! This new technology is quite astonishing.'

'I know,' Anna laughed, taking her by the arm. 'Come on – let's have lunch . . .'

Stella Timpson indicated left as she moved into the slow lane of the motorway, ready to take a break at the next service station. Still livid about the developments since she'd last talked to Philip Jackson, she'd decided to take the matter into her own hands. Swifford Lea and the Blessed Rhianna bloody Summers were not sacrosanct. There was no law against going there and no law to say she couldn't ask a few questions of her own. Bloody Philip may have a bloody contract, but he didn't have a monopoly on ordinary, everyday questions and conversation.

She glanced at her watch as she marched into the women's toilets, a grim smile etching itself across her features. She had been at a conference in London, making for a long day and an even longer drive, but with any luck, she'd be in Swifford Lea around 7 o'clock this evening.

Fletcher Godfrey was in a daze, mind numb, almost physically reeling from the shock of what had happened. His head throbbed, blood seeming to pulse in his ears like the rush of a river in flood.

He was seated in the shed at the bottom of his garden, on the old collapsible stool he used to use when he went fishing. He leaned forward, vision swimming as he tried to calm himself. The shotgun lay on the workbench, along with what he'd found. At the Hanging Tree.

Oh God – what he'd found . . .

Time and reality seemed to have no boundaries as he relived the morning's experience. After loading the shotgun he had walked towards the tree, with quite what intention in mind, he didn't know. And then he'd lost it – completely lost it, as he'd roared his own guilt and pain and confusion, inviting confrontation with whatever force it was that had wreaked such terrible vengeance throughout the Swiffords.

'Come on, then – show yourself, you bastard!'

He had circled the tree, faster and faster, knowing it was stupid, that at any moment, he might trip and with the shotgun loaded and the safety off, that could prove fatal. Finally, overcome by giddiness, he had stopped, his breath ragged, chest heaving and burning, his last few steps nothing more than a straggling shambles as he'd sat down abruptly, head between his knees, mumbling, 'I'm sorry . . . I'm sorry . . . I'm sorry . . .'

It was only as he'd tried to push himself upright that he'd felt it. The sharp prick of a thorn in his hand. He'd glared sideways, affronted by the pain, staring stupidly as his brain tried to make sense of it.

A rose.

He had staggered to his feet, turning to look at the base of the tree.

More roses.

It was a wonder he hadn't sat on them.

He had stood staring, counting, trying to understand.

A circle of roses. No – not quite. Nothing but the head of one in the centre. The others were long-stemmed, complete. One above it, one below it, one to the left – the one he'd put his hand on, but nothing to the right.

Not yet.

Fletcher Godfrey had been Swiffords born and bred, and knew his local geography well.

With sudden, horrifying clarity, he had understood.

The centre was for the Petersons; the top – north – was for Swifford Maisey, where Reverend Fury had died; the left – west – was for Swifford Holt and Emily Parsons; the bottom – south – for Swifford Fen and the Morgans.

No wonder there was no rose on the right, in the last space remaining. Right was east and Swifford Lea.

It was waiting for him.

Early evening in The White Hart saw Anna and Maggie standing at the bar, ordering drinks.

'Didn't think we'd be seeing you tonight, Maggie – isn't Jack due back?' Pat Barker handed over the change.

'He was.' Maggie smiled. 'He's decided to stay a few days extra with my sister. Can't say I blame him. He said he hasn't felt so normal for God knows how long. I'm just worried about his studies. It's going to be hard for him, coming back to this lot.'

'You going to be all right on your own? How have you coped so far?'

'I haven't. I've been staying the night with Anna, who, bless her cotton socks, has agreed to carry on the arrangement until Jack comes home.'

'Got to keep at least one of the Swifford Two out of Trouble!' Anna grinned.

Pat rolled her eyes. 'I'm doing my best with the other. Keep him in the kitchen as much as possible, that's my motto.' She glanced over the two women's heads as silence descended in the bar.

Idly, Anna thought it was like the night she'd first walked in, when every eye had turned to look at the newcomer. A stranger, then. She turned. And found herself doing a disbelieving double-take as Stella Timpson walked towards her.

Stella paused as her own eyes lighted upon the other woman.

'Well, well – if it isn't the Blessed Rhianna Summers! Drinking, too. Sure it won't mess up your medication?'

'I'm not on medication, Stella. But thanks for your interest.' How could her voice sound so normal? Anna had the strange sensation that she was somehow outside herself, yet experiencing fire in her head and ice in her heart simultaneously as part of her lived the encounter while another part observed it.

'I'm not interested.' Stella's voice, like her gaze, was cool, calculating. 'But you surprise me. I would have thought, living in the middle of what's been going on around here, that you might need something to keep your emotions in check. It takes a while to recover from a breakdown, so I'm told.'

A murmur rippled through the bar at her words. Maggie, looking at the big stranger as if she were something unpleasant a dog had brought in, opened her mouth, but Anna's hand sped to her arm, warning her to keep quiet.

'You haven't changed a bit, have you, Stella? What are you doing here?'

'Is there a law that prevents it? This was still a free country, the last I heard. Strikes me, you're feeling a little paranoid, perhaps. Understandable, given the state of your mental health, and let's face it, if you cock things up and Philip has to pull you out, well – it'll be me who will be taking over here.'

'Over my dead body!' Anna laughed. 'You're wasting your time. I'm not going to rise to your gibes, so why don't you just leave?'

'Whatever for? I think I'll stay for a drink.'

'You'll not get served here.' Pete's voice came from behind Anna's back, and she turned to see him standing beside his wife.

Stella strode toward him, undeterred. 'And why not?'

'Why not? I don't even have to answer that – this is my pub and I serve who I please. And I'm not pleased to serve you, when you've just insulted a friend of mine.'

Anna had a feeling of *déjà vu* as people moved to the sides of the room. Another rerun, this time of the night of Pete's confrontation with Dave. Yet not everyone had moved. She was keenly aware of Adam Etheridge, his eyes on her face, still standing in the centre of the bar.

'You should pick your friends more carefully,' Stella told Pete. 'She may look like butter wouldn't melt in her mouth, but believe me, she drove her husband and child to their deaths, and I would have thought you'd had more than enough of that around here of late.'

Anna felt Pete attempt to lift the bar flap, but blocked his exit with her body. Her voice, when she spoke, was barely able to contain the fury she felt as it built in her chest like waves.

'You are so unspeakably vile, Stella. To stoop that low. But nothing should surprise me, should it? Coming from a woman who plagiarises her own students' work; who has driven one to suicide by her unwelcome advances, and ...'

'Slander! Oh dear, oh dear, Summers!' Stella turned towards her and shoved her face into Anna's. 'Slander and a pub full of witnesses! And just for the record – I didn't drive Chantelle to kill herself – your husband managed that when he ended their affair.' Stella punctuated her last few words with her index finger, prodding Anna's chest.

'Don't touch me, Stella ...' Anna's voice was cold.

'Or what? Or what, eh?' Each word was accompanied by a further prod.

Anna released Maggie's arm. 'I warned you not to touch me ...'

There was a communal gasp of disbelief as Anna swung a sudden right at the bigger woman's jaw – and connected. Stella staggered backwards as Pete burst through the bar and hurtled towards her.

'Let go of me!' Stella roared in outrage as two pairs of hands grabbed her – Pete and Adam Etheridge had moved in a pincer formation to restrain her.

'Out! And don't come back!'

'This is assault! I'll have you, Summers! I'll have the police on you!'

The rest of her diatribe was muffled as Pete closed and bolted the front door behind her. His wife had moved to do the same with the one leading to the car park.

'Are you all right?' Maggie looked at Anna in astonishment. She would never have believed she had it in her.

Anna was breathing deeply and nursing her right hand. Pete clapped his arm around her shoulders.

'I don't know how you restrained yourself for so long!' He turned to his wife. 'Get the woman a drink!' His eyes swept the bar. 'And what are you lot gawping at?'

People began to shuffle back, one or two glancing at the doors.

'You can leave as soon as that evil bitch has cleared off.'

'She's stamping across the Green. Talking into a mobile. Well – shouting by the look of things.' Chris, the Morris Man, was peering out of the window and reporting back, enjoying every second by the sound of it.

'That'll be Janice turning up next, then ...' Pete grinned at Maggie as he passed Anna a glass of wine. 'Looks like the Swifford Two are about to become the Swifford Three ...'

Chapter Thirty-six

Molly Webb barely registered the grandfather clock chiming 2 a.m., too absorbed in her project to let it intrude. There! That was as much as she could do for now. Slowly, she got up from her seat, turning off the sewing machine and carefully hiding the evidence of her night's work. She had thought of using one of the old hand or treadle models, for fear of waking Alice, but the way Alice slept lately, it would take the Last Trump of the Second Coming to manage that. *Not like Marcus Beardsmore, poor man. He was wakened by the dead . . .*

Molly rubbed her hands as she limped to the bathroom. Poor things they were, these days, because of the arthritis. She did so hope there would be something in the medicine cabinet to ease the pain somewhat. *Deep Heat or Tiger Balm – something like that.* As she opened the mirrored door to peer at the contents, a similar olfactory memory struck out of the blue. *How extraordinary!* She wrinkled her nose in distaste. She hadn't thought of that in years. *Gordon Claybourne. That was what he had smelled of. Most distinctive. Hadn't Alice said it was some concoction he made up himself?* She shook her head. *Such a shame. What a terrible thing to have done. What state of mind must people be in, to take their own lives?* Molly pondered for a moment, unable to imagine herself ever wanting to do such a thing. Almost. She winced. A combination of applying the ointment she'd found and allowing in memories of the dark days when she had realised that Robert wasn't coming back for her. Misery, like a great black cloud, had hung over her for months, all the time hidden away from Mother and Alice, hugged to herself until she had thought she would die of suffocation.

I was always vaguely surprised to wake up in the mornings. Would not have cared, had I not. And yet I never thought of actively taking steps to annihilate myself. Still – all of us are different, and one never knows the private griefs carried by others under the daily façade of cheerfulness.

Not that Gordon had ever been cheerful, of course – not by any stretch of the imagination. No. A terribly morose man. *Perhaps that was it. Some permanent inborn state of depression. As if the trials of farming had not been bad enough. How awful.*

Molly began the journey back along the corridor to the bedroom where Alice lay sleeping. *Strange, what one thinks about as one gets older. Or perhaps not. Mortality. That's the thing, isn't it? 'The only certainty in life,' Father used to say.* She smiled to herself as she realised how, of late, and for reasons quite different from those she had thought of earlier, she had felt surprised to wake in the morning. A pleasant surprise. *Still here? How nice. Such a bonus, another day. And at least, I'm still fit and healthy. Well – as healthy as can be expected, given my age. Which is what? Am I ninety-one or ninety-two? Goodness, I'm not sure . . . Never mind. I'm all right, that's the thing. Poor old Marcus Beardsmore, though – not that he was old, of course, but to become unhinged, the way he had . . . Dear me . . .* Molly realised that she had used Alice's terms, Alice's frame of reference. To her sister, there was no other way to describe what had happened to Marcus Beardsmore. It had to have been madness, and was not something one could talk about. Molly did not share this view, however, and mulled the business over as she got back into bed. *It really has been a most peculiar day. And I don't like what happened this evening at all. Perhaps I should have telephoned Dr Summers. At least Dr Summers is a* nice *young woman, and has manners. Yes. Well . . .*

She turned over, easing her aching bones, as the decision came to her. *Whether Alice jolly well likes it or not, I shall give Dr Summers the Marcus Beardsmore material. Just as soon as I can lay my hands on it . . .*

The house was in darkness. *If whatever it is, is coming after me, let it think I'm sleeping.* No alcohol tonight, despite the temptation. *Can't take a chance on a fuddled brain. Besides, it sends me to sleep, and sleep is not what I want. Not tonight. Not with that thing after me.*

How slowly the time passed. Eyelids drooped, overcoming resolution, thought and dreaming sliding, merging, until they reached a stage where they were indistinguishable.

A jolt into waking – or was it? How long did he think he could keep this up? What was he going to do – sleep during the day and stay awake at night? Every night? Who was to say it wouldn't get him in the daytime, anyway? The vicar's death had been in the day, even if his death didn't fit the pattern. Emily, too. Over the cliff. In daylight.

Maybe what the Voice said was true. That there was no escape. Day or night, it didn't seem to matter. It was hunting down and killing those it held responsible.

Shadows swam like murky river currents in the darkness as Fletcher Godfrey's gritty eyes fought off the demon images that came out to haunt him. *How long do you think you'll last, man? You can't go on like this. Not indefinitely.*

When the Voice came, it was almost a relief.

No escape eh?

The loaded shotgun had sat stretched across his knees throughout his vigil. When the Voice came, Fletcher knew what he had to do.

Kisses.

Deep.

Slow.

Sensuous.

Incense breathing its way into her lungs, suffusing her body with weightlessness.

Her mind with clarity.

Her heart with love.

Hanging, hanging, hanging . . .

Until leaden limbs came alive, tingling with desire.

Pheromones. Lightning coursing down to the depths of her, waking her womanhood till her vagina was wet, vulva glistening, ready, ready, aching with the wanting, the heat of it burgeoning, unbearable, aching for release.

Yes . . . Yes . . . Oh God . . . Please . . . Yes . . . Please . . . Now . . . Now . . .

Straining, hips lifting, feeling the heat, the hardness, opening, opening for it, gasping as it entered her, stretching her to her limits as it began its thrusting drive to ecstasy, mounting, grinding, causing the breath to explode from her stifled chest.

Aaahh . . . aaahh . . . aaahhh.

Faster now.

Faster . . .

faster . . .

frenzied . . .

Hotter and harder until she thought she would split, unable to contain it, then – *oh* – *oh* – OH . . .

spurting . . .

spurting . . .

spurting into the very depths of her and she couldn't breathe and still it went on, exploding inside her until all became blackness again.

Chapter Thirty-seven

Saturday November 19th

The sky was barely touched by the kiss of morning as Janice Mills drove along the deserted road towards Swifford Lea. Her head ached and her limbs were still heavy with tiredness as she stifled a yawn. Hedges had given way to a long, unbroken stretch of trees on both sides of the road and she slowed as a splash of colour announced itself amongst the virtual monochrome silhouettes of the early hour.

She stopped as she drew abreast. A yellow car sat on the grass verge on the opposite side of the road. Not one she recognised, but then, she didn't know every vehicle in the vicinity. A prickle of unease ran between her shoulder blades. Putting her own vehicle in reverse, she backed it up until she could read the number plate. *No point inviting trouble by getting out at this stage. Let's run a check* ... She had the answer in minutes. Frowning, she turned off her engine, got out and walked over to the car.

No sign of anyone inside. Engine cold. Why park here? There was nothing to see and no houses for a good couple of miles in any direction. A toilet stop, perhaps? It seemed unlikely, but you never knew. Janice stood, uncertain of what, if anything, to do next. She took a couple of steps into the trees. The prickle of unease shivered between her shoulder blades again. *Don't be so daft. The worst you're likely to see is someone having a pee.* No. There was no reason to take this any further. She was about to turn back when another flash of colour signalled on the perimeter of her vision. *What the hell's that ... ?* A few further steps revealed it to be a bicycle. Frank Arnold's by the look of it. She blinked, facts sorting themselves through her brain. Wasn't Fletcher using that at the moment? Doing the paper round or something? Then why would he be out here? It didn't matter, anyway, she told herself. If it was Fletcher, there was nothing to worry about. Or was there? Whatever his reasons for being out here, Fletcher was an ex-cop. Suppose he'd seen the yellow car, too, and decided to investigate? *Shit!*

Janice was uncomfortably aware of her heart thudding against her ribs. *I ought to call for back-up.* Almost as fast as the thought came into her head, she dismissed it. *What – get people out here to find Fletcher having a pee or a secret assignation with the driver of the car? I don't think so. As if we haven't got enough on our plates already ...*

'Fletcher! You OK? It's Janice – and Pete.' Her voice was strong and confident, belying the true state of her feelings. And the lie about Pete, she told herself, was unnecessary, just a sensible precaution. There was no reason to think anything was wrong. Except for that bloody prickling between her shoulder blades ...

She made her way forward, senses alert. *You're going to look such a fool, my girl. Fletcher's not going to thank you if ...*

She stopped, heart lurching to her mouth as she entered the clearing, senses reeling, recoiling, as her eyes screamed information to her brain. No. No. It couldn't be. It couldn't be. It ...

The rope, suspended from the tree, seemed to mock her as it creaked beneath the weight of its burden.

Bile rose, burning, into her throat as Janice Mills turned on her heel and ran.

There's a little green urinal to the north of Waterloo ... Anna slammed her hand down on the work surface of the Misses Webb's kitchen. *Oh shit! Why can't I get that bloody thing out of my head? Don't let me be cracking up. Please.* Please. With shaking hands, she drew a glass of water from the tap and drank it. *Why did she have to come to the Swiffords? Why?* Her stomach fluttered as she thought of the confrontation with Stella. Of what had happened afterwards ... *Oh Christ! What the hell was I thinking of? How could I have done it? And what the* hell *do I do now ... ?*

She was seated at the table, searching in her handbag for painkillers when Molly came into the kitchen.

'Are you all right, dear? You look a little peaky, if you don't mind my saying so.'

Anna tried to smile. 'Just a bit of a headache. I'll be fine. Lunch won't be long now. How's Alice today?'

'Behaving as if she has a hangover. She's refusing to get up. I should like my lunch downstairs, though, if you don't mind. I'm looking for something. If you just let me know when it's ready . . . ?'

'Of course. Can I help at all?' Anna stood up.

'No, no. You have enough to do. And you wouldn't recognise it. I must talk to you, though – perhaps when you've seen to Alice?'

'Certainly. I'll just go and check on her.' Anna started for the hall, remembering what Sally had said. *As long as there's no sign of a stroke. Would I* know *if she's had a stroke? Hell – what Molly said about a hangover – does she mean slurred speech?* That *could be a sign. Oh, shit. All I want to do is go and have a shower and forget what happened. How could I have done it? How* could *I?*

Her foot was on the second stair when the doorbell rang. She turned back and went to the door. *If that's Sally's niece, I'll let her take over. More than gladly, given the circumstances . . .*

She stared blankly for a second at her visitors. Janice Mills and two other uniformed police officers.

'Dr Rhianna Summers?' one of them asked.

'Yes.' She looked at Janice for an explanation, but the woman stood, grim-faced and silent.

The officer who had asked her name stepped forward and continued to speak. 'Rhianna Summers, I have to tell you that I am arresting you on suspicion of the murder of Professor Stella Timpson . . .'

Chapter Thirty-eight

It was almost 7 p.m. by the time Anna had her first formal interview. Dressed in a paper boiler suit and with the tapes running, she was singing like a bird – but not singing the tune the investigating officers were looking for. She had stressed to the duty solicitor that she had nothing to hide and would quite happily answer any questions the police wanted to ask, but was far from happy with the way things were turning out. She felt as if her every reply was being twisted, making her behaviour seem all the more suspect.

'There must have been quite some bad blood between the two of you for that fight to have blown up as quickly as it did.' DC Ryan looked at Anna across the table.

'Well, of course there was! Years of it! But I didn't kill her! For Christ's sake – I only hit her once – and that was to stop her pushing me around!'

'No one's arguing with that. There was a bar full of witnesses, all of whom are agreed that you didn't start the altercation. But you should have left it at that. What made you go after her?'

'I didn't!'

'It's understandable, I suppose, that you didn't want to let it lie. She'd humiliated you in front of a lot of people. Cast slurs on you and your marriage. Perhaps it just boiled over, eh?'

'Nothing boiled over! Dear God, I hated the woman, yes. Have done for years, but you have to understand . . .'

'What? What do we have to understand, Dr Summers? Why don't you tell us the background?'

Anna clasped her hands on top of her head and closed her eyes. Sleeping nightmares were bad enough, but this was infinitely worse. Right then, she would have given anything to wake up and find that it *was* a nightmare.

'Talk to anyone who knew her. She was trouble on two fronts. God knows, there were enough complaints, but she had friends in the right places – either that, or had the dirt on people – I don't know. But she'd write papers and use other people's research, just absent-mindedly "forgetting" to credit them. Several cases of outright plagiarism, but it was hushed up or paid off. That's on the academic front, right? But there was her personal life, as well. She was ...' Anna ran her hands through her hair. 'Had she been a male lecturer doing what she did with female students, she'd have been bounced through the courts for sexual harassment.'

'But the boys liked it – is that what you're saying?'

'Boys? No – she was a lesbian.'

'You have a problem with lesbians?'

'No, I bloody don't! My youngest sister is gay, but she's a decent human being, not some predatory monster who preys on the very students she has a responsibility for and duty of care towards! I'm not even sure it was genuinely the way Stella was – it seemed more like she was making a political statement. There were rumblings, but she was clever. Played the innocent. But she went too far – there was ...' Anna broke off, tried to compose herself. 'I had a star student. Did her MA with me. Hugely talented.' Her smile was bleak, as the pain of memory clouded her eyes. 'They're such a rarity. You get one, now and again, who is just ... how can I explain it? They shine. They're head and shoulders above the rest. Chantelle was one of those. Full of life. Absolutely first-class mind. She would have gone far.' There was silence as she gathered her thoughts. 'She went to Stella's institution to do her PhD. Stella was her supervisor. We had hoped to keep Chantelle with us, but they offered inducements, and God knows, students need all the help they can get these days. We couldn't match them, so we lost her. Anyway – it wasn't long before she ran into difficulties. Stella was giving her the come-on and Chantelle wasn't interested. Stella took her revenge by undermining her work. One thing led to another.' Anna bit her lip and cleared her throat, struggling to contain her emotion. 'To cut a long story short, Chantelle killed herself.'

'And you blamed Professor Timpson for that?'

'You're bloody right I did! At least the stink from that was something they couldn't brush under the carpet. Not completely, at any rate. Even so, Teflon bloody Timpson was sent on an enforced sabbatical, rapped over the knuckles, but went back to work a year later, promising to be a good girl and still insisting it had all been a terrible misunderstanding.'

DC Ryan leaned back in his chair and gave Anna a long look. 'That's only your story, though, isn't it, Dr Summers? According to witnesses at the pub, Professor Timpson claimed that this Chantelle killed herself after your husband finished an affair with her.'

Anna's laugh rang hollow around the interview room. 'Guy and Chantelle? Believe me – she wasn't his type.'

'Meaning other women were?' DS Cooke leaned forward now, her face sympathetic.

'You're really digging the dirt, aren't you? Yes, other women were. A succession of them, once I was pregnant with Jamie. And no – before you ask – I didn't go off sex. Christ, what is this? You want to know about my marriage? I'll tell you about my marriage, shall I? The outwardly perfect marriage that became an utter bloody farce – and how Stella bloody Timpson even got in on the act there! Guy and I – we should never have married in the first place. I was on the rebound and he – well, not that I knew it at the time, but –' Anna spread her hands in a gesture of helplessness. 'I knew he was competitive. It was one of the things I liked about him at the time. What I didn't realise was that he had this thing going with Ian – the guy I was on the rebound from. No –' she shook her head at the expression on DC Ryan's face. 'They weren't gay. But they had to score points off each other. Ian got a new music system – Guy would have to get a better one. Ian got a new car – Guy had to have a faster one. You get the picture?' She didn't wait for the police officers to reply.

'Well – I wasn't, as it turned out, Guy's type of woman. Air-heads with big tits were more his line, but it seems – not that I was aware at the time – that because Ian had had me, Guy had to, as well. Whether I was a novelty for him, or what, I don't know. But we got married. And it seemed to work. Until I got pregnant and suddenly he didn't want a clever working wife anymore. He wanted me to stay at home, give up my career. We rowed more and more about it, and that's when he went back to seeing his bimbos. And you know what? I was going to divorce him. But I never got the chance. Because that bloody woman ...' Anna gave a low moan, her last evening with Guy burned into her brain and corrosive, now, in her belly.

'We'd been rowing even more than usual. I was knocked sideways by Chantelle's suicide. Determined that Stella should get her come-uppance. Guy was taunting me, saying what was the point – it was too late for Chantelle – she was dead, there was nothing I could do. He said I was fixated on Stella. Maybe he was right.' She shook her head. 'Anyway. He lost his temper, big style, when I said I was leaving him. It didn't suit his outwardly successful image, and it meant – as he saw it – that he'd failed to tame me.' She looked up, her mouth twisted. 'Those were the words he used. As if I were a bloody dog. And he snatched Jamie up and stormed off. In the car.'

The tapes ran on through a silence in which one could have heard the proverbial pin drop.

'He was speeding. He had an accident. The police said he hadn't fastened Jamie into the child seat properly. They were both killed.'

An almost imperceptible nod passed between DS Cooke and DC Ryan before the latter spoke.

'That seems like a powerful motive for murder, Dr Summers. You held Professor Timpson directly responsible for your student's suicide and indirectly responsible for the death of your husband and son. Simmering away all this time. The fight in the pub just bringing it to a head ...'

'No!' Anna shouted as the duty solicitor laid a hand on her arm. 'I didn't kill her! Christ knows, I could quite cheerfully have done, but I didn't. Good God – I was lucky even to land the punch I did. She's a big woman. I'd have had to mow her down in my car, unless I wanted to risk a pasting myself.'

'So why did you leave the pub just after she did? And where did you go? Mrs Taylor was supposed to be staying the night with you in April Cottage, was she not? Because she was worried about being alone while her son was away. You had that arrangement, did you not?'

'Yes, but ...'

'But you phoned her and asked if she could stay at The White Hart instead, because you wouldn't be coming back that night. And when she said that she hoped that you'd calmed down after the fight, you said . . .' DC Ryan glanced at his notes ' ". . . calmed down? I could kill the bitch." Isn't that right?'

'Oh God!' Anna slumped forward, head in hands. 'Yes, that's what I said! But I didn't mean it literally!' She looked up, thumping the table in frustration.

'So where did you go after leaving the pub, Dr Summers? Back to April Cottage? Is that where you got the knife and the rope? And more to the point – where did you spend the night?'

Chapter Thirty-nine

Sunday November 20th

Pete Barker eyed Maggie Taylor as the last of the Sunday lunchtime punters left his pub.

'Come on up, Maggie – you look done in.'

She followed him upstairs to the living quarters and sank gratefully on to the sofa, kicking off her shoes.

'Bloody hell – I wouldn't like to work in a shop – or a bar! I don't know how you do it, being on your feet all day.'

'What have you been up to, then?' Pat Barker smiled as she entered the sitting room.

'Helping Frank and Sally. Mavis wouldn't work a Sunday, and with Fletcher out of action, Frank had to do the paper round. They thought Jack might do it, but he's staying with my sister for another week. What a bleedin' mess, eh?'

'Bet Sal's none too happy about April Cottage. Plods in and out of there all day yesterday. Christ knows what kind of mess they've made. No news of Anna, I suppose?'

Maggie shook her head. 'Fletcher's due out of hospital, though. Frank's going to pick him up.'

'I still don't understand what happened.' Pat frowned.

'Do any of us? It's Chinese Whispers gone mad at the moment, isn't it? I've heard God knows how many versions since yesterday morning, each one more lurid than the last. But if he's coming home today, I take it it wasn't a heart attack?'

'No. I think that's what Janice suspected when she found him near the dead woman, but Sally says it seems he was concussed.'

'So – what? He fainted? Hit his head?' Pete looked from Maggie to his wife.

'Something like that, I expect. Seems like he was the one that found her, at any rate. Must have been an awful shock.'

'But why is it being treated as murder if the woman was hanged? I mean, suicide would be more likely with a hanging, surely?' Pat's voice betrayed the frustration they were all feeling at the lack of reliable information.

'Exactly. And after seeing that woman in here the other night, can you believe a little slip of a thing like Anna could have hoiked her up a tree with a noose around her neck? It doesn't make sense, does it?' Maggie wiggled her toes. 'There must be something they're not telling us.'

'Typical,' Pete grunted. 'So all we get is rumour and speculation.'

'There's been rather more of that than I care for in the bar. Talk of mutilation, for instance, and some very nasty insinuations doing the rounds. And we've been besieged with reporters – it was bad enough when it was journalists, but with the TV cameras – you can't walk down the street without being stopped and asked for a comment, or interrogated about whether you knew any of the victims.'

'I know.' Maggie's face was sombre. 'We had 'em hanging round the village store, intercepting people. Frank had a bit of a barney with one of 'em. Right cocky madam. It's just inflaming things.'

'Tell me about it!' Pete's laugh was far from amused. 'I've banned 'em from the pub. Vultures, the whole lot of them. Like living under siege. Which reminds me, babe –' He turned to his wife. 'You done the notice yet?'

'Give me a break! I'll have it ready for when we open again!' Pat protested.

'What notice?' Maggie looked from one to the other.

'Telling all media scum to piss off to the shit pit over the road.'

'Not quite as bluntly as that!' Pat rolled her eyes. 'It's getting bad, though – one or two folk who ought to know better are talking about ...' Her speech was interrupted by the unmistakable ringing of a mobile phone. Maggie's face flushed.

'Sorry – I must have forgotten to turn it off.'

'Don't worry about it. What's a mobile when a homicidal maniac is on the loose?' Pete waved at her to answer it.

Finally retrieving it from the depths of her shoulder bag, Maggie frowned as she looked at the display.

'Who the hell's this? I don't recognise the number . . . 'Ello?' She listened intently before saying, 'Don't worry – I'll come over now. No – no, it's not a problem – honest.' Ending the call, she looked at Pete and Pat. 'That was Anna – the police are letting her go.'

Maggie slid into the seat opposite Anna. Unlike The White Hart, The Royal George in Market Eaton was open from midday on a Sunday.

'There you go, girl. You look like you need it.' Maggie pushed the drink towards her.

Anna looked at the large glass of red wine and laughed, biting off the near hysteria she was feeling. 'I'll be under the table if I drink this! Oh – to hell with it!' She picked it up and took a deep draught, bringing colour to her pinched cheeks.

'Thanks, Maggie. Thanks for coming. I don't know what I'd have done if you hadn't, and asking Roly to buy underwear and God knows what, would have been the last thing I wanted.' Anna looked down at herself in some bemusement. 'So thanks to Pat for the clothes. What must I look like?'

'Better than you did in a paper boiler suit, that's for sure.' Maggie eyed her critically. 'Given that Pat's taller and bigger than you, think of it as BoHo chic or something.'

'Maggie –' Anna set down the glass and reached for the other woman's hand. 'I did not kill Stella Timpson. I swear. I hated her guts, and I know I said I could kill her, but I didn't.'

Maggie's glance did not waver. 'I had to tell the police what you said. You know that.'

'Of course I do. And you were right to tell them. I did say it. But I didn't kill her.' Anna released her hand and took another drink. 'I don't know what I'd have done if you hadn't come to get me. It's all such a mess. The police have got my car, my clothes . . . Oh shit! What am I going to do?'

'But they've let you go. That's a start, right?'

'Yes. I'm on police bail. Have to go back in two weeks' time. Bloody hell, Maggie! How I wish I'd just taken the drink Pete offered me and gone home with you.'

'Where did you go?' Maggie had never been a believer in beating about the bush and didn't mean to start now.

Anna looked at her, her eyes watery. 'I was so upset. So *angry*. And you don't know the background between me and Stella. I left the pub to come here, to Market Eaton. To see Roly.'

'The feller with the flowers?'

'Yes.' Anna remembered the delight on Roly's face when she'd turned up; how quickly it had turned to anger as she'd described what had happened.

'He was so good. Calmed me down. Bought me dinner in the hotel restaurant. It was after that, that I phoned you. I'd had a couple of drinks – knew I wouldn't be safe to drive back. I felt awful, letting you down, but figured you'd be able to stay with Pete and Pat.'

'Which I did. But we were worried about you. And you didn't say where you were. Not that you're answerable to anybody else, of course, but ...'

'I know. And I'm sorry. But oh *shit*, how I wish I'd stayed with you.'

Maggie's eyes narrowed. 'What are you getting at, Anna?'

Anna slumped back in her seat and looked at Maggie, her face bleak. 'I don't know what I was thinking of. And drinking didn't help. What with all the turmoil ... I've known Roly a long time, Maggie. He's been a good friend over the years – all the more so since my husband and child died.'

'I didn't know you had a child! Bloody hell, Anna – I'm really sorry.'

Anna shook her head. 'Jamie. He was two. Anyway. Roly – he's always had a thing for me. Wanted us to get together. I just never felt that way about him. But since I've been here – in the Swiffords – and he's – don't say anything, but he's involved, as a consultant, with the murders – the curse stuff – well – I don't know why, but I've hardly been able to get him out of my head. But still – I don't think of him like that – you know – sexually.'

'It's either there or it's not, the chemistry.' Maggie shrugged.

'Yes, but – well, I wasn't fit to drive back to Swifford Lea. I should have got a taxi. But I didn't. I stayed the night. With Roly. One thing led to another ... Oh God, Maggie – when I got up the following morning, I thought it had all been a dream. Then I went to the loo and ...'

'... it wasn't a dream at all.' Maggie finished for her.

Anna nodded. 'I felt awful. It should never have happened. The last thing I wanted was to give him the wrong idea.'

Maggie gave Anna a long look. 'He didn't rape you, did he?'

Anna shook her head. 'Just the opposite. He was tender and gentle and – oh, shit, Maggie – he told me he loved me, had waited all his life for me. And I just want to scream. I don't want him. I don't love him. Not like that.'

'So he's your alibi for Friday night?'

'Yes.' Anna's face was the picture of misery. 'He was all up in arms about me being taken in for questioning. Wanted to run me back to the village himself or, better yet, have me move into the hotel for the time being, and I just couldn't face it, Maggie. I needed to think, to get my head straight. Needed another woman to talk to. That's why I called you. I just feel ... I don't know – so confused. So *unclean*. I'm not making any sense, am I?'

'Oh, I dunno.' Maggie's eyes took on a faraway look. 'I had a couple of one-night stands. Years ago, it was. Worse bloody things I ever did. I reckon I felt pretty much the same.'

Anna sighed. 'So – what's happening in the village? What kind of reception can I expect?'

Maggie pulled a face. 'Mixed, I should think. I have to be honest – the place has been buzzing. You know the way people's minds work – no smoke without fire, and all that.'

'Philip'll love me.'

'Who?'

'Philip – my boss. For the Swiffords project. He'll probably think I killed Stella! What a bloody mess. And my position with the project is untenable, with this hanging over my head. Oh hell ...' A further implication hit Anna. 'What about Sally and Frank?'

'Mmm.' Maggie's expression was unreadable. 'You'd best speak to them yourself, I think. The police were in and out of April Cottage all day yesterday. Forensics, I expect. Took a load of stuff away.'

'So they'll probably want me out.'

'That's not what I said. But I shouldn't think they're too happy, no.'

'They're not going to want me near Alice and Molly, either, are they? Can't say I blame them. They *are* all right, the sisters? The police said Janice had arranged for Sally's niece to go in after I was taken away.'

'Yes, they're fine. They weren't told why you'd left, by the way. That's to say, they were told the police needed your help urgently. Nothing about the murder or the fight.'

'Right. Well ...' Anna finished her drink, and rose, unsteadily to her feet. 'I suppose I'd better go and face the music, then.'

The one-way system through Market Eaton took them back past the police station.

'I don't need a reminder, Maggie!' Anna protested as Maggie slowed the car to a crawl.

'Oh shit – it's not a reminder, Anna – it's Adam! This is just what we reckoned might happen.'

'What?' Anna watched, uncomprehending, as Adam Etheridge was led inside, just as she had been the previous day.

'Stands to reason, doesn't it, now they've let you go? He'd be next on the list if you're looking for people with a motive to kill that Stella woman.'

'Adam kill Stella?' Anna laughed, the wine having gone straight to her head. 'Why on earth would he do that? How would he even know her?'

Maggie put her foot down and accelerated away, her mouth set in a grim line.

'Oh, he knows her, all right. His ex-wife, Maxine, ran off with her.'

Chapter Forty

Fletcher Godfrey had said hardly a word since Frank Arnold had picked him up from Market Eaton hospital. His mind seemed numbed by an inescapable fog whose lurking folds thrust forward image after image to haunt and taunt and torture his already overtaxed brain. Outwardly silent, inside he was howling with the pain of shock, revulsion and sheer terror, tremors taking hold of him and shaking him as if in punishment for the garbled half-truths he had told to the police.

Eyes closed, head back against the car seat, he could not shut out the memory of what had happened, could not stop the macabre death-dance he had witnessed. Why had he gone back, yet again? He must have been out of his mind through lack of sleep, sitting up, as he had, with the shotgun across his knees, screaming at the Voice, the Voice, the bloody Voice ... And to think he was going to go out and do the paper round as if nothing had happened.

He'd gone out too early for that, wobbling all over the road on Frank's bike, headed for the Hanging Tree with the shotgun in his poacher's pocket, just like before. Only this time, he'd had it in his head that he would find whoever or whatever was leaving the roses there, would have a target, a tangible enemy, to confront.

Barely a blush of sunrise when he'd got there and had his first surprise, with the discovery of the car. What had he felt when he'd seen it? A leap, a fierce leap of exultation in his chest, thinking it was the bastard he was after. Oh yes. A car. Something solid, real, an ordinary, everyday object. This was no phantom in the night. He'd felt no fear at all, as he'd set down the bike and moved with as much stealth as he could muster through the verge and the undergrowth and the trees, into the clearing. It was as if he were invincible, focused so fine and fierce on finding the bastard. And then … and then …

Frozen. Rooted to the spot. For one awful moment believing time had warped and he was back all those years ago, 'finding' Gordon's body. He'd expected what he'd 'found' then, of course, having helped to hang the man. This was different. This was altogether different. No pre-knowledge. Just the shock, the horror, the failing to comprehend, especially the garlands, the streamers. There'd been none of them with Gordon. Just hanged. So why, in this instance, was the body adorned? And then he'd realised – God Almighty – they were not garlands at all, but guts spilling out, some draped round her neck and …

'You all right, Fletcher? Want me to let the window down?'

'Pull over!'

Frank barely had time to do so before Fletcher staggered out of the car and vomited into the side of the road. Frank shook his head as he offered paper hankies.

'I hope they know what they're doing, letting you out. You look bloody awful to me.'

'I'm fine. Just the motion of the car on top of these pills I'm taking. I'll be all right once I get home, get myself to bed.'

'Long as you're sure.' Frank waited until Fletcher was belted up and settled before setting off again.

Fletcher felt a shaking inside, like rising hysteria. Home? Safe at home? Who was he kidding? Maybe he should have stayed in hospital, if they'd let him. Not that they would have, with the wards chock-a-block. But at least he'd felt safe there. No Voice in the night. No killer on the loose. But going home … He'd be a sitting duck. If he could just get through a day or two, maybe he'd be fit to drive himself to his sister's. She lived over a hundred miles away. Surely it couldn't follow him there? He couldn't stay in Swifford Lea anymore, that was certain. He'd sell up. Move someplace else. *Anywhere*, as long as it put as much distance as possible between him and whatever this monstrosity was.

'That's some shiner you've got there,' Frank commented. 'Don't think I've ever seen one that bad.'

Fletcher grunted in reply. 'Can't see a bloody thing and it hurts like hell. Still – I should count myself lucky I didn't lose the eye. Must have gone down like a ninepin when I saw the body.'

'You don't remember?'

Fletcher started to shake his head and stopped, wincing with pain. 'They weren't sure whether I fainted or had a fit or what the hell happened.'

'Good thing Janice found you when she did. She thought you'd had a heart attack.'

'They checked for that as well. How is she, by the way?'

'Janice? Bearing up. But I shouldn't wonder if she jacks the job in, after this lot. What she's seen these past few weeks doesn't bear thinking about. Where's it all going to end, eh? That's what folks are asking, and there doesn't seem to be an answer. A couple of families are already talking about moving, putting their houses on the market – if they can get a buyer after this. They'll lose a lot of money.' Frank shook his head.

'Aye, well it was outsiders that pushed the house prices up in the first place. People paid well over the odds and drove out them that was born and bred in these parts. Can't say I blame them, mind – for moving, I mean,' Fletcher conceded. 'There's more to life than money, at the end of the day, and when people are being murdered in their beds ... well, I have to be honest and say it's crossed my mind.'

Frank glanced at him. 'I don't know what the world's coming to. And the police don't seem to be getting anywhere.'

'Must be a nightmare for them. Folks don't realise how many officers a murder investigation ties up. Even one murder in a large town would stretch resources. With everything we've had – Christ, I wouldn't like to be footing the bill for this little lot. There's been no developments while I've been in hospital, I take it?'

Frank snorted. 'They arrested Dr Summers – you know – came to work with the Misses Webb.'

'What? You're having a laugh, aren't you?' Fletcher's voice was incredulous.

'No. She had a fight – and I mean a fight, not an argument – with the dead woman the night before you found her. Sounds like there was a lot of bad blood between them, from what I've heard.'

Fletcher fought to keep images of blood and entrails out of his head. 'You can take it from me, she didn't kill her. Little chit like that? No way, Frank. And it doesn't explain the others, does it? Or are they trying to pin the lot on her?'

'Not as far as I know.'

They drove on in silence, Fletcher's mind grasping at straws as they approached Swifford Lea. The vicar, as he'd thought all along, was an oddity. Now this woman. And technically, the Hanging Tree could be said to be in Swifford Lea. What if *she* was the one to die there, not him? Then why had the Voice taunted him, told him he was next? It didn't make sense.

'Well – here we are.' Frank pulled up outside Fletcher's cottage. 'Take your time getting out. Do you want me to open up?'

'Aye. Thanks.' Fletcher handed over his keys and remained seated as Frank got out of the car and headed for the front door. The trembling was worse now he was back. He couldn't spend another night here alone. He just couldn't. Reluctantly, he swung his legs out of the car and straightened up, walking unsteadily down the path. Frank had the front door open and was bending down to pick up something on the step. He turned to Fletcher, smiling.

'Looks like somebody loves you, anyway.'

'What?'

Fletcher's eyes widened with shock as Frank handed him a long-stemmed, blood-red rose.

Chapter Forty-one

Anna saw him as they approached the Green. 'Oh shit ...'

'What?' Maggie followed her gaze towards April Cottage and the man leaning against the wall outside it. 'That's him, isn't it? Your flower man – alibi?'

'Roly. Yes.' Anna closed her eyes. How in God's name was she going to deal with this? As if she didn't already have enough on her plate ...

'Not taking "no" for an answer, eh? Want me to drive past?' Maggie was now keeping her eyes strictly to the front.

'No.' Anna's voice was resigned. 'He'll probably wait all night. I just have to get it over with, I'm afraid.'

'You sure? If you need any help, you know – I'm just next door.'

'Thanks, Maggie.' Anna barely had time to unbuckle her seat belt before Roly was at the passenger door, waiting for her to get out.

'Rhianna!'

She was pulled into an embrace that left her breathless. Struggling to free herself, she thanked Maggie for her lift.

'No problem. Well ...' Maggie stood awkwardly for a moment. 'I'd best leave you to it, then.' She nodded at Roly before walking away.

'I don't understand you, Rhianna! You know I would have been happy to give you a lift! I made that quite clear and – God! I've been out of my mind with worry! Darling, we need to talk.' Roly moved to embrace her again, but Anna side-stepped him and walked down the path to April Cottage.

'Rhianna ...'

'Oh my God ... !' Anna stopped abruptly as she viewed the apparent devastation inside.

Roly peered over her shoulder. 'They certainly don't believe in clearing up after themselves, do they?'

Anna bit her lip to stop herself from crying. Everything had been gone through, and little or nothing replaced. It all shrieked at her senses with an air of defilement, intrusiveness and trespass. 'God – now I know how people feel after a burglary!'

'You must let me help you clean up –'

'No!' Anna's voice was sharper than she had intended. 'Look – I'm sorry, Roly, but after everything that's happened – I just want to be left on my own.'

'You can't be serious! Rhianna ...'

'Roly, please – I appreciate your coming. And I'm grateful that you were able to tell the police that I was with you ...' She looked at him, hovering on the doorstep, and beckoned him inside. More fuel for the rumour mill, no doubt, but she was past caring.

'It was simply the truth. How could I do less?' His voice was gentle now, his face concerned. 'It was easily proved, Rhianna. The receptionist remembered your arrival – you were rather distressed at the time – and everything followed on from there. We were remembered at dinner, then in the bar, and it's probably a good thing we called room service. The hotel also has CCTV in the car park, and both our vehicles were clearly there all night. Rhianna ...'

'Roly, I'm sorry.' Why did she feel as if she were wavering? 'I'm really grateful for everything, but this has all been an awful ordeal. I had to go all through the background between me and Stella. I had to talk about my marriage – things I've never told anyone. And now – well –' She walked through to the dining room, flinging out her arms. 'Look at this! I have to square it all with Sally and Frank, then there'll be Philip to speak to tomorrow – this has probably put the kibosh on the project. Oh shit!' She stared at the table. 'They've taken the laptop. The tapes. Buggeration!'

Roly moved behind her, massaging her shoulders, ignoring the way she hunched them under his touch.

'All the more reason you should let me help. Rhianna, you know how I feel about you ...'

'Roly ...' Anna pulled away, turning to face him. She took a deep breath. 'I can't tell you how bad I feel about the other night. It – it should never have happened.' Roly recoiled as if she'd slapped him. 'I'm sorry.' Anna shook her head, feeling utterly wretched. 'I was feeling vulnerable and you've always been such a good friend ... I should never have let things go as far as they did.'

Roly stood silently, the working of his jaw muscles the only outward evidence of his reaction. Finally, he stepped back, palms held out as he conceded defeat.

'You need space, Rhianna. You're obviously and understandably overwrought by everything that's happened, and it's insensitive of me to crowd you at this time. All I ask – please – is that you don't throw away what we have. Give it time. Think it over. Please?' He stepped towards the living room. 'I'll see myself out. I'll ring you tomorrow. See how you've got on with Philip, OK?' He looked at her expectantly.

'OK.' Anna watched him disappear, heard the closing of the front door, then sank into the nearest chair and wept.

It was early evening and already dark when Anna squared her shoulders and opened the tall back gate leading to Frank and Sally Arnold's house. The kitchen light was on and Frank answered her knock almost immediately.

'Dr Summers.'

'Hello, Frank. I thought I'd better come and talk to you and Sally after what's happened.'

'Best come in, then.' Frank stepped aside to lend her entrance. 'I was just making coffee. Do you want one?'

'Please. White, no sugar.' She wiped her feet on the mat as Frank crossed the room.

'Go on up.' He inclined his head towards the stairs. 'Shan't be a minute.'

Anna knocked on the living-room door before entering.

'Well, well!' Sally was sitting on the sofa, her plaster-casted leg elevated on a footstool. 'I wondered when you'd be round.'

'Sally, I'm awfully sorry about ...'

'Met Fletcher, have you?' Sally indicated the man sitting in an armchair by the fire.

Anna looked at him, shocked at his haggard appearance. 'Yes. I believe so.'

Fletcher stood up, hand outstretched. 'That fight over the goats, wasn't it? Your friend helped save the day.'

'Dare I ask what happened?' Anna asked as she shook his hand.

'A murdered woman's what happened,' Sally put in. 'Fletcher found her. I assume that's what you're here to talk about.'

Anna glanced round as Frank entered the room with a tray.

'Yes. Look, whatever anyone may think, I didn't kill Stella Timpson. I hit her – yes. But I didn't kill her. And I'm really sorry about the police turning over April Cottage. I've made a start on cleaning up ...'

'So where were you that night? After you hit her?' Sally's cool gaze belied her tone of voice.

'Sal!' Fletcher was embarrassed on Anna's behalf.

Frank passed her a mug of coffee and Anna was grateful to hide her face in it for a second.

'No – it's a legitimate question,' she said. 'I was upset after the confrontation with her and went over to Market Eaton to see my friend, Professor Featherstone. We had dinner and I drank rather more than I should. I couldn't drive back in that state, so I stayed the night.'

'I didn't realise you were so close.' Sally arched an eyebrow.

'I'm not.' Anna felt herself colour. 'Nonetheless, I did stay the night with him and the police have finished questioning me for the time being.'

'On police bail, are you?' Fletcher asked.

Anna nodded. 'You were the police officer here before Janice, weren't you? I've been meaning to talk to you about one or two things, but I've been so tied up with the sisters ...'

'That's something we need to get straightened out right now,' Sally interrupted. 'I don't think it's viable to have you seeing them while this thing is hanging over your head.' Frank moved to the sofa and sat beside her, all too obviously signalling a unified front. 'We're responsible for their safety, and all, and ...'

'That's OK. You don't have to justify it.' Anna's voice was level as she set down her mug on the coffee table. 'I do understand. I have to say, if our positions were reversed, I'd do the same thing, under the circumstances. But I really didn't kill Stella.'

'I'm not saying you did. But we can't take any risks with the sisters' welfare.'

'Fair enough. I'll talk to my boss tomorrow.' Anna paused. 'I take it you want me out of the cottage, too?'

'That would be appreciated.'

Anna nodded her assent. 'If I could have a day or two – the police have kept my car for forensic examination and I don't know when I'll get it back. I may have to make alternative arrangements to get home. And, as I said – I need to clean up after the forensic people.'

'By the end of the week will be fine.'

'OK. I'll obviously reimburse you for any damage and replace the knives.'

'The knives?' Sally and Frank exchanged a glance.

'The police took all the kitchen knives and the meat cleaver. I presume you'll get them back at some point, but I don't want to inconvenience you.'

'Me or Frank will come and check the place over before you leave. In the meantime – I believe you still have a spare key for Broomwood House?' Sally watched as Anna struggled to free it from her key ring. 'Thank you,' she said as it was finally handed over.

'Right. I'd better be going, then. I'll let you know when I'll be leaving.' Anna left the room, fighting back tears once her back was turned, the more so when she heard Frank's footsteps on the stairs behind her.

'Mind how you go.'

'I will. Goodnight, Frank.'

'Goodnight.'

Anna nodded without looking back as she made her way down the garden path.

Chapter Forty-two

Monday November 21st

Anna's eyes darted ever more frequently to the clock as the hands dragged themselves inexorably towards 9 a.m. when she knew she would have to phone Philip. She had slept only fitfully and had been up for hours, cleaning and polishing, rehearsing in her mind the conversation she would be faced with once Philip was in his office. She felt light-headed and sick to her stomach. Was there *anything* she could do to salvage the situation? She had been over and over it, worrying at it like a dog with a rat. 8.45. This was no good. Overruling the nausea she felt, she forced herself to eat toast and drink tea before finally picking up the handset and dialling Philip's number.

'Rhianna! My God, I . . .'

'Philip, before you even ask – I didn't kill her.'

'Well, I hardly thought you did! But how are you? Are you all right?'

'I'm fine, Philip, but the project will have to be handled differently, due to what's happened. Obviously, it's sensible for me to stay away from the sisters while everything is hanging in the air, but the main project – the Swiffords research itself – there's no reason why that shouldn't continue. I thought about moving to Market Eaton until things have calmed down. I can use the library and the Records Office.'

There was silence.

'Philip?' Anna's heart was hammering.

'Yes, that sounds good. But I think we need to talk first. Face to face. A sort of debriefing, if you like, before we commit ourselves to finalising the best way forward.'

Shit! He's going to pull me off it! 'Philip – I would just like to ask – on the record – whether I still have your confidence?'

'That goes without saying, Rhianna. Absolutely. It's more the ... shall we say, the public relations side of things. How soon can you come in?'

'The police still have my car, Philip, so I'll have to come by train, and I don't feel I can do that for a couple of days at least. There's a lot of sorting out to do here – cleaning the cottage and so forth. The forensics team left it in rather a mess.' *Stall for time. It's the only thing you can do.*

'I see.' Philip's voice was grim. Anna could clearly imagine the expression on his face and didn't like it one bit. 'And what exactly is your legal position as far as the police are concerned at present?' Philip continued. 'Just so I know before I see you?'

Before he pulls in the university PR machine for damage limitation ...

'I'm on police bail, Philip. I have to go back in two weeks' time, unless they call me in earlier. You should know, too, that I have a rock-solid alibi for the night Stella was murdered. That's why I'm out on bail, rather than in custody. I haven't been charged with anything.'

'Does this bail have conditions?'

'No, Philip. Only court bail has conditions.'

'Right. Well. Where are we? Yes. How about Wednesday, then?'

'Thursday or Friday would be better.'

'Thursday then. Shall we say 11 o'clock?'

'That's fine, Philip. Goodbye.' Anna hung up, breathing deeply to control the trembling she felt. He wasn't convinced. There was doubt in his mind, she could feel it. He was probably back-pedalling like hell, wishing he'd never asked her to get involved. *His reputation's on the line and he'll sacrifice me to save it. Shit!*

'What did you expect?' She spoke the question aloud. Academia was just as cut-throat as any other business these days. Was *run* as a business these days. Just one of the reasons she'd left, she acknowledged, even though it had been buried under the trauma of the accident that had tipped her into a breakdown.

She sighed heavily, got to her feet and looked around the room, wondering what to do next. *Pat's clothes!* She had washed them last night, put them in the tumble dryer this morning. She went through to the utility room and opened the machine, shaking the clothes before folding them and putting them into a plastic bag. At least drying them this way had obviated the need to iron them. She sighed again. *Come on, Summers – pull yourself together! This isn't going to go away, so face it with the best grace you can muster!* Crossing to the kitchen door, she almost collided with Maggie on the step.

'Blimey, girl – you look rough! Didn't sleep well?'

Anna shook her head. 'Too much on my mind, I'm afraid.'

'I do wish you'd have stayed with us at the pub last night.'

'It was a kind offer, Maggie, but I don't want to cause any more difficulty for anyone. You and Pete and Pat have to live here, even after I leave.' She held up the bag of clothing. 'I was just on my way round to return Pat's things and say thank you.'

'Right.' Maggie paused, then, colouring slightly said, 'Look – there isn't an easy way of saying this, so I won't beat about the bush – I just had a phone call from Sally. Molly Webb phoned her, quite agitated, apparently, insisting on seeing you. So she asked if I'd go over with you to find out what she wants.'

'A baby-sitter, eh? Just to make sure I don't run amok?' Anna shook her head. 'I feel like I've got "SK" tattooed on my forehead – Suspected Killer.' She forced a smile. 'Don't worry – I do understand. And I'm sorry if it's putting you out.'

'It's no problem, Anna.' Maggie watched as Anna locked the door and they set off together. 'Sally would have come herself, if she'd been fit, but what with Frank having to do the paper round this morning, and Fletcher's staying with them and not feeling too good . . .'

'I saw him there last night,' Anna told her. 'I'm surprised he's been discharged from hospital so soon.'

'Well, he insisted he was OK, but he had a bit of a funny turn when he got back home, apparently. Frank said he nearly keeled over on the doorstep – he was all for taking him back, there and then, but Fletcher reckoned it was just the stress, and he'd be all right. Anyway, Frank decided it'd be best to take him home with them – at least that way, there's someone to keep an eye on him. Wouldn't do to have him collapsing at his own place, what with him living alone and all.'

The two women turned down the lane leading to Broomwood House.

'Did Molly say why she wanted to see me?' Anna asked as they climbed over the stile. Maggie shook her head.

'Sally couldn't get it out of her. Seems she insisted only you would do.'

Bet that went down like a lead balloon, Anna thought, noting also, as they approached the house, that Maggie was now apparently Guardian of the Spare Key. Maggie glanced at her as she rang the bell and fitted the key into the lock.

'Sally said you gave yours back. What with the investigation going on.'

Anna had no time to reply, as the door was opened almost immediately.

'My dear Dr Summers! I'm so glad to see you! Do come in!' Molly stood aside and leaned on her stick as the women entered.

'How are you, Molly? And how's Alice? Is she feeling better?'

'I'm feeling perfectly all right apart from Molly making my life a misery.' The voice came from the end of the corridor, where Alice stood, ramrod straight and dressed in her tweeds. 'Come on through and see what she's done!'

Anna and Maggie glanced at each other, mystified, as they followed Molly down the entrance hall and through to the Arts and Crafts Room.

'Oh my Gawd!' Maggie's hand flew to her mouth. 'Have you called the police?'

Alice frowned. 'Why ever would we do that?'

'Well, you've been burgled again, haven't you? You poor things!'

'No, we have not. This is all *her* doing.' Alice inclined her head in the direction of her sister, fighting down the impulse to point, which she had always been taught was rude.

'Molly?' Anna helped her to the nearest chair, having to clear things from the seat before the old woman could sit down. 'What's been going on?'

'I was looking for something, dear – for you. I started before you went away, but it's even more important now.'

'Stupid woman!' Alice interjected. 'If she'd told me what she was looking for in the first place, I could have told her where it was! The original, at least. The facsimile went missing in the burglary.'

'Had I told you what I was looking for, you would have told me not to bother because you're always embarrassed by it! And you weren't well, so I didn't want to bother you.'

'Bother me? Ha! This mess bothers me! And who's going to clear it all up, that's what I want to know!'

Anna and Maggie exchanged another glance. The room looked like a bomb site. 'I'm sure we can help,' Anna began '... but what was so important?'

'The Marcus Beardsmore document.' Molly said the words as if they were self-explanatory.

'Stuff and nonsense!' Alice snorted.

'Alice – I don't care whether you think it's stuff and nonsense or not!' Molly raised her voice, shocking her sister into silence. Turning to Anna, she said, 'I was thinking of giving it to you, anyway, but it was that dreadful woman who made up my mind.'

'What dreadful woman?' Anna was baffled.

'The one who came here on Friday night.' Molly leaned forward. 'The one who was murdered.'

'Stella? Professor Timpson? She was here?' Anna's head spun.

'Oh yes. Left her business card.' Molly fumbled in the pocket of her cardigan and held it out. Anna stepped forward, then stopped herself.

'Maggie – check it, will you? I don't want my fingerprints on it.'

'OK.' Maggie took it and held it up for Anna to see. 'Bloody hell!' she muttered under her breath. 'She's right.'

'What on earth was she doing here?' Anna directed her question to Molly.

'Being rude about you. We can't bear bad manners, can we, Alice? Our mother always used to say that manners cost nothing, and she was quite right.

'Smelled of drink, too,' Alice offered.

'Stella did?' Anna looked at Maggie. 'But she wasn't served at The White Hart ...'

'Then she must have been in The Penny-Farthing,' Molly told her. 'It's the only other public house in the village now, I believe. There used to be six, you know – The Wagon and Horses, The King's Arms, The Golden Rod and the May Tree. The Penny-Farthing is still The Penny-Farthing, but The White Hart was called The Innkeeper's Rest, back then – this was the 1930s, you know.'

'Molly –' Anna tried to bring her back to the present. 'Do you know what time Professor Timpson was here?'

'Oh, we know that all right!' Alice put in. 'We were just sitting down to watch a programme on television which commenced at 9 p.m. Only it must have been a little late starting, because I distinctly heard the church clock strike the hour before it began, and then, just as the announcer said – we couldn't see him, you know – it was just his voice – just as he apologised for the delay, the doorbell rang and it was That Woman.'

'But we didn't know until this morning that she'd been murdered, did we, Alice? It was only when we saw her picture on the early regional news.'

'Yes, and we thought we'd better tell you, because of how rude she was about you.'

'Have you told the police? This could be really important . . .' Anna was cut short by Molly, still in Friday evening mode.

'Not that she was rude to whoever she went off with – oh no! Her voice was quite different, then.'

'She was with someone?'

Alice and Molly looked at each other, shaking their heads. 'Not *with* someone, exactly. That is to say, she came here alone, and there was no one else in her motor car. You did say there was no one else, Molly?' Alice turned to Maggie and Anna. 'Molly still had her distance glasses on, but I had already changed into my close-up ones.'

'That's right. But when we finally managed to close the door, well, we . . .' Molly flushed at the memory. 'To be quite honest, we were a little alarmed by her and wanted to be sure that she was, indeed, going away as we had asked her to do . . .'

'. . . so we stood with our ears pressed to the door to make sure. In fact, I had mine by the letter flap. Just *slightly* open, you understand. And that's when we heard him.'

'Who?' Anna asked.

'Why, the man she went away with! The one who told her he had the – what was the phrase he used, Molly?' Alice frowned as she tried to recollect the words.

'It had something to do with electricity, I think.' Molly sounded dubious. 'It reminded me of it, at least. We didn't have electricity in the village until 1945, you know.'

Anna and Maggie were almost holding their breath, willing the sisters to remember.

'Generators – that was it! Do you remember when we first had generators for the function at the village hall, Molly!' Alice turned to her visitors, face aglow.

'Generators?' Anna's heart sank. This wasn't making sense at all.

'Not generators – that's what reminded Molly of electricity! No, dear – the man told the Professor that he had "all the gen" she needed.'

'Thank you, ladies.' Anna's relief was heartfelt. She turned to Maggie. 'Why don't we make a nice pot of tea and phone Janice . . .'

It was early evening when Anna and Maggie finally made their way to The White Hart, Maggie sweeping her way to the bar with a grin that belied her cry of, 'God – we're exhausted!' The pub was unusually quiet and both Pete and Pat were behind the counter.

'What have you been up to then? Anna – welcome back!' Pete's smile was genuine as both he and his wife extended handshakes to her.

'Thank you. And thank *you* –' this to Pat '. . . for the loan of the clothes, herewith returned, washed and dried.' Anna handed over the bag as Pete poured her a glass of wine.

'On the house.'

'No, really . . .'

'We insist. Oh – here he is! That's all the Usual Suspects, then!' Pete nodded and Anna and Maggie turned to see Adam Etheridge emerge from the men's toilet.

'Adam! They let you go!' Maggie rushed to greet him and was enveloped in a hug.

''Course they did! It was a no-goer from the start.' He looked over her shoulder and took in Anna's presence. Releasing Maggie, he moved towards her. 'Dr Summers. Nice to see you.' He held out his hand. Anna took it cautiously. Warmth seemed to flood up her arm as she was held in his grip. 'Before you ask – I didn't kill the woman.' His eyes were clear as he spoke.

'Neither did I,' she answered, her voice even.

'Good – that's that out of the way, then . . .' Pete began.

'You don't know the half of it!' Maggie glanced over her shoulder before scooting everyone into a huddle around the bar.

'Turns out that that Stella woman went to see the Misses Webb on Friday night!'

'What?' Pat's voice reflected the bafflement that Anna and Maggie had experienced earlier.

'Yeah – that's what we thought. Seems she turned up there around nine o'clock – bit the worse for wear, from the sound of it – and I'm not referring to Anna's jab at her nose, either.'

'She must have gone to The Penny-Farthing after we kicked her out, then,' Pete observed.

'Right.' Maggie stifled a giggle. 'Poor Anna got a lesson in how many pubs there used to be here and what they was called ...'

'I would have done the same.' Anna's voice was thoughtful.

'What you on about?' It was Maggie's turn to look mystified.

'If the positions had been reversed. It's probably why Stella came in here in the first place. Pubs – especially in rural communities – are the centre of village life. You want to know anything – that's where you ask. I've done it before, as I'm sure Stella had.'

'And she went from the pub to the sisters?' Adam frowned.

'Yes – around nine o'clock – when Anna was having dinner in Market Eaton with a restaurant full of witnesses. Where was you then, Adam?'

Pete spluttered into his mineral water.

'No, no – I didn't mean it like that!' Maggie protested. 'If the police has let you go, same as Anna, there must be a good reason. I wasn't accusing you of anything.'

'That's all right then,' Adam smiled. 'I was very lucky. I'd only popped in here on Friday night to drop off an estimate for some work for Pete and Pat. Me and Dad had been working late – it's not been easy getting a replacement for Dave, so he's come out of his semi-retirement until I find somebody. The thing is, we had something arranged – a mixture of work and social, if you like.' He turned to Pete and Pat. 'Do you know Alan Crossthwaite in Market Eaton?'

'A lawyer, isn't he? I've heard of him, but not met him.' Pete shook his head.

'Well, him and Dad were at school together. They're still mates – play golf and go to the footie. Alan's wife was off visiting her mother in a nursing home down south and Alan wanted a bit of a refurb on the kitchen while she was away – as a surprise. And him and Dad being mates, like – well, we were invited down on Friday night, have dinner, play some snooker and what have you – ready for an early start on Saturday. We were going to work right through the weekend.'

'So you were at his place.' Maggie nodded her satisfaction.

'Too right! Sat up watching an Al Pacino film till turned one in the morning. And he lives in some style, so he's got alarms all over the place. If I *had* decided to go and murder Stella Timpson, I'd have set the place off like a nuclear alert.'

'You don't know the combinations, then? Even being a builder and your dad being his mate?'

'Maggie!' It was Pat's turn to protest.

'He knows what I mean, don't you? And the police must have asked you the same thing.'

'They certainly did. And the answer's no. Not even my dad knows Alan's security codes.'

'Two of you on police bail then, eh? Let's just hope they get whoever did do it, and pronto.' Pete's face was serious.

'That reminds me ...' Pat turned to her husband. 'You heard the latest about the goats?'

'No – what?' Pete and Maggie spoke the words together.

Pat rolled her eyes. 'Chris was telling me earlier – seems the police aren't seeing it as open and shut with Carol and Bill ...' Maggie made a disgusted sound of protest, but Pat held up her hand. 'No – listen to this. Someone – anonymous, as far as I know – put them in the picture about Pete chucking Dave out, and what Dave had said about the goats and all. So they've hauled *him* in for questioning about it.'

'Bloody hell!' Maggie shook her head in disbelief.

'It's a wonder there's anybody left in the village who *hasn't* been hauled in for questioning over one thing or another! How many of us are on police bail now?' Pete asked.

'Well, there'll be more yet!' Maggie announced. 'Isn't that right, Anna?' Anna seemed reluctant to reply, so Maggie carried on without her. 'The sisters said that Stella whatsername went off from their place with a local man.'

'What? Well, who?' Pete looked from one person to the other.

'That's just it – they don't know,' Maggie told him. 'Not for sure. Only that he was local – because of his accent. We've had a right time there, haven't we, Anna? Molly had turned the place upside down looking for something that turned out to be in the safe all along, and me and Anna has been clearing up while Janice come over to take their statements – and afterwards. Every room except one! That was Molly's work room, because she said she knew it wasn't there. And Alice really had her hair off about it. She was right about the mess, though – we thought they'd been burgled when we first got there, didn't we?'

Anna smiled at the memory. 'It really was a mess,' she agreed. 'Anyway – look – I should really get going.' She looked at her watch. 'But thanks for everything. I really do appreciate it.'

'You want to stay here tonight?' Pat asked.

'That's all right,' Maggie interrupted. 'She can stay at mine. Two of us together, we'll be fine.'

'As long as you're sure?' Anna smiled at her, grateful for the renewed confidence.

''Course I'm sure. How about we have dinner here first, eh? You as well, Adam? Celebrate being out on bail and all that?'

'That'd be lovely, Maggie. Thank you,' Adam smiled.

'Oh, I'm looking forward to this!' Pete rubbed his hands together before handing them the menu. 'Let's see what tickles your fancy ...'

Chapter Forty-three

Maggie waited outside April Cottage while Anna dropped off the box she had brought from Broomwood House and collected her ight things. Moments later, they were safely inside Maggie's iving room.

'I don't know about you, my girl, but I'm done in! I'll show you where everything is and leave you to it, if you don't mind.' Maggie stifled a yawn as she spoke.

'No problem. It's been quite a day for both of us.' Anna ollowed Maggie into her house and up the stairs.

'I hope Sheila got the old girls settled all right. Far too much xcitement for 'em. I couldn't believe it when Alice blew a gasket ike that.' Maggie clucked her disapproval.

'Well, to be fair, Molly had made one hell of a mess,' Anna aid.

'Yes, but throwing that box at her! Molly was awful upset. Said he'd kept that old schoolwork all sorted by – what was it?'

'Year order, with alphabetical order within that,' Anna told her. She, too, was beginning to yawn. 'It'll be easy enough to sort out. 'll do it tomorrow – it shouldn't take long.'

'I'll leave you to it, then. It's a shame, though, isn't it, when they start losing their marbles? Makes me worry about getting older myself, especially if I'm on my own.'

'Oh – I wouldn't put it as strongly as that,' Anna said. 'Thank God they were lucid about Friday night. I do think having the TV and their new glasses is doing them good.'

'Yes, but Alice was furious that Molly had been in her room, and Molly was insisting it was all to do with the cocoa or something. Asked me to stop Sheila leaving it for them.' Maggie shook

her head sadly. 'I had a quiet word with her when she arrived an
she looked at me as if I'd gone off my rocker.'

Anna raised her eyebrows.

'She doesn't leave 'em a drink for late at night,' Maggi
explained. 'Says they'd have trouble with the bathroom and al
So one of the sisters must be doing it themselves. Poor things
not even remembering. Which makes you worry on all kinds o
fronts, doesn't it? And how much store do you reckon the polic
will set by their account of Friday night given that they're lik
that?'

'They were pretty lucid about it,' Anna repeated. 'And more t
the point, they had Stella's business card, which proves she wa
there. Let's just hope they settle down in the next few days.'

'Yes. Well, goodnight, Anna. See you in the morning.'

''Night, Maggie. Sleep well.'

'You, too – you look like you need it!'

Anna quickly unpacked the few things she'd brought with he
and made her way to the bathroom. A shower would have to wai
until the morning, she decided, settling for washing her face an
brushing her teeth instead. *Well, at least the day's ended bette
than it began*, she thought. The sisters' evidence may hav
provided valuable new clues to Stella's murder, and she had had
warm reception at the pub and a lovely dinner with Maggie an
Adam. She tried to push thoughts of him out of her mind
Obviously at ease with Maggie, he was surprisingly warm an
funny when he relaxed. There was something about him … sh
raised her face to the bathroom mirror and said, 'No!' Aloud. An
firmly. And none of Maggie's nonsense …

Her face flushed at the memory. Adam had gone to the bar an
Maggie had grinned at her, saying, 'Adam's sweet on you!'

'Don't be so ridiculous!' Anna had protested. 'He doesn't eve
call me by my first name! I'm still "Dr Summers" to him, in cas
you hadn't noticed!'

'Oh, I have – and that's how I know he's sweet on you.' Maggi
had tapped the side of her nose. 'Trust me!'

Enough! Anna padded back to the guest bedroom. Adam's ex-
wife had left him for Stella Timpson. Appallingly bad taste o
anyone's part, in Anna's opinion, but to have encouraged Maxin
to do a degree and have her leave him for an academic – well, tha
should be enough to put him off academics for life. *Not that I stil*

n *an academic. Not really. But I am to* him, *hence the 'Dr ummers' appellation. And that's all there is to it.*

Disgruntled with herself now, Anna got into bed. *God! I hope m not going to lie here thinking about Adam bloody Etheridge!* ne sat up, turned on the light again. *How do I take my mind off m? Food. Think of the meal. Pete really is a master chef. We had* . This wasn't going to work. Thinking of the meal and the pub itomatically meant thinking of Adam. *Shit! As if I don't have iough man problems at the moment!* Anna got out of bed and pened the bag she'd used to bring her things over for the night. he'd left the box of Molly's school books back at April Cottage, it had brought the stiff-backed envelope from the safe with her. iven that Molly had been to such trouble, which had, in turn, iused such trouble between her and Alice, it hadn't seemed right abandon it. Anna took it out and turned it over, picturing again e devastation that had been wrought in Molly's attempt to find it. /hat could be so important about this Marcus Beardsmore docuent? And why did the sisters argue over it? There was only one ay to find out. Getting back into bed, she adjusted the bedside ght and drew out the contents.

Concerning a most shameful and wicked episode in the Year of Our Lord 1732 and how it came to be unearthed on All Hallows Eve, 1888, in the village of Swifford Lea, as sworn by my own hand this day. A tale so fantastical that, had it been told to me by any person else, I should have believed them unbalanced of mind. Indeed, I am barely able to believe the veracity of my own senses, having always counted myself a man of both rational mind and superior intellect. How much more, then, is doubt bestirred when the fact of the matter is, that it was a dream that led to me to the unearthing of such hitherto buried deeds; a mere phantasm of the night. And yet the fact remains. What I dreamed was true, for upon waking I was compelled by the overwhelming reality and anguish of him who spoke to me to go and seek what he told me of in the place which, in such dream, he did show to me …

nna was suddenly wide awake. This, surely, was the document tella had had! A part of it, at least. She read on.

. . . I race ahead of myself. I must tell my story in its proper sequence. I had come to Swifford Lea ahead of my brother, Arthur, and his family, who are to take up residence here in Broomwood House. I was happy to do so, having over-exerted myself of late, and therefore glad to avail myself of time alone in the wholesomeness of countryside isolation. What could be farther removed from the turmoil in the City where 'Murder' is shrieked from every street-corner in the wake of the rash of abominations in Whitechapel! So here I came and swiftly arranged for a local woman to take care of needs until such time as Arthur and Beatrice arrive with their little ones when more permanent arrangements can be made for the acquisition of servants.

I am not a fanciful man; logic and science have ever been my pursuits and strengths; indeed, I have endured disapproval on more than one occasion with regard to what others perceive as my lack of imagination. I confess, in an effort to address such deficiency, I have resorted to the sort of reading that in normal circumstances, I should not dream of undertaking, but found myself greatly entertained by Mr Stevenson's tale of The Strange Case of Dr Jekyll and Mr Hyde. *Indeed, perhaps his portrayal of a man of like profession was what allowed me to be drawn to this shilling shocker. Likewise, the recent* A Study in Scarlet *of A. Conan Doyle stimulated me immensely. Would that his Mr Sherlock Holmes could cast his eye on the foul deeds afoot in Whitechapel of late. These literary diversions, however, entertained me for their scientific approach to their themes; hence I can reiterate – I am not a fanciful man.*

Dreams, for instance. I have never set store by dreams; in fact, I can barely recall a dream in my entire life. Yet the very first night I spent here at Broomwood House, I experienced one of startling clarity and intensity. It was, in fact, as if I had awoken in the night and there, at the foot of my bed, stood a fellow whom I should have taken for a burglar had I not immediately noticed his attire, which showed him clearly to be a gentleman. And yet, a gentleman of more than a hundred years ago. My heart began to race, despite the fact that I was able to assure myself that this was only a dream because:

1. *The gentleman's attire proved he could not be present in any real way and must therefore be a figment of my imagination.*
2. *The fact that I could see him at all bespoke a dream – there was no light in the room yet he was visible to me through the darkness, haloed, as it were, by a strange luminosity.*

I shook myself, therefore, stating aloud that this was only a dream. Making myself lie down again, I considered whether I may have eaten or drunk something which could have brought about this phenomenon. It seemed unlikely, but I felt the need to bring my reasoning faculties to this strange experience. Having cast my mind around for answers, I opened my eyes once again – and the figure was still there!

I confess, I took fright at this occurrence and jumped from the bed, whereupon the figure turned and walked to – nay – walked through *the door of my bedchamber, beckoning me to follow him. I did not do so, fumbling instead to light the lamp and dispel such imaginings from my brain through the introduction of light.*

I was disturbed no further that night, but the same thing occurred on the following one and the one after that. And last night – All Hallows Eve – I could bear it no more and this time, when beckoned, I followed, carrying the lamp with me, surprised to find that light did not dispel my visitor nor make him any less clear. Along the corridor we proceeded, and down the stairs and through the kitchen until it became obvious that I was to be led outside. Near farce ensued at this point, for I had to collect the key and unlock the door, sure that at any moment, my visitor would disappear and I should awake in my bed.

It seemed, however, that he understood, and when, at last, I proceeded behind him into the garden, he began to walk more and more slowly, and I sensed, rather than heard, some great anguish emanating from him. Finally, he stopped and pointed to the ground. I saw nothing but flag-stones. How, I cannot explain, for it was entirely without words, but he communicated to me that I should lift up one in particular. This proved no mean feat, especially with such feeble illumination as I had, but, with the aid of certain gardening implements, at last I succeeded.

To my great astonishment, I found a box buried in the soil beneath, and within the box, a document. The story it tells is an horrific one; the tale of how Megan Painter, an innocent woman, was hanged to cover up the vice and debauchery of men of authority. It should serve as a warning and a lesson to us all that the Almighty will not be mocked, and that those who commit such heinous crimes will, even in the afterlife, know no rest while their evil deeds are hidden from the light. It is my firm belief, after my experience, that the figure I saw and which led me to the burial place of this document, was none other than William Warrender himself. Examination of the document will show why I believe this to be so.

This account, I do swear, is true in every respect.
Marcus Beardsmore.
1st November 1888.

Fingers trembling with excitement, Anna held her breath as she turned to the even older pages and began to read ...

Chapter Forty-four

Molly Webb sat at the table in her work room trying to make sense of the events of the day. She felt horribly flat, thinking of herself like the remains of a bottle of ginger beer that had been shaken up and fizzed over, the dregs now undrinkable. *What a strange image! I did so use to love ginger beer when I was a little girl.* She looked around the room absently, trying to muster her thoughts. She had meant so well and it had all, somehow, gone wrong. *So* much trouble over the Marcus Beardsmore document and it wasn't really her fault; not really. It was all very well Alice saying that if she'd asked, she could have told her that the original was in Father's safe, but that's *not* what Alice would have said at all. *Alice* would have been the one going off like a bottle of exploding ginger beer because she hated anything to do with it. Molly reflected on that. Had it not been for Father insisting that it be saved for posterity, she had no doubt that Alice would have destroyed it. Stuff and nonsense! What a flap over nothing! Alice confessing – only if pressed, mind – that she was embarrassed by the supernatural aspects of the thing, believing it to be, in fact, a sign of mental disturbance. Tommyrot! The very fact that Marcus had dug up the William Warrender document was evidence that, dream or otherwise, his instincts had been correct. How, then, could he be mad? The William Warrender document existed, and that was an end to it. Not for Alice, though. Alice lied about her reasons for wanting the Marcus Beardsmore document forgotten, and those reasons were ... Molly struggled to remember. It was to do with Marcus himself, and something to do with dates, but she couldn't quite put her finger on it. *Damn and blast my memory! One minute it's there and the next it's slipped away, like a radio signal fading in and out. Why do I even bother?*

She thought of her sister, fast asleep in bed and snoring like a pig. *I can't seem to get* anything *right – I* told *them not to leave cocoa, and what happens – they left Horlicks instead! I thought I'd made it clear that we shouldn't have a drink at bedtime at all. And Alice wouldn't miss it, if it weren't left ready. She never needed night-time incontinence pads before. Not until Sheila started leaving the cocoa. And she's so grumpy, nowadays and ... How can I make myself clearer?*

Molly stood up slowly, moving to the doorway and looking across the corridor at what used to be Alice's bedroom – still was, except Alice chose not to sleep there anymore. *Was it so wrong of me to have looked for the Marcus Beardsmore document in there? It's not as if I were prying, or anything. Not into her personal things. I know jolly well what it looks like, and I wasn't looking at anything I shouldn't.* She shuddered, thinking about Alice's reaction. Incandescent. That was the only word for it. My, my – she hadn't seen Alice so angry for ... the calculation failed her, but it was a very, very long time. And dear Dr Summers and her friend had been quite happy to set everything to rights, and it was when they were replacing the dresser drawers that Alice had screeched at her and gone through into her work room and flung her box of tutorial books around, asking how *she* would like it. Molly shook her head in dismay and returned slowly to the table. She hated to admit it, but Alice's outburst had shaken her up quite badly. Alice had always had a quick temper, of course, but she had never been one for physical violence. And the box of books had very nearly hit her, and given everyone a fright, and Dr Summers' friend had taken Alice away and Dr Summers had come into the work room and picked up the books and comforted Molly and ...

Molly's thoughts faltered ... *and what?* Something was stirring at the back of her memory and she couldn't pin it down, elusive as a fluttering butterfly. *Oh well ... Best get on with the wedding gown.* Another deflating thought. *At one time, I could have whizzed along with it. Now ... inch by painful inch. Like drawing teeth with a pair of pliers. I wonder – did I tell Dr Summers about when old Baxter, the dentist, used to do that, with his patients stretched out on their own kitchen tables ...?* She found that she had wandered, not to where her work-in-progress was hidden away, but to where the box of books had been. *Oh dear. I don't remember taking off my cardigan . . .* She picked it up and draped it over one arm, its soft folds feeling somehow not quite right. Moving back to the table, she spread it out, tutting under her breath. *What is that inside? I only ever keep my handkerchief . . .* Gnarled hands turned over the garment until she had access to the guilty pocket. Ah yes. As her fingers closed around its contents, illumination came. *Dr Summers said it was trapped between drawers and gave it to me, though why, I don't know, because I'm sure she said it was from Alice's room – except she seemed to think Alice's room was mine. And I must have slipped it into my pocket without looking because Dr Summers' friend shouted up the stairs to say that the police were here to talk about that rude woman who died. Perhaps that's why I took off my cardigan. I was hot after the fright of Alice throwing the box and I didn't, in any case, want to look a fright to a police officer.*

Seated now, and with her reading glasses on, Molly looked at what it was that Dr Summers had given her. The top of it gave her no direct clue, appearing simply to be folded paper. She removed it, but before looking at it, her eyes were drawn like magnets to what had been hidden beneath it. She blinked, the sudden uncomfortable lurching of her heart making her feel quite light-headed. She breathed deeply, trying to steady herself, blinking rapidly now. There was no doubt about it. What she had in her hands was a small bundle of air mail envelopes addressed to herself. Letters that bore Canadian stamps and Captain Robert Strachan's handwriting . . .

Chapter Forty-five

Tuesday November 22nd

Anna was half-way down the steps outside Market Eaton police station when there was a flurry of feet behind her and a hand came down on her shoulder.

'Rhianna! What are you doing here? They've not hauled you in again!'

'Roly! No – I came to volunteer some information. About Megan Painter's curse.'

'But ...' They came to the bottom of the steps together and Roly turned to look at her straight on. 'But you said you knew nothing about it! That you'd let me know if you came across anything!'

'Roly –' Anna pulled away, running her hand through her hair. 'I *didn't* know anything. Not until late last night. And I've made you a copy. The important thing was to get it here to the police straight away. If nothing else, it may have bearing on Stella's murder. And I hate to disappoint you, but there is, in fact, no Megan Painter's curse. The whole thing was a hoax.'

'What?' Roly moved across the forecourt with her, his face thunderstruck. 'But the murders – the graffiti ...'

'I know. Which begs the question, who else knew about this stuff besides the sisters?'

'The sisters?' Roly grabbed her arm. 'You're not making sense. Look – I was just about to go for lunch – why don't we go somewhere and talk?' Anna hesitated and Roly used the all-too-brief moment to press his advantage, steering her towards the main street. 'Please – this is far too important to let our ...' He struggled for words '... personal difficulties get in the way. We need to pool resources, and fast.'

'All right.' Allowing his appeal to logic to overcome her reluctance, Anna dropped into step beside him.

Moments later, they were seated in the dining room of an old-fashioned hostelry where booths of dark oak afforded more than the usual amount of privacy. Anna waited until their orders had been taken before telling Roly about the previous day's events with the Misses Webb, ending her story on how she had only begun to read the Marcus Beardsmore document when she went to bed at Maggie's.

'... it was a shock, seeing the words Stella had read to Philip over the phone, but an even bigger shock, reading the documents that accompanied it.' Rapidly, she went into her account, drawing a photograph of the documents from her briefcase as she did so. 'William Warrender was the owner of Broomwood House back in 1732. Along with two friends, John Nettleton and Samuel Garwood, he aided and abetted a plot to help out Nathaniel Parry, the most prominent person in the area, who had, shall we say, a penchant for exercising *droit de seigneur* on whosoever took his fancy. Which was just about any female not buried, by the sound of it.' Anna made a moue of distaste. 'Well, to cut a long story short, Megan wasn't having any of it and things got out of hand. She was paraded in a scold's bridle and accused of doing away with her neighbour's child, which, being one of Parry's bastards, had been spirited away to aid the case. The whole thing was a set-up, and the poor girl was hanged. *But* – and this is where things get really interesting – all four men received something known as Megan Painter's Curse shortly after her execution.' Anna pointed out the page. 'As Megan was illiterate, as well as dead, to say it put the wind up the lot of them is something of an understatement. Warrender says only that he believed the source of the curse was some nebulous group called The Guardians. The name obviously meant something to him, but he doesn't go into any detail about them. He did, however – and the others along with him – fear them enough to take the curse seriously. Within the year, all four families had decided to leave the Swiffords and start afresh in the New World. Even so, before they left, Warrender himself was plagued by nightmares to such an extent that he wrote his account – confession, if you like – and buried it in the garden of

Broomwood House, praying that the curse would be buried with i
and unable to cross the ocean after him.'

'Standard stuff about putting water between yourself and a witch,' Roly commented. 'So maybe they inferred, from this intervention from The Guardians, that although they'd stitched up Megan on false charges, they had inadvertently killed a witch.'

'What also interests me,' Anna continued, 'is the fact that this Swiffords project was funded by Americans who trace their ancestry back to these parts. I'll check it with Philip when I see him on Thursday.'

'You think they could be the descendants of Warrender and the rest?'

'It would be an ironic twist, wouldn't it?'

Roly scooped the papers off the table as their lunch was served.

'My God – I can't believe the old girls have been sitting on this!'

'Oh, I can!' Anna leaned over as he replaced the photocopied pages by the side of his plate. Finding the Marcus Beardsmore document, she tapped it with her forefinger. 'Take a look at these dates ...'

Alice Webb had been acutely aware of Molly's absence all day. Not that she was absent from the house, of course – that would have been unthinkable as well as physically impossible – but whenever she had entered a room, her sister had left it. They hadn't spoken at all. Well, she herself had spoken to her sister, but had not been afforded the courtesy of a reply. And for the past few hours, she had heard a series of drawers being opened, bumps and bangs, starting in the library but, more recently coming from upstairs. Alice closed her eyes. What if Molly was turning the place upside down again? What if she were in Alice's old bedroom? *I should have checked, before I retired last night. I should have, but I forgot. And Molly's silence today ...*

A particularly loud bang emanated through the ceiling. Expelling a puff of air, Alice could bear it no longer. Slowly, she walked through to the hall and up the stairs, at the top of which she stopped dead.

'What on earth do you think you're doing?'

'What does it look like?' Molly snapped. 'You have new spectacles, as well as I do. I'm moving you back to your own room.'

'But ... but *why*?' Alice stood helpless as she took in the trail of her belongings scattered along the corridor.

Molly drew herself as upright as she could manage. 'Why? *Why?*' She limped towards her sister, an expression on her face that Alice had never in her life seen before. Involuntarily, she stepped backwards, almost toppling down the stairs before grabbing the banister and finding firmer footing.

Molly's eyes were like gimlets, boring into Alice with laser-like hatred.

'You are a wicked, wicked woman, Alice Webb, and I shall no longer share a bed or a room with you.' Reaching into her pocket, she brought forth a bundle of letters. 'I have been examining my journals today. After I read these last night. After Dr Summers gave them to me. After she found them where you had hidden them.' With trembling hands, Molly unfolded the first of the bundle, which had no envelope, and read it aloud.

Vancouver,
Canada
July 14th 1948

My dearest Molly,

I cannot tell you how your last letter cheered my heart. And I hope that this will cheer yours, my darling. You will see from my new address in the west that things have gone even better than expected. So much so, that I am now in the position where I can, at last, ask you again to marry me. I know, my darling, what courage it will take for you to make such a decision, but I swear that, should you accept me, you will never regret it. I send you this ring in token of my undying love, sincerity and utter commitment to you.

Molly, Molly, Molly – your name is music to my ears, nectar to my soul. 'So fair art thou, my bonnie lass, and deep in love am I, and I will love you, oh my dear, till all the seas gang dry ...'

Write soon, my darling, knowing that you will make me the happiest man on earth should you consent to wear my ring. As soon as I hear from you, I shall make arrangements for your passage. Oh Molly – how you will love it here! How you will thrive! I enclose some photographs – they do not do the land justice, but you will at least have some idea. And the house – it is mine, my darling. OURS, if you will have me.

Love, love and always love,

Robert.

Alice's head was bowed, her skin as pale as parchment as Molly's voice faded on Robert's name.

'I never saw this letter. Nor the photographs. I never received any ring.' Molly's voice broke as she blinked back tears.

Alice said nothing.

Molly waved the rest of the bundle at her. 'Nor did I receive these! Robert writing in increasing despair, coming to believe not only that I had spurned him, but that I had not even afforded him the courtesy of a reply or the return of his ring.' She half-staggered as she limped towards her sister.

'How could you do it, Alice? How could you!' Waving the bundle again, this time right under her sister's nose, Molly gasped, 'I should tear your heart out, Alice Webb, for you have surely broken mine ...'

Adam Etheridge was locking the door of Fletcher Godfrey's cottage.

'Ay up, Adam!'

Adam turned to see Chris, the Morris Man, at the garden gate.

'Chris.' He acknowledged the man with a curt nod as he walked down the path towards him.

'I thought Fletcher wasn't back yet.' Chris stared pointedly at the darkened windows.

'He's not. But he's probably coming home tomorrow. I've been doing some minor work for him. Good opportunity while he's not there.' Adam walked through the gate, closing it behind him.

'Still with Frank and Sally, eh? Saves disturbing him. Quite.' Chris glanced hurriedly over his shoulder. There was no one else around. 'Well – I'd best be off then.'

'Sure. See you in the pub later, maybe.' Adam watched as Chris scuttled away. Only when he was out of sight did he turn and start walking down the lane, face grim. Pulling his mobile from his belt, he punched in a short-cut number as he approached his van, face betraying none of the impatience he felt.

'Sal? Adam. You can let Janice know I've done what needed doing. But we need to meet. Urgently. All Four of us. About Fletcher ...'

Chapter Forty-six

Anna, alone in April Cottage, was experiencing mixed feelings about her last evening in Swifford Lea. As she checked her list, to see what else was left to do, she weighed things up in her mind. Yes, it would be good to get away from the oppressive atmosphere generated by the murders, but on the other hand ... *I can't stand the thought of being pulled off the project. It's as if, even in death, Stella is reaching out and throwing a spanner in the works. And the sisters – what if anything happens to them? They're old, they could die at any time, and all their experience, their memories, will be lost for ever. Even if I'm pulled off the project* temporarily, *that could still be too long as far as the Misses Webb are concerned. But what can I do? Even* if *I can convince Philip that I didn't kill Stella, there's the problem with Sally Arnold. So even* if *Philip lets me carry on general research, I won't have access to the sisters unless I can convince Sally of my innocence. And it would be no good appealing to their solicitor – he'll be guided by Sally's opinion, and rightly so, given the circumstances.* That was a hell of a lot of 'ifs', she realised.

Feeling all too glum at the prospects ahead of her, Anna fastened her suitcase. This was not at all what she had planned or hoped for during the past few weeks. Despite her innocence, the village as a whole would see her departure in terms of her leaving under a cloud. Maggie was going to run her into Market Eaton tomorrow morning, from where she could catch the train home, spending just one night there before going for her meeting with Philip.

Taking a last look around the bedroom, she wrinkled her nose as her eyes fell on the basket of dried flowers. She sighed and chewed her lower lip, thinking about what to do. *With the basket, or Roly?* she asked herself, already knowing the answer was 'both'. Decision made, she picked it up and carried it, lugging the suitcase in her other hand, to the top of the stairs. *I'll throw it out. There's no way I'm taking it home with me after what's happened. It would just be a constant reminder of a major misjudgement on my part. How I'm going to put it right, I don't know. And I'll have to ...*

Unbalanced by the weight of the suitcase and distracted by her thoughts, Anna missed her footing on the narrow staircase, skidding down several steps before handing heavily on her bottom. The basket went flying, only to be crushed as the suitcase landed on top of it.

Bloody hell! Shaken, Anna got to her feet, looking down at the mess at the foot of the stairs. Crushed petals and stalks littered the carpet, a pungent and rather unpleasant smell seeming to waft through the air. *Just what I need! I'll have to hoover again!* She limped to the utility room, rotating her shoulders and rubbing her hip. It could have been worse, she conceded, telling herself to be thankful she hadn't broken any bones. Retrieving a black bag from the cupboard, she lumped the vacuum cleaner through to the living room and set about tidying up. Moving her suitcase to the front door, she picked up the remains of the basket and jammed it into the rubbish sack before scooping up the larger bits and pieces of its contents.

What the hell ... ? Anna did a double-take. It couldn't be, surely? There in her hand, along with broken stalks and flower heads, was a large gemstone. She held it up to view it better, a sudden wave of nausea sweeping over her. *If this is real ...* As the emerald caught the light, Anna's head seemed to spin. *There's a green-eyed yellow idol to the north of Kathmandu ...* She threw the stone into the sack as if scalded. *Green-eyed yellow idol? That poem – that's what the pastiche was about – the little green urinal to the north of Waterloo! But what does it mean? And what the hell is the matter with me? Feeling sick? Oh God – what if I'm pregnant?* Running through to the downstairs bathroom, she scrubbed her hands, soaping and rinsing them several times, telling herself that she wouldn't feel sick this quickly, frantically trying to remember when she'd had her last period. *God! If I'd had my wits about me – if I hadn't been arrested – I could have gone and got the morning-after pill. Oh SHIT! What am I going to do?*

Breathing deeply to steady herself, she collected a dustpan and brush before returning to the living room. Nothing seemed to be making sense. All she knew was, she did not want to touch the remains of the basket again. Did not want be pregnant with Roly's child. Did not want any of this bloody mess to be real.

Moments later, the carpet had been hoovered and the bag and its contents were in the dustbin outside the back door. Anna took stock. All the cleaning had been done and all her belongings were packed. Best stop worrying and get them – and herself – round to Maggie's. She glanced at the clock. *Damn! I'll have to hurry! Our table's booked for nine …* She had invited Maggie for a meal at the pub to thank her for her help and to mark her last evening in the village. She checked quickly to make sure that all the windows were locked and lights were out before closing the door of April Cottage for the last time. *Not quite the last*, she reminded herself. *Frank or Sally will be round in the morning to check it out and give me a final bill.* Although they'd given her until Friday, Anna had changed the arrangement, deciding to get it all over with now, rather than having to come back again.

Walking the few yards to Maggie's house, Anna duly deposited her suitcase and waited while Maggie finished applying a fresh coat of mascara.

'Right then!' Maggie picked up her handbag. 'Looks like we're ready for the off!' She pulled her coat around her as they stepped outside. 'It may only be a short walk, but, bloody hell, it's cold!' Frowning, she glanced up at the sky. 'Clear as a bell – the temperature will plummet.'

'There's already frost on the cars,' Anna observed.

'Oh well – at least it'll be warm in the pub!'

They had barely passed April Cottage when Anna's mobile rang. She pulled it from her pocket.

'Rhianna Summers.'

'Dr Summers – I'm so sorry to bother you.' Molly Webb's words were infused with barely suppressed panic. 'I'm so sorry,' she repeated. 'It's just that … well … I can't find Alice …'

Chapter Forty-seven

Anna laid her hand on Maggie's arm, bringing her to a halt.

'I'm sorry, Molly – what did you say? You can't find Alice?'

Maggie's eyebrows shot up as she heard what Anna said. She stood and listened as Anna asked a couple of questions and finally ended the call by saying, 'OK, Molly. Don't worry – we'll be with you in a minute or two.'

'What's going on?' Maggie asked.

'Molly can't find Alice. Apparently they had a row – a big one, from the sound of it. Molly thought Alice was in her room, sulking, but can't find her.' Anna bit her lip. 'I'm sorry – I told her we'd go over. She's awfully upset.'

'No problem. Come on – we'll take the car.'

The women turned and trotted back to Maggie's cottage. As they got into the car, Anna had a sudden thought.

'We ought to let Frank and Sally know. They might not be too happy, me going over there.'

'Bugger that! It's an emergency.' Maggie tutted her disapproval, but nonetheless pulled her mobile from her bag and dialled their number. 'No reply. Oh well. Let's go. Gawd – I hope nothing horrible's happened.'

'I know.' Anna had been trying various scenarios in her head. 'What if Alice has had a fall or – I don't know – a stroke or a heart attack and is lying behind a door or something.'

Maggie shook her head to try and rid herself of the images Anna had conjured up, swinging the car round the Green and heading it towards the lane which led to Broomwood House. Moments later, she brought it to a halt and turned to Anna. 'Right then. Let's see what's what.'

Anna rapped the Green Man knocker and shouted through the letterbox.

'Molly! It's Dr Summers and Mrs Taylor.'

They heard the chain being removed within seconds.

'Thank you so much!' Molly's hair was dishevelled, her eyes red from crying. 'I'm so sorry to bother you. I tried Sally's number, but there was no reply.'

'That's quite all right.' Anna moved to Molly's side. The old woman was limping heavily. 'Can I give you a hand?'

'Thank you, dear.'

Maggie closed the door behind them and they made their way along the corridor to the Oriental Room. Anna got Molly seated before asking any questions.

'Why don't you tell us what happened?' She knelt on one side of Molly's chair, Maggie pulling up a stool on the other.

Molly's face crumpled. She stretched out her hand and took a photograph from a side table, showing it to Anna.

'We had such an argument. It was Robert, you see. She'd hidden his letters, let me believe that he'd forgotten about me – that he didn't care. and all the time ...' She took a deep, shuddering breath. 'All the time – he'd asked me to marry him. Had even sent a ring.' Her hand moved again, this time producing a box of deep blue velvet. Anna opened it, gasping at the sight of the ruby and diamonds nestled inside.

'It was bad enough that she'd done it. But to keep the things, all this time! Have them hidden away! And do you know what she said?' Eyes overflowing now, Molly pulled a sodden handkerchief from her pocket, mopping ineffectually at her face.

Maggie fished in her handbag, pulling out a wad of tissues. Molly took them, but was unable to speak for several minutes. Finally regaining her composure, she took up the story again.

'She said she'd done it for the best. For my own good. And she wouldn't just have got rid of the letters and the rings because that would have been stealing. Stealing! When she stole my happiness by withholding this from me! And in the end, she confessed – said she didn't want to lose me, and how could she have looked after Mother and Father without me. I could have killed her! Robert meant everything to me.'

Maggie and Anna looked at each other as the old woman wept. Anna took Molly's hand in her own.

'Molly – you said you thought Alice had gone into her room in a sulk?'

'Yes. Hours ago. But I hadn't heard anything for a while and when I went upstairs, her door was open and she wasn't there. And I looked for her and couldn't find her.'

'All right.' Anna got to her feet. 'Maggie and I will take a look. You just stay here, OK?'

Molly nodded and clutched at the balled-up tissues as the younger women left the room.

Closing the door behind them, Maggie braced herself, raising an eyebrow.

'How do you want to do this?'

'I'll start upstairs – you start down here.'

Maggie nodded her agreement and she and Anna went their separate ways.

It didn't take long for them to conclude that Molly was right. Alice was nowhere to be found.

Maggie had a sudden, horrible thought. 'You don't think she would have taken the car? Tried to drive off somewhere?'

Anna shook her head, even though they had both turned to go through the kitchen to the garden.

'Molly's hearing is quite good – she would have heard the engine start. And I'm sure Sally said that Frank had removed the starter motor. The old girls think it doesn't work any more – he took it out to stop them driving off on their own.' It was with some relief that they found the car untouched.

Walking back into the kitchen, Maggie stopped to fill the kettle. 'What do we do now, then?'

Anna thought. 'I don't know if the police would want to get involved at this stage. But if Alice is out there ...' she gestured through the window '... we need to find her – fast. We don't know what she's wearing and even if she *is* wrapped up warm, it's bitterly cold, as well as dark. She could get hypothermia.'

The two women looked at each other, faces bleak as they considered the possibilities.

'I'll give Janice a ring,' Maggie said. 'In the meantime, why don't you whip over to the pub and see if you can raise a search party. I'm sure people will turn out, once they know what's happened.' She put her hand in her pocket and tossed the car keys to Anna. 'It's insured for any driver. You'll be OK. I'll stay with

Molly – get a cup of tea down her neck or something.' Her eyes scanned the kitchen surfaces and came to a halt. 'Is that the box of books you sorted out for her?'

Anna nodded. 'I took them to Sally's so that her niece could return them.'

Maggie pulled out the first one and flicked through it. 'Perhaps I'll get her to tell me about her teaching days. Take her mind off things, you know?'

'Good idea. These are from home coaching, after the sisters retired.'

'Right.' Maggie picked up the box and walked with Anna along the corridor. 'Off you go then. And I'll keep things under control, this end.'

Anna let herself out and jumped into Maggie's car, cursing as she crashed the gears and the car shuddered its way down the drive. *God! This clutch!* The headlights cut a swathe through the inky blackness of the lanes and it was with relief that she finally turned on to the main road with its street lights, swinging her way around the Green before turning into the car park of The White Hart.

Heads turned as she ran through the back door. Chris, the Morris Man, shook his head and clucked like a mother hen, tapping the face of his watch.

'You're late for your dinner booking! Pete won't be happy about that! Where's Maggie?' He was staring into space behind her, as if expecting Maggie to materialise at any second.

Anna didn't bother to reply, hurrying past him and only stopping when she reached the large brass bell by the bar, which was used to call time. She jangled it with full force, bringing the place to a standstill. Pat stood open-mouthed and Pete appeared from the kitchen, his face like thunder.

'Your attention, please! I need to organise a search party – Alice Webb is missing.'

A ripple of shock ran round the bar, every eye on Anna as people waited with bated breath.

'She and Molly had an almighty row, but we're not sure how long she's been missing or what she's wearing. She's definitely not in the house, however, and Maggie's phoning Janice to see if the police will help. In the meantime ...'

Several people were already on their feet, understanding the seriousness of the situation.

'Thank you,' Anna continued, heartened by the swift response. 'We're going to need all the help we can get.' As she paused for breath, a shrill ringing cut the air. She glanced behind the bar as she pulled the mobile from her pocket, but Pete made no objection.

'Rhianna Summers ...' She glanced round the bar, holding up her hand for silence. 'It's Maggie.' Listening intently, her eyes widened in disbelief. 'What?!' She listened again, so focused on what Maggie was telling her that she was unaware of the collective holding of breath as people waited for the news. Ending the call, she seemed to need a moment to gather her thoughts.

'I'm sorry – and thank you, all of you. Alice is in hospital in Market Eaton.'

'What?' Pat's voice echoed the question in everyone's head.

'I don't know all the ins and outs, but it seems she'd got herself over there and gone to the theatre. Apparently she collapsed in the bar during the interval of the play. The hospital phoned the house – she must have had some sort of ID on her – trying to ascertain what medication she's taking.'

'Christ! What is it? Heart attack? Stroke?' Pete's face was sombre.

'I don't know. I'll go back and talk to Maggie. Sorry about the booking, Pete – we ought to stay with Molly until we know how bad it is.'

'Sure. Don't worry. And if you need anything – just give us a shout.'

Anna nodded her acknowledgement and set off back to Broomwood House, mind buzzing with worry over what had happened to Alice. *At least she's in the best place, and not out in the cold and dark. But Market Eaton? The theatre – oh hell! I said I'd take them, and forgot all about it. But I didn't book tickets – not for this week, I'm sure.* She thought back to the trip to Market Eaton. *Alice went into the theatre while I took Molly to the loo. But the musical wasn't on until next week, surely ... ?* She was more puzzled than ever by the time she was let back into the house by Maggie, who ushered her through to the kitchen.

'How bad is it, Maggie?' Anna came straight to the point.

'I don't know. I don't think *they* know.'

'What, *what* is it? Stroke? Heart attack?'

Maggie shook her head. 'That's the weird thing. That's why

they phoned, asking about her medication. They *think* it might be a reaction between drugs and alcohol. She was having a glass of wine in the bar and her symptoms ... Well, I didn't know what to tell them. Molly says Alice doesn't take any medication, and I couldn't find anything in the bathroom cabinet or the kitchen cupboards except stuff for Molly. All I could do in the end was tell them who their GP is.'

'Damn! And we don't know if she's going to pull through?'

'They ain't saying much at the moment. I told 'em Sally's the closest they've got to next of kin, and gave them the name of their solicitor as well. I still haven't been able to get hold of Frank and Sally, mind.'

'What have you told Molly?'

'Just that Alice is safe and well and in hospital.' Maggie grimaced as she said it. 'Two out of three's truthful, at any rate.'

'Whatever happens, she's not going to be coming home tonight, is she?'

'No. And I wouldn't feel right, leaving Molly on her own. Trouble is, it'd be no good taking her back to mine because she'd never manage the stairs. And Frank and Sally's is even worse. I think we'd be best staying here with her overnight, don't you?'

'I don't see what else we can do,' Anna conceded. 'It would also be less disruptive for Molly, too, given that she's already distressed. I think Sally and Frank ought to know, though – especially as they're not keen on me being here.'

Maggie pulled out her mobile and tried their number again. She shook her head. 'Still no reply.'

'Haven't they got an answer machine?'

Maggie laughed and shook her head. 'In a village shop? They'd have people on the blower at all hours, pleading for a pint of milk or a tin of dog food. So not on the landline, no. If it's urgent, you either know them well enough to be privy to their mobile, or you go round and risk their wrath if it's not genuine. But I'm getting nothing on their landline *or* the mobile – and the mobile usually diverts to Sheila's if they're out for an evening – because of the old girls. There's no panic though, is there? I mean, we're here and we've got everything under control.'

'Yes, but Sally might know something about Alice's medication that Molly doesn't,' Anna said, 'so why don't I swing round there? The phone could be off the hook or something. And if they're not at home, then Fletcher Godfrey's bound to know where they are – I saw him in the pub. If he's staying with them, he'll either have a key or know where we can reach them. And the guys in the pub will be glad of an update on Alice's condition. Not that we can tell them much ...'

'OK,' Maggie agreed. 'I'll see if I can find some spare bedding while you do that, and when you come back, you can stay with Molly and I'll go and collect some bits and pieces from home. Your stuff's already packed, so that will be easy enough. If you don't mind?'

'Sure. No problem.'

'Right. I'd best make it look like I came through here for a purpose. Why don't you go and have a chat with Molly while I make a drink? Do you want one?'

Anna shook her head. 'No, thanks. I'll leave you to it, then.'

She knocked gently on the door of the Oriental Room before entering, trying to make her face show a brightness she was far from feeling.

'Hello, Molly – Maggie won't be a minute. What have you been up to, then?'

'Oh, we've had a very nice time, thank you, dear.' Molly's arm swept over a scattering of books across the table in front of her. 'Talking about when Alice and I used to tutor children in the three Rs.' She lowered her voice. 'I think she's trying to take my mind off Alice, you know. You've heard that she's in hospital?'

'Yes.' Anna sat down beside her. 'At least she's in the best place, Molly.'

'But whatever was she doing at the theatre? How did she get there? Oh Lord – I do hope she didn't drive.'

'No, no – the car's in the garage. I would assume she took a taxi.'

'I never heard one pull up. And no one knocked on the door. Perhaps a bus, do you think?'

'Who knows? But she's all right – that's the main thing.'

Maggie came into the room, bearing a tray.

'Here we are then – I made you a nice mug of Horlicks.'

Molly pulled a face. 'Oh dear – I know I asked the girl to stop leaving cocoa, but I didn't expect Horlicks instead. I don't particularly like it, you know.'

Anna and Maggie exchanged a glance over her head.

'Well, it'll soothe your nerves. Mine, too. I brought us some biscuits as well, or there's a nice piece of Bakewell tart.'

'Oh lovely! I'm quite partial to Bakewell tart.' Molly's face lit up.

'I'll just pop it down here, shall I?' Maggie moved towards the table, and Anna scooped the exercise books out of the way. She stood up, moving them to the seat of the chair, a piece of paper fluttering to the floor as she did so.

'I'll be off, then, and see if I can find Frank and Sally.' She bent to pick up the paper, eyes running idly across it. 'Oh my God ...'

'What?' Maggie looked at her curiously. 'You all right? You've gone white as a sheet.'

Anna barely heard her. Her eyes were transfixed by the hand-written words that were burning themselves into her brain.

'The soals of the corrupt shall rise as the smoak of incense, being a sacrifice pleasing before the Lord.'

Chapter Forty-eight

Anna tried to keep her voice casual. 'Molly – where did this come from?'

'What is it, dear?' Molly took the paper from her and fumbled for a moment, changing her glasses in order to be able to read it. 'Oh this!' She chuckled, a wonderfully warm, throaty sound. 'We had such fun with it!' She handed it back to Anna, her face alight with the pleasure of memory. 'My goodness, it must have been – let me think – all of twenty-five years ago. The story was Frank Arnold's idea . . .'

'Frank?!' An image of the huge, bear-like man cannoned into Anna's mind.

'Yes, dear. He ran the village youth club back then, you know, but this was a story done specially while Alice and I were tutoring Adam Etheridge and Gideon Claybourne – just before Gideon and his mother left the village. They moved to Okehampton, I believe. He wasn't well enough to go to school, poor thing, so . . .'

'He doesn't live here anymore? Gideon?'

Molly's expression was pained but habit kept her voice patient. 'No, dear – as I just said – they moved to Okehampton. Twenty-five years ago.'

'So there was some sort of story that Frank made up and you used it in tutoring the two boys? Did you use it for anyone else?'

Maggie was frowning and opened her mouth to speak, but Anna raised a hand, warning her not to interrupt.

'Oh no.' Molly smiled with the pleasure of recollection. 'No – it was done particularly for Adam and Gideon – atrocious spellers, the pair of them, although using archaic language in the story didn't help. But it wasn't really their spelling we were concerned about just then. More some fantasy to …'

'Thank you, Molly.' Anna's heart was hammering and she thrust the piece of paper into her pocket. 'I'll be back a.s.a.p., Maggie.' She strode to the door.

'But …' Maggie was half on her feet, bewildered, but Anna left without explanation. She sank down again, shaking her head and taking a sip of her Horlicks. She would much have preferred a brandy and Coke, but still … She handed Molly a slice of Bakewell tart.

'Oh thank you, dear. Would you mind passing the remote control device? There's a programme on in a few minutes about aircraft of World War II. We had a Junkers 88 shot down just over the back here, you know. Saw it with my own eyes. I heard the rattle of machine-gun fire – I was in the kitchen at the time, and went outside to look – and down the Junkers came with his port engine on fire. For one awful moment, I thought he was going to hit the house, but he came to earth in Foxton's Field.'

'I know it well,' Maggie told her, thinking back to the day she'd sat there, crying, after discovering the vicar's body.

Molly's eyes became unfocused as she allowed her memories to transport her back in time. 'Well, it was two Hurricanes that got it. I saw them doing a victory roll. The wreckage was scattered all over the place.' She blinked and looked at Maggie, back in the present. 'November 1940, I think it was. Of course, that would be before you were born …'

Anna drove the car only a short way down the lane before pulling it over and taking out her mobile.

'Rhianna! I was just on my way over to see you. I was hoping we could have a drink before you leave. I didn't want …'

'Roly – something's come up,' Anna interrupted. 'I think you'd better get hold of whoever's dealing with the murders.' Rapidly, she explained what had happened, culminating in her discovery of the paper and Molly's explanation of it.

'Good God!' There was silence for a moment as Roly took the information on board. 'And Frank's the postmaster. And Adam's the one you saw with the goats when you first arrived. *And* the one they had in after you in connection with Stella's murder?'

'Yes, but he had a cast-iron alibi. Staying with a lawyer.'

‘I’m going to hang up, Rhianna, and contact the police. In the meantime, I want you to stay out of their way and stay in a public place until I get to you.’

‘I can’t leave Maggie . . .’

‘Rhianna – I’m sure I don’t need to remind you that the course of these events has been taking an anti-clockwise circle. And you’ve seen the Marcus Beardsmore document – brought it in, for Christ’s sake! The next murder will take place in Swifford Lea. What you’ve found out this evening has given the best clue yet as to who’s behind it. I’ll call you back.’ The line went dead.

‘Shit!’ Anna spoke aloud. ‘Now what do I do?’ She tried to gather her thoughts. She was *supposed* to be going to check on Frank and Sally. To let them know what had been happening at Broomwood House. Was that a good idea in light of what she’d just learned? *No. But if I hadn’t come across this paper, I would have gone, as promised. It would be the natural thing to do. They need to know what’s happened to Alice, and that Maggie and I are there. And what if Maggie’s got through on the phone in the meantime and told them that I’m on my way? It would look bloody suspicious if I* don’t *turn up.*

She put the car back into gear and set off. *Just keep it natural. You have good reason not to stay – no going in or hanging around. You have to get back to Maggie and Molly.* She felt a prickle of fear. The whole thing seemed so terrible. Frank and Adam? Or Frank *or* Adam? Either way, she felt sick to her stomach. *Not that again. Oh hell!*

Stopping the car a short distance from the back entrance to Sally and Frank’s house, Anna turned off the lights and ignition and sat for a moment, surrounded by the darkness. Frank was huge. He’d have no problem killing anyone, if physical size was what it came down to. She shivered. And Adam? She thought again of how he’d pulled his fleece off in the living room of April Cottage, of the muscles he’d exposed. How those muscles had felt when she was in the fireplace with him . . . *Stop it!* The rush of sensory remembrance threatened to overwhelm her and she brought her attention back to logical thought. The goats. He’d *said* that he’d been unaware of her presence on Bonfire Night, but what if he hadn’t? What if he’d been planning to kill the goats then, and she’d effectively disturbed him, causing him to delay his plan? She suppressed a bitter laugh as she remembered how he'd apologised for frightening her. She felt an overwhelming need for fresh air and lowered the window, the chill striking her face and pinching her nostrils. *This is ridiculous! They're normal people. Nice people.* She leaned her head on the steering wheel. *What do you expect, Summers? An old-fashioned movie where the bad guys wear black hats? Don't be so bloody stupid! If evil was that obvious, we'd all run a mile.*

She lifted her head and froze. Just yards away, Janice Mills, Frank and Sally Arnold and Adam Etheridge came out of the back gate, the women, shivering despite their sweaters, staying huddled in the entrance, while the men, dressed for outdoors and carrying torches, stepped on to the path. Anna, despite the darkness, found herself sliding down in the driver's seat, heart hammering, praying for invisibility as she kept them barely in view through the spokes of the steering wheel. Sally, leaning on her crutches, turned her head.

'Is that the phone?' Her voiced carried easily to Anna's ears.

'I'll get it,' Janice said.

'No. Leave it for now. So,' Sally's voice was tight. 'Fletcher Godfrey. Death by Air. No wonder he was so keen to get to his sister's.'

'And to get out of his cottage.' It was Adam who spoke.

'Well, we helped him do that, I'm afraid.' Frank's tone was grim.

'Let's see if we can help him again, shall we? Bring him in.' Sally looked at the two men before manoeuvring herself on her crutches to return to the house, helped by Janice.

Anna watched as Frank latched the gate behind her before he and Adam strode off down the lane together, heading for the main road. The blood seemed to rush and swirl in her ears as the enormity of what she had heard sunk in. *Oh my God ...* Not just Frank and Adam, but Sally and Janice as well. And Janice a police officer! Pushing herself upright, Anna watched the men until they disappeared from view, turning right, towards the centre of the village. Frantically punching Roly's number into her mobile, she gave him no time to speak, merely reporting what she had witnessed.

'It'll take them several minutes to get to the pub on foot. Oh Christ – I hope they're not picking up a car round the corner! Roly

– I have to go! I have to get to Fletcher before they do.' She ended the call, throwing the mobile on to the passenger seat and starting the car.

Seconds later, she was out on the main road, heart leaping as she passed Frank and Adam, who, still on foot, had not yet reached the car showroom. Shooting across the car park of The White Hart, she was out of the vehicle in a flash, leaving the engine running as she ran towards the pub in search of Fletcher Godfrey.

Chapter Forty-nine

The pub fell silent as Anna entered through the back door, every face swivelling expectantly in her direction.

'Everything all right?' Pat asked.

'Fine. Just thought I'd let you know that the hospital has things under control, but no further news as such.' Anna forced herself to smile, scanning the faces, searching desperately for one she could not find. *Shit!* Adam and Frank would be here at any minute. 'We've been trying to raise Sally and Frank – where's Fletcher? I thought he was here – would be able to give them a message.'

'Oh – you just missed him! He's popped home to get a few things he forgot – he's off to his sister's tomorrow. Chris gave him a lift.'

'The Morris Man? Right. Not to worry, then.' *Not to worry?! Stall, woman – stall!* 'Well – I'll get off back to Maggie and Molly. But if you see Frank or Sally, would you let them know that the hospital would be glad of a word about Alice's medication?'

'Sure. Will do.'

Anna forced herself to walk normally until she was out of the back door, when she sprinted for Maggie's car for all she was worth. At least if Frank and Adam did call into the pub, expecting to find Fletcher, they'd be held up for a couple of precious moments and, even if they decided to go to his house, she had a head start, especially given that they were on foot. Getting to his house first and getting him away was all she had in mind at present. What she would do then, she hadn't yet decided. *Hell, I'll drive him to Market Eaton police station myself, if I have to. Maggie and Molly will be OK, and hopefully Roly will be here soon, along with reinforcements.*

She frowned as a sudden, fierce spattering of raindrops hit the windscreen, virtually obliterating her view. *Where the hell did that come from? And where the hell are Maggie's windscreen wipers ... ?* She fumbled until she found the right lever. *Why don't they make things standard in all vehicles? It's on the other side, in my car.* She had slowed down and hunched forward in the seat, peering through the windscreen as her headlights cut a swathe through the roadside darkness, showing the upcoming junction. Left for Broomwood House. Right, and just a short distance straight on, to Fletcher Godfrey's cottage. There! She breathed a sigh of relief as she saw light in the window. Quite what she was going to say to him, she didn't know. But at least she'd got to him first.

Once again, she left the engine running as she ran up the path to the front door. He had to be made to hurry. The sooner they were away, the better. She hammered as loudly as she could.

'Mr Godfrey! Fletcher! It's Dr Summers!'

She wiggled her knees with impatience. He would have had to be deaf, not to have heard her. She lifted the knocker and hammered again.

'Mr Godfrey! It's urgent! Please!'

The door opened at last, Fletcher Godfrey standing semi-silhouetted as his body blocked the light from the room behind him.

'Yes?'

Anna took a deep breath. 'I know this is going to sound crazy, but I have reason to believe that your life is in danger. I don't have time to explain until we're away from here, but please believe me – it's this curse business – I believe you're next! It's all to do with Adam and Frank and some story for a boy named Gideon Claybourne.' Anna tugged at his sleeve. 'Please – just get in the car. Adam and Frank are on their way here now, with orders to pick you up.'

Fletcher stepped backwards into his living room and Anna followed him, wanting to scream with frustration. It must be shock. He wasn't taking it in. How on earth was she supposed to get the danger across? She sensed, rather than heard, the front door close behind her.

'Oh dear. Not quite what I had in mind. But thank you for the warning.' The hair stood up on Anna's neck. The voice behind her. Fletcher's stricken, sweating face in front of her. Slowly, she turned. To find herself staring down the barrel of a gun.

Roly Featherstone didn't bother turning into the car park of the pub, opting instead to pull up on the verge outside its frontage. Striding through the main entrance, he headed straight for the bar where Pat's eyes crinkled in welcome as she recognised him.

'Hello! It's Anna's friend, isn't it? What can I get you?'

'Directions only, I'm afraid – to Broomwood House. I understand there's been some trouble and thought I'd go and keep the girls company.'

'Oh, that's kind.' Pat reached for the notepad by the till and sketched a map. 'We're here, see? So you need to go back round the Green and up the lane, then turn left and left again when you come to the T-junction. Broomwood House is down there on the right – nice big drive – you can't miss it. About a mile and a half.' She handed it over, smiling.

'Thank you.' Roly cast his eye over it before turning to leave.

'Shame, really – that you weren't here a few minutes ago,' Pat commented. 'Adam was driving up that way – he could have gone in the lead for you.'

Sally Arnold was speaking to her niece, Sheila Finney, on the phone when she heard the thunder of her husband's footsteps on the stairs.

'Sal – something terrible's happened!' Frank burst into the room looking like a drowned man.

'I know.' She turned back to the phone, telling her niece that she had to go, and hung up. 'It's all round the village. Somebody from the pub rang Sheila when Dr Summers said she hadn't been able to get hold of us, and she just rang me. What I don't understand is, why didn't calls to this line divert to your mobile, where they could have left a message?'

Frank shook his head, angry with himself, spraying water like a dog. His temper had not been helped by having to run home in such a squall. 'It's my fault, Sal – I thought I'd put the mobile on silent and I'd switched the bloody thing off instead.'

'I told you you needed your eyes testing! So what's happening? And where's Fletcher?'

Rapidly, Frank recounted the message he'd been given when he and Adam had arrived at the pub.

'But Alice doesn't have any medication!' Sally exclaimed. She frowned, trying to make sense of the matter. 'Oh strewth – what if she's been taking stuff prescribed for Molly! I'll give the hospital a ring now. But what about Fletcher?'

'Adam's gone to get him. Apparently Fletcher went home to collect some bits and pieces. I came straight back here when I couldn't get through to you on the phone – you were engaged. Where's Janice?'

'Gone up to Broomwood House,' Sally told him. 'Once I knew they'd been trying to get us, I rang back, but the line was dead.'

'Probably this storm.' Frank shivered. 'It's blowing a gale out there and the rain's nearly horizontal.' He pictured Broomwood House in his mind. 'All it would take is a couple of old branches to come down and take the phone lines with them.'

'Well, I don't like it. Seems to me like things are getting completely out of hand.' Sally looked at her husband, water dripping from him into a puddle on the living-room carpet and smiled suddenly. 'And it looks like you need taking in hand! Go and get out of those wet clothes before you catch your death!'

Adam Etheridge used his sleeve to wipe condensation off the inside of the windscreen as he turned right at the T-junction, heading for Fletcher Godfrey's cottage. He had picked up his van from the car park at The White Hart and frowned as he now brought it to a halt, seeing a vehicle parked outside. Wasn't that Maggie Taylor's car? What was she doing here? Taking his flashlight as he got out of the van, he jogged towards it, rapping on the driver's window when he realised that the engine was still running. Empty. That didn't make sense, not with all the lights off at Fletcher's. If Fletcher wasn't home and Maggie wasn't in the car, then where could she be? He opened the door, bending to peer into the interior, startled, as he did so, by the ringing of a phone. What the ... ? He half drew back, then realised that, if it were

Maggie's mobile ringing, it could be Anna with more news about Alice, or Jack trying to get hold of his mum, and the boy would worry if he got no reply. He pulled off his hat and followed the sound, feeling around on the floor until he found the mobile beneath the passenger seat.

Pressing 'answer', he had no time to speak before his ear was filled with the sound of a male voice, frantic with worry.

'Rhianna! For God's sake – I've been trying to get hold of you for the last few minutes! I'm on my way to Broomwood House now! Rhianna? RHIANNA!'

Adam backed out of the car and straightened up, his skin crawling with unease. Anna's phone in Maggie's car and no sign of either of them? About to answer, his free ear was caught by a different sound as the wind gusted from behind Fletcher Godfrey's house. His blood running cold, Adam dropped the mobile and ran.

Roly Featherstone screeched to a halt outside Broomwood House, catching a startled Janice Mills in the glare of his headlights. He flung himself out of the car and ran towards her.

'Who the hell are you?'

'Janice Mills. Local police. Professor Featherstone, I presume.'

He glanced from Janice to the door of Broomwood House, looking ready to take it off its hinges. 'I'm sorry about the misunderstanding. Rhianna just answered her mobile – or someone did – but she didn't speak.' He pushed past her, hand raised to take hold of the Green Man knocker. Janice's hand snaked around his wrist, surprisingly strong.

'No point. No one's answering. I've shouted through the letterbox as well. I was just about to try the back.'

Roly was down the steps before she was, running ahead of her round the side of the house.

'What the hell's going on?' he hissed as they crouched below the unscreened kitchen window.

Janice raised herself slightly, peering inside before standing up.

'That's what we're trying to find out. And just for the record, Professor – I'm not involved in some bloody black magic group trying to kill Fletcher Godfrey.'

Roly's face flushed. 'Market Eaton told me you'd already phoned them – something about Adam Etheridge finding hidden microphones in the man's cottage when he was doing repair work.'

'That's right.' Janice stamped her foot in annoyance as the back door proved to be locked. 'I sent Adam and Frank to pick him up for his own protection. God alone knows what's going on.' She looked around desperately. Roly, guessing her thoughts, picked up a heavy stone garden ornament and wrapped it in his now sodden jacket before smashing the kitchen window. Janice was inside like a shot, warning him that the sink may not take his weight and telling him, needlessly, to mind the glass. He was in and out of the sink before it could decide to give way, and they stood together by the kitchen table, straining their ears for sounds of life.

Wordlessly, Janice signalled to Roly to follow her, moving to the side of the kitchen door before opening it. Below the loud and sonorous ticking of the grandfather clock, a muffled sound could be heard, emanating from along the corridor. After listening again, Janice began to inch her way towards its source. Stopping outside a closed door, she indicated to Roly to position himself on the other side of it. Their eyes met for a brief instant before she stretched out her hand and twisted the knob. There was no human reaction, only increased volume of the sound they'd heard. Janice rushed in, throwing the door back to its fullest extent, Roly hard on her heels and breathing heavily.

The only light in the room was that which flickered from the TV screen as it showed, in black and white, an aircraft, on fire, spiralling its way towards a watery grave in a choppy sea. Their eyes must have lighted on the women in the room simultaneously, as both Roly and Janice spat, 'Shit!' within a split second of each other. Roly headed towards an old woman, sprawled sideways on the sofa, while Janice approached the armchair cradling the slumped form of Maggie Taylor. Her mouth was dry as she felt for a pulse in Maggie's neck, relief exploding when she found one.

'Alive – she's alive!' she croaked.

'Same here. What do we do?'

'Put them in the recovery position. Do you know it?'

Roly nodded, lifting Molly Webb in his arms before laying her gently on the floor to do so. Janice was already speaking into her mobile and he hurried across the room to do the same with Maggie, before disappearing through the doorway.

Janice flew after him as he bounded through the house, flinging open door after door and shouting for Rhianna.

'You're buggering up a potential crime scene!'

'Fuck that! Where the hell is she?'

'You said she answered her mobile – or someone did. Try her again.'

He did so, following Janice back to the room where they'd found the women. She knelt and checked their breathing again, telling him the ambulance was on its way before rising to her feet.

'Nothing!' Roly smashed one fist into another in frustration. 'It's just giving an engaged tone. Where the HELL is she?'

Janice shook her head, baffled, moving across the room towards him as he sank onto the sofa, head in hands. All of a sudden, his shoulders stiffened and he leaned forward, picking up an open book. 'What's this?' He sprang to his feet and went into the hall, which was fully lit, to look at it, tilting it to show her when she joined her.

'What on earth ... ? No – it wouldn't make sense.' Janice looked up into his face, her expression dubious. 'But then again ...'

'What?' Roly shouted. 'What does it mean?' He looked back at the drawing in his hands. The figure hanging from a tree, face grotesque in close-up, while in a circle around it, smaller figures stood, so fiercely delineated that the pen had gone almost through the paper. 'Is this meant to be Stella Timpson, or what?'

Janice shook her head. 'No. Much too old for that. But it can't be right – see ...' Her stabbing finger led Roly to a scrawled signature at the bottom of the page. Janice spoke the name as he struggled to make it out. 'Gideon Claybourne. Must have drawn it after his dad hanged himself. But it was only Fletcher that found him – he was the local bobby then – not a group of people, like this.' She looked up at Roly again, her face pinched in concentration as facts tumbled into focus. 'Thinking about it, though – oh shit! – where Stella Timpson was found – that's where Gordon Claybourne topped himself.'

'Then Fletcher Godfrey found both of them!' Roly's mind went into overdrive, back in the incident room in Market Eaton, seeing the map of the area, the photographs. Flinging the book to the floor, he turned and ran towards the front door.

'What are you doing? You can't just . . .' It was too late.

Before Janice had a chance to stop him, Roland Featherstone was gone.

Chapter Fifty

Anna was brought to her knees as Fletcher Godfrey fell. Handcuffed together, and Fletcher with a rope around his neck, they had been dragged across fields and pulled through hedges, battered and bruised and soaked to the skin.

'Gideon ...' Fletcher's voice was almost blown away on the wind, which was now gusting at gale force, shrieking and whipping through each obstacle it met, bending all in its path to its will. What could not bend, broke, ominous creaks of protest seeming to come from all around them.

'Get up!' Gideon Claybourne pulled Fletcher roughly to his feet, jerking Anna with him.

Teeth chattering, body shivering violently, Anna stumbled on alongside him, no longer able to feel her sodden feet. She blinked back tears, swallowed up in the acid rain which lashed at her face, plastering her hair to her head and dripping into her eyes, which stung relentlessly as she fought to see her way ahead. Her breath, like Fletcher's, came in ragged, panting gasps, as much from fear as from the violent exertion enforced on their fragile frames.

Gideon Claybourne seemed immune to the elements, possessed of a strength and purpose aided all too well by a body maintained at the very pinnacle of fitness. Anna's mind crawled back to the moment when he had yanked her and Fletcher out of the back door of the house, to the look on his face, at which the blood in her veins had turned to ice. *Oh God – we're going to die ...*

She lifted her head and let out a crazed cackle of laughter, unnoticed or ignored by Fletcher and Gideon, struck, irrationally, with what a mess she would look as a corpse, soaked to the skin and covered in mud. Above her, the sky seemed to spin, a huge bank of multi-layered cloud looming and threatening and roiling as it unleashed its contents on to the earth below, acting like a giant diffuser for the light of a moon just past full.

Anna cried out in pain, tasting blood as thorns whipped across her face, ripping skin, just missing her eyes. Another hedge gone through, feet squelching in sheer mire now. She struggled desperately to stay upright as fresh panic filtered through. *If I fall face down, I'll drown! Drown in mud!* She fought to free her right foot, resistance sucking at her ankle. When, at last, she lurched forward once more, left hand flapping uselessly as it failed to find grip, she felt sure she had lost her shoe. Maybe it was her imagination. Maybe it was all just a bad dream, but oh God, she wanted to wake up – she *had* to wake up.

She skidded and fell, the reality of her situation brought home with full force as Fletcher crashed down, a stifling weight, on top of her. A scream rose in her throat as she felt her nose, her entire face, forced down through the squelching, liquid earth. Panicking wildly, she flailed helplessly, red and black, red and black flashing behind her scrunched eyelids, feeling that her chest was about to burst, until Gideon Claybourne lifted her from the ground and shook her like a dog. Her anguished howl was carried on the wind as she and Fletcher were pulled forward afresh, the beam of Gideon's torch now picking out, at its furthest reach, the straggling edge of a band of trees.

Even carrying Sally, Frank Arnold tore down the stairs, her arms tight around his neck, her plaster cast covered in a plastic bin liner. Janice Mills, holding the crutches he had thrown down to the kitchen first, hovered outside the back door, running, as soon as his legs were visible, to open the door of the summerhouse, where Sally was hurriedly deposited.

'Go! Go!'

They needed no further telling. Janice had left her car, engine running, outside the back gate, and Frank barely had time to fasten his seat belt before Janice was out on the main road and gunning the engine until the tyres screamed.

'What the FUCK is going on?!' Frank was forced back in his seat by the acceleration.

Never taking her eyes from the road, Janice began to talk at speed, hoping that this time, she could make her earlier, garbled phone call intelligible.

'Featherstone had just left Broomwood House when I had a call from Adam. Gideon Claybourne – at least we're assuming it's Gideon – has got Fletcher and Dr Summers. Adam's following on foot, at a distance, but we're fairly sure he's headed for the place in the woods where his dad topped himself. Adam says he's armed. Shit! This is a mess!' Janice swore again as she swerved to avoid a fallen branch.

'But what . . . ?'

'I don't know, Frank!' Janice snapped. 'I'm as much in the dark as you are! I daren't phone Adam for an update in case the ringing of his mobile gives him away. Molly Webb and Maggie Taylor are out for the count up at the house – drugged, is my suspicion, but I don't know because I couldn't hang around for the medics to arrive once Adam told me what was happening. I got Pat from the pub to come up and stay with Maggie and Molly while I came to get you.'

Another oath escaped Janice's lips as the back end of the car slid on the unlit road, now running with water. 'We can't get the air ambulance or the police chopper up, in this weather, and whilst an armed team is on its way, it's going to take them forever in this. Our one advantage – we hope – is that Gideon doesn't know we're after him.'

'Then we'll just have to call in every other kind of help we can get.' Frank closed his eyes, tuning in to his wife, The One, who was even now raising power back in the summerhouse, calling on every ally they possessed.

Roland Featherstone crouched in the undergrowth, every sense straining against the elements, seeking some clue as to where he was and, more to the point, where the damned tree of death was located in relation to his present bearings. He had been stupid to attempt this alone, he knew, but his fear of losing Rhianna – losing her to death – was stronger than logic, stronger even than the fear of what he might have to face out here in the wild darkness. He had been confident enough to start with, buoyed up by adrenalin, thinking that even if he had to slow the car to a snail's pace on the unlit road, he would be bound to see police tape marking the spot where Stella Timpson's car had been found. But he had had to abandon the car when the road was blocked by a fallen tree, sure, even so, that he was no more than half a mile from the point where he needed to turn off into the woods. He had scrambled over the toppled trunk, torch beam bobbing as he was bowled along by a wind, the force of which threatened to send him somersaulting along the drenched grass verge. And surely the tape would no longer be there, whipped away by the fierceness of the primal air that screamed through the night.

The tape *had* been there, however; tattered and broken, it was true, but flapping and snapping in the wind, the white and blue of it illuminated before his eyes with startling clarity. He had stopped then, breathless, closing his eyes and forcing himself to bring his breathing under control, to picture, once more, the diagrams, the maps, before heading in what he believed to be the right direction. The thickness of the trees with the resulting near absence of light soon had him hopelessly disoriented and it was not long before he realised, from his all too infrequent glimpses of the moon, that he was moving, not diagonally, as he had supposed, but in a meandering circle. And so he crouched now, taking stock.

He could be within feet of Rhianna and not see her. *I don't need to see her. There are other ways to sense ...* But there was neither time nor need to do so. Close by, and to his right, came the unmistakable sound of a gunshot.

Adam Etheridge's breath went out of him in an explosion to match the sound he'd heard. *Anna! Oh no ...* He forced himself to focus, turning in the direction of the fast fading noise, conscious as he did so of a sense of support washing over him. The trees were thinning rapidly now and he could no longer risk even the shielded beam of his flashlight for fear of giving himself away. Snapping it off, he lowered himself flat on his belly and began to crawl as a sudden, eerie silence descended all around him. The gale no longer blew. The deluge slowed to a sulking spatter. As suddenly as it had started, the storm was over.

Adam's relief was short-lived. The elemental savagery had provided much-needed cover for his approach. With that gone, he would be able to go no further without risk of discovery. *Right then, Etheridge? Now what ...?*

Anna's ears were ringing from the gunshot as Gideon bludgeoned Fletcher Godfrey to the ground. Gideon had been about to release the handcuffs shackling Fletcher to Anna, when Fletcher had made an ill-advised attempt to overpower his captor. Gideon's booted foot lashed out, finding its target three times before he bent down and dragged Fletcher to his knees.

'Stupid move, old man! And you try another, it won't be you who gets it – it'll be her.' Gideon pulled at Anna, holding the gun to her head.

'Gideon!' Anna's knees buckled at the sound. 'Gideon – it's Adam! I'm on my own and unarmed.'

Gideon swung round, dragging Anna and Fletcher with him. Now the sky had cleared, the moon shone down into the clearing, casting a pale wash of light which made stark silhouettes of the trees at its edge. Adam was clearly visible as he walked forward, hands held high.

'Adam! Long time, no see!' Gideon's torch beam swung through the clearing. 'Where's Frank Arnold? Anna here said the two of you were coming for Godfrey.'

'That was the plan. Unfortunately – because she thought we were out to kill him – she put a delaying tactic in place. We got a message about Alice Webb when we called at the pub. Said the hospital wanted details of her medication. Frank couldn't raise Sal on the phone, so Frank went home to tell her.'

'Leaving you to pick him up, eh?'

'That's right. What the hell's going on, Gideon?'

'Justice. Somewhat delayed, but better late than never, eh? That's far enough.'

Adam stopped, slowly lowering his hands.

'Keep them where I can see them, Ad! No funny business if you want her alive.'

Adam glanced from Anna to the stricken Fletcher, retching on to the ground.

'What's this about, Gideon?' Adam repeated.

'Why don't you ask him?' Gideon tugged at the rope round Fletcher's neck. 'Come on then, old man – make your confession, like a good boy! Don't you want to get it off your chest, after all this time? What's the matter – cat got your tongue?' Fletcher shuddered violently, but made no reply. 'I'll fill in the gaps for him, then,' Gideon said. 'He killed my dad. Him and the others.'

'What? Gideon –' Adam took a step forward, halted as Gideon

pressed the gun into Anna's temple. 'Gideon – your dad killed himself. He ...'

'No – he's right.' Fletcher's voice was hoarse. He struggled from his knees to his feet. 'Gideon – let them go. Do what you want with me, but please – let them go. They've never done you no harm.'

The only sound was the steady dripping of rainwater from the trees.

Gideon's voice was hard as flint as he replied. 'You're in no position to drive bargains, old man. I'm the one here with the power of life and death. I'm the one in control. Just like you were, all those years ago. I didn't hear anyone pleading for my dad, then.'

'Hear?' Fletcher's eyes were wild with shock.

'How else do you think I knew? I was here. I saw it all. Heard it all. And what would you have done if I'd rushed forward, trying to save him, eh? Killed me with him?' Gideon motioned to Adam to come closer, signalling when 'closer' had become close enough. 'And who'd have believed me if I'd told? The word of an eleven-year-old against the respected citizens of our community? Against the village policeman? The *law*?' He kicked at Fletcher again. 'You made a mockery of the law that day – all of you.'

'Fletcher –' Adam turned to face him. 'Fletcher – why? What the hell had Gordon done?'

'Nothing! He'd done nothing!' Gideon's voice was brutal. 'They just *thought* he had. Judge, jury and executioners, all.'

Fletcher drew in a deep breath as he spoke, his words little more than anguished sobs. 'But we were so *sure*. We ...'

'That's why there's due process!' Gideon flung at him. 'That's why we have investigations and trials. That's why – in a supposedly civilised country – we *don't* have lynch mobs.'

'What did you think he'd done, Fletcher?' Adam asked.

'We thought – believed – he'd been interfering with kids.' Fletcher's next words came out in a rush. 'He hadn't. I admit that, Gideon – you're right. But I didn't know until years later! And the others – the others never knew.' Fletcher's voice was desperate now. 'It was my fault. My responsibility. I should never have gone along with it.'

'How right you are. But it's a bit late now, isn't it? Some pervert got away with it while my dad – an innocent man – paid the price.

And now it's your turn. The last one left. Your turn, to pay, Fletcher.'

'Wait!' Adam interrupted. 'Fletcher – if it wasn't Gordon – then who was it? And what the fuck was going on?' He stalled for time, praying that Frank and Janice would get here before it was too late to stop his boyhood friend carrying through his plan.

Adam's voice seemed to fade as a scene flashed into Fletcher's mind in answer to his question. The scene that had taught him their mistake. *Oh God, no!* Life had gone on since the execution of Gordon Claybourne. Years had passed – many years – and the business of the Hanging Tree was left behind, buried deep in some fenced-off recess of the mind. There had been no more reports of abuse, so maybe his conscience had come to an accommodation over the lynching. It had seemed a small price to pay for the right result.

Fletcher's day had started out ordinarily enough. It was summer and the air had been heavy – muggy – as if readying for a storm to break. It was his Swifford Lea part of the round, and he was doing it on his bike. He always liked to see things properly, talk to people, make sure that he himself was visible, approachable. 'Keeping his finger on the pulse' was the way he thought of it. He'd been right out on the edge of the village, just past the midday point of his circuit, if you thought of the round as a clock face, when he noticed it. A milk bottle sitting on Percy Ashcroft's doorstep. He'd frowned, dismounted, knocked. It didn't look good, even at that stage. All the front curtains still shut at eleven o'clock in the morning. He'd thumped on the door with the big brass knocker but it had mocked him with its lack of response.

He'd walked round to the back of the house, then, peering in through the kitchen curtains. Pink and yellow check, they were, and didn't quite meet in the middle. Nothing. Just the kitchen table and chairs. Still no sign of Percy. It had never entered his head that the man could be away. He'd have known if he were – everybody knew everybody else's business – and, besides, Percy would have cancelled the milk.

Shit! He'd sworn under his breath, knowing he'd have to break in. A security-conscious man, was Percy. No keys hidden under doormats or flowerpots or the fifth stepping stone down the garden path. Fletcher had used his elbow, padded as it was by his uniform sleeve, to break a pane of glass in the kitchen door. No shirtsleeves in summer, back then.

It hadn't been enough, mind. Breaking the glass. When he'd reached inside, he'd found no key in the lock. He could see it, hanging on a nail on the other side of the room. Sensible, of course, had it been a burglar trying to get in, but that hadn't been much comfort to Fletcher.

'Percy! Percy! You all right?'

Still nothing.

He'd sworn again, and started putting his shoulder to the door before smashing the other glass panel and kicking out the wood in between them. With a big enough gap made, he'd stepped through, stooping to avoid clouting his head, feet crunching over the shards of glass now littering the kitchen floor.

'Percy!' He'd shouted again, knowing already that it was useless. Percy would have been through, playing merry hell by now, had he been able to.

He had stood for a moment, listening. Nothing but the muffled ticking of the grandfather clock which he knew stood in the hall beyond the inside kitchen door. And so he'd opened it, stuck his head into the living room before turning back and going up the stairs. They'd creaked as he'd ascended, and he'd called out, 'It's me – Fletcher!', still eliciting no reply. The bathroom door, to his right, was half-open. He'd pushed it back, glanced inside, before moving to the tiny spare room at the back of the house. That had been empty, too.

He'd often wondered, afterwards, why he'd left the main bedroom till last. Probably, he'd conceded, because he'd known in his heart of hearts what he would find there, and was unconsciously giving himself time to prepare.

But he *hadn't* known what he would find. Not quite. Oh yes – he'd expected to find Percy dead. But dead in bed. Dignified. In his sleep, so to speak. The reality had been altogether different.

He hadn't understood quite what he was seeing, to begin with. The bed was empty. His eyes did a sweep, coming to rest on Percy, who was sitting with his back to him, at a desk in the corner of the room. Fletcher remembered quite clearly the gentle humming sound that had pervaded it, the glow of a screen, shielded by the dead man's body, seeming to sneak around its outline, casting ghostly white light that barely penetrated the darkness, made more intense by the thick curtains which kept out the sun. He had stood motionless, feeling for the light switch, before stopping himself and crossing the room.

'Percy?'

It was as he'd come up close that he'd been able to see over the dead man's shoulder. His right hand, moving to touch him, to feel for the pulse in his neck, had stopped, quick-frozen by the sight that had met his eyes. He heard the noise from far away, as if someone else had made it, but was aware that it was he himself letting out a strangled cry that was half shock, half utter disgust.

He'd stepped back then, hand over his mouth, brain screaming. It was a computer screen he'd seen. He hadn't even known Percy had one. And it was filled with ...

The image had haunted him ever since.

A tiny child, impaled on an engorged penis.

Letting out a rasping sound and gasping for air, he'd moved to the side of the dead man, horror striking his eyes again as they fell on another penis, this one all too real, dead flesh, still gripped in Percy's right hand, spilt semen staining the infant knickers into which he had been masturbating.

Without anything else, it would have been bad enough.

But it was made infinitely worse by the realisation that, years before, just as he'd protested at the time, struggling for his life as they'd thrown the noose around his neck, he and Mike Morgan and Seth Peterson and Emily Parsons had, indeed, hanged an innocent man.

He'd tried to rationalise it. They'd been right, and Percy was just another of the same ilk, albeit one who just looked at pictures of kids, rather than doing things to them. How could he ever have tried to believe that? But he had. For about ten minutes. That was how long it had taken him to make a cursory search of the bedroom. And then he'd known. For sure.

The smell was the thing that had convinced him and the others that it had to be Gordon who had done it. The kids, although they'd never seen the bastard's face, had talked about his smell. And only one man in these parts had smelled like that. Or so they thought. Some peculiar stuff he used for his muscles. And now he'd found that same stuff – home-made, by the look of it – in Percy Ashcroft's bedroom. It had made him vomit, when the realisation had hit him. Percy had been quite calculating. Deliberately throwing the scent – literally – on to another man. An odd man, whom no one had ever really liked or tried to fathom because he'd kept himself to himself. Didn't socialise. Didn't like his wife doing so, either, and, some said, would have kept his kid at home were he not likely to be prosecuted if he'd kept him away from school. You'd see him, surly, in the fields or on the roads. Came into the pub once a week. Drank one pint and one whisky chaser, and buggered off home with no word beyond his order to anyone.

Perfect, really. The kids had never seen the pervert's face. He'd never said a word in a normal voice. Just grunting and heavy breathing as he'd carried out his foul deeds, followed by rasping threats if they told. But the smell ... Oh yes. That was unmistakable. That couldn't have been anyone else.

Only it was.

It had come out in dribs and drabs, kids too frightened to spill the beans. Nightmares. Bed-wetting. Those had been the first signs. And when it had become clear what had happened, their parents had come to him, but wanted to keep it off the record. Didn't want their kids put through the mill. Didn't want them to have to give evidence. Didn't want social workers involved in their family business. Didn't want the bastard getting away with it, either ...

The clincher had been when Emily had walked into the shop with Ben just as Gordon was coming out. Screamed the place down, the child had, although he'd never even set eyes on the man before. It was the smell. Gordon's smell.

So the day he'd found Percy was the day when Fletcher knew his career was over. He'd cleaned up. Removed evidence – including the computer and its filth. Told people he'd found Percy dead, which was true, but hadn't told them anything more than that, certainly not he'd had his knob out and been wanking into kid's underwear. He'd thought, in one horribly irrational moment, of trying to move the body, stick him in his bed, but knew that post-mortem lividity would give the game away. So he'd done what he had to do before quietly getting the doctor in and following the proper procedures. And shortly after that – not so shortly that anyone might think there were a connection – he'd resigned.

It had been the trophies that had bothered him most. The absolute clincher, even above the liniment. He had felt personally defiled, touching them. In Percy Ashcroft's bedroom, along with more kiddie porn than anyone should ever have to see, he'd found Ben Parson's underpants. Chrissie Peterson's knickers. Stewart Morgan's socks.

Two of those marriages had split because of what had happened. Only Em and Henry had stayed together, Henry, being semi-invalid, never even knowing about the abuse. The others – the wives, at any rate – had left, taking their children with them. Both Seth Peterson and Mike Morgan had remarried, had more children, though Seth's second wife – Karen's mother – had been killed in a road accident when Karen was little. And now they were all dead, too.

Which just leaves me ... Fletcher blinked, back in the present, looking at the faces around him in the clearing. Dr Summers. Adam. Gideon Claybourne – his father's avenging angel. Shocked rigid, all of them. Because he had been not only remembering. He'd been reciting aloud as he'd revisited those memories. And now they all knew. His guilt was out in the open. He was truly, in all respects, a finished man. Fletcher smiled as the pain gripped him. A smile that ended in a grim rictus etched across his face as his heart finally gave way under the onslaught of the attack it had been brewing for so long.

Chapter Fifty-one

'I've no beef with you, Adam. You were the best – the only real friend I had here when I was growing up.'

'Let Anna go, Gideon, please.' Adam glanced in her direction, willing her to move. She had gone down like a ninepin beneath Fletcher's toppling weight, Gideon refusing help for either of them until he was satisfied that Fletcher was dead.

'He had no right to cheat me.' Gideon shook his head. 'This wasn't what I had in mind for him at all.' He laughed now, as Anna began to stir. 'Anna. Yes. She's had your knickers in a twist, hasn't she? I reckon I did both of you a favour, getting rid of that Timpson bitch.'

'You killed Stella?'

'Like I said, Ad – you're the only real friend I had. I spent a long time setting all this up.' Gideon waved an arm towards Fletcher's body. 'Learned a lot, living in the attic at Broomwood House. Perfect, really. Stage a break-in – everybody assumes the burglars have left the premises, not that they've installed themselves and a load of high-tech surveillance equipment. It was a long and careful operation, Ad. They had to suffer like we suffered – me and my mam. And what better way? I remembered the stories we made after – when Frank was trying to help, and you and me went to the old ladies for lessons. They were being kind. Letting me let off steam through writing, even if I couldn't spell for shit. Broomwood House is wired, Ad. Helped enormously. Women do love to talk, don't they? Sally and Sheila, as well as the sisters. I knew about Maxine running off – and when I'd found the photocopy of the Marcus Beardsmore shit – well, it seemed too good to miss. I thought she'd get the job, you know, but Anna got it instead, so when Professor Timpson turned up, slagging her off and giving the old ladies a hard time – well – she deserved everything she got. I just slipped out the back, came round the side and chatted to her like I was family, just about to leave, apologised for the old girls – they can be so *awkward* at that age, can't they?' Gideon mimicked the way he'd spoken to Stella. 'I told her I knew exactly what she was after. Greed, man – greed. She fell for it hook, line and sinker. I had her unconscious and away in no time. Unplanned, but a nice little bonus for you. I've learned to improvise, over the years. What else can you do, when you've seen what I did? I learned a whole lot of other things, too. Lying. Stealing. Killing. And I'm a whizz on the surveillance, Ad. So much call for it. Industrial, corporate – you name it.'

'And all the time you had this in mind? Avenging your dad?' Adam's eyes flickered to Anna.

Gideon shook his head. 'Not all the time – no. I thought – I really thought, for a while, at least – that what I was doing was a service. As a mercenary. On the side of justice. That's what I told myself, but you know what?' His voice was stark with bitterness. 'They're all the same. *It's* all the same. Doesn't matter where you go. Kids roasted alive in Africa. Old women raped in Bosnia and Albania. Men mutilated everywhere. How anybody can believe in God, I don't know. Nor the devil, either. Evil's man-made, Ad. Every fucking time.'

'Joseph Conrad said much the same thing. What was it? "The belief in a supernatural source of evil is not necessary; men alone are quite capable of every wickedness." '

'Too fucking right.' Gideon looked from Adam to Anna, who now sat, shivering violently, teeth chattering, by the side of Fletcher Godfrey. He pointed towards her. 'Walk towards her real slow, Ad. I'm going to give you the key. You're going to unlock her from dead meat, there, and fasten yourself to her instead. Properly, mind. Then I'm going to walk away, and you don't make a move. You got a watch?' Adam nodded. 'See it in the dark?' Adam nodded again. 'Right then. Not for half an hour. You don't move. You got that?'

'She'll freeze if she doesn't move. She's in shock.'

'She'll die if you come after me. Do it!'

Adam picked up the key, illuminated in the light of Gideon's torch. Anna's eyes drank him in as he crouched beside her, before flickering to Gideon, as a strange sound rent the night, widening as she saw, too late, the movement of his arm as he raised the gun ...

Sally Arnold's body jerked convulsively on the summerhouse floor. Frank and Janice, about to turn off the verge into the woods, stopped dead, looking at each other wordlessly, faces stricken. Blinking rapidly, Frank breathed one word before plunging into the trees. 'Adam ...'

Gideon Claybourne stopped what he was doing and looked into Anna's face.

'Another change of plan, then. I would have let you go – you're no danger to me. Ad was. But I didn't think he'd lie to me. This changes everything. I may need you.' He pulled her roughly to her feet. This time, she was the one with a rope around her neck. Gideon listened for a split second before dragging her away, the baying of dogs hard on their heels.

'This is hopeless, Frank! They could be anywhere!' Janice raised her head, her eyes squeezed shut in frustration.

'No, Janice! If we just ...' Frank's voice tailed off, his body hair rising in response to the sound that echoed through the trees. 'Do you hear that?' His voice was no more than a whisper.

Janice stood stock still, hardly daring to breathe.

'It can't be ... he's not ... ? He wouldn't – surely?' Her face was aghast.

'He bloody well has ...' Frank grabbed her arm, and, praying for all he was worth, ran on. Janice, a few short paces behind him, stumbled suddenly, hitting the ground with a thump that knocked the breath out of her. Frank turned to help, stopping short as she raised one hand, the frozen fingers of her other scrabbling desperately for the vibrating mobile in her pocket. Pushing herself to her feet, her eyes held fresh fire as she said, 'The chopper's up, Frank! They've got the chopper up! It's on its way!'

Any minute now, and they would hit the road. Gideon Claybourne knew every inch of this countryside, by night as well as day. Maybe there'd be a car to hijack; maybe not. Were it not for those bloody hounds, he could let the woman go. She was the weight that could tip the balance of the scales – either way. Without the dogs, he'd be quicker on his own. With them on his heels, she could be a pawn, a hostage, a bargaining chip. Cursing, he yanked at the rope around her neck, cursing again, as she stumbled. He slapped her face as he pulled her to her feet.

'Keep up, or you're expendable!'

Anna nodded mutely, sick at heart, pulse racing as he dragged her onwards. What . . . ?! She fell forward, hands grasping at the noose as she landed, heightened consciousness bringing through the sounds of the struggle taking place.

Breathing heavily, Gideon Claybourne got to his feet, training the beam of his torch on the figure on the ground in front of him, rolling it on to its back with the toe of his boot.

'Well, well! If it isn't the goat-killer!' His voice was dry. Anna's eyes widened as she was pulled forward to see. 'Friend of yours, by any chance?'

'Roly! It's Roland Featherstone.'

'Rhianna . . .' Roly's voice was thick.

'Ah – that's who he is, is it?' Gideon laughed, an unpleasant sound. 'I've been hearing a lot about him. You should choose your friends more wisely.'

'But he can't have killed the goats! He . . .'

'Saw it with my own eyes.' Gideon shook his head, cocking an ear to the sky as he heard the baying of the hounds, closer than ever. 'I never could stand cruelty to animals . . .' He pulled Anna away before loosing a shot that bucked Roland Featherstone's body before he became still.

Anna screamed before the sound was cut off in her throat by the tightening of the noose.

'According to Adam's lot, he was a black magician. "Adept of the Dark Side" was how I think they referred to him. Sounded like bloody Star Wars, to me. Or it did, until he killed the goats.'

Gideon was hauling Anna along with renewed urgency now, and she gasped as her feet suddenly found grass verse, followed by the tarmac surface of a road, jarring her knees after the sodden surfaces she had become used to. 'Know about Ad's lot, do you?'

Anna shook her head, too breathless to speak.

'If I got it straight, Sally's Aunt Ida was what they call The One, but when she died, Sally became The One. Seems to have run aunt to niece, rather than mother to daughter, and Sheila Finney, she's in training to take over when Sally dies. There's four of 'em – one for each of the directions – and they call themselves Guardians of the Keepers of the Old Knowledge. They all have apprentices. The Four are the top dogs, the Elders. Their job – all of them – is looking after the land, or some such shit. Reckon they have an unbroken line going back to the 900s AD. Over a thousand years ago! They've got to be bullshitting, right?'

Anna was stunned. The Guardians? Descendants of those mentioned in the document that Marcus Beardsmore found? Her head swam.

'I heard a lot of conversation between Sally and Sheila. They reckoned your mate Featherstone, apart from whatever other shit he was up to, was trying to corrupt you, seduce you. Funny word, in this day and age, eh? Quite a conversation the women had about it. Seems there was disagreement, to begin with, about whether you were already on the Dark Side. It was Adam that fought your corner, from all accounts.' For a moment, Gideon said nothing further, turning his head in all directions, listening, looking, even, it seemed to Anna, sniffing the air.

'This way.' Mind made up, he hauled in the rope, shortening the distance between them as he ran straight over the road, dragging Anna with him.

Oh my God! How wrong could I have been? About everything? Anna's heart ached as she thought of Adam, thought back to that moment in the clearing when Gideon had raised the gun. *Oh shit . . . !* Anna closed her eyes as the hedge loomed in front of her, yowled in pain as she was pulled through its thorns. *Where are we going? Where's he taking me?*

Pushing her forward to the other side, Gideon Claybourne seemed remarkably calm as he said, 'Situation like this, a man needs to keep his options open . . .'

He was quite unaware, as he forced Anna into a fresh run, of the figure hugging the hedge behind him.

Janice, running ahead of Frank now, screamed in terror as a hand – it felt for all the world like a hand – snaked around her leg, toppling her off balance to land, face first, in the waterlogged earth.

Frank's torch beam caught him before her own did. 'Featherstone!'

Janice scrabbled backwards, crab-like, using the trunk of a tree to help her to her feet.

Roland Featherstone blinked in the light, frowning as he fought to speak.

'Shot me. The bastard shot me.' Disbelievingly, his hand moved to his ribs.

Frank's skin crawled as the baying of the Hounds, in front of them now, seemed to echo through the darkness. When he spoke, his voice was rough.

'You called them up – created them – call them off.'

Featherstone smiled, shook his head. 'They have work to do. You should know that.'

'If Anna's with him, they'll kill her, too.'

'No. She's mine. Holds my signature. My semen.' Featherstone's voice was triumphant.

'Bastard!' The word exploded from Frank's mouth.

'I'll make an honest woman of her, if conception has taken place. She only took a little persuading ...'

Janice swore under her breath. Featherstone turned to her and laughed. 'You're out of your league. All of you.'

Janice turned to Frank, stopped and pulled out her mobile as its vibration signalled another call. 'Adam!' Her voice soared, body going limp with relief as the two men beside her tensed. 'We thought you were dead! We ... what? Where?' She listened, ended the call, started to make one of her own, punching in numbers as fast as she could. 'Gideon's taking Anna to the river.' Her eyes darted to Frank, dark with anxiety. 'Adam thinks he's heading for the old lifeboat station ...'

Anna's heart hammered, every step adding to the rising fear that threatened, at any moment, to overwhelm her. Knee-deep, now, in mud, the earth itself seemed to be as much her enemy as the man who held, in his own way, her life in his hands, at the end of a rope.

'Come on! Not much further! I may even be able to let you go!' Gideon, taller than she, was far less hampered by conditions underfoot, far more sure of himself, the more so now he had the river in view. Anna had seen it, too, and balked with fear at the sight of it. The water coursed, swift and swollen, dark and turbulent, almost bursting its banks and carrying in its swirling currents debris and broken wood whose branches reached for the sky like the futile hands of drowning men.

The rope bit into Anna's neck as Gideon pulled, impatient now. A car may never have come along the road, but here, there was a chance. Once they'd crossed the river, the dogs would lose the scent and he could lose the woman, lighten the load, give himself full advantage. Laughing now at the sound of the dogs behind him, Gideon upped his pace still further. He wasn't finished yet. Not by a long chalk.

Adam almost fell into Frank's arms as the big man and Janice ran to meet him.

'It's as I thought – he's heading where I thought he would.'

'Then we've still a chance, if we use the road! We can run quicker along here than he can through the fields! We can get there first! Are you all right?' Frank held the younger man at arm's length, eyes searching Adam's face.

'Gideon slugged me. Nothing broken, I hope. Just a bloody splitting headache.' Adam looked past Frank, to a figure moving more slowly along the road. 'Featherstone!' His body bristled. 'What . . . ? We have to get him to call off the Hounds! Anna . . .'

Frank shook his head. 'He's been shot. And he won't. And the Hounds won't attack Anna. Adam . . .' Frank didn't need to say more. The realisation was already in Adam's face. 'We can take her away from him, afterwards. It can be undone – you know that.'

'Not if she doesn't believe . . . Shit!' A wave of despair swept through Adam as the Hounds howled again.

'Fight it, man! Don't give him anything else to work with! Come on –' Frank started to run, the others beside him, as Janice made another call to confirm their whereabouts and, more importantly, that of Gideon and Anna.

'Why didn't Gideon just let Anna go? She's slowing him down – he must know that!' Janice's panting voice signalled her desperation.

'The Hounds,' Adam told her. 'He thinks there's a search party out with tracker dogs, is my guess. Keeping Anna as his ace in the hole.'

'He can hear them? It's not just us?'

'He can hear them, all right – with his sickness, his hatred, the blood on his hands, Gideon's aura has holes in it you could drive a truck through. He's perfect prey for the Dark Side, just doesn't understand what it is that's after him. He heard them the same instant I did. That's when he clobbered me.'

All three of them were breathless now, pushing themselves beyond their limits as they veered from the road and scrambled for the hedge on their right. Impeded by the mud on the other side, they were forced, at last, to slow their pace.

'Come on!' Frank urged again. 'At least we have a straight run for it now.' He pointed across the field. There, below them, holed roof stark in the moonlight, was the abandoned lifeboat station.

The clatter of the helicopter rose in the darkness as it swooped through the sky, searchlight cutting the blackness, like a bird of prey, seeking its quarry. Gideon ducked and swore, dragging Anna to the sodden ground beside him. Seizing her by the scruff of the neck, he dragged her the last few yards to the back of the wooden building, kicking a hole in its rotting timbers and thrusting her inside. Wrapping the end of the rope around his hand, he swung the torch as the sound of the dogs rose to a frenzy of excitement, sending fear coursing through Anna's veins.

'Let her go, Gideon.'

The torch beam swivelled. Adam stood just yards away, empty hands at his sides.

'You don't give up, do you?' Once again, Gideon forced Anna's body in front of his own. Once again, the gun was pulled. 'You lied to me.' Gideon's voice was flat.

'No. I was alone and unarmed, just as I said.'

'But now there are others. Too many others. I can't let her go, now, Ad. You must know that.'

'No.' Adam shook his head. 'Come on, Gideon. You and I were friends, once. Good friends. There's been more than enough bloodshed.'

'So what's a little more? Who cares?'

'I care. I care about Anna and I care about you. There's an armed response team, man. If you don't give it up, you'll die.'

Gideon laughed, a hollow echo that rang through the rafters. 'You think I care about that? I'm not afraid to die.'

'Maybe not. Maybe your own life means nothing to you now. But what about Anna's? What about mine?'

'Playing the sympathy card? It's too late for that, Ad. Much too late.' Gideon pulled the gun away from Anna's head, swung it towards Adam.

'No!' Anna drove her elbow back as hard as she could, bending forward as she did so, sending the shot wild as she crashed down, sprawling under Gideon's weight. As he rolled to right himself, there was a splintering sound as the floorboards gave way, opening beneath Anna's body as the rope slipped from Gideon's hand.

'Anna!' Adam leaped over him, landing flat out, grabbing wildly for the rope as it slithered like a snake, away from his hands, across the fast disappearing floor. There was a further shot, a crash, then Adam's eyes were locked with those of Frank Arnold as the big man skidded on his belly, arms outstretched, one hand curling, like lightning, into a fist, the end of the rope within his grasp.

'I've got her! I've got her!'

Dangling in the water beneath, Anna's hands clawed frantically at the noose as it tightened around her neck, legs thrashing helplessly against the current as it tried to tear her away from the saving, strangling grip. To strangle or to drown ... What an abject choice ...

Janice Mills, outside the building, signalling frantically to the helicopter hovering above, watched in horror as two grappling figures emerged in the swathe of the searchlight beam. She had not seen, as Adam had, how Roland Featherstone had thrown himself at Gideon, facilitating Frank's passage to Anna's aid, and could only marvel at the strength shown by the wounded man as the sound of the Hounds, even above the whirring rotor blades, reached a crescendo of furious anticipation. The two men, Featherstone and Gideon, seemed caught up in some macabre dance, staggering and slithering across the ground together in their fight for possession of the gun. She never heard the sound of the shot, just saw the jolt as one figure tensed before sliding reluctantly to the ground like a rag doll as it was released from the arms of the other. Then Frank and Adam were out of the building, too, Anna held between them, and – *Oh God ... Oh no ...*

Three pairs of horrified eyes watched as Featherstone, swaying above Gideon's body, turned to see the Hounds he had summoned, slavering with hunger, maddened by his own destruction of their prey, throw themselves upon him in a feeding frenzy. At which point Anna, blinking away water as she followed their gaze, opened her eyes and *saw* . . .

The helicopter crew, with Roland Featherstone captive in their searchlight, could only watch in bafflement as the man below jerked and thrashed, raking at the air as he tried to run, legs held strangely immobile below the knee, as if by some invisible force.

'Christ! Is he having a fit, or what?'

Their eyes transfixed, they looked on as the man toppled, then crumpled in a heap, thrashing and convulsing before finally becoming still.

Chapter Fifty-two

Friday November 25th

In a side ward of Market Eaton hospital, Anna was dozing, tired after a steady stream of visitors. The police, of course, but more well-wishers than she had ever expected. Philip, ecstatic to report that the Americans who had financed the Swiffords project were, indeed, descendants of the very men who had murdered Megan Painter.

'They want to commission a memorial for her. And they're more keen than ever for you to complete your research as soon as possible. You will stay on, Anna? Rhianna – sorry.'

'Anna is fine,' she had smiled. 'And yes, Philip – I'd love to stay on – providing, of course, that I have your full confidence?' She hadn't been able to resist the dig and Philip had had the grace to blush.

Then there had been Pete and Pat, full of plans for a celebratory party at the pub as soon as everyone was allowed home. *Tomorrow evening, then*, she realised, acknowledging too, how much she was looking forward to another of Pete's wonderful meals. Maggie, thrilled to have Jack back with her, was obviously fully recovered from her imbibing of drug-laced Horlicks.

'We've had to compromise, mind – at the party,' Maggie had warned her.

'Compromise?' Anna had been wary.

'Well, seeing as how the whole village is involved, so to speak – the bloody Morris Men are going to be doing their thing out front! As an act of thanksgiving.'

Anna had laughed, seeing the discomfiture in the woman's face.

This was going to be a sight for sore eyes. Something else had been a sight for sore eyes, too. She remembered the look of astonishment on Maggie's face at the broad smile on her own as she had come back from the bathroom.

''Ere – are you all right?' Maggie's voice had been anxious. 'Can I get you anything?'

'Oh, yes, please, Maggie –' she had replied '– Tampax!'

She stirred from her reverie as a tap came on the door of her room.

'I brought someone to see you.' Adam pushed in Molly Webb, in a wheelchair.

Anna struggled to sit upright, blushing at the sight of him, thinking what a wreck she must look.

'How are you?' she asked. He looked none too bad after his concussion. In fact he looked ... *Don't!* she warned herself. Lord! What would he think if he knew what she'd dreamed about him?

'Fine. How about you?'

'Fine. Just tired.'

'Well that's good, then,' Molly put in firmly.

'How are *you*, Molly?' Anna laughed, turning towards her. 'And how's Alice?'

'We're both fine, too,' Molly beamed, 'and Alice is coming home this afternoon. Did you hear that we're to have a live-in companion? A nurse?'

'Yes, I did. How do you feel about that?'

'Oh, we like the idea very much. Just as long as she doesn't make Horlicks. Or cocoa.' Molly's face darkened. 'That was a wicked thing, drugging us. Mrs Taylor and I only slept, of course, but Alice – drinking alcohol on her excursion – well – she could have died, you know!'

Adam leaned forward and squeezed her shoulder. 'But she didn't.'

'How ever did she get to Market Eaton, Molly?' Anna asked. 'And what was she doing there? It wasn't the right time for the musicals we talked about.'

'I should say not!' Molly started on a giggle that turned into the dirtiest laugh Anna had heard in years. 'Booked herself a taxi cab, on the sly. Had him pick her up at the end of the drive. And do you know what she went to see? That play with the naked men!'

'What?!' said Anna. 'It's a wonder she didn't have a heart attack!'

'She said it was bad enough that she was going to die a virgin, so she damned well wanted to get a look at a man's plumbing before she turned her toes up! Pardon her language and mine ...'

Adam's shoulders shook as he tried vainly to suppress the laughter that racked through his body.

'Oh my word ...' Anna wiped her eyes. 'But Molly – about the trouble between you ...' She searched for a tactful way of raising the delicate matter of Molly's foiled love affair.

'What's done is done. Though I'm not sure I shall ever completely forgive her, you know. I did so love Robert, and for him to have thought that his love was unrequited ... But still. Alice is my sister, and although we had a falling-out – well ... when I thought she was going to die from the combination of drugs and alcohol, it was love for her and fear for her life that was uppermost. Love has to be what counts in the end, doesn't it?'

'Indeed it does, Molly.' Adam patted her hand.

'And now you're taking her home.' Anna smiled.

'Quite. With this young man's help. Which brings me to the other reason for coming to see you, my dear,' she smiled at Anna, '– besides checking on your health, that is!' Molly rummaged in her handbag. 'You have your own key, now, to Broomwood House! We shall be happy to see you at any time and as often as possible. Lots to do! Professor Jackson told us how delighted everyone is with your research. And with the Marcus Beardsmore document!'

'Which I wouldn't have seen, had it not been for you, Molly!' Anna acknowledged as she accepted the key.

'I'm glad you talked to Alice about it.'

Adam raised an eyebrow and sat on the end of her bed.

'Alice had a secret fear that Marcus Beardsmore was Jack the Ripper,' Anna told him. 'Because of the dates, and various things he mentioned.'

'And you were able to set her mind at rest?' Adam smiled, bringing an unbidden flush to her cheeks.

'Even better than that – I told her that I had photographed something in Broomwood House that came from the hands of Jack the Ripper himself!'

'What?' Adam laughed.

'I'm serious,' Anna assured him. 'It's a painting by Walter Sickert.'

'And he was Jack the Ripper?'

'According to Patricia Cornwell, the crime writer – yes. He's been mooted as a suspect for years, but she spent millions of dollars of her own money investigating the case. She even bought thirty-two of his paintings, as well as his desk and painting table and personal effects.'

'Well, I'm not sure we'll want to keep that painting on the wall, after this!' Molly grimaced. 'But we've turned up a journal of Marcus Beardsmore's now!'

'No!' Anna sat bolt upright.

'Yes!' Molly clapped her hands with excitement. 'It was in a trunk in the corner of the attic. The police went through it with a fine-toothed comb, you know, after Gideon . . .' Molly took a deep breath. 'Poor boy! One can't help but feel sorry for him – for what he must have suffered. But what he did – it was shocking! Wrong – so wrong.' She shook her head sadly. 'Do you think you'll ever find out who they were?'

'I'm sorry?'

'Those Guardian people who put the wind up the fellows who killed poor Megan Painter?'

Anna studiously avoided Adam's eyes as she made her reply. 'Oh, I very much doubt that, Molly. If even the people concerned at the time didn't know who they were, I don't see how I could get to the bottom of it, after so many years.'

'But that's just what this woman did with Jack the Ripper, isn't it? You said so yourself!'

'Molly! I don't have several million dollars, and we don't have any forensic evidence or any further clues!' Anna laughed, adding, for good measure, 'And I'm not a miracle worker!'

'What a shame! It's such a wonderful mystery! The forces of light, driving out the evil in their midst . . .' The old woman sighed.

'You're just an incurable romantic, Molly!' Adam got up from the bed and kissed her cheek. 'I'd best get you back to Alice, or she'll think I've run off with you!'

'Chance would be a fine thing! Doesn't Anna get one as well?'

'What?'

'A kiss. You can't show favouritism, you know. Not unless you've made a Declaration of Interest. That would be ungentlemanly.'

'I'm sorry.' Adam turned to Anna, the laughter in his eyes fading as he took in her tousled hair and flushed cheeks. 'May I?' His voice was soft.

'Well – yes, please.'

He sat on the bed and took her face in his hands, his hair brushing hers, lips brushing hers, gentle and tantalising, before melting into her own to send liquid fire rushing through her veins. He pulled away reluctantly, eyes locked on hers, slowing his breathing before turning back to Molly.

'Right then!' He took the brake off the wheelchair and pushed her out of the room, as Anna sat, breathless, rooted to the spot, heart pounding.

'Oh, by the way . . .' His head reappeared round the door.

'Yes?' It was all Anna could to, to speak.

Adam crossed the floor to her bedside, one arm behind his back. 'Did Molly give you her little booklet on *The Swiffords' Own Language of Flowers*?'

Anna nodded.

'Good. Then you'll know what these mean . . .'

He brought the hand from behind his back.

A bunch of red tulips.

A Declaration of Interest.

'About time, too!' Molly chided as Adam wheeled her down the corridor.

On Saturday evening, Anna sat in the Arnolds' living room. Her eyes swept the faces around her; Sally and Frank, together on the sofa; Janice, dark smudges beneath her eyes, but very much off-duty and with her hair loose to her shoulders; and Adam, sitting to her right. The Arnolds had shut the shop early, ostensibly so that they could prepare for the evening's party at The White Hart, but in fact to talk to Anna before she made her re-entry into the life of the village.

Janice brought her up to date on the findings of the police investigation.

'That was quite some show Gideon had going. They reckon the attic at Broomwood House looked like something out of *Mission Impossible*. Hi-tech wasn't the half of it – he was working cutting-edge technology.'

'What a shame he couldn't have put it to better use.'

'Quite. He'd kept logs – a journal – since he got there. Meticulous record-keeping of how his plans were coming along. Emily and Fletcher were easy, living on their own, but even the families – Morgans and Petersons – he had their routines sussed so well, he knew when Karen and Gavin would be in on their own. Had it all down to a fine art.'

'But what about Emily Parsons? And the vicar – I still don't understand how he fitted in.'

Janice blew out a long breath. 'Emily had arranged to meet him at the churchyard – you knew that much, yes?'

Anna nodded.

'She was almost certainly going to spill the beans about how they'd hanged Gordon. And Gideon had heard, through conversations between Sally and Sheila, about the vicar's views on burying suicides and killers. Well, he didn't want anyone else getting the credit for what he'd done, and it made the nice touch, if you'll pardon the expression, of bringing in the earth element of the curse. He actually got there first, ahead of both Emily and Reverend Fury, defrocked him, rolled him unconscious into the part-dug grave, and filled it in, making sure enough of his arm was exposed so that Emily would see. Then Gideon snaffled Emily when she arrived and led her to the grave. She screamed the place down, as you know, and he was lucky to whizz her away when Fletcher and Maggie arrived on the scene. The water element didn't quite come off with Emily, of course, because she was actually dead before he sent the car over the cliff.'

'He drove it?'

'Oh yes. All the way. Whether Emily was alive or dead during the ride, we're not sure. If she was, she must have been terrified.'

'That was the point though, wasn't it? To terrify everyone? Make them suffer?'

'Yes. And he had the flexibility to improvise and work around anything that came up. He'd originally planned to burn the Morgan house down – would have killed them first, before setting fire to the place, but Gavin's death at the party – entirely unforeseen – changed his plans. Hence a car bomb, which still kept the fire element going.'

'Do you know what his plans for Fletcher were?'

Janice nodded. 'Fletcher should have been death by air. He'd planned to hook him up to the exhaust of his car after making him write a confession. That went out of the window after Fletcher moved here, to Frank and Sal's, especially as Gideon knew he was planning to go to his sister's – make his escape, as Fletcher saw it.'

Anna sat back and closed her eyes. 'The whole thing was a nightmare.'

There was silence for a moment, everyone caught in their own sombre reflections.

'Anna –' It was Sally who spoke. 'We need to talk about what you saw the other night.'

'The Hounds.' Anna nodded.

'The medics thought you were babbling from shock and exposure.'

Anna took a deep breath before she spoke. 'I think you need to know – before I say anything else – that Gideon had heard other conversations between you and Sheila in the sisters' kitchen. "Did I know about Ad's lot?" That was how he put it. And when I said I didn't, he told me what *he* knew.' Anna ran through his account, ending simply with, 'So I know that you're The Four. The Guardians.'

'OK,' Sally said at last. 'What do you intend to do about it?'

'Do?'

'You're a researcher. Isn't this just what you need? Especially to tie up the Megan Painter business?'

Anna shook her head. 'As far as my researcher hat goes, I never heard any such information. But, assuming you knew what your predecessors had done – knew about the so-called curse – it must have been a hell of a shock when this business kicked off.'

'You're not wrong …' Sally's mind flew back to the first Council Meeting they'd held about it, when she had called upon each of them, and they upon her, to swear by the vows and penalties of their calling, that they had had nothing to do with it. 'And we didn't know, of course, about the buried confession, nor the Marcus Beardsmore document.'

'So you thought the curse may have been activated?' Anna ventured.

'Good Lord, no! There was no curse. But we were desperate to find out what was really going on. Not that we were successful. And we may harm none – we protect. So – you're not planning to expose us, then?'

'Absolutely not. You saved my life – all of you. Kept

yourselves hidden for more than a thousand years. I'm not going to put my oar in on that.' She gave a wry smile. 'Off the record – can you really trace yourselves back to the 900s?'

'Off the record – yes. Unbroken, to the time when King Athelstan of Wessex became King of all England. And we were probably around in one form or another, even before then.'

'Athelstan … 937,' Anna murmured. 'Shades of the Old Corporation of Malmesbury, in rather a different form. They still have their Turfing and Twigging ceremony and gained rights and privileges for helping Athelstan repel the would-be invasion by the Danes and Celts.'

'There's more than one way to protect the land …' Frank's voice was soft.

'So I'm learning. There's something else I need to know, too.'

'Go on.'

'Not about you, specifically. About Roly. I know he killed the goats, and again, Gideon told me things he'd heard about him.'

'What things exactly?' Sally's voice was level and Anna was aware that, to her right, Adam had become very still.

'He told me that Roly was a … an adept of the Dark Side.' Anna was embarrassed by the terminology.

'Right. We've known about him for years. Anyone in a similar position to us knew that.'

'And he said that – that Roly was trying to corrupt me and trying to … seduce me.'

'And?' Sally's eyes were full of compassion as she looked at Anna.

'Well … he did.' Anna's face flushed scarlet and she fought to stop herself turning to Adam.

'We know that.'

Anna groaned.

'Don't you go worrying. It's nothing for you to be ashamed of. He used what might be termed highly unlawful means. Anything done against anyone's will, or without their permission, is black magic. We believe killing the goats was part of it.'

'Roly said –' Anna was remembering her conversation with him, angry now to think he had been mooting theories when he himself was guilty of the crime. 'About blood – power –'

'When we went through April Cottage, while you were in

hospital – to cleanse it of his influence – we found a flower arrangement in the rubbish. And an emerald.'

'You think … ?'

'Almost certainly, he charged the emerald with the blood of the goats and cast a powerful spell that drew you to him against your will. Did you have … strange dreams?'

Anna nodded. 'And I had a parody going through my head – you know the Green Eye of the Little Yellow God? Well, it was a student skit on it, but I didn't realise until I threw the flower arrangement out.'

'Your subconscious trying to warn you, more than like, but when you're not aware …' Sally grimaced.

'I dreamed of an abyss – being pulled in two directions. As well as other things.' Anna flushed again.

'The other night, my girl, you chose the right way to go. That's the important thing. You were already on what we call "Edge of Sight" when you arrived in the village.'

'My eyes were opened on Tuesday night, all right. To a lot of things.' Anna felt Adam's hand find her own, give it a gentle squeeze. Still, she didn't look at him. 'What do I need to do? To get rid of the … contamination of Roly, or whatever?'

'Do you still feel contaminated?'

Anna thought about it, surprised by her own answer. 'Well no – now you come to mention it, I don't. Not since I woke up on Wednesday morning.' She dared a look in Adam's direction this time, comforted by the warmth of his gaze. 'It wasn't just because of Roly's death, though, was it? And it wasn't a dream …'

Light was dawning on her face.

'Tell us your dream that wasn't a dream, Anna.' Adam squeezed her hand again.

'It was a dark place. But I wasn't there – I was seeing it. Sally and Frank and Janice were kind of … I don't know – guarding me? And you, Adam – you went into the dark and found Roly. It was …' She shuddered. 'That part of the dream was horrible.' She composed herself. 'You asked him to give it back – something that he had that belonged to me, and he didn't want to let it go, but somehow – and it took some time – he did. And you carried it out of the darkness – like a crystal light in your hands – and you brought it to me and kind of … breathed it into me – *back* into me.'

'It was yours all along.' Adam smiled. 'A part of you that he stole, for want of a better word.'

'How could Roly have done all that? How can you think you know someone and they're secretly doing such things?'

'The important thing to remember, Anna,' Frank said, 'and the best way to remember him, is that he effectively gave his life for you. If he hadn't tackled Gideon when he did, I would never have been able to save you. So – if you want to think in terms of "redemption" – he did the right thing in the end. There are those of his ilk who would have been only too happy to take you with them.'

'There's so much I need to learn.'

'Only when you're ready.' Sally smiled.

'Talking of ready ...' Frank helped his wife to her feet. 'I think it's time we made an appearance at the pub!' He smiled at Anna. 'You know where we are, if and when you want to learn more in a private capacity, so to speak ...'

They made their way to the party in two vehicles, Janice going with Frank and Sally, while Anna went in Adam's van. Chris and his Morris Men were visible from quite some distance away, dancing and jingling and thoroughly enjoying themselves. Inside, The White Hart was packed to the beams, with the Webb sisters present as special guests of honour, delighted to be part of the celebration and bursting with memories of the building's past history and reputation, not to mention those of its landlords.

'It's like a whole new spirit of goodwill is afoot,' Maggie smiled.

'What's that?' Chris had come inside to order drinks for his dancers and caught her conversation as he tried to squeeze past. 'Did I hear you say "goodwill", Maggie Taylor?'

'It has its limits, Chris ...' Maggie narrowed her eyes.

'Such a shame. I can see I'm going to die an unfulfilled man ...'

'What *are* you on about?'

'I always wanted to kiss you, Maggie. Ever since you came and yelled at me, wearing your dressing gown and a face like thunder that May Day morning ...'

'Are you out of your mind?'

'No – just in lust with your luscious lips.'

'I'll luscious lips you!'

'If only ...'

Maggie banged her brandy and Coke down on the windowsill. Heads turned. Chris was really in for it, this time. But not quite the way everyone expected. Especially not Chris himself. Throwing her arms around his neck, Maggie planted the kiss to end all kisses on his mouth as a roar of laughter and delight swept through the bar. Anna looked at Maggie, astonished.

'My God! That's taking it a bit far, isn't it?'

Maggie gave a wicked little smile. 'Who me? He just got a lot more than he bargained for. Like a mouthful of garlic ...'

Pete moved to the table of one of his diners, as the man signalled him. He was in a good mood tonight. Nothing was going to spoil his evening. Nothing could. Look at all these happy people on his premises ...

'Chef! This bouillabaisse ...' Heads turned.

'Yes?'

'Very good, but I have to tell you that we've eaten it in France and they serve it with the fish heads.' Silence fell.

'Really? But it tastes all right? You liked it?' The entire pub seemed to wait with bated breath for the reply.

'Oh the taste was superb – nothing wrong there at all, but ...'

'But this is England, not France,' Pete told him. 'And the English, on the whole, don't like fish heads in their soup.'

'Well, be that as it may, old chap, I do think that if one is going to cook such a superb dish as this undoubtedly is, it should be served authentically.'

'Oh shit ...' Maggie and Anna exchanged a knowing look.

'Authentically?' Pete stepped back. 'Right. One moment ...'

Seconds later, he had returned from the kitchen, a bin bag in his hands.

'There you go, sir!' Pete splattered a pile of fish heads into the diner's dish. 'Bon appétit!'

'So much for goodwill!' someone groaned.

'Don't talk wet – it's brilliant!' Maggie declared. 'It means we're back to normal ...'

'That reminds me ...' Molly leaned close to her sister's ear, as uproar resumed. 'I must get on with Anna's wedding dress.' She looked at the couple across the room, as they left the pub together.

'What? Anna's getting married?'

'She will be, Alice – yes. In the spring, I should think.'

'Molly – even supposing this is true – how can fish heads possibly remind you of weddings? Or don't I want to know ... ?'

'Not fish heads, Alice. Bouillabaisse. It made me think of oysters, you see, which are an aphrodisiac, and Aphrodite being the goddess of love ...'

Adam and Anna walked the short distance to April Cottage. She unlocked the door, a great waft of warmth greeting them now that the chimneys were fully in service again.

'Come in.' Anna moved ahead of him, disappearing from view. Adam stood uncertainly, turning to face her as she came back into the room with one arm behind her back.

'I thought you might like this ...'

She held out a red tulip with a green ribbon tied around it in a very particular fashion.

A Declaration of Interest.

Accepted and reciprocated.

Acknowledgements

The Old Corporation of Malmesbury is real and I am indebted to Chris Hall and his article 'Malmesbury's Turf Lores' in *Wiltshire Life* magazine for bringing this to my attention.

Special thanks go to Jackie Pritchard, who gave me the inspiration for Maggie Taylor, and whose home, complete with chimney problems, became the April Cottage of this book; to Alex and Alison at The Tollgate in Holt, Wiltshire, for fantastic food and hospitality; and to Betty and Sam, their goats, who are still alive and well at the time of writing; and extra special thanks to D.C. for being a veritable fountain of knowledge on all manner of unlikely subjects, more of which will undoubtedly find their way into future books . . .

Thanks also to Dave Avery, Community Liaison Officer, for putting me in contact with Sgt John Skilling of Gloucestershire Constabulary, who kindly spent time to explain police procedure and the likely timetable involved in Anna's arrest. Any errors or liberties taken are mine.